║║║║║║║║║║║║║║║║║║║║║║║║║║║║║

✧ **T5-CQC-294**

FRIENDLY PERSUASION

"I can't believe how lucky I am to have you as a friend," Audrey said happily, throwing her arms around Landon in an exuberant embrace.

Not one to ignore such a grand opportunity, Landon rested his hands at her waist and held her near. Gazing down into her upturned face, he said, "And I am just as lucky to have you for my friend."

"I'm serious," she said, unable to believe he could honestly think himself lucky when she had done nothing for him except cause unnecessary gossip. "Landon, because of you, many of my dreams are finally coming true."

Overwhelmed by the unbridled emotions bursting inside her, she leaned forward and kissed him. Not just a friendly little peck on the cheek like she might give her brother. Instead, she wrapped her arms firmly around his neck and pressed her mouth hard against his, with all the unrestrained passion she possessed.

Landon was not about to let this unexpected opportunity pass him by. Eagerly, he fastened his arms around her and drew her body hard against his.

Audrey was too full of joy to worry about any complications falling in love with Landon might cause for her, about the painful heartaches that might lie ahead. Instead, she gave herself up to the overwhelming fulfillment of his kiss, eagerly accepting his ardent embrace, aware of the intimate way their bodies touched—and just as aware of where the sensations building rapidly inside her could lead. . . .

Elusive
Caress
ROSALYN ALSOBROOK

ZEBRA BOOKS
KENSINGTON PUBLISHING CORP.

ZEBRA BOOKS

are published by

Kensington Publishing Corp.
475 Park Avenue South
New York, NY 10016

First printing: April, 1990

Printed in the United States of America

DEDICATION

This book is dedicated to the loving memory of two great storytellers: my father, L.E. Rutledge, M.D., and my grandfather, Harry F. Rutledge. With these two men to influence, love, and guide me, is there any wonder I turned out the way I did?

chapter one

May, 1870

The house was magnificent. Maybe it wasn't *the* largest nor *the* grandest of all the houses that had been built in the more affluent neighborhoods of upper Fifth Avenue, but to Audrey Stoane, the stately three-story brownstone had a special pride all its own. To Audrey, the house represented not only wealth, because undoubtedly it was worth a small fortune, but it also symbolized the sheer power and the undeniable respect that came from having such wealth. To her, this one house represented all she'd ever wanted out of life.

Designed with a tall mansard roof, pale sandstone trim, wide clustered chimneys, and surrounded by parklike grounds, the house truly fascinated her—and had since the first day she saw it. It was the sort of house she'd always dreamed about; and if everything went exactly as she'd planned, both she and her brother would soon become a very real part of that household. At long last, their lives would be heading in the right direction.

"Come on, Sis, let's get on home," Seth Stoane said, breaking into his sister's faraway thoughts, unaware she had a special reason for lingering outside the house a little longer than usual that night. Shifting his weight impatiently, he reached up to push his thick brown hair

7

away from his face. "It's nearly eight o'clock and neither one of us has had any supper yet."

When she turned and tilted her face to look at him, Audrey showed no indication that she had even heard her brother's complaint. Instead, she leaned back against the five-foot tall stone wall, which completely circled the house, then offered a wistful smile. "Seth, wouldn't you do or give just about *anything* to be able to live in a wonderful house like this some day?"

Seth sighed heavily, having heard his sister's foolishness too many times before. Though two full years had yet to pass, it seemed to Seth a lifetime ago that Audrey had suddenly decided they should leave the southern regions of Louisiana and move to New York to seek their fortunes in the city of opportunities. Some fortunes. Some opportunities. They both now worked twelve hours a day at jobs they hated, and they barely earned enough money between them to feed and clothe themselves. Though they did indeed earn higher wages in New York than they ever had in New Orleans, they were no better off. Living expenses were also higher, much higher, and had proved just as impossible to meet.

"Of course, I would enjoy living in a big house like this," he admitted grudgingly as he peered down at his sister's dark form.

Though Audrey, at the age of twenty-three, was a full fourteen months older than Seth, because of his large size, he appeared older. He had already surpassed her in both height and weight back before their mother had died from starvation over nine years ago, leaving the two to fend for themselves. In fact, he had been a good two inches taller than Audrey when they'd stood side by side at their mother's funeral. But even so, Audrey, being the elder, had immediately taken charge—and had remained in charge ever since. Yet, in all honesty, Seth did not mind, because he loved his sister dearly and he trusted her judgment in most cases.

He just wished she would give up her foolish notions of

8

one day overcoming her poverty-ridden past and suddenly turning into a rich and well-respected lady of society—for her own sake. "I think most folks dream of living in such luxury one day; but let's be practical. On what I make lugging freight around at that warehouse all day and on what you make stitching those fancy dresses at Miss Nadine's, we're lucky to afford that one-room hovel we live in now."

"Don't remind me," Audrey said, frowning as she turned to gaze at the house again, admiring the way the warm glow of the lanterns nestled in the plush flower beds gave the house a strong sense of dignity. Tiptoeing, she laid her arms along the top of the wall with her elbows angled out, then rested her chin on the backs of her folded hands, her face filled with as much longing as a small child standing dazed in front of a candy shop. "But what if something happened that changed all that? What if we were indeed given a chance, a real chance, to live in a house as grand as this?"

"And what if we could afford those fancy clothes you sew for the rich ladies and expensive coaches with noble black steeds?" Seth asked, clearly mocking his sister, still wishing he could make her stop dreaming the impossible —but pleased she always included him in her fantasies. "Come on, Sis. We've been standing around out here for over twenty minutes now. Why can't we go on home? I'm hungry."

"You're always hungry," she pointed out, not taking her eyes off the house. After tugging her dark blue cotton shawl closer about her shoulders, she waved him away with a quick bounce of her hand. "Go on along if you want, but I'm staying here a while longer."

"You know I can't leave you out here by yourself," Seth complained. His whispered voice rose a degree, further evidence of his mounting frustration. "The streets aren't safe for a woman to be out alone after dark—not even one as mean and stubborn-headed as you."

9

"True," she said agreeably, but did not bother glancing at him again. Nor did she attempt to step away from the dark shadows that allowed them to linger outside the stately home without much chance of being detected from within.

Seth shifted his weight from one long, powerful leg to the other in a show of impatience, while his stomach grumbled aloud with angry protest. Catching a whiff of freshly baked bread that drifted on the gentle night breeze, he closed his eyes and willed himself not to strangle his own dear sister. "Will you at least tell me how much longer you plan for us to stand out here gawking at that house?"

"Not much longer," she told him, glancing up and smiling at him at last. But because of the dense shadows created by the overhanging tree limbs, he was unable to clearly see her pleased expression.

The nearest street lamp was several hundred feet away, and with a six-foot hedgerow directly behind them, a five-foot brick wall directly in front of them, and the huge shade tree draping its dark green branches low over their heads, she could hardly make out his glowering expression, even though he towered well above both the wall and the hedgerow. But then, she didn't need to see his expression. She knew by the gruff tone of his voice that her brother was not at all happy with her.

"It's not as if you've never seen the house before," he pointed out, knowing it was one of her favorite places to stop and look. Whenever the two of them took a late evening stroll along the city streets, more often than not, they ended up in this neighborhood—usually in front of this very house. "Come on, let's go. Before a policeman happens to spot us and decides to arrest us."

"Nonsense," she snapped, weary of his complaints. "There's no law against looking at a house." Besides, she knew that the policeman who patrolled the quiet neighborhood had already come by once and was not expected to come back for another two hours.

"Please, Sis? Tomorrow is a work day. We both have to get up early," he said, trying a whole new approach. "Not yet."

"How about if I promise to come back with you on Sunday? Neither of us has to work then. We can come back early in the afternoon and look at the house in the daylight." His stomach growled loudly, as if to hail his fine judgment, and Seth patted it reassuringly but waited until the slow, hollow clip-clopping of a passing carriage had faded into the distance before adding, in a most pitiful voice, "Please, Sis?"

Audrey shook her head, fully aware Sunday would be too late. Unbeknownst to Seth, she had invested the last forty dollars of their emergency fund toward tonight's little venture and she was not leaving until she'd seen it through. She was sick of being looked down upon as one of the "dirt poor," tired of barely having enough money to make ends meet each month and never having anything extra for a luxury or two. Therefore, she was finally going to do something about it. The time had come to take her fate into her own hands. Through the use of her own cunning and wit, she would not only have the wealth, but also the power and respect she'd always wanted—and deserved. And she'd have them while she was still young enough to enjoy them . . . no matter the risks involved.

"You'd be able to see all those pretty flowers a lot better in the daytime," Seth prodded, still hoping to convince her to leave, before his grumbling stomach staged a full-scale rebellion. "Besides, it's nearly time for the owner to come outside for his nightly walk."

Exactly, Audrey thought, and glanced again at the house. She had studied the man's nightly habits for several weeks and had discovered that he was quite a stickler for routine. It was what had encouraged her to set such an improbable scheme into motion to begin with.

Aware of everything that could go wrong, as well as the trouble that would result if anything did, her heart

11

pounded against her chest with incredible force. Every nerve and every muscle in her body ached with an overpowering mixture of anticipation and fear. Her whole future lay at stake and she knew it. With growing apprehension, she listened for sounds in the night while she waited, hoping against hope that this time everything would turn out right.

"There he is," she gasped softly when the front door opened just seconds later. It was as if Seth's casual mention of the man had willed him to appear.

"Let's get out of here," Seth pleaded one last time. "What if he decides to come this direction for some reason? He might see us."

"So what if he does? We have just as much right to be out here as he does," she whispered adamantly, aware the man was not yet close enough to hear them.

"Yes, but what right do we have to be hiding in his hedges?" Seth quickly reminded her, then turned and parted the tall bushes in hopes that she would take advantage of the opening and step out. "Let's get on out of here while we still can."

"Too late. He's already at the steps. He might see us if we leave now," she said, then motioned for her brother to sink down and be quiet. Because Seth was several inches taller than the neatly trimmed hedge that ran the length of the front wall, conveniently providing them with a dark, narrow hiding place, she was afraid they would be spotted if he continued to stand.

Grumbling softly to himself, Seth obliged. Though he didn't like the thought of hunkering down in the bushes like some sort of common thief, he felt it was better than having to explain to the man what they were doing there. Exactly how did one tell the rest of the world that his only sister was so obsessed with being rich someday that it had robbed her of all common sense?

Audrey, too, had crouched low, peering cautiously over the top of the wall, ready to duck out of sight should the man turn his head in their direction for even a moment. With her hand pressed lightly against the throbbing hollow at the base of her throat, she watched with ever-mounting apprehension as he slowly descended the massive steps in front of the house, as he did nearly every night.

As expected, a single male companion appeared behind him, pausing just long enough to close the front door, then followed at a short distance.

Curling the hand at her throat into a tight fist and pressing it against her collarbone, Audrey watched breathlessly as the two proceeded briskly toward the front gate. Everything was going exactly as it should, exactly as she knew it would, until suddenly the front door opened again, throwing a wedge of light across the front porch as out stepped yet a third person.

Audrey's heart knotted painfully in her chest. The thin, very pale man who followed directly behind Marshall Steed, she had expected; but this other man was a different matter entirely. He could easily ruin everything.

Though it was darker in the main part of the yard and the third man was still some distance away, Audrey could see him well enough to know he was a much younger man, far more agile than the other two. He moved with the strength and the grace of a man who handled himself very well—too well. While she waited to see if he planned to join the first two in their nocturnal stroll, her breath caught deep in her throat and held there until her lungs felt as if they were on fire.

She watched helplessly while the first two men paused along the walkway long enough for the taller, younger man to catch up to them. They exchanged words. Then, to Audrey's overwhelming relief, the third man spun away only seconds later and went immediately back inside.

Slowly, she released the trapped air, then replaced it with a long, fresh breath while she watched Marshall Steed again turn and head for the street. As soon as he

13

stepped through the front gate, he turned right and, as was his custom, proceeded down the narrow walkway at a brisk pace, his companion remaining always a few feet behind, struggling to keep up.

Suddenly, two unsavory-looking characters appeared out of a tall hedgerow farther down the block and moved quietly into Marshall Steed's path. Audrey's heart froze. Each man brandished a large gleaming knife and stepped forward with a determined air. While the shorter of the two held the frightened companion aside with a steel blade pressed firmly against the side of his neck, the other dragged a startled Marshall Steed down the street toward a parked carriage, waving his knife in front of the man's face as a warning. Marshall attempted to break loose, only to find the sharp blade placed against the base of his throat.

Audrey gasped, parting the hedge with her hands as she stepped immediately out onto the sidewalk to get a better look. Though her long skirts caught on one of the lower branches and tore loose part of her hem, she hardly noticed as she turned to see what Seth intended to do about the situation, only to find that her brother had yet to emerge from the hedge.

"Seth, that man's in danger. You have to help him," she cried out, and within a heartbeat, Seth had come out of the hedge and was on his way to do just that. Being so impressively large and undeniably strong, one sound blow to the left jaw of the man who kept trying to shove Marshall Steed into the dark confines of the awaiting carriage sent both attackers running into the night. One of the men was so eager to be gone that he did not stop to retrieve his knife when it clattered carelessly to the sidewalk only a few yards away.

Caught off balance by his unexpected release, Marshall fell sharply against the side of the carriage, then stumbled backward to the ground. By the time he'd recovered his wits and had pushed himself up off the street to stand erect, Audrey was there, helping him to straighten his coat, using her wadded shawl to dust away some of the dirt he'd collected during the fall.

His companion was still too wide-eyed and weak in the knees to be of any assistance at the moment. He had leaned his slight weight against a nearby hitching rail until he'd regained the strength he needed to stand alone again.

"Sir, are you hurt?" he asked when he was finally able to speak.

"No. But little thanks to anything you did, James," Marshall snapped, glowering at his assistant while he wiggled his arms, adjusting the fine silk of his shirtsleeves beneath his smudged coat. "Why on earth didn't you use your gun?"

"I—I couldn't. It happened too quickly," came James's reluctant reply. His hand went automatically to where he'd hidden a small pistol in the special leather holster beneath his coat.

Audrey's stomach knotted at the mere mention of a gun. It had never occurred to her that either man might carry a weapon. Someone could have been killed. Suddenly, her own legs felt weak.

"I'm just glad this young man was nearby and so willing to come to my rescue," Marshall said, glancing then at Seth, who had stepped back out of the way. Though Marshall was tall by most standards, he had to tilt his head back to look into Seth's concerned brown eyes. "Young man, you may very well have saved my life. What's your name?"

"Seth. Seth Stoane."

"Pleased to meet you, Seth," Marshall said, and thrust his hand out for a proper greeting. "My name is Marshall Steed, and I'm glad to know there are still people around like you, people who are willing to risk their own necks in order to help another man in trouble."

Reluctantly, Seth stepped forward and accepted the handshake from the older man. "Pleased to meet you, too, sir; but I didn't do nothing nobody else wouldn't have done."

"You are wrong. You saved my life and I think you deserve a reward," he said. Marshall reached immediately into his coat for his wallet . . . a wallet he was very pleased to still have in his possession.

"I don't deserve no reward," Seth said, backing away again, feeling embarrassed by the whole situation. "I didn't do nothing."

Audrey cringed at her brother's poor use of English. Of all times to show his lack of a proper education!

"You are far too modest," Marshall told him as he opened his wallet and slipped the rounded tips of two manicured fingers inside the main fold.

"Sir, please," Audrey said, quickly placing her hand over his to stop him. "We can't take your money."

"And are you his wife?" Marshall wanted to know, clearly surprised that she had intervened.

"No, I'm his sister; but I know Seth well enough to tell you that he's as serious as he can be about not wanting any reward for what he did. He did it because he wanted to help."

Seeing that they both undoubtedly meant to decline his offer, Marshall frowned. "But I want to do something to show my gratitude. After all, your brother saved my life."

"Well, there is something . . ." Audrey put in swiftly, then glanced timidly away, hoping to seem anything but bold.

"Name it," Marshall insisted, feeling quite benevolent by now. "Name it and it's yours."

"Forget it, sir. I really couldn't ask it of you," she said in her softest southern drawl, shaking her head as if she'd undergone a sudden change of heart. "Forget I said anything. Your verbal thank-you was quite enough. We'll be on our way now."

"No, please." Marshall reached out to capture her by the elbow when she moved away from him. "I want to do something to show my gratitude. What were you about to ask me?"

Audrey hesitated, glancing momentarily at Seth before turning her large brown eyes to meet Marshall's blue gaze straight on. She opened her mouth as if to reply, but no sound came forth. Finally, she shook her head again. "No, it would be too much to ask."

"Come now. Out with it," Marshall insisted. "Let me be the one to decide if it is too much to ask."

Finally, Audrey replied, "Well, I was sort of hoping you might know of a couple of decent-paying jobs around here. My brother and I are both looking to find better work and would appreciate it if you could put in a good word for us somewhere. We are both very hard workers."

Marshall stared up at Seth for a moment, judging both his size and strength. "Come to think of it, I may know just the job for this young man."

Seth's eyes widened at the prospect of a new job . . . anything to get away from that warehouse. He was tired of working twelve to thirteen hours a day, six days a week, for a slave driver like old man Johnson. "What sort of job?"

"Follow me and we'll discuss it further," Marshall said as he turned and headed back toward the gate.

Audrey's heart jumped excitedly against the inner muscles of her chest when she realized Marshall Steed did indeed plan to invite them into his home . . . into the beautiful house she'd admired for so many months. Thus far, everything was going exactly as she'd thought it might. She just hoped McKinney's jaw wouldn't be too sore the next morning, but she was certain the forty dollars she'd paid him to stage the fake kidnapping would help him overcome his pain. Remembering how she had clearly warned him of the risks involved, she felt very little remorse. At the moment, she was far too pleased with herself to feel anything but pure elation as she and Seth followed Marshall Steed up the wide steps toward the front door.

"Everett," Marshall called out the moment he had

17

pushed open the door and stepped inside. "Everett, where are you?"

Following him inside, Audrey glanced around, expecting the young man she'd seen earlier to appear in response to Marshall's loud, demanding voice.

"Everett, we have guests."

Suddenly, a thin, elderly gentleman appeared in the marble hallway just beyond the main entrance. He was dressed in a dark gray uniform with double rows of black and silver braid stitched across his shoulders and huge shiny black buttons aligned in two neat rows down the front of his coat. His pale green eyes swept over the two guests curiously, resting momentarily on the wadded cotton shawl in Audrey's hands, then on the common material of her skirt and blouse. His eyebrows rose with obvious disdain when he asked, "Will you be wanting tea?"

Marshall glanced back at Seth and Audrey only a moment before responding. "Yes, please. And if we have any crumb cakes left, bring some of those, too. We'll be in the library."

Seth's eyes widened at the mention of crumb cakes. Food at last. His stomach grumbled appreciatively.

Audrey shot him a disapproving glance.

"Come along," Marshall said, obviously unaware of the exchange between sister and brother. He motioned them to follow him, then proceeded immediately down the massive hallway, passing to the left of a grand curving staircase as he headed toward a pair of carved oak doors that were thrown wide to reveal the lighted room beyond.

Audrey missed nothing of the grandeur that surrounded them, pleased to discover the inside of the house was even more elegant than she had imagined. As they passed beneath the gleaming chandeliers that sparkled high over their heads and beside the intricately designed oak hall table with its matching set of Windsor chairs, she held tightly to the hope that the job Marshall Steed wanted to discuss would indeed allow them to live, or at

18

least work, in such glorious surroundings. Her heart thumped with wild anticipation as she followed him into the huge book-lined room at the farthest end of the hall.

"Have a seat," Marshall told them, then crossed the room to a tall cabinet with a leafy design carved along the outside and began to pour himself a drink from a small crystal decanter. Turning to Seth, he asked, "Would you care for a glass of brandy?"

"No, sir," Seth answered uncomfortably as he settled his large frame into one of the four elegant hand-carved rococo arm chairs that sat facing the man's leather-topped writing desk at opposite angles. "I'm not a drinking man."

"Good for you," Marshall said, nodding approvingly. Immediately, he set aside his own glass, then turned and watched as James quietly closed the doors, walked across the room, and stood to one side.

With both hands clasped behind his back, Marshall waited until both Audrey and Seth were comfortably seated before he sat down in his huge desk chair facing them. He studied Seth for several moments before he spoke. "Seth, what would you think of coming to work for me? I assure you, the wages would be more than fair, though the hours might prove impossibly long."

Audrey's stomach twisted frantically while she waited for her brother's response, knowing that if he refused the job, whatever it was, she would murder him on the spot.

"What sort of job do you got in mind?" Seth asked, shifting his weight forward in the chair to get a better view of Marshall's face. He grimaced when the delicate chair creaked in protest to the abrupt movement of his heavy bulk.

Before Marshall could tell him more about the job, there came a sharp rap at the door. Then, before anyone could answer, the doors parted and in walked a tall, broad-shouldered man. As Audrey watched him enter, she guessed him to be about twenty-six years old and, judging from his size and the authoritative manner in

19

which he carried himself, knew immediately that he was the same man who had come outside to speak with Marshall earlier . . . the same man who had caused her such a fright, making her worry that all her carefully made plans had been for naught.

Her pulse raced with renewed vigor as she waited for him to come closer still. There was just something about his manner that both enthralled and frightened her.

"Ah, Landon, I'm glad you're here," Marshall said, rising from his chair and coming around the desk to meet him halfway. "I have someone I'd like for you to meet."

Landon? Immediately, Audrey knew that this man had to be Landon Steed, Marshall's only son and a millionaire in his own right. Having thought Landon to be middle-aged, since Marshall was undoubtedly in his mid to late fifties, she was startled to find that he looked so young.

"I passed Everett in the dining room and he told me we had guests," Landon replied, glancing curiously at first Seth, then at Audrey. "Not having been warned of any expected guests, I thought I'd better come see for myself."

"Actually, they are more than guests," Marshall explained, then led his son toward Seth and Audrey. "And they were hardly expected."

Audrey watched with breathless fascination while the two wealthy industrialists moved closer. Just knowing how very important these two men were in the financial world was enough to set her heart into rapid motion. But when Landon Steed stepped closer and she got her first good look at his well-defined features, the response inside her was astounding, for he was without a doubt the handsomest, most virile man she'd ever seen . . . ever even imagined. Everything about him spoke of perfection, from the sheer confidence in his walk to the deep, golden timbre of his voice.

When he then stepped even closer, she noticed that his eyes were the most startling shade of blue she'd ever seen, almost colorless in contrast to his dark eyelashes

20

and his deeply tanned face.

The rugged line of his jaw revealed an unrelenting male strength that sent shivers through her. Yet, there were enough tiny lines at the outer corners of his eyes to hint at an equally viable sense of humor. His dark brown hair lay in thick waves around his face and had been cropped, though not recently, in the very latest of men's fashion. His clothing fit perfectly against his wide shoulders and lean, muscular thighs, revealing the sort of man that made women take second notice—and Audrey proved no exception. Suddenly, she wished she'd taken the time to repair her hair after getting finished at work, or at least to change from the simple muslin skirt she'd worn all day into something with a little more eye appeal.

"Son, I'd like for you to meet Seth Stoane," Marshall said as he continued with his introduction. "I think it might interest you to know that Seth here just saved my life."

"Saved your life?" Landon's eyes widened. His attention, which had been divided between the two guests, immediately focused on Seth. "What happened?"

"As you already know, I had started out on my nightly jaunt, with James right behind me as always, when a ragged pair of rowdies suddenly jumped out of the hedgerow in front of us. They both were armed with knives, and while one of them held James back, threatening to slit his throat if he so much as breathed, the other tried his best to force me into a nearby carriage." Marshall shuddered at the frightening memory. "Happened right in front of the house. I hadn't even had time to take out my cigar yet."

Landon's gaze shifted from Seth to Audrey to James, then back to Marshall while he listened to a full account of what had occurred right outside their own home.

"So, when I learned he was looking around hoping to find a better job, I decided that the best thing would be to hire him myself," Marshall said, ending his explanation.

"As what?" Landon asked. He stared again at Seth,

21

who by this time had risen and stood awkwardly before them, dividing his attention between Landon's probing gaze and the thick blue carpet beneath his scuffed work boots.

"Why, as my personal bodyguard, of course," Marshall announced, as if that should have been a foregone conclusion. "You know as well as I do that any man who has attained my financial status makes lots of enemies . . . enemies that apparently think nothing of causing me great harm. What almost happened tonight really opened my eyes. An armed assistant is not enough protection. I'd feel much, much safer knowing I had someone like Seth watching over me, too. Just look at him. He's as big as an ox. Don't you think he'd make a good bodyguard?"

"He's certainly got the build for it," Landon agreed as he carefully studied the man in front of him. Though at six feet two Landon was himself considered a tall man, Seth indeed stood a full three inches taller than he did and was every bit as broad across the shoulders, if not more so. And judging from the fit of his clothing, none of his bulk was wasted fat. The man appeared to be solid muscle. "But has he had any experience?"

"I think his actions tonight more than qualify him for the job," Marshall insisted, hoping to dispel any lingering doubts his son might have. "You know, you really should consider hiring a bodyguard for yourself. I realize you don't have as many enemies as I do, but still, it's better to be safe than sorry."

"I have neither the patience nor the desire to put up with a bodyguard, but what you do is your own business," Landon said, then for the first time, he addressed Seth. "What do you think about all this?"

Seth glanced at Landon, then at Marshall, his dark eyebrows drawn into a perplexed frown. "I'm not sure what I think. What exactly does a bodyguard have to do?"

"In your case, very little," Marshall said, laughing.

"Most ruffians will take one look at you and be long gone before they'd even *consider* starting any trouble."

"Still, it sounds like a very dangerous way to make a living," Audrey stated, also standing, tired of being left out of the conversation and just as upset that no one had thought to introduce her to Landon, something she wanted very much, though he was not yet a part of her plans.

When she felt his attention turn to her at last, her pulse stirred, throbbing rapidly at her throat. Again she wished she had taken the time to do something to improve her appearance, perhaps an upswept hairstyle that would have been attractive yet still allowed her to look businesslike and self-assured. "How much does the job pay?"

"Who's she?" Landon asked his father, glancing quizzically at her, as if he'd just now realized someone else was in the room. "His wife?"

"No, that's his sister, Audrey Stoane," Marshall supplied. "She's the one who let me know that Seth was interested in finding a new job."

"Oh," Landon said, as if that bit of information had told him a great deal about her. Raising his hand to his chin, he studied her for a moment, then let his gaze dip down to glimpse the womanly figure so aptly displayed beneath the well-fitted lines of her white blouse and dark blue skirt, before finally coming to rest on the sheer determination that glowed from her light brown eyes. "How nice that you are so concerned about your brother."

Insulted by his bold perusal, Audrey bristled, curling her hands into tight fists at her side as she thrust her chin forward, though she was determined not to let her anger get the better of her. "No one has yet bothered to answer my question. Before Seth would even consider working at such a dangerous job, I think he should be told exactly how much he could expect to be paid and what other sort of benefits he might receive."

Marshall and Landon exchanged glances, then looked at Audrey as if not quite sure what to think of her.

"My sister takes care of all our finances," Seth explained with a reassuring nod, then drew her into the protective curve of his arm.

"Is that so?" Landon responded with a raised brow. Slowly, he smiled, revealing startlingly white teeth. A doubled set of curving dimples formed in his tanned cheeks. "Then I take it your sister has a good head for figures."

"That's for sure. She hasn't had a whole lot of schooling, but she's got a real good head for figures. Comes by it natural, I guess."

"No doubt," Landon said, again letting his gaze dip boldly down to assess the only sort of figure he appeared interested in at the moment.

Audrey stiffened at such brash behavior, finding it harder to control her anger but knowing she must. She wondered how long before Seth noticed, too, fearing that in her defense he would do or say something foolish to jeopardize the new job.

"Yes, no doubt," Marshall repeated, clearly disinterested in what Audrey could or could not do. Turning sharply away from her—his way of dismissing her entirely—he spoke directly to Seth. "The job pays well: thirty dollars a week. And you'll be given a large bedroom upstairs, plus three solid meals a day."

"Thirty dollars a week?" Seth remarked, unable to believe his good fortune. It was five times what he made at the warehouse. "And meals too?"

"I realize it seems a bit generous, but that's taking into consideration the hours I will expect you to work. I'll want you with me whenever I leave this house, day or night, Sundays included. Of course, I will let you have an afternoon off now and again to visit your sister, but other than that I will want you near me at all times."

"Visit my sister?" Seth asked, puzzled. "Won't she be living here, too?"

24

Audrey felt her world crumble around her. She was not going to be allowed to live there after all. Tears stung her eyes, but she refused to blink them back. Instead, she stared straight ahead.

"I see no reason why she should," Marshall answered, frowning at the thought. "You are the one who will be working here, not her."

"But I thought you planned to give us both jobs," Seth said, then slowly shook his head. "I'm sorry, but if Audrey's not going to be given a job, too, then I'll have to turn down your offer. I don't like the idea of her living alone in this city, especially in the neighborhood where we live."

Audrey couldn't believe her brother had done such a foolish thing. Just because she wouldn't be allowed to live there didn't mean he should give up his big opportunity. She'd make out all right living alone, and Audrey had opened her mouth to state as much when Landon's next words cut her short.

"Father, if you really want this hulk of a man for your bodyguard, I suggest that you find some sort of work for his sister, too," he pointed out unnecessarily, then looked at her with a doubtful expression. "Surely, there's something she can do."

Marshall twisted his face into a thoughtful frown while he considered it further. "Well, Kelly has been complaining again. Claims she needs another helper in the kitchen, though I'm not so sure she does." He turned to Audrey, studied her for a moment, then heaved a noticeable sigh. "Can you cook?"

"Can she cook?" Seth asked, grinning instantly, as if unable to believe the stupidity of such a question. "There's nothing she can't cook. In fact, she's been cooking for me ever since our folks died."

"And how long has that been?" Landon wanted to know. His attention again focused on Audrey in a most disturbing manner.

"Nine years ago," Seth quickly supplied.

"Fine," Marshall stated, bringing what he obviously felt was an unnecessary discussion to an abrupt end. "Then she can go to work in the kitchen. I'll pay her six dollars a week, which is what I pay the other girls. And I'll supply her with both a room and meals. How's that?"

Seth looked at Audrey questioningly.

chapter two

Delighted that everything had indeed worked out—
even *better* than she'd dared hope—Audrey nodded
agreeably. The animosity that had been gradually
building inside her was quickly forgotten as her
excitement took over. Not only would they be working
and living in that glorious house, where opportunities
awaited them at every turn, but their wages were to be far
more than she'd ever dreamed possible. It took all the
self-restraint she had to keep her wits about her and
calmly ask, "Will I also be allowed an occasional
afternoon off?" What would be the point of having all
that money if she didn't have enough time to do anything
with it.

"Of course," Marshall responded. "All the domestic
help gets one day off each week. But it'll be up to Kelly to
decide which day that will be. She makes all the decisions
when it comes to the girls."

Audrey wondered just how many "girls" there were in
his employ, but she decided it would be wiser to wait and
find that out later, from Kelly—whoever that was. For
now, it was enough to know her scheme had worked. She
and Seth were well on their way to a better life. Thanks to
a little personal ingenuity and a well-placed forty-dollar
investment, their days of being "dirt poor" were over
because, with an open ear and a careful eye, it wouldn't

be long before she discovered ways to increase their good fortune even more. Suddenly, she believed there was no limit to what the future might bring.

"So, do you accept the jobs or not?" Marshall asked, growing impatient.

"Of course they accept," Landon said, nodding with cool self-assurance, as if he'd possessed the uncanny power to read her thoughts and, by having done so, understood the real reason they were there.

Shifting nervously, wondering just what he did know, Audrey answered with a polite smile. "Yes, sir, we'll gladly accept the jobs." They would be fools not to.

"Good," Marshall said. His face suddenly lifted into a pleased smile that closely resembled his son's. "Then, it's settled. You'll both start work tomorrow, just as soon as you can get all your belongings put away."

"Tomorrow?" Seth asked, surprised they would start that soon. "But shouldn't we give some sort of notice to our present employers?"

"First thing in the morning, you can tell them you've found better jobs. Shouldn't take five minutes," Marshall pointed out, not wanting to be bothered with such unimportant details.

"Even so, it'll take us hours to pack our things and then hire someone to carry them over here."

"You'll have all night to pack, and I can send one of my own wagons for your belongings in the morning. The sooner you start protecting me, the better," he answered, giving no consideration to the fact they might have need for some sleep in that time. Then, before Seth could come up with any other reasons to protest, he turned his attention to Landon. "Why don't you have Everett show them to their rooms, so they'll have a better idea about what they will and won't need to bring with them. No sense having them haul in a lot of unnecessary furniture. Oh, and be sure to tell Everett to put Seth in the room right beside mine, so he'll be within calling distance in case someone tries to break in and do something terrible

28

to me in the middle of the night."

"That won't be necessary. I was just on my way upstairs. I can show them to their rooms."

Marshall shrugged. "Doesn't matter who does it, just as long as Seth ends up in the room next to mine."

"What about his sister?" Landon asked, tilting his head in Audrey's direction. "All the servant quarters are being used at the moment. Where do you want me to put her?"

"I don't care. Find some place. Just see that she's made comfortable." Then, without further word to anyone, Marshall spun about and left the room. James immediately followed.

Seconds later, Landon led Seth and Audrey out of the library and up the stairs, glancing back occasionally to be certain they still followed. He paused outside a large bedroom near the top of the stairs. He was not very pleased with his father's decision to hire total strangers without first having checked their credentials. "Seth, this is where Father wants you to sleep. Those next two doors lead directly into his rooms."

Seth stepped inside to look around, his mouth agape at the sight of such lavish furnishings.

"Go ahead and get acquainted with your room while I show your sister to hers," he said, then proceeded immediately down the wide, carpeted hallway with long, easy strides.

Audrey had no choice but to follow. Curious to know if her own bedroom would be as elegant as Seth's, she followed closely at Landon's heels. Her insides fluttered with excitement at the thought of actually living in such grandeur. At that moment, she felt very much like a princess from some fairy tale who had just been granted her first wish, and Audrey refused to let anything dampen that giddy feeling—not even Landon's overbearing silence. Or the reasons for it. Instead, she sought to start a conversation that might ease the tension building between them.

"So many different rooms in one house. How do you ever find a use for them all?"

"We don't. We have several guest rooms that are never used, especially now that Father has stopped entertaining here. But most of the rooms along this short stretch of corridor are used by the family. As you may have overheard me tell Seth, the two connecting rooms off to your right are my father's. Those on the left belong to my little sister."

With a light wave of his left hand, Landon gestured toward a set of closed doors as a way of clarification. At the mere mention of his sister, his harsh expression dissolved into a teasing grin. "Rachel has gone to bed early with another one of those headaches she always gets when she wants to be left alone so she can read the latest romance novel she's bought, or so she can write scandalous lies in her diary. I doubt you'll meet her until sometime tomorrow."

"You have a little sister? How old is she?" Audrey asked, though she already knew. The name Rachel Steed was constantly mentioned in the different society magazines, especially now that she was engaged to marry Preston Windthorst, the oldest son of the renowned iron and railroad magnate, Anthony Windthorst.

"She just turned twenty," he told her, unaware that to Audrey this was old news. His long crescent-shaped dimples deepened to a fascinating depth when he added, "But Rachel rarely acts like a young lady of twenty. In fact, she rarely acts like a young lady of any age, which drives poor Father to the edge. He blames himself for her sometimes inappropriate behavior, thinking that if he'd only remarried after Mother's death, Rachel might have had enough proper guidance to teach her to be a true and proper lady. As it is, he hopes her approaching marriage will help settle her down some, but I don't really look for that to happen."

"Why not?" she asked, aware she had stumbled upon a subject he discussed willingly, almost eagerly. Despite

30

his uncomplimentary words, he obviously loved and admired his little sister very much, which Audrey decided was to his credit.

"Too much free spirit in that girl," he told her, still grinning. "Though, at the moment, she really seems to like the idea of being married, Rachel will never be able to conform to everything that will be expected of her, to all those confining rules of social etiquette that seem to go hand in hand with being married—especially if she ends up married to someone like Windthorst. His family is one of those who live under strict social protocol. Rachel's far too independent to comply with such nonsense for very long."

"Is that why you have never married? Are you also too independent for such nonsense?" she asked, knowing she was asking personal questions that she had no right to ask, but so curious to find out why such a rich and devastatingly handsome man had not married.

"And what makes you think I'm not married?" he wanted to know, glancing curiously at her as they turned the corner and progressed along yet a second corridor.

Audrey felt her stomach grow painfully taut. Other than the information that occasionally appeared in the financial section of the newspapers, there really had been very little written about Landon Steed. She thought she remembered having read something in the society columns about his having attended the Vanderbilt Cotillion with some rich socialite, but she could be mistaken. Maybe he *was* married. For all she really knew, he could have children, too. Oddly, the thought of Landon with a beautiful wife and adoring children made her insides ache.

"*Are* you married?"

"No."

"Because you are too independent for such nonsense?"

"Because I've never found anyone worth the time or the effort."

Having similar views about marriage, Audrey relaxed a

31

degree and asked, with genuine interest, "Is that how you see marriage? As a time-wasting effort of some sort?"

"Isn't that how you see it?" He glanced at her face to study her expression. "Isn't that why a pretty young woman like you has never married?"

Now it was her turn to look questioningly at him. "And how do you know that I'm not married?" A tiny smile toyed at her lips while she awaited his answer.

"Lucky guess," he said. His blue eyes sparkled with amusement when he looked at her again. "Most married women don't spend quite as much time taking care of their brothers as you seem to. Nor do they continue using the same last name as their brothers. And, as a rule, most married women wear wedding bands as proof of their marriage vows."

He turned another corner, this time with no forewarning, and continued down yet a third corridor, glancing back to make sure she still followed. "But, then again, I guess you could be a widow who had to sell her rings to help meet expenses, then possibly returned to using her maiden name to help draw attention away from her previous marriage. Is that the case? Are you a widow?"

"No," she answered, and wondered exactly when the conversation had shifted its focus from him to her.

"I thought not," he said, then before she could comment further, he paused outside one of the few doors along the small end-section of hallway they'd entered and gestured toward it with his hand. "Here is the room where you'll be staying. I think you'll enjoy being in this part of the house. It's quiet . . . well out of everyone's way."

To Audrey, it sounded as if he had chosen this particular room as a sly way of getting rid of her, as if he felt her presence might cause some embarrassment. Out of everyone's way, indeed! Angered by the mere thought of it, she fought the urge to lash out at him, knowing how gratifying it would be to reach up and slap that arrogantly handsome face. But his next words came like a cold slap against her face, cooling her sudden burst of anger and turning it into cold apprehension.

"Except mine, of course," he said, smiling down at her while he awaited her reaction.

"Yours?" she asked with uncertainty, notching her eyebrows as she looked up at him.

"Yes. Those are my rooms directly across the hall," he said with an outward wave of his hand.

Audrey glanced at the two doors he had indicated, then at the hallway itself, quickly assessing the fact that there were no other rooms along this portion of the hall other than his and hers. She would indeed be out of everyone else's way—except his.

Tiny prickles of apprehension skittered across the back of her neck when she glanced back at him and noticed that his gaze had again trailed boldly downward, lingering momentarily at the base of her V-shaped neckline. She brought her wadded shawl up to cover herself, then folded her arms protectively over her chest.

"Doesn't anyone else live in this part of the house?" she asked, swallowing nervously, wishing she had chosen to wear a dress with a high, stiff collar. But then, judging by the devilish glint in his pale blue eyes, a full suit of armor might have been an even wiser choice. The muscles around her stomach twisted into a firm knot while she tried to think of a logical way out of her present dilemma. She'd read enough romance novels herself to know that such a situation could prove very dangerous . . . very dangerous indeed.

"No. Until now, I've had this entire section to myself," he responded, moving closer, all the while gazing deeply into her soft brown eyes.

Audrey felt a perplexing leap of her senses when she realized his intentions were far less than honorable, and she quickly took an awkward step back.

"Then I can't possibly accept this room," she said. But in an attempt not to sound ungrateful—which she wasn't—and certainly not wanting to sound as if she was terrified to be so close to him—though she was—she quickly added, "I couldn't invade your privacy like that. You are too used to having the area to yourself. Surely there is another room available in a house this size."

"Half-a-dozen, at least," he agreed, then slowly took yet another step in her direction, his eyes still gazing intently into hers, his purpose apparently unchanged. "But *this* is the bedroom I want you to have. It's larger than most of the other bedrooms on this floor. You might at least go inside and have a look around. I really do think you'll like the room once you've seen it."

Finding it a good way to put needed distance between them, Audrey did just that. Turning cautiously away, she stepped into the room, but she was too concerned with the fact that he had followed her to pay much attention to her elegant surroundings.

"Do you like it?" He stood only a few feet away from her while he motioned about the room with agile movements of his wide masculine hand. "It has everything you could possibly need—and more. As you can see, there are two tall dressers as well as a large double-door armoire for your clothes. There are several easy chairs and matching sofas to relax in and read from if you like. There's even a vanity for your toiletries and, what's more, your own bathing cubicle for—"

He hesitated as he motioned toward the tall silk-covered screens that hid most of the white porcelain bathtub from view. His blue eyes sparkled with amusement when they dipped down to look at her appraisingly.

"Yes, I know what the bathing cubicle is for," she swiftly informed him, tapping her foot impatiently, wishing he would hurry with his ridiculous explanation of the room so she could be rid of him. His presence was far too distracting. "If you are, in your own less-than-subtle way, making reference to the grime on my dress and hands, I have a good reason for being this way. I got dirty while helping to brush the street dust off your

34

father's coat after his fall."

Quirking his mouth into a wide grin, pleased by her temper, Landon gestured toward the far side of the room where an immense bed, adorned with a pale yellow satin coverlet embroidered with bright splashes of gold, stood on a raised dais beneath a draping canopy of yellow, gold, and white, "And, last but hardly least, there's the bed itself. I assume you also know what *that's* for."

"Sleeping would be my guess," she responded abruptly, then crossed her arms and locked them in place, to indicate that was the *only* use she had for a bed. Though she knew it was a fairly common practice for the rich to dally with their help, for which they offered the generous benefits of favoritism, Audrey had no intention of becoming a rich man's plaything. She had too much self-respect for that sort of thing. And if that was what Landon Steed had in mind, then he'd better do some serious rethinking on the matter.

"Yes, sleeping is one possibility, all right." Landon nodded, clearly delighted by her answer. "Why don't you try it out? See if it is comfortable."

Audrey didn't care for the husky timbre to his voice. "I'm sure it will be fine, though I'd still rather have a different room, preferably one that's a little closer to my brother's bedroom."

"It really is very noble, this concern you continue to show for your brother," he said. His smile stretched wider across his face while he slowly advanced toward her again. His long eyelashes lowered over sultry blue eyes while his gaze slid over her with slow, searching intensity. His deep voice became soft as velvet when he spoke again. "You two really are a remarkable pair. Father was certainly lucky that you both just happened to be right outside our house when those two bumbling idiots tried to abduct him."

A cold, wavering chill of apprehension bounced back and forth along Audrey's spine before centering itself in the hollow pit of her stomach—a reaction caused more by what he'd just said than as a result of the male hunger that radiated from his eyes. The careful way he had worded that last comment made her wonder if, somehow, he suspected the truth.

The color slowly drained from her face while the blood went to the aid of her roiling stomach, even though she tried her best to convince herself she was imagining things. If he'd really suspected the truth—that the whole thing had been set up to get them jobs in that house— he'd have said something earlier. He never would have allowed his father to hire them. Or would he? When she looked at him then, she wished she could read his thoughts.

"I'm just glad my brother was able to stop those men before they could do much harm." She made every effort to keep her mounting apprehension out of her voice. If he didn't yet suspect her, she had no intention of giving him a reason to. The last place she wanted to spend the night was in jail.

"Yes, it worked out rather well, didn't it?" Landon agreed. He studied her beautiful upturned face while he continued to move toward her, slow and easy, like a wild animal stalking its prey.

"Why do you say that?" she asked uneasily. Her mouth felt as dry as dust when she bravely met his gaze.

Landon shrugged, as if that should be obvious. "If Seth hadn't been there to rescue Father, then you wouldn't be here with me now, and I never would have had the pleasure of meeting you." He was close enough now to reach out and touch her, which he did, lightly across the cheek.

A shocking array of tingling sensations scattered wildly through her body, making her more aware of his magnetic charm. She tried to look away from the mesmerizing depths of his blue eyes but found it impossible. Suddenly, it became difficult to swallow and to draw a needed breath. Audrey immediately attributed her unusual reactions to the very real possibility he suspected the truth about her—that he saw her for the opportunist she really was. She refused to consider that her odd responses could have anything to do with the fact that Landon Steed was so undeniably handsome, or that he had a very disturbing habit of standing a little too close.

He reached out to touch her cheek a second time.

Clearly, he was intent on seducing her, or he was possibly testing her in some manner. Either way, the danger was clear when his fingers trailed lightly against the delicate curve of her cheek and a startling wave of vibrant warmth cascaded down Audrey's spine, settling quickly in her toes. Tiny bumps of pure sensation formed just beneath her skin, causing her to take a quick step back, hoping again to put substantial distance between them.

Mesmerized by the startling clarity of his eyes as he slowly countered each of her movements with one of his own, she felt her knees growing rapidly weaker . . . so weak that she feared they might not continue to hold her weight. She chose to believe this sudden infirmity to be the direct result of having neglected to eat any supper. But Audrey knew that lack of food was not her problem. Landon was. She had to get out of there. She had to get away from him before her knees collapsed entirely, leaving her completely at his mercy.

"If my brother and I are to get everything packed by morning, then we'd better be on our way," she said just before bolting suddenly past him, unaware it was exactly what he'd expected her to do.

Audrey and Seth spent the rest of that night packing their meager belongings, too excited to sleep anyway. By daybreak, they had loaned what little furniture they had, but would no longer need, to friends and had boxed up everything else to carry with them. They were ready to begin their new jobs.

As promised, shortly after six a carrier arrived for their things, and at six-thirty they were on their way to tell their previous bosses that yesterday had been their last day of work. By nine o'clock they had arrived at the Steed mansion and were rapidly putting their things away so they could begin their new duties.

To Audrey's relief, Landon and Marshall had both been out of the house when they'd arrived and she was able to unpack her things without any interference from either one. Though she was certain Landon had understood her silent, yet determined message the evening before, she was just as certain he was the type to pay it no heed. Until he proved to himself that she was truly not going to give in to his wanton desires, he would continue to do all he could to seduce her. She was aware it would take time to convince him that she was truly not interested in anything like that, but how much time? Days? Weeks? Just how long would it take for him to tire of such foolishness? An entire month possibly?

She shook her head at the thought. A month was a long time to have to fend off his unwanted advances. But fend them she would, because she did not need to add further complications to her life at the moment. If she intended to take full advantage of her new position in the Steed household, she needed to be able to center her attention on everything that went on around her, and not on keeping Landon Steed out of her bed. Though she was determined to one day be both rich and powerful, she was just as determined that she attain those goals by her own wit and resourcefulness, and not by sleeping with the boss's son—for whatever rewards it might bring.

With so much plaguing her thoughts, it was almost noon before Audrey finished with her unpacking and was finally ready to report to the kitchen, wherever that was. But before going downstairs to find out, she stopped by Seth's room to wish him luck, only to discover he had already finished putting his belongings away and had left his room.

Sighing heavily, she turned to go on downstairs alone when she noticed that a large, rosy-cheeked woman dressed in a pale gray uniform and a crisp white apron was already on her way up. Deciding to wait until the stairs were clear, Audrey stepped back to let her pass.

"You Audrey Stoane?" the woman asked, halting a few steps from the top. Her gaze quickly swept the length of her, as if trying to judge her worth.

"Yes," Audrey answered timorously. She felt uncomfortable with the way the woman tilted her head from side to side to get a better view of her.

"Ya'll do, I guess," she finally decided with a slight Irish lilt, then waved for her to follow. "Come along, let's get ya started. I was hopin' Ruby's uniforms would fit you, but I'm afraid they'd have to be cut down too much. I guess we'll have to have yer uniforms made up from scratch. It'll take a few days longer. I hope ya have enough of those old clothes ya've got on to last until then."

Audrey glanced down at her skirt and blouse while she followed the woman down the stairs. True, the clothing she wore was not new, but they were among her better garments and it hurt her pride to have them referred to as "old clothes." With a stubborn lift of her chin, she decided the first thing she would buy with her next pay would be a pretty new dress—from a regular dress shop and not from a second-hand store. After all, if she intended to better her station in life, she would need to look the part, and since she would have no other expenses while living at the Steed mansion, she could afford to splurge a little.

"I want to be sure Andre gets yer measurements before he leaves. He's in with yer brother now," the woman went on to say as she turned toward the back of the house. "Oh, by the way, I'm Kelly Meagan. I suppose Mr. Steed told ya that I be in charge of all the domestic help around here. I'll be the one tellin' ya what to do. I'm also the one ya should come to if ya have any complaints."

"I'm pleased to meet you." Audrey hurried to keep up, surprised by the large woman's agile movements as she breezed along the hallway, her wide skirts dancing in lively animation behind her.

"Do me a good job and ya will find I'm easy to get along with. But if I catch ya loafin' about when ya should be a workin', or find that ya've put some of yer duties off on someone else, ya'll rue the day ya ever met me," Kelly continued, not mincing her words. "I expect an honest day's work out of everyone, no matter who they are or why they were hired."

"Of course," Audrey stammered, a little taken aback by Kelly's abruptness.

"As long as we understand each other."

Audrey followed alongside the woman in silence for a moment, wondering if she should ask any questions about her duties yet or wait until after they'd reached the kitchen, which she assumed was where they were headed. She had a feeling that Kelly was used to breaking in new girls and decided to wait and see if she had any questions once she'd heard everything the Irishwoman had to say.

"Later on," Kelly said, effectively interrupting her straying thoughts, "I'll give ya a complete tour of the house. That way, ya'll be knowin' yer way around if, for some reason, ya're needed in another part of the house. There may be days when ya'll have to help with the regular housework, but for now, ya will mainly be a workin' in the kitchen. I was told that ya already know a lot about cookin'. Is that true?"

"I know the basics," she admitted, turning her head first in one direction then another, able to do little more than catch tiny glimpses of the lavishly furnished rooms they passed while she continued the struggle to keep up with Kelly's hurried gait. "I've never really had the opportunity to prepare anything fancy, but I can cook a hardy meal out of very little."

"For now, ya won't have to worry about preparin' anything fancy. We'll start ya out doing simple things like choppin' vegetables, keepin' the fires goin', and washin' the pots and pans as they're used. Eventually, though, I'll expect ya to take yer turn plannin' the menu, settin' the dinin' room table, and servin' the family meals, which I'm afraid can fall at the oddest hours around this house."

Following Kelly when she made an abrupt turn at the end of the hall and entered a second, smaller corridor, Audrey listened while she further explained what her duties would include. By the time they had reached the kitchen, she pretty much understood what would be expected of her and had found none of it to be truly objectionable. After all, it was only a temporary position as far as she was concerned—a stepping-stone to better things.

Upon entering the kitchen, Audrey first noticed the size, for it was huge, then she noticed how modernized the equipment was, some of which she'd never seen the likes before. It wasn't until she was fully inside that she realized there were four other women in the room, and all of them had stopped what they were doing to look at her.

"Girls, I want ya to meet Audrey Stoane. She'll be a-workin' in the kitchen with ya," Kelly announced, though obviously it was not news to anyone in the room.

"So that's her," someone mumbled loud enough for Audrey to hear, yet not be able to pinpoint the direction from which it had come. "No wonder she rates a room upstairs."

Audrey glanced around in hopes of determining who had said such a thing, but she was unable to tell which of the four women had spoken, though she suspected it was the plump little blonde who stood near the larger of the two stoves, staring at her as if she were some ugly spot on the wall that needed to be cleaned.

"That's quite enough," Kelly admonished, giving them all a meaningful glance. "If ya have any complaints, bring them to me. Otherwise, be keepin' them to yerself." She paused to see if there would be any response to that, then immediately proceeded with the introductions.

One by one, Audrey met all four of the women assigned to the kitchen: Cora Fagan, Harriet Martin, June Ballard, and Molly McMillain. Cora was in charge of baked goods and, according to Kelly, did little else. She rarely was asked to serve, nor was she ever asked to set the dining table. Cora had been there the longest and was clearly the oldest of the four, though not quite as old as Kelly, who appeared to be in her forties. Cora was also the only one in the room who wore a white mobcap to protect her hair. Tiny wisps ducked out beneath the ruffled edge, letting Audrey see that Cora's hair was curly and light brown, matching the color of her thin eyebrows. Audrey could tell that Cora was very proud of her position in the Steed household.

Harriet, who it turned out had just recently been hired, was probably the youngest and definitely the prettiest of the lot. Still undoubtedly in her teens, her massive mane of coal-black hair was piled high atop her head and held into place by two large combs and at least a dozen hairpins. Her big green eyes were friendly, matching the smile that came easily to her lips. Audrey immediately liked Harriet and thought that if she ever needed a friend, this girl would be the most likely candidate.

June, too, was quick with a smile, yet just as quick to tuck that smile away, which made Audrey nervous. She was tall, thin, and rather plain-looking, but obviously interested in everything that went on around her. Audrey was told that June, who looked to be about her own age, had worked there for over five years and seemed as if she would be quite satisfied to continue working there for forty more.

Molly was the watchful blonde near the stove. She was the short and, kindly put, roundest of the four women, with ample amounts of both bosom and hips filling her crisp gray and white uniform. Clearly, Molly resented

Audrey's presence and didn't care that everyone knew it. Audrey could not imagine why she had taken such an immediate dislike to her and decided to do what she could to show the girl she meant her no harm.

"I'll go get the measuring tape so we can get yer measurements," Kelly said, distracting Audrey from her thoughts. "The sooner Andre gets started on yer uniforms, the better." Before sweeping from the room, Kelly again looked at Audrey's attire as if it were little more than rags, leaving her standing awkwardly before the rest of the women, wondering what she should do first.

chapter three

Seth took readily to his new job, though he found it hard to believe that the most difficult thing he'd been asked to do that first day was to stand around in stuffy office hallways and wait. Being as large and as brawny as he was, he was used to doing strenuous jobs. At the warehouse, he'd spent most of his days hauling heavy crates and barrels from the loading docks to the storage area, or from the storage area back to the loading docks, to be hoisted onto a customer's wagon. Whenever there was something particularly heavy to be moved, Seth was usually the first one to be called, and he was usually told to hurry.

After having been measured for the suits he was expected to wear during work, which he felt had taken a ridiculous amount of time, he'd discovered that about all his new job really consisted of was following Marshall Steed around from place to place, waiting for him to get finished with his different meetings.

Though he didn't particularly enjoy waiting outside office doors while Marshall conducted his daily business, Seth truly enjoyed the rest of his job. He liked riding in Marshall's fine, high-sprung carriage and even enjoyed accompanying him from building to building. It felt good to be out and about, breathing fresh air for a change. To him, his new job was a dream come true, so much so that he easily put up with all the hours spent waiting alone in dark hallways or cramped outer offices.

At first Seth could not understand why James, who also accompanied Marshall everywhere, was allowed to go inside with the boss while he, himself, was not. But Seth soon learned that James was more than a personal assistant or an armed bodyguard; he was Marshall's business secretary and, as such, kept careful records of all the different meetings that went on during the day and sometimes well into the night. Several times, Marshall had referred to James as his right-hand man and swore he could not get along without him.

Audrey, too, had quickly accustomed herself to her new job and, before long, was familiar enough with the kitchen to find whatever she needed without anyone's help.

Soon she had learned that Cora, Harriet, June, and Molly worked exclusively in the kitchen in two separate nine-hour shifts that overlapped by three hours at midday. The only time that all of them were in the kitchen working together was from noon until three o'clock.

Shortly after the tall case clock beside the dining room door had chimed three, Cora and June left. Having begun their work shift at six o'clock that morning, the two were finished for the day. Harriet and Molly, who had not come in until noon, were expected to remain until nine. Occasionally, the latter group had to work a little later than nine o'clock, if there was a special late-night dinner planned, but the women were always well rewarded for their overtime. Kelly saw to that.

Audrey was delighted to discover that she, too, would be expected to work only nine hours a day, yet would still earn six dollars a week as promised—a full dollar for each day she worked. Accustomed to jobs that required twelve and thirteen hours of work each day for far less pay, she

45

felt as if she were on holiday.

Having also learned that she was to be a part of the second shift, working from noon until nine every day except Thursdays, Audrey realized she would have the mornings to do whatever she wanted—a luxury she'd never before been afforded. Why, she could sleep until the sun came up if she took a notion to! And she'd still have the rest of her mornings and all day Thursday to relax or go out and spend her money any way she saw fit. She could hardly believe her good fortune and worked hard to assure she did not lose the job before she got from it exactly what she wanted.

That first afternoon passed at a dizzying pace, while Audrey struggled to keep up with the continuous pile of dirty dishes Harriet and Molly produced as they prepared first the afternoon tea and then the evening meal. Meanwhile, she also had to keep the fires in the two stoves evenly stoked and make sure nothing in the pots on top of the stoves ran dry of liquid or got too hot.

Before Audrey knew it, the clock revealed that the hour had passed eight. Supper had been served promptly at seven, and all that was left for them to do before retiring for the evening was to wash and dry the dessert dishes Molly had just gathered from the dining room and then put them away.

Though Audrey had worked hard to prove her worth to both Kelly and her coworkers, and despite the fact that she had not slept at all the night before, when the time finally came to drop her dirty apron into the hamper and leave the kitchen, she was too full of repressed energy to sleep. Instead, she went to Seth's room to wait until her brother retired for the night. She wanted to hear all about his first day as Marshall's bodyguard and tell him a little about her new job.

In the many hours that had passed since morning, she'd seen her brother only once, while he and several of Marshall's other male employees were served their supper at a large dinner table near the back of the

46

kitchen. It was the same table where she and the other women who worked for Marshall later ate their evening meal, which had been a thick, hardy stew made from the mutton left over from the family's dinner the night before.

"What are you doing still awake?" Seth asked when he entered his room shortly after nine-thirty and found his sister curled up on the blue and white silk-covered couch, staring past the ornate metal fender into an empty fireplace, her eyes wide with distant thought.

"I wanted to hear how your day went." Startled from her reverie, she did not bother to get up while she watched him shrug out of an unfamiliar light gray summer coat. When he then grabbed for the ends of his black necktie, tugging frantically in his haste to be rid of it, she fought the urge to laugh. "Where'd you get those clothes?"

"From some shop over on Broadway. Mr. Steed bought them for me to wear until my own clothes get ready. Seems he likes for his employees to look their best at all times," he explained. His nose wrinkled at the idea of having to wear such finery every day, while he continued to struggle with the stubborn knot at the base of his throat. "I'll have to wear one of these ridiculous neckties and some sort of fancy day coat from now on, even in the summer. But then again, I was assured the coats Mr. Andre is making for me will fit me much better than that confounded contraption."

Though finally starting to make a little headway with the tangled knot, he scowled disgustedly at the wadded pile of light gray material he'd just tossed haphazardly across the closest chair.

At last, he'd ridded himself of his tie, then arched back his head and stretched out his tired arms in an effort to relax his cramped muscles. He frowned at the ripping sound that resulted and peered down at the gaping hole he'd just created along the narrow seam just below his right sleeve. Shaking his head tiredly, he fumbled with

47

the tiny pearl buttons along the front of the flimsy white garment. "I sure hope the shirts he's sewing for me will be made of sturdier material and allow for a little more moving room than this one did."

Audrey laughed at her brother's disgruntled expression. "I'm getting new uniforms, too," she informed him, glancing down at the faded blue skirt tucked neatly around her folded legs. It pleased her to know that she soon would be able to toss her well-worn garments aside in favor of newer frocks.

"I know. I was in the room when Kelly brought Andre your measurements. He seemed far more pleased with your size than mine. Every time he went to write down another one of my measurements, he mumbled to himself something about it being easier to clothe a tree." Seth grinned, then changed the subject as he sank down onto the Grecian couch beside her, plopping his feet across the top of the tiny marble-topped table in front of him, one leg at a time, one atop the other. "So, how did your day go?"

"Fine," she told him, then quickly recounted all that she had done that day and everyone she'd met thus far, including the other four cooks, the six housekeepers, a real-live lady's maid, and of course, Kelly, who oversaw everyone else's work. Most of the women she had met only briefly during supper and had yet to learn everyone's name, but she had remembered far more about them than she'd expected.

Thinking everything she'd done and heard that day and everyone she'd met quite fascinating, she left nothing out as she responded to her brother's query with eager enthusiasm.

Soon, Seth was nodding sleepily at her side and Audrey realized that he did not share her excitement for all that had happened that day. She noticed he was desperately in need of sleep. Rather than keep him awake any longer, she bent forward and placed a sisterly kiss at his temple, then left the room so he could go to bed before he actually fell asleep sitting straight up.

Still bursting with far too much inner exuberance to actually sleep, Audrey was reluctant to head for her own bedroom but really had nowhere else to go. Though she would have enjoyed a late night stroll through the lovely gardens that surrounded the house, she was not certain employees were allowed such privileges and quickly decided against it. She did not want to chance making any mistakes that might jeopardize her job before she'd accomplished everything she had set out to do. Instead, she decided to go on to her room and enjoy the beautiful lamp-lighted gardens from her window.

Having been too busy that afternoon to think of anything beyond mastering the different tasks at hand, Audrey had not had many opportunities to think about Landon, nor about his forward behavior of the evening before. But, while she slowly walked along the main corridor that eventually led to the shorter corridor where his bedroom lay positioned directly across the hallway from hers, his handsome image came quickly to mind.

Her insides fluttered nervously while she wondered if he was still downstairs talking with his father or if he'd already come upstairs for the night. She had heard that the rich were accustomed to staying awake until all hours, then lying in bed until long after the sun came up; but then, again, Landon did not seem to be typical of most wealthy men. His muscular shoulders and sun-tanned skin were the most baffling. They didn't quite fit with what one usually expected of the rich, nor did his odd habit of staying home at night and, thus, out of the different society pages.

When Audrey turned that last corner and entered the short section of hallway to her room, she was relieved to discover Landon's two doors already closed. At least she would not have to put up with a repeat of the previous night's activities. Quietly, she slipped past the two closed doors and entered her own room, expecting to find it empty as she gently closed the door.

49

Because someone had been kind enough to light the small sconce gas lamp nearest the door and leave it burning low—probably when the hall lamps had been lit earlier—all Audrey had to do to fill the room with a rich, warm glow was to twist the tiny brass knob half a turn to the right. When that side of the room slowly brightened, she became immediately aware that someone else was in her room. A slight movement along the outer circle of her vision made her glance up in time to watch Landon move away from the semi-shadows near her open window into better light.

"I was starting to think you'd gotten lost," he commented, moving casually to one of the damask-covered sofas nearby and sinking comfortably into its soft depths, as if he had every right to be there. "How was your first day?"

"What are you doing in here?" she asked, ignoring his question, furious that he had felt it perfectly all right to make himself so comfortable in her bedroom.

"Waiting for you," he answered honestly, then reached up to slowly undo the top three buttons of his shirt, making himself all the more comfortable—and Audrey all the more *un*comfortable. "You probably noticed that I had to be out of the house most of the day taking care of several business problems, one of which occurred at the last minute. I barely made it back in time to get dressed for dinner, so I never had much of a chance to drop by the kitchen and find out how your first day was. I hope everything went well."

"It went as it should," she told him with a curt nod, but offered no further comment while she studied him warily from across the room. Though her first inclination had been to show her outrage and demand that he leave her bedroom immediately, screaming if she had to, she'd quickly decided against such brash action. She knew that to anger him in any way might result in the sudden loss of her job, and that would never do. She needed this job. She needed the contacts she expected to make while working in this house. She would have to handle her present plight firmly, but very, very carefully.

"There were no little problems you'd like taken care of?" He tilted his head while he studied her with lazy interest.

"If there were any problems, I'd report them to Kelly," she stated matter-of-factly.

Landon smiled that endearing smile of his that had probably melted many a female heart, but Audrey was determined to remain unaffected by it. Crossing her arms over her thudding heart, she stepped back. She tried to look only mildly annoyed while she sought to steady herself by leaning back against the edge of a nearby dresser.

"You look tired," he said, then patted the cushion beside him. "Come and sit down."

"I'm not at all tired," she answered honestly, *perhaps a little weak around the knees, but not at all tired.* "I'd much rather stand."

He shrugged, reclining comfortably, stretching his arms across the curved back of the pale yellow cabriole sofa. The light blue material of his dinner shirt stretched taut across his muscular chest. Audrey wondered again how a man of his apparent means managed to keep so fit as she tried unsuccessfully not to notice where his shirt had gaped open at the collar, revealing a lightly tanned throat and a portion of the dark, curling hair that swept across his chest in soft, smooth patterns. She couldn't imagine a man of Landon's wealth lifting as much as a finger to do anything he could pay someone else to do for him. Yet the sturdy muscles across his shoulders and along his arms and thighs proved he did something in the way of regular exercise. Something more than take a nightly walk to smoke a cigar like his father did.

Having noticed where Audrey's gaze had drifted, Landon's smile deepened, forming long, narrow dimples at the outer corners of his mouth. "I guess Seth told you that Father reported last night's incident to the police," he stated, casually waving his hand, though he watched her carefully for a reaction.

A cold feeling of apprehension crept over Audrey when the full implication of what he had just said sank in. Wondering why he thought she should care one way or the other about his father's visit to the police, she felt her stomach slowly tighten. Again she wondered if he had somehow discovered the truth. He certainly sounded suspicious of her reason for being there. And if that were true, she had to next wonder what he intended to do about it, aware blackmail would not be beneath the likes of him.

"Oh?" she muttered in a voice that had not sounded quite as strangled as it could have—considering the jagged lump that had formed in her throat.

"Yes, I thought you'd be pleased to know that the police think they've already captured the two men who attacked Father and James last night. In fact, Father has been asked to go down to the station tomorrow morning and make an identification. I imagine they'll want James and Seth to do the same."

"How do they know they have the right men?" she asked, hoping against hope that her part in the incident would go undetected. She knew no one else, not even Seth, could possibly understand her reasons for taking such desperate measures, which is why she'd never let him in on the scheme to begin with. As far as Seth was concerned, he had truly saved Marshall Steed from great harm and had been justly rewarded.

"They don't know for certain . . . and won't until Father has had a chance to go down and look them over. The captain sent a messenger by here earlier, requesting that he stop by the station sometime tomorrow morning to identify the two. But I thought you'd be pleased to know that there's a very good possibility the two culprits who caused all that concern last night are probably already in jail. You won't have to worry about Seth having to go up against them again. And, if the police are able to find out who put them up to it and arrest that person, too, then you won't have to worry about anyone else being hired to finish the job."

"What makes you think someone put them up to it?" she asked, swallowing with panic.

"Because those two men can't possibly have the good sense it takes to think out such a workable plan. It's pretty obvious that someone studied the situation carefully enough to have learned my father's nightly habits. They picked just the right moment to make such an attempt—while Father was alone with only James to protect him. Yet, even so, they managed to bungle the job."

"Couldn't it have been blind luck that they picked just the right moment?" she asked, and wished he'd never reached such a conclusion. Suddenly, she had a horrifying vision of being carted off to jail and tossed into a dark, dank cell with only bread and water for meals.

"It could have been blind luck, I guess, but I really don't think so" is all Landon had to say on the matter before suddenly changing the subject. "Say, Seth told me that he worked at a warehouse down near the docks before he got this job as Father's bodyguard, but he didn't mention where you worked. Just what sort of work did you do?"

"I worked as a seamstress," she answered, relieved that the subject had been changed but feeling uneasy that Landon had decided to change it so abruptly.

"You can sew as well as cook?" he asked, surprised. He looked at her with renewed interest.

"I can do lots of things," she said in ready defense of herself.

"Can you now?" he asked. His brow rose high and his blue eyes sparkled with bedevilment while his gaze swept over her. "And are you quite talented at all these *other* things you do?"

Knowing the direction his thoughts had taken and wondering if she'd been purposely tricked into saying

53

something like that, Audrey tossed her shoulders back and leveled her gaze at him. "I'm quite good at *everything* I do."

"I have no doubt that you are." His mouth stretched into a pleased smile. Slowly, he rose from the sofa and moved toward her.

Instinctively, Audrey drew in a long, deep breath to steady herself while she watched him cross the room with an air of nothing less than smooth sophistication. Her eyes remained bright with determination when he subjected her to yet another of his leisurely appraisals.

"I'm not the least bit intimidated by you," she stated defiantly when he had finally come to a halt only a few feet in front of her. Though her heart rampaged wildly out of control, she continued to lean casually against her dresser with her arms folded over her chest, hoping to appear totally unaffected by his sudden closeness.

Landon's gaze lingered on the soft curve of her lips while she spoke, then lifted to her shining brown eyes. "You're not in the *least* bit intimidated?"

"No, not in the least bit," she repeated, though with far less conviction than before. Aware he was now close enough to capture her in his arms and force a kiss from her—or whatever else crossed his mind—she waited cautiously for his next move, praying that it would be in the direction of the door.

Landon looked at her with an arched brow, clearly doubting her statement. "And nothing I can do will change that?"

"No, nothing."

"Then it won't make any difference if I kiss you," he muttered before reaching quickly forward to do just that.

Before Audrey actually realized what was happening, though she had halfway expected it from the beginning, his hands had already caught her upper arms and had pulled her sharply against his long, hard frame. His mouth silenced any startled protest she might offer with the confident movement of his lips over hers.

Audrey was stunned by the erotic sensations that shot through her like hot bolts of summer lightning. They were not at all what she'd expected. In the past, only clumsy and grossly inexperienced suitors had tried to kiss her, and she had easily ignored their efforts. But Landon's kiss was neither clumsy nor inexperienced. Nor did it leave her cold like the other kisses had. In fact, his kiss had just the opposite effect. He definitely knew what he was doing, easily awakening a heady response inside her that both amazed and alarmed her. It took all the self-restraint she could muster to remain perfectly still and show no response while his masterful kiss cast wave after wave of pure ecstasy through her body, leaving her weak and light-headed.

Having discovered years ago that the quickest way to cool any man's ardor was to pretend to be completely unaffected by his kiss, she held her body rigid and tried to keep her breath under firm control. Just when she felt she was about to lose the battle raging inside her, Landon's arms loosened their hold and she moved away from him. The woozy feeling in her stomach caused her to reach again for the solid support of the dresser.

"You know, I really ought to slap you soundly for having taken such liberties with me. Or at the very least, I should have my brother call you out and demand satisfaction," she said with amazing calm, though her senses still reeled from the unexpected onslaught of his kiss. "But if you'll leave this bedroom immediately and promise never to try anything like that again, I'll pretend it never happened."

Landon looked as if he'd *already* been slapped. "Do you mean to say that kiss did nothing to you?"

"Should it have?" she asked innocently.

He studied her a long moment, clearly perplexed. "I— I guess not."

"Then you'll leave now, with no further incident?"

She held a deep breath while she waited for his answer, praying it would be yes. Another minute in his presence, and her firm resolve just might turn into pure jelly, and then where would she be?

Landon shifted his weight to one leg while he studied her a moment longer, clearly bothered by her stony reaction. His brow notched, forming a narrow ridge in his forehead while he continued to gaze curiously at her. How could that kiss have left her so totally unaffected when it had left him so unexpectedly shaken?

"And just what did you find wrong with that kiss?" he finally asked, unable to believe that the power from that kiss could have been so one-sided.

"Nothing. I'm just not that sort of girl," she told him with a firm shake of her head, knowing she did not need to complicate her life by lending her heart to someone like Landon, someone who would use her until he eventually tired of her, then cast her easily aside. The rich were notorious for their casual affairs. It was the one thing she did not plan to indulge in once she, too, had money. "Now, if you don't mind, I'd like to go on to bed."

"But I thought you said you weren't tired," he quickly reminded her, as if trying to find obvious discrepancies in her behavior.

"Good night, sir," she stated in a determined voice, and moved across the room to open the door for him before turning to stare at him expectantly.

"I'm leaving, I'm leaving," he muttered, still deeply perplexed by her reaction to his kiss—or rather total lack of it. He'd put his all into that kiss. She should have felt *something*. He certainly had.

Pausing in the doorway, he looked back at her again but said nothing before stepping out into the hall.

Relief washed over Audrey as she watched him leave, but it wasn't until she had the door securely closed and the brass bolt shoved firmly into place that her stomach

56

finally ceased its frantic churning and her heart settled down to a far more normal rate.

"It was just a little horse race. I don't know why Father is so upset about it," Rachel wailed as she entered the house through the kitchen door.

Audrey glanced up in time to see the young blonde fling her riding crop across the room, knowing immediately that she had just caught her first glimpse of Landon's little sister but, at the same time, surprised to see such a stark contrast between the two. Rachel was as short as Landon was tall, barely an inch over five feet, with long honey-colored hair falling in soft, bouncy waves to the small of her back.

"You know how Father feels about such things," came Landon's response just moments before he appeared only a few yards behind his sister. "He desperately wants to make a lady out of you, and racing horses in Central Park is not exactly what most people consider ladylike behavior. What would Preston think if he found out about your latest escapade?"

"He'd be proud that I won," she said with a defiant toss of her head, and continued to march across the kitchen with amazingly long strides for such a short person.

"Would he really?" Landon asked in a skeptical tone.

"No," she finally admitted. Her shoulders sagged with defeat as she spun about on the heels of her riding boots to face her brother, her pert mouth twisted into a curious frown. "He'd have a full-blown fit."

"That's what I thought," Landon said, shaking his head while he patted his sister's shoulder in a show of brotherly affection. "You are just going to have to make up your mind, Little Bit. Either you want to marry Preston enough to change your errant ways, or you don't. And if you don't, you really should consider

57

calling the engagement off—before it's too late."

"You don't like Preston, do you?" Rachel tilted her head to one side while she gazed questioningly at her brother with shining blue eyes.

"I'm not particularly fond of him, no," Landon admitted. "I don't think he's at all the sort of man you should marry."

"But he's rich," she swiftly pointed out as she spun cheerfully back around, heading again toward the dining room. "And his family is one of the most prominent in all of New York. Don't those facts account for anything?"

"Not much," Landon responded, glancing up to notice the three sets of eyes upon them while he followed his sister across the room. His gaze locked with Audrey's for a brief moment, as if to question what she found so interesting.

Surprised he had noticed her, her heart reacted by slamming sharply against her breastbone, which set off a rippling effect through her entire body. Quickly, she glanced down at the dishwater, where her hands suddenly came back to life.

"Not when you consider that your dearly devoted Preston has done very little to help his father manage his estate," Landon went on to explain, still following Rachel, though his gaze lingered on Audrey. "I realize the Windthorst fortune was acquired long before Preston ever became of age, but Preston has since seen little need to do anything to help his father in any way."

"True," she answered agreeably just seconds before she reached forward to push open the heavy swinging door. "But he's still young. There's plenty of time for him to learn how to handle his father's finances." She gave her brother one quick backward glance before she disappeared from sight.

"Learning to handle his father's finances isn't going to be his biggest problem, I'm afraid," Landon muttered as he, too, disappeared through the door. "His biggest problem will be learning to handle his fool-brained wife."

As the heavy dining room door swung shut behind the pair, the kitchen fell oddly silent while Audrey, Harriet, and June exchanged startled glances, then suddenly burst into a fit of giggles.

"Imagine racing horses right there in Central Park? Do you suppose her father is going to go through with his threat to lock her away in her room?" Harriet asked, blinking back the tears that had resulted from her uncontrollable laughter.

"Well, he warned her. One more incident and he'll lock her in and put a guard at her door," June said, reaching up to dab away her own tears.

"Yes, but knowing Miss Rachel, she'll just climb out the window instead," Harriet said, obviously delighted by the girl's unfailing audacity.

"Not if I put locks on her windows, too," came a dark, deep voice from behind them, startling the three into immediate silence.

"Mr. Steed, we didn't hear you come in," Harriet stammered apologetically, her green eyes wide with horror.

"Obviously," Marshall stated in a brusque tone as he stalked angrily into the room with James at his heels and Seth bringing up the rear.

"And to answer your question, yes, I do plan to lock that girl in her room. And I will indeed post a guard at her door. She's going to learn to behave like a proper lady, even if it means locking her away for the rest of her life!" Marshall's nostrils flared as he huffed out an angry breath.

Everyone in the room stood stone still while they waited for him to finish his tirade. Even Kelly, who had just entered the kitchen from the back stairs, had frozen in her tracks, refusing to as much as blink.

"This is the last time that girl is going to defy me!" he shouted, turning to glare at them over his shoulder as he stormed toward the dining room door, with James and Seth following quietly at his heels. "She's gone too far this time. I'll see to it that she never, ever, *ever*—"

The rest of his angry speech was lost to the rest of them as the dining room door swung shut behind Seth.

Startled by the man's behavior, Audrey glanced wide-eyed at Kelly, who was slowly shaking her head as she moved farther into the room. "What's he going to do to her?"

"For now, he'll do exactly what he said he'd do," Kelly told her. "He'll indeed lock her away in her room with a guard of some sort posted at her door. But soon enough, he'll calm down, she'll smile that pretty smile of hers, and she will again be free to do exactly what she wishes. He never stays angry with her for long, no matter what she does, and believe me she's done much worse than this."

"Then you heard about the horse racing in Central Park?"

"Yes, I was on my way down the stairs when they came in. But, when ya consider some of her other escapades, this one matters very little."

Audrey was extremely curious about those other escapades, but she knew it was not her place to encourage such gossip. "You don't think he'll take a strap to her, do you?" she asked, truly worried for the girl, whom she'd immediately come to like.

"Oh, no, he never does anything like that," Kelly quickly assured her, then let out a wry chuckle as she again shook her head. "Though sometimes I think maybe somebody should."

chapter four

"But, Father, surely you're not serious," Rachel cried, gazing up at him with an expression of utter disbelief in her wide blue eyes.

"Oh, but I am," Marshall said firmly, crossing his arms across his chest and glowering angrily at his unruly daughter. "I warned you, Rachel. One more such infraction and you'd find yourself confined to your rooms for an undetermined length of time."

"But you can't mean to keep me in *tonight*. Preston and I have already made plans to go to the theater. It's opening night for John Minter's new play at Booth's. Everyone who is anyone will be there," she wailed, her eyes bright with unshed tears. "What will he think when he comes calling for me this evening, only to have you tell him that I will not be permitted to go, that I've been locked away in my rooms like some small child?"

"You should have thought of that before goading Samuel Ewan into that horse race," Marshall shouted. "Besides, after I've explained the situation to Preston as it truly is, I'm certain he will not only understand, but will support my decision wholeheartedly. He cannot allow his future wife to be out gallivanting around on horseback like some wild bantling, any more than *I* can allow it of my daughter. You are not a child anymore, but as long as you continue to misbehave like one, you will be

61

punished like one."

"A child? You think I acted like a child? No *child* that I know could ride Thunderhead with the same expertise I just did. Why, there's hardly a grown *man* that can do as well," Rachel was quick to point out, angry that he had belittled her obvious skill. Wasn't that just like a man? "I daresay *you* wouldn't last ten minutes on that horse's back."

"I wouldn't last ten minutes on any horse's back," Marshall readily agreed. "But that's not the point. The point is, you defied me again and will now pay the price for having done so."

A deathly silence fell over the room.

Seth stood outside the door, trying not to listen to the heated exchange between father and daughter. But he couldn't help overhearing most of it. Neither could James, who stood in the hallway beside him with his hands folded behind his back. The two exchanged uncomfortable glances, knowing full well that Marshall's anger could eventually spill over onto them.

"Why can't that girl simply do what she's told?" James muttered so only Seth could hear. "Why does she always have to push her father to the very limit?"

Seth shrugged. Being only his second day in Marshall Steed's employ, he did not know enough about the situation to make any sort of judgment. All he knew was that his boss was already in a foul mood from having learned that the two men the police were holding in custody were not the two who had jumped him the evening before, and now this. His own daughter, a mere slip of a girl, had clearly defied her father's wishes and had caused a household disturbance by doing so. And it was obvious that this was not the first time she had rebelled against her father.

"Seth!" Marshall's voice shot out into the hall in an angry burst, startling both men. "Seth, get in here!"

"Yes, sir," he called back immediately, casting James an uneasy glance while he hurried toward the doorway.

Stepping inside, he found Marshall and Rachel in the center of the room, standing only inches apart with their arms crossed and their eyes boring into each other. The scene struck Seth as comical, considering Marshall was a good foot taller than his daughter and twice as broad; yet she continued to meet his gaze squarely, as if she were his equal, if not his better.

"Can I help you, sir?"

"You most certainly can. I want you to stand guard outside these two rooms for the rest of the day. You will not let anyone into either room except for Emma or me. Rachel is not to be allowed to leave these rooms, *for any reason*, unless I instruct you differently. She is not even to speak to anyone except you, me, or Emma."

"What about Landon?" Rachel asked, more in a display of continued defiance than anything else.

"Landon shows you too much sympathy," Marshall countered quickly. "I think it would suit my purpose better to ask him to stay away."

Seth peered at Rachel, giving her sufficient time to respond before he awkwardly cleared his throat and asked what he felt was a foolish question. "Who is Emma?"

For the first time, Rachel glanced away from her father and turned her wide, luminous eyes to Seth.

An uncomfortably warm, tingly feeling washed over him, making him shift his weight nervously from one leg to the other. The eyes that now gazed curiously up at him were the dark, vivid blue of sapphires, fringed with heavy lashes and slightly tilted at the corners. They were the most beautiful eyes he'd ever seen. She was the most beautiful *girl* he'd ever seen, but he'd noticed that right away. Her skin was flawless, the color of rich cream. Her hair lay in soft, shimmering waves of spun gold past her shoulders. Her pert nose was perfectly shaped and her mouth softly inviting, despite the harshness of her frown and the determined set of her jaw.

Aware he was staring, Seth tried his best to look away

but couldn't. His gaze was captured by her beauty.

"Is this your new bodyguard?" Rachel asked. Though she spoke to her father, her eyes remained on Seth. Clearly, she was impressed by his size.

"He was, but for now, he's to be *your* new bodyguard. He's now been assigned the duty of keeping you confined to your rooms," Marshall answered with an adamant nod, very pleased with his decision. "He's to stay right out there in that hall and will be under strict orders to do whatever is necessary to keep you from leaving these rooms until I say differently."

"But what about supper?" she challenged, cutting her gaze to her father, but only for a moment. "Surely I'll be allowed to come downstairs for meals. You don't intend to starve me, too, do you?"

"I'll have Emma bring you a tray. I'll have her bring Seth one, too, since I don't want him leaving that hall even long enough to eat." He glanced at Seth to be sure that he had heard him, too. "Is that understood, Seth?"

"Yes, sir, fully understood," he answered, nodding sharply. The last thing he wanted to do was cause Marshall any further aggravation. Rachel had already caused plenty.

"Good, then find a comfortable chair and make yourself at home out there. I'm afraid you may have to be out there for quite a while," Marshall said, then spun about and headed for the door. "I'll find Emma and tell her what's been decided here. I'll see to it she brings you both some supper when it's time."

Seth watched his boss with raised eyebrows, feeling awkward at having been left behind, standing alone in the middle of his daughter's bedroom. Turning back to find Rachel still staring up at him with wide, curious eyes, he offered her an off-centered smile and wondered what he should say to her, for she was clearly waiting for him to say something.

"I . . . uh . . . I'm truly sorry about all I . . . uh," he muttered, floundering for the words that might explain

64

how he felt.

"I know. And I also know that none of this is in any way your fault," she quickly assured him, forming a smile so warm and so sensationally beautiful that it sent shock waves of awareness leaping through Seth's entire body, unnerving him to the point of distraction.

Tiny sets of crescents formed in her lower cheeks when her smile deepened, revealing shiny white teeth when she spoke. "Please, don't be too concerned about me. Father won't stay angry with me for long. He'll calm down soon enough, probably by this evening. And as soon as he does, I'll be allowed out of my rooms again and you can then go back to your regular duties." She stepped closer to get a better look at him.

When Seth got a closer view of Rachel's upturned face, he came to the conclusion that her eyes had to be the bluest blue he'd ever seen. Raising a hand that was not quite steady, he quickly swept it through his thick hair, awkwardly returning her smile. "I'm glad you're so understanding about all this, Miss Steed. I really am. I wouldn't want you to be angry with me for something I don't got any control over whatsoever. Your father is my boss. I have to do what he tells me or chance losing my job."

"Please, my name is Rachel," she told him, and deepened her smile even more, until Seth felt such a blaze of tempestuous desire burst to life inside him that he had to take a step back to better control the sudden unsteady pounding of his heart. Her gaze continued to search his, as if she wanted to look right into his very soul.

"I—I don't dare call you by your given name." His dark eyes grew round with concern.

"But I hate it when someone calls me Miss Steed. It makes me feel like some withered old spinster," she protested, pouting prettily.

"But what if your father was to hear me call you Rachel?" Seth asked, swallowing hard around the bulky lump that had formed in his throat. "I'm sure he wouldn't like that one bit."

"Then call me Miss Steed whenever he's around, if it makes you feel better. But when we are alone like this, I'd much rather you call me Rachel."

Alone like this? The words struck Seth hard across his stomach, making him suddenly aware that she was absolutely right. They were indeed alone—and in her bedroom of all places, which was extremely improper. What had gotten into him? He should have immediately followed Marshall out of the room. What would the man think if he and this person Emma were to return and find him still in Rachel's bedroom, standing there alone with his beautiful daughter? As protective as Marshall seemed to be, there was probably no limit to what he would do. Seth's pulse raced at an alarming rate.

"I—I don't think it's proper for us to be in here by ourselves . . . together . . . alone." Slowly, he started backing toward the door, his face deathly pale. "I'd better get on out into the hall before someone comes back and finds us like this. It would be sure to ruin your reputation."

Rachel tilted her head to a beguiling angle and moved toward him, clearly unconcerned about what others might think. Her blond hair swept forward to caress her shoulder in a way that made Seth envious. "Are you afraid of me, Seth?"

"No, ma'am, of course not," he lied, when suddenly he was terrified of her. Terrified of a little slip of a girl who looked as gentle and as vulnerable as a four-week-old kitten. So terrified of her he could hardly speak.

"Then why are you in such a hurry to leave? Don't you like me?" she asked, studying the shimmering depths of his soft brown eyes.

"Oh, yes, ma'am, I like you all right," he admitted, bobbing his head to emphasize just how much he did like her. "It's just that I don't think it's quite proper for me to be here in your bedroom alone like this. It could get us

66

both into a heap of trouble, and it appears to me that you already got yourself in enough trouble as it is."

Rachel continued to advance toward him, smiling playfully, until he felt compelled to take another step backward to avoid letting her come too close. His heart pounded against the wall of his chest like a massive train engine that had gone haywire.

"You are too afraid of me. Why? What have I done?"

"Nothing," he admitted, stumbling clumsily over a small decorative table near the door while he continued to back away from her. "Nothing at all."

Her gaze refused to leave his face. Tiny bumps of apprehension formed beneath his skin, covering him from his head to his toe—which was a considerable area, indeed.

"Then you'll agree to call me Rachel?" she asked, her eyes wide with hope.

"Yes, ma'am . . . ah . . . I mean, Rachel . . . ma'am," he stammered. He tried to swallow again, but this time his mouth was too dry. "But only when your father is not around. I don't dare call you by your given name when your father is present."

"And may I call you Seth?"

"Sure, if that's what you want."

"I do. I want that very much," she assured him, reaching out to touch his arm lightly.

Even though he had both a shirt and coat sleeve covering that arm, it felt to Seth as if her gentle touch had burned right through to set him on fire. "I—I . . . uh . . . I'd better get on out there and find me a chair to sit in. Your father could come back any minute and he'd sure rather find me out there than in here."

"I understand," she said brightly as she watched him stumble out of the room. "And Seth?"

He paused just outside her door, his heart frozen in mid-beat while he waited to hear what else she had to say.

"Thank you." Her voice was soft as a summer breeze, setting off yet another wave of sheer bedlam inside

67

his chest.

"For what?"

"For being my friend. It means a lot to me." Her gaze met with his, as if to convince him she spoke the truth.

Something about the way she looked at him made his insides ache. "I—I'll talk to you later. I—I got to go now," he stammered. He did not know what else to say. Having made his excuse, he immediately ducked out of sight. With his hand pressed firmly against his hammering chest, he hurried down the hall and into his room to get a chair, unable to believe that such a wee girl had caused his sturdy knees to tremble with something so very akin to fear and his heart to quake with such complete uncertainty. What had taken hold of him? And why, even now as he leaned heavily against his closed door, did her beautiful image come unbidden to mind, sending a whole flood tide of unfamiliar sensations through him?

Confused and shaken, he tried to figure out just what had happened to him in there, when suddenly the answer struck him like a thunderbolt. He was physically attracted to her, as any man would be attracted to so beautiful a woman. But that was ridiculous. She was Marshall Steed's daughter. He shouldn't allow himself to have such feelings for a girl of Rachel's high stature. Why, she was from a whole different world, a world of wealth, glamour, and proper breeding. It was wrong for a nobody like him to have any feelings at all for someone like her. But what could he do about it? The feelings had formed unexpectedly and were already very much a part of him.

The best thing for him would be to avoid Rachel whenever possible, which he decided should not be too hard. Seth had been hired to help protect Marshall, and he knew that as soon as the man was over his anger with his daughter, he would order him back to his regular duties, which would include very little opportunity to be alone with anyone other than Marshall himself. If Seth could just endure Rachel's confinement, then his problem would eventually resolve itself, he told himself as he picked up a chair and left his room to begin his guard duty.

"Well, what did you think of my little sister?" Landon asked, startling Audrey as she entered the dining room to return the clean china to its proper place in the massive glass-encased Edwards cabinet near the kitchen door.

"You frightened me," she admonished as she very nearly lost her grip on the expensive stack of plates and saucers she carried. "What are you doing in here at this time of the day?"

"I was on my way to the kitchen." He shrugged in that cavalier way of his while he continued across the room with long, easy strides. He paused near the table, still at what Audrey considered a safe enough distance away, yet close enough to cause her heart to hammer.

"Since I missed out on tea again this afternoon," he said happily, "and it's hours yet until supper, I thought I might be able to persuade Kelly into letting me have a crumb cake or two to tide me over."

"Kelly is not in there," Audrey quickly informed him while she set the china down on the sideboard, giving herself reason to place her back to him. The less she had to look at that impossibly handsome face, the better for her equilibrium. "Seems Mop has had her kittens in a very unlikely place somewhere in the attic. Kelly left more than fifteen minutes ago to help Norma and Regan get the cat and her kittens into a basket and moved to a more suitable spot."

"That cat," Landon chuckled, bringing to mind an image of the long-haired white cat with big blue eyes and funny little gray markings at her ears, nose, paws, and down her long, fluffy tail. "It appears that Kelly's efforts to prepare a nice, cozy place for her in the laundry room went for nothing."

69

"Evidently Mop had her own ideas about where she wanted to have those kittens," Audrey said as she opened the cabinet doors and began to place the plates and saucers on the proper shelves. She refused to let Landon deter her from the job she had come to do.

"Sometimes that cat is a little too independent for her own good. But that probably comes from being around my sister so much. Some of Rachel's stubborn ways must have rubbed off on the poor animal. How many kittens did she have this time? Did either housekeeper say?" he asked, suddenly moving closer, until he stood only inches from where the last of the china remained in a small stack on the sideboard.

Audrey attempted to show no reaction to the fact he'd come closer, though she was clearly aware he now stood only a few feet away. Without looking up, she carefully continued to rearrange the saucers she'd already placed on the shelves. "Regan mentioned that she thought there were five, but couldn't really be sure until they got up into the little cubbyhole where Mop had them and coaxed her away from them. That's why Regan and Norma came downstairs to get Kelly. With Rachel locked away in her rooms at the moment, Kelly seemed the next likely person to be able to get Mop to cooperate."

"Only because Kelly is the one who feeds her," he pointed out, knowing full well where that spoiled feline's loyalties lay. He studied her beautiful face for a moment. "Have you heard anything from your brother about whether or not the two men at the police station were the two who tried to kidnap Father?"

Icy prickles of apprehension snaked their way around Audrey's stomach. Again, she wondered if he suspected that she were in some way connected. "No, why do you ask?"

"No reason," he answered innocently, tilting his head to one side. "It's just that I haven't had a chance to ask Father about it and thought maybe you knew."

"Well, I don't," she said, trying her very best to sound unconcerned, though her insides were a cauldron of frightened emotions. When she then stepped over to pick up another plate from the sideboard, she found Landon's hand resting lightly along the edge. "I need those plates," she told him in her most polite southern drawl, hoping he would remove his hand and allow her to proceed with her work so she could leave the room as quickly as possible. After what had happened last night, she felt very nervous about being alone in the same room with him, even a room as large and as open as the grand dining room.

"These plates?" he asked, his blue eyes wide with innocence. "Here, let me hand them to you."

"That won't be necessary," she assured him, her insides fluttering at the thought. "If you'll just remove your hand, I can get to them easily."

"Please, be nice to me. I only want to help. It will help make up for last night."

"There's no need to make that up to me. As far as I'm concerned, it is already forgotten."

"Make it up to *you?* I meant your being nice would be a way for *you* to make it up to *me.*"

"What did I do?" she asked as she turned to face him with wide, disbelieving eyes.

"You crushed my male pride," he said in a voice so ludicrously serious that Audrey could not believe she'd understood him.

"I what?" Instinctively, she took a step back.

"How do you think it made me feel to discover my kiss had left you completely unaffected? You could have at least *pretended* to be overwhelmed with passion."

"I'm not very good at pretending such things," she told him, and took yet another step back. Her heart hammered furiously at the mere mention of that kiss. She wondered what he would think if he knew that the kiss had indeed affected her, so much that she'd spent

71

several impossible hours trying to fall asleep afterward.

"And I'm not very good at admitting defeat," he said, leaning his head forward as he took another step toward her. Slowly, his long, silky lashes lowered over sultry blue eyes like they had the night before, making his intentions instantly clear. "Somehow, I have to get a positive reaction out of you. I have to know that I have not lost my touch."

"What do you mean?" she asked, hoping that she had misunderstood. Every muscle in her body tightened in preparation for the worst.

"I mean, I intend to kiss you again, only this time I aim to put all the expertise I have into it. I can't allow your cold reaction to stand on my record," he told her, and continued to move steadily toward her with slow, deliberate steps.

"Don't you dare come near me again," she cried out. Her heart filled with panic as she reached for something to protect herself, finding only a gold-edged dinner plate within reach. "I told you I'm not that sort of woman."

"Ah, but I am that sort of man," he countered, never pausing in his advance upon her. His gaze bore directly into hers, demanding that she give in to him.

"Stay away from me," she warned, holding the plate up against her chest like a soldier's shield while she carefully continued to back away from him.

"Or you'll what? Scream? My ears can stand it," he said, obviously unconcerned that the scream might also bring the entire household rushing into the room.

"But can your hard head stand having this dinner plate smashed over it?" She raised the plate high to show she was serious.

"You wouldn't dare."

For every backward step she took, he offset it with a long, slow, agile step forward, until it became clear he was closing the gap between them.

"I'm warning you, stop right where you are," she said

when she realized he'd advanced to within arm's reach. She brought her hand back as if to fling the plate at him. "Don't you dare come any closer."

When he then reached out to capture her in his arms, her hand reacted instinctively. She brought the plate crashing down on top of his head. Broken pieces of china showered the floor at their feet.

Landon stared at her without moving, stunned that she'd actually done it. He blinked once, then slowly reached up and brushed the tiny shards of porcelain from his hair, his eyes as wide and as round as the dinner plate had once been.

Audrey watched in horror. Her hand flew to her mouth when she realized the trouble she had no doubt brought down upon herself. The sound of rapid footsteps on the stairs outside the main doors caught her attention and she knew, without actually seeing, that Kelly was on her way to investigate.

"What happened in here?" Kelly demanded to know, a large picnic basket clutched in one hand and a very disgruntled-looking white and gray cat tucked up under her other arm.

Audrey felt the color drain from her face when she turned to face the large woman, whose gaze had already taken in the fact that one of Marshall's dinner plates lay in a dozen broken pieces on the carpeted floor at her feet.

"I—I—" she tried to explain, but could not bring herself to admit what she'd done—though she felt she had justifiable reasons for having done it. Never had she felt so helpless.

"I'm afraid we broke one of Father's plates," Landon quickly offered. "It was an accident."

"We?" Kelly asked, clearly relieved to hear that Landon was in some way partially to blame.

"Yes. I was handing the plates to Audrey one at a time, thinking only to help; but before she had a good grip on this last one, I let it slip from my hand and it fell to the floor. I'd hoped the carpet might cushion its fall, but the fool thing hit my boot instead. Shattered into pieces."

Audrey glanced at him, unable to believe he had taken the blame. "It was as much my fault," she inserted quickly. "I should have reached for it sooner."

Kelly studied the two for a moment, as if trying to decide if she fully believed their story or not. Eventually, she let out an exasperated sigh and started back for the door. "Better be gettin' the mess cleaned up. I'll go tell Marshall about the accident as soon as I've found a suitable place to put these kittens."

"Tell him that I'll run down to Tiffany's and buy a replacement for the broken plate first thing in the morning," Landon called out to her as he knelt beside Audrey and began picking up the larger pieces.

"Why did you do that?" Audrey wanted to know as she, too, collected the jagged pieces, placing them in the crook of her apron.

"Do what?" He paused to look at her.

"Take the blame for the broken dish?"

"Because I was to blame. You warned me. I just didn't believe you would go through with it." He smiled at her with pure amusement when he reached up to touch the place where the plate had made contact with his head.

"And you aren't angry with me?"

"For what? Defending yourself against an arrogant rake like myself? Hardly," he said, laughing as he studied her startled reaction. "But don't go thinking I've had any change of heart. I always find a way to finish whatever I start. And I think I should warn you: We Steeds are quite accustomed to getting what we want."

"Meaning?"

"Meaning that I still intend to break through that invisible barrier you have thrown up around yourself, but at a time when you are not so aptly armed."

Audrey's insides tightened into a hard, painful knot as she wondered how far he intended to carry his scheme to seduce her, suddenly aware of the very real danger he represented. "Even though I don't want you to?"

"Especially because you don't want me to." His eyes then locked with hers when he reached forward to place the broken pieces he'd gathered into the fold of her apron with the rest. "I'll win you over yet, Audrey Stoane. Might as well get used to that idea, because it is inevitable."

chapter five

At five minutes to seven, Marshall came upstairs to tell Seth that he and James were headed to the Fifth Avenue Hotel for a dinner meeting with someone from out of town. He admitted he was not at all pleased with the thought of going out without the added protection of his new bodyguard, but he was determined to see Rachel's punishment through. For that night only, he planned to take Everett with him, as an added show of force, though he wasn't sure how forceful the thin butler would appear. Even so, he asked Seth to stay right where he was, watching both locked doors until his return, which could be as early as ten o'clock or as late as midnight. Then, almost as an afterthought, he handed Seth the door key, telling him to use it only in case of an emergency.

"And don't fall for any of her trickery," he warned, keeping his voice low so as not to attract Rachel's attention. "If she realizes that I've given you the key, she'll try to figure out some way to get you to open that door. Don't do it. Tell her you are under strict orders to keep the doors locked. Only Emma has permission to unlock the door, and that's so she can go in and out herself."

"Yes, sir," Seth answered firmly as he pocketed the key, knowing he had no intention of opening that door. He had yet to recover fully from his last glimpse of her.

76

To see her again might be his complete undoing.

"Remember, no matter what she does, no matter what excuses she comes up with—and I warn you she's a clever girl when it comes to creating excuses—you are not to open that door for her. That key is to be used *only* in an emergency."

Seth nodded that he understood. "You can trust me."

"Good," Marshall said, also nodding. "Then I'm off for the evening. I'll see you later tonight."

No sooner had Marshall disappeared from sight than Seth heard a light tapping on the door from inside. "Seth? Are you still out there?"

Seth's pulse leaped at the mere sound of her voice. Not having had a chance to sit back down yet, he stepped closer to the door to be able to hear her soft, sensual voice a little better. "Yes, ma'am, I'm still out here."

"Yes *who?*"

"Yes, Rachel, I'm still here," he amended, grinning when he remembered how determined she was to make him use her given name.

"That's better," she commented, obviously pleased that he had remembered. "Was that Father's voice I heard?"

"Yes."

"Did I hear him say he was leaving for the evening?"

"Yes," Seth admitted, wondering how she'd possibly heard what had been said, unless she'd had her ear to the door the whole time.

"Good. Now you can open this door so we can talk."

"I can't," he said hesitantly. His stomach twitched nervously at the thought.

"Why not? Didn't Father give you the key?"

"Yes, but I promised him I wouldn't open that door for any reason."

"How's he ever going to know? I'm certainly not going to tell him. Please, Seth. Open this door. Just for a few minutes. I promise not to leave my room. I just want to talk to you for a while."

"I can hear you just fine," he told her, pressing an unsteady hand against the door frame for support. Just knowing she was on the other side of that door, barely inches from where he stood, made him feel all funny inside.

"But I want to be able to look at you while we talk," she reiterated, her tone pleading sweetly for him to do her bidding.

"What do you want to see *me* for?" He closed his eyes in an effort to regain better control of his hammering heart, only to find her beautiful image waiting for him in the resulting darkness. Slowly, a smile formed on his face.

"I don't know," she admitted, her voice as soft as Italian silk. "I just want to see you. Is there anything wrong with that?"

"No."

"Then open this door so we can talk."

"I told you, I can't," he tried to explain again. "Your father ordered me not to open this door for anything except an emergency."

"This is an emergency," she suddenly decided. "If you don't open this door and let me see you, I'll die from a broken heart."

Seth thought that an odd thing to say. "Why should not seeing me make you die from a broken heart?"

There was a long pause. "Don't you know? Are you really so blind?"

Seth felt a vibrant wave of emotion flood his body, causing his toes to tingle and his heart to throb hard against the walls of his chest. "Blind? About what?"

"About us, you silly. About how interested I am in getting to know you better. Surely you are aware of the overwhelming effect you have on women."

Unable to believe she could possibly be serious, knowing full well he had never had much effect on women—other than to frighten them away because of his size—Seth shook his head and stepped back from the

78

door. "Your father done warned me about your tricks. He told me you might do or say just about anything to get me to open this door. He also told me you were pretty much used to getting your way. I'm sorry, but nothing you say or do is going to get me to open this door." He raised his voice so she could still hear him while he returned to his chair with plans to resume his vigil. "You might as well go on back to doing whatever it was you were doing before you heard your father's voice."

"Don't you care about me at all?" she asked, unable to believe anyone could be so cruel.

"I care more about my job. I'm not opening that door."

Seth grinned at the loud thud that sounded near the middle of the door, followed by a sharp yelp of pain. Quietly, he sank down into the chair and played with the idea of what it would be like if she had been serious about being interested in him. Though he knew it was ridiculous, it still was something to help pass the time until supper arrived.

Forty-five minutes later, Emma and Kelly finally came upstairs carrying two large silver trays. By the time Seth heard them coming up the stairs, he was starved . . . so starved, he actually smelled the rich aroma of food long before he saw the tall silver domes on the trays that meant supper had arrived at last.

While Emma paused to unlock Rachel's bedroom door, then quickly carried her tray on inside, Kelly set hers down on one of the narrow hall tables carefully spaced along the wide corridor. Seth watched Emma disappear from sight before turning to give his attention to his own food.

"Here's yer supper," Kelly told him unnecessarily while she lifted the largest silver dome high into the air.

Seth smiled eagerly when a cloud of steam curled out from beneath the tall metal dome, assuring him that his meal was still hot. "Thanks."

"No need to be thankin' me. I'm just doin' me job," she

responded with a bright smile as she set about uncovering the rest of his food, placing the metal food domes on the table out of Seth's way. "Though, I will admit, it was me own idea to fill yer plate with such large servings. I remember from yesterday just how hardy that appetite of yers can be."

"I appreciate it," Seth told her, running the tip of his tongue over his lower lip while he eyed the largest plate, which was piled high with a steaming slab of roasted beef, two heaping mounds of braised potatoes, and smaller mounds of cut corn and glazed carrots. A meal fit for a king. Quickly, he tugged off his coat and looped it over the back of his chair so he could be more comfortable while he ate. "Even though I haven't done nothing but sit here and stare at those doors for the past four hours, I'm still as hungry as a bear."

"And as big as one, too." Kelly laughed while she took the napkin from the tray and handed it to Seth. "I'll send Audrey for the tray after everyone has finished up eatin' downstairs. Yer sister also said to tell ya that she'll be a comin' upstairs to keep ya company for a while as soon as she's finished in the kitchen. How long will ya have to sit here like this?"

"Don't know. Until Mr. Steed gets back, which might be as late as midnight."

Kelly shook her head, sharing his misery, then glanced at the closed door. "If I get a chance, I'll come up and relieve ya a spell when I finish with some of my chores downstairs. That way ya can take care of any . . . ah . . . personal matters ya might need to be a tendin' to."

Seth felt his cheeks grow hot when he realized what she meant and looked away while he quietly muttered his thanks. After having been stuck in the hall for over four hours, he already had "personal matters" that needed to be taken care of and had considered slipping off to do just that more than once. He shifted uncomfortably in his chair while she handed his tray to him.

"Tell Emma when she comes out that I've gone on

back downstairs to get our own supper on the table. Since Landon is the only family member eating in the dining room tonight, we should be able to eat a little earlier than usual."

Seth wondered why Kelly was allowed to refer to the family members by their given names, even in their presence, but decided it was none of his business. As long as neither Mr. Steed seemed to mind, why should he? "I'll tell her."

By the time Emma had left Rachel's room, careful to relock the door behind her, Seth was already halfway through his meal. He paused only long enough to give Emma the promised message, then resumed devouring everything on his plate. But shortly after he'd finished and had set the tray aside, his need to attend to "personal matters" became too great, and though he had promised not to abandon his post for any reason short of catastrophe, he decided it was better than abandoning something else in the middle of the hallway floor.

After checking the stairs to make sure no one was on the way up who might catch him neglecting his duties, he hurried to the water closet at the far end of the hall and took quick care of his needs. When he came back down the hall, he heard Rachel calling out his name at the top of her lungs.

Panicked at the thought of having left his post when he shouldn't have, and instantly aware of the intense fear in her high-pitched tone, he quickly reached into his pocket and pulled out the key Marshall had entrusted to him. Fumbling momentarily with the lock, he finally managed to get the door open and rushed inside, ready to do battle. His heart froze, a result of both his fear and uncertainty, when he found her standing in the middle of her bed, wearing nothing more than a white silk nightgown. She held a similar dressing robe clutched to her breast.

"What's wrong?" he cried out, glancing in all directions, trying to find a reason for such odd behavior.

"A spider!" she wailed, pointing toward the bedstead

with a trembling finger. "A big, black, hairy spider!"

Seth felt his whole body go weak with relief, having instantly conjured up all manner of imminent danger. "A spider? Is that all?"

"Is that all? I'm afraid to death of spiders! Get it out of here. Toss it out the window. Hurry, before it comes any closer!" Her voice rose with each word, until it strained at the very top of her vocal cords.

"All right, all right," he said, his own voice deeply reassuring while he slipped his handkerchief out of his vest pocket. Gently, he bent forward and captured the tiny creature in the folds of the cloth, carried it to the window, then pushed out the wire screen just far enough to drop it onto the narrow sandstone ledge outside. As he pulled the screen back into place, he turned and smiled. "There, now. It's gone. You're safe."

"Are you sure there was only one spider?" she asked, still eyeing the bedstead fearfully.

"I only saw the one." Seth refolded his handkerchief and tucked it back into his pocket. "But if it will make you feel any better, I'll look again to make sure."

"Please," she pleaded, her voice a mere whisper.

Unable to believe this was the same courageous girl who had so openly defied her father only hours before, Seth stepped forward and examined the bedstead carefully, looking both along the front and in the crevices behind.

"No more spiders," he assured her, straightening as he turned to look at her again. He shifted his weight cautiously to one leg when he realized she was no longer standing in the center of her bed. Instead, she had taken several steps in his direction and stood now only inches away from him, gazing up at him with open gratitude. A strange sense of panic pulsated through his veins while he struggled to find his breath in a room that had grown insufferably warm.

"Thank you," she whispered in a deep, sultry voice. Her gaze moved from his eyes to his lips, then back to his

82

eyes. "When you didn't come right away, I was frightened. I thought you'd left my door."

"I had left, but for only a moment. I came just as soon as I heard you calling," he explained as he stared into her upturned face, her golden hair spilling softly about her shoulders. Again, he thought her the most beautiful creature ever to grace the earth. His blood raced hot, random trails while he, too, let his gaze drop from her pale blue eyes to her parted pink lips. He tried to swallow but found it impossible. His heart beat painfully in his chest.

"I think you deserve a reward for your bravery." She reached up to rest her hands on his broad shoulders. "My, but you are tall," she added in a deep, throaty whisper, as if making the observation to herself.

A waterfall of tiny shivers cascaded over him when he felt the gentle pressure of her touch. "Reward? For what? For tossing a spider out of your room? I don't deserve no reward for something as simple as that."

"Yes, you do," she said, her voice very determined as she reached up and placed a gentle kiss on his cheek, pulling back only a few inches to be able to gaze longingly into his eyes.

The resulting jolt left Seth momentarily speechless while he continued to look into her beautiful face, thinking himself to be the luckiest man alive to have received such a treasured reward. Then, when she bent forward and placed a second kiss on his other cheek, he decided he was no longer the luckiest man *alive*, like he'd just assumed, because he was now certain that at some point he'd died and slipped off to heaven, for surely hers was the kiss of an angel. His heart beat a crazy rhythm, causing his legs to feel funny and his throat to swell shut. To his further disbelief, her arms slid slowly around his neck and she moved closer to kiss him on the mouth.

Caught completely by surprise, Seth's senses spun at an alarming rate, leaving him light-headed and barely able to catch his breath. Unable to remember why he'd sworn to stay away from her, knowing only that he desired her more than he had ever desired any woman, he caught her up in his arms and drew her closer in a passionate embrace. Slowly and gently, he let her body slide down the length of his.

Rachel responded by tightening her arms around his neck, drawing his mouth closer. Hungrily, she pressed her body harder against his by pushing her foot back against the side of the bed, eager to make the kiss more intimate.

Seth moaned aloud. He felt her young breasts splay invitingly against the hard plane of his chest. Slowly, he lowered her onto the bed, coming to rest lightly to the side of her. With a hunger he had never before experienced, he devoured her with kiss after kiss, dipping his tongue repeatedly into the sweet depths that beckoned him.

It drove him to the point of sheer madness to feel her hands pressing hard into his back, urging him on. Eagerly, he slipped his hand between their bodies and felt first her delicate ribcage before moving up to one of the thrusting breasts beneath him. The tip was rigid to the touch, making him instantly aware of her own needs . . . needs any man would gladly fulfill. But something inside him caused him to stop. With a willpower he was not sure he possessed, Seth pulled away from her.

"I'm sorry," he apologized between hard, ragged breaths as he pushed himself up off the bed and stood again on unsteady feet. "I didn't mean for that to happen."

Rachel looked up at him through eyes still dark with unfulfilled passion, her expression puzzled. "I did. I've wanted to kiss you from the very first moment I saw you. I've wanted to feel your arms around me, holding me close."

Taken aback by such a confession, Seth didn't know quite how to respond. "You have? But why?"

Rachel lay before him, her cheeks flushed, her breasts

rising and falling rapidly, her hair spilling about her in wild abandon, making it that much harder for him to resist the temptation that still awaited him.

"I don't know why," she answered honestly, her gaze searching his. "I just know that I want you. More than I have ever wanted anything in my life."

"But you can't," he replied, hoping to reason with her, still unable to believe any of this was happening.

"But I do," she responded quickly, then, as if to prove something to him, she reached up with delicate fingers to untie the tiny white sash that held the top of her nightdress together. "Go and shut the door, and I'll show you just how much I do want you."

Seth ached with a need to do just that: shut the door and enjoy whatever pleasures Rachel had to offer him. But he couldn't. Something he could not put a name to was holding him back. "Rachel, you don't know what you're saying. I'm just a man who works for your father. I'm not good enough for someone like you."

"Why don't you let me be the one to decide that?" she told him, never taking her eyes from his while she gently tugged again on the silken tie.

Seth watched with growing fascination when the tiny strap gave way easily to her touch. The gown parted in a wide V beneath her throat, revealing the creamy white skin between her breasts. She had never bothered to get up from the bed, and continued to lie before him in a most beguiling manner.

"Please, Seth, go and shut the door. I want you. I want you so badly, I'll do anything to make you want me, too." She swallowed hard in anticipation of his response. "Please, Seth. Give me a chance to prove it to you."

Then, with the hand of a practiced siren, she ran her thumb beneath the lacy edges of her parted gown, pushing the garment open further, until he could see all but the tip of her ripe, young breast.

Seth stood staring down at her breathlessly for only a moment more before turning away and heading for the door, not knowing if he intended to close it and return to her like she had asked, or walk right on out of her room like he knew he should. When he reached the door and it was time to make the decision, he turned back to look at her, which proved to be his undoing, because she had risen up on one elbow, allowing her garment to gape open enough to reveal her entire breast to him. Desire for her shot through him. He could no longer deny his own needs—nor hers.

Knowing full well what was at risk but no longer caring, he slowly closed the door and turned to face her. He considered darkening the lamps before returning to her, but Seth knew he wanted to see whatever was about to happen and left them as they were. With trembling hands, he began to unbutton first his vest then his shirt, and by the time he had reached the bed, he had tugged off the two garments and had tossed them both easily aside. He paused at her bedside long enough to discard the rest of his clothing. When he lay down beside her only seconds later, he was naked.

Rachel, too, trembled with desire when he bent forward to kiss her again. Leaning back against the softness of her mattress, she slid her arms around his strong neck and drew him to her. She moaned softly as she parted her mouth to accept his kiss.

Lying more to the side of her than on top of her, so as not to crush her with his weight, Seth allowed his hand to gently explore the soft curves of her body while he proceeded to kiss her thoroughly. First he ran his fingertips over the smooth, silky fabric of her gown, then quickly dipped beneath it to feel the delicate softness of her ivory skin. Having seen the advantage of the wide opening at her neck, he slid his hand inside and cupped the treasure that awaited him beneath. He found deep pleasure hearing her sharp intake of breath the moment his thumb came into direct contact with the hardened tip.

While his mouth continued to sample the sweetness of her lips, he continued to tease the peak of her breast lightly with his fingertips until she moaned aloud with pleasure. She trembled in anticipation when he then reached down and brought the gown up over her head. He wanted her just as gloriously naked as he was. A scant second after the unwanted garment had been discarded, he pulled her firmly against him, pressing her soft, warm curves against his hard frame. Her fingers dug deep into his back when his mouth left hers to trail hungry kisses down the slender white column of her neck, pausing at the pulse point in the hollow of her throat before resuming the path downward.

Rachel's breaths came in short, rapid gasps when his mouth finally neared its destination. Her hands pressed harder into the muscles along his shoulders, urging him on. But Seth needed no urging. Seconds later, his mouth finally moved to claim the straining peak. Rachel quivered in response, arching her back to give him easier access to the sweet mound he'd so eagerly sought.

Tenderly, he suckled the breast while fondling the other with his hand, bringing her more and more unbearable pleasure, until her head tossed restlessly from side to side. His desire grew with each tiny whimper that escaped her lips, until he knew he could wait no longer. Gazing down at her beautiful, passion-filled face, pleased to find her eyelids pressed closed from the sheer weight of her own desire, he moved to take her gently. He was as shocked as she was when he met with resistance and his first forward thrust resulted in a sharp cry of pain.

Anger surged through him at the realization that he'd just taken a virgin to bed, and his first instinct was to pull away. But the arms holding him tight and the breasts still rising and falling rapidly beneath him beckoned him to continue. He was beyond stopping.

With deliberate slowness, he moved within her, allowing her time to get over the initial pain and become used to the feel of him. After he sensed her body gradually relax, he moved with more force, until she started to move with him. Soon they reached the same frenzied level of passion as before.

"Seth, oh, Seth," she called out in short, raspy breaths as she soared ever higher into the unknown. Her entire body ached for release. "Seth, please." Then, in almost the same earth-shattering moment, the two lovers crested the zenith of their passion. They gasped aloud at its body-shuddering force again and again before drifting ever so slowly down into the hazy realms of fulfillment.

For several moments, Seth lay beside her, holding her in his arms like a precious jewel, not knowing what to say, still too stunned from discovering he had been her first to think rationally. The way she had come on to him earlier, and knowing how loose the morals of the wealthy were said to be, he had thought her a well-practiced seductress. Had he known she was a virgin, he would never have closed the door and returned to her bed. How could he have been so easily fooled?

"Seth," Rachel's voice called his name softly, breaking into his miserable thoughts with the same effect as if she'd shouted.

Responding to her gentle voice, he gazed at her, amazed at the adoring look in her huge blue eyes when they really should be filled with hatred.

"Oh, Seth, I knew from the many different books I've read that it would be wonderful, but that was even more beautiful than I'd ever imagined. I do so love you. You are the strongest, yet the gentlest and most enticing man I've ever met."

Seth couldn't have been more shocked. "That's foolishness. You can't possibly love me. I already told you, I'm not worthy enough for someone like you. I'm just a poor boy from the South who has always had to scrounge for a living the best way he could, which many times bordered on the dishonest. You, on the other hand, are a rich, beautiful socialite from the city who is used to having the best of everything. The two of us should never even associate with each other, much less do what we just

88

did." He closed his eyes as a sickening pain wrenched his gut. How could he have allowed such a thing to happen? "Besides, you're already engaged to be married. Have you forgotten about that?"

"I don't feel the same way about him as I do you. He doesn't stir my blood with fire the way just looking at you does."

"But you don't even know me. You never even saw me before this afternoon," Seth tried to reason with her, almost pleading in his attempt to get her to listen. He'd already caused enough damage. To let her believe that she loved him would only make things worse for both of them—if that were possible.

"That's not true. I've been watching you from a distance ever since you started to work for Father, and I knew from that first glimpse when you passed my room in the hallway that I loved you. You are truly the most handsome man I've ever seen."

"That's ridiculous. Besides, love isn't something you can decide instantly from a distance. It's not something that happens just because you like the way someone looks. It takes time to develop." Or so he'd been told. Quickly, he climbed out of her bed, snatching up his clothes. "I can't believe we let this happen. It was wrong. It must never happen again."

Tears filled Rachel's eyes. Suddenly, she felt the need to cover herself with her robe. "Don't you care for me even a little?"

Seth's heart went out to her, for she clearly believed she was in love with him. In that moment, he wanted to tell her just how much he did care, and that he, too, had fallen under some mystical spell, a spell that closely resembled all he'd ever heard about love; but he had to keep her best interests in mind. She deserved a far better life than what he could ever offer her. Taking a deep breath to fortify his rapidly wavering strength, he looked at her lying there, her eyes wide with hope, and flatly lied to her. "I care, but not in the way you want me to."

Seeing the pain on her face, he quickly cushioned that remark with gentle pepperings of the truth. He started out by quoting something he'd heard his sister say many times whenever she was intent on cooling the ardor of the different men who had become infatuated with her. "The problem is that I'm not really ready to fall in love with anyone. Rachel, you are the most beautiful, the most alluring woman I've ever met, and if ever I do fall in love, I truly hope it is with someone just like you."

"Why can't it *be* me?" she wanted to know, her expression still hopeful.

"I told you. We are all wrong for each other. And you are already engaged to marry someone else, someone who obviously loves you a great deal. Besides, it may be years before I'm ready to fall in love with anyone."

"I'll wait," Rachel said as she bravely sniffed back a tiny sob.

"I don't want you to wait," he said firmly, his heart breaking into a thousand pieces while he hurriedly put his clothes back on. When he was finally dressed, he knelt at her bedside, gazing tenderly into her tear-dampened eyes. "Rachel, what happened between us shouldn't have. I really think it would be better if we both tried to forget it ever did. You should go on with your plans to marry your rich fiancé and live the sort of life you were meant to live."

"But what if somehow he finds out about tonight? He'd never marry me then. If he ever found out about us, he'd break our engagement and immediately find someone more appropriate to marry."

"He'll never hear it from me," Seth promised. "No one will."

"But what if—" she paused as the realization struck her fully, "what if what we did tonight has put a child inside me? I could never marry Preston, knowing I was carrying another man's child. Besides, he would eventually realize it was not his child and he'd divorce me anyway." She closed her eyes against the thought of such a disgrace.

Seth grimaced, his stomach turning to cold lead, for it was clearly a possibility. "If that turned out to be the case, I'd marry you."

A tiny ray of hope shone again in Rachel's eyes. She searched his face for evidence of the truth. "Would you? If it turns out I'm with child, you would indeed marry me?"

Hanging his head, Seth felt as if the weight of the world had fallen on him. Reluctantly, he answered, aware it would be the ruination of Rachel's carefree existence. He knew that even though she presently believed she loved him, she'd soon come to resent him for being as poor as he was, and eventually she'd resent their marriage. "Yes, if that ends up being the case, I'll do the right thing and marry you."

If she carried his child, what choice would he have? Her reputation would be ruined and she could no longer hope to get another husband, so the responsibility to provide for them both would be his. He knew he would do all he could to make her happy but, at the same time, knew that would be impossible. He could never fit into her world. She was too used to the finest life had to offer. Any marriage between them would be doomed right from the start.

Maybe it wouldn't ever come to that.

chapter six

Cracking the door open a few inches, Seth carefully listened for the sound of footsteps either out in the hall or on the nearby stairs before quietly slipping out of Rachel's room. Miserable to the point of despair, still unable to believe what had happened between them, he stared idly off into space while he gently closed the door behind him, fully aware what a hornet's nest he'd stirred to life.

"Seth! I've been looking everywhere for you! What in the world were you doing in Rachel's bedroom—with the door *closed?*" Audrey's voice came out in an angry, accusing whisper.

Seth spun about, startled to discover his sister standing only a few yards away, her hands planted firmly on her hips. "Rachel called me inside to get rid of a spider for her."

"Therefore, you closed the door so it couldn't get away?" she asked, tossing her hands into the air, clearly distraught over Seth's lack of good sense. "Seth, use your head! What if Marshall Steed had returned in time to catch you slipping out of his daughter's bedroom like that? What do you think his reaction would be? It's bad enough that you were in there at all, but to have closed the door like that was just plain foolish! What were you thinking?"

"I wasn't thinking," he admitted, wondering what his sister would say if she knew the whole truth. Unable to look her in the eye, he bent his head and studied the thick piling of the dark gray carpet at his feet.

"You certainly *weren't* thinking! Don't you realize that when you do something so foolish you put both our jobs at risk? The only reason I'm working here at all is because of you. We both know that. If you do something thoughtless enough to get yourself fired, it would be the same as getting me fired, too! I don't know about you, but I am very happy working here. I have great plans for the two of us, which can only come about if we keep these jobs. Please, don't do anything that could ruin it all for me."

"I'm sorry." He met her angry gaze only briefly before glancing back down at the plush hall carpet. "All I can do is promise not to let anything like that happen again."

Studying his forlorn expression, Audrey drew in a long breath, then slowly let it out. With it went some of her anger. "And I'm sorry I got so upset with you. It's just that I came up here to look for you, and then when I couldn't find you, I became immediately upset thinking you had left your post. And then when I saw you come out of her bedroom like that . . . well, I was shocked. And hurt, unable to believe that you could risk both our jobs like that."

Seth's shoulders sagged. He knew how very important such a good-paying job was to her. It meant finally having a chance to get ahead in life. It meant never having to beg for food or clothes again. Glumly, he wondered what his sister would do if Rachel did indeed become pregnant as a result of his foolishness, for surely Marshall would fire them both and send them far away. Audrey would never forgive him, any more than Rachel would. His brief moment of weakness could very well have cost them everything.

All he could do was repeat his promise never to let it happen again—the same promise he had made Rachel only moments before.

Audrey felt very much like a nagging fishwife when she studied her brother's sullen reaction. Smiling, she reached out and hugged him close to show all was forgiven.

"So, were you successful?" she asked, in an effort to relieve some of the tension she'd caused between them.

Seth's back stiffened at the implication. "Successful?"

Audrey glanced at him, puzzled. "In getting rid of the spider?"

"Oh, that. Sure. I tossed it out the window. I imagine it was about as happy to go as Rachel was to see it gone."

Audrey studied the pale color of his cheeks and the way he seemed to avoid her direct gaze. "It's hard for me to imagine Rachel being afraid of anything, especially of a little spider."

"You know how women are," he said, grinning for the first time since he'd left Rachel's room.

"No, how are we?" Audrey challenged, as if daring him to speak badly of the female gender. "Perhaps you think us fickle?"

"I was thinking more along the lines of unpredictable," he answered wisely, for he knew Audrey didn't mind the thought of being unpredictable. There were times that she even took great pride in it.

"Are we now?" she bantered, smiling back at him approvingly. "And do you think that's good or bad?"

Rather than pursue a conversation that could eventually take a wrong turn and lead to trouble, Seth quickly changed the subject by asking a question of his own. "Do you have time to sit and talk for a while before going back downstairs?"

"Back downstairs? Seth, it's almost nine-thirty. Why would I be going back downstairs? I'm through for the night."

Unable to believe the time, for that meant he'd spent well over an hour in Rachel's room, Seth reached inside his vest pocket to check his watch. When he did, he discovered the watch gone. His heart froze with panic while his gaze moved fearfully to Rachel's closed door. He'd had the watch just moments before going into her room.

"But didn't you come up here to get my tray and carry it back downstairs?" he asked, hoping to get her to admit she was wrong about the hour. But a quick glance at the table where he'd left the empty tray revealed it was already gone. Suddenly, he felt ill. Fear ran through him like ice water.

"No, Kelly came and got it earlier," Audrey told him, finding his obvious memory lapse a little queer. "She came to get Rachel's, too, but Rachel wasn't through with her meal yet."

Seth's insides coiled into a hard, tight knot as he wondered what Kelly had thought of his absence in the hall. Could he possibly convince the observant housekeeper that he'd been in the water closet taking care of those "personal matters" when she'd come upstairs for the tray, or was she perhaps already aware of the truth? Is that why she'd made excuses for not returning downstairs with Rachel's tray? If so, how long before she told Marshall of their indiscretion?

"Well, if it's already nine-thirty, then I guess you're pretty tired," he said, trying to keep the panic that gripped his chest out of his voice. "I'll understand if you'd rather go on to bed and get some sleep than sit up and talk to me." Inside, he prayed she'd agree. He wanted to get back inside Rachel's room and let her know that Kelly had come upstairs while they had been together. In all likelihood, the housekeeper knew enough to get them both in serious trouble. But, just in case all was not yet lost, he needed to get his hands on that watch before someone else went in and discovered it.

"Actually, I am pretty tired," Audrey admitted. "But I haven't had much of an opportunity to visit with you since we started to work here. I'll stay and keep you company for a little while." Audrey offered a sisterly smile as she pulled a small Chippendale chair away from the wall and set it near the large upholstered chair Seth had brought out of his room for his own use. "Besides, I imagine you are bored silly having to sit out here all alone the way you are."

What she refused to admit, even to Seth, was that the real reason she was so eager to stay and visit was that she hoped to give Landon plenty of time to settle into his room and be fast asleep before she ventured into that part of the hall. After what had happened earlier in the dining room, she did not want to risk yet another confrontation with the man. She wasn't sure her heart could stand it. She'd been a nervous wreck ever since he'd openly declared his intention to pursue her until she finally gave in to him.

"I don't mind sitting out here alone, so there's really no need for you to give up your sleep just to keep me company," Seth assured her. "We can visit some other time. Your rest is far more important."

"Oh, but I want to hear about your day. Did you go to the police station with Marshall to help identify those two men who jumped him the other night?" Her breath held while she waited for his answer.

"I went with him, but it wasn't the right men."

Audrey was overwhelmed with relief. "That's too bad. Maybe they will have better luck next time."

"I doubt it. None of us could remember enough about them to give the police a very good idea of what they looked like. I remembered them both being kind of short with light brown hair, and James remembered them being tall with coal-black hair."

"And which description did Marshall agree with?"

"Neither. He claimed that the one who had him was tall, like me, but that the one who had James was short and spindly. As for hair, he wasn't sure they even had any."

"I see where the police would have a problem coming up with any real leads," she said, chuckling with delight.

At that moment, the sound of heavy footsteps on the stairs caught their attention. Audrey's heart jumped with the thought it might be Landon, though she'd understood Kelly to say he'd gone up to bed over half an hour ago, shortly after a brief stroll through the gardens. Even so, Audrey's heart hammered hard against her chest with fearful anticipation.

When the sound grew louder, she and Seth both turned toward the stairs in time to watch Marshall Steed come into view, wearing dark gray trousers held up by black suspenders and a stark white dinner shirt with the sleeves rolled almost to the elbow. It was the first time either of them had seen him without a coat, and somehow it made him seem less forbidding. Still, Seth's stomach knotted, remembering the terrible thing he'd done an hour earlier.

"As you can well see, I managed to get back from my meeting a little early," Marshall said as he approached the two with his usual long strides. The man was forever in a hurry. "Has Rachel caused you any trouble?" He nodded toward his daughter's door while he continued in their direction. Everett followed only a few steps behind him, carrying Marshall's coat over his arm.

After Marshall stopped in the hallway to speak further with Seth, Everett stepped over to one side and continued on past them, disappearing seconds later into Marshall's bedroom, where it was his duty to take care of his master's clothes and turn back his bedcovers.

"No, no trouble," Seth answered hesitantly, glancing first at Audrey, briefly at Marshall, and finally at Rachel's closed door.

"Good. Maybe my punishment has done some good after all. Hand me the key. I'd like to go inside and tell her good night before I retire," he said, holding out his hand. "Meanwhile, I guess it'll be all right for you to go on to your room and get your rest. As late as it is now, there'd be no place for her to go should she somehow discover a way to get out of there. I'll let you know first thing in the morning whether or not you'll have to continue your vigil at her door. A lot will depend on her attitude tonight."

Reluctantly, Seth reached into his vest pocket and felt for the key.

"Well, where is it?" Marshall asked, growing impatient while Seth fumbled first with one pocket then another.

"Just a moment, sir. I have it here somewhere," he said. Fear-stricken, he considered that the key might have gone the way of the watch. The thought of having to come up with a logical reason as to how the key he'd been entrusted to use only in case of an emergency had actually gotten inside her bedroom terrified him. When his fingertips finally touched the smooth metal surface as he dipped his hand deep into his trouser pocket, he was so overwhelmed with relief that his legs felt momentarily weak.

"Ah, here it is."

"Good. Hand it to me," Marshall insisted, still holding out his hand for the key.

"Here, let me unlock it for you," Seth said, knowing he had not yet bothered to lock the door again, something Marshall would surely notice. Quickly, he stepped toward the door, aware he also needed to find some excuse to follow him inside so he could try to find his missing watch before Marshall spotted it. No telling where it had fallen out of his pocket. The thought of the man finding it right beside Rachel's bed sent sickly chills through him.

"That's all right. I can manage. You go on to bed," Marshall insisted as he reached for the key, taking it right out of Seth's hand. "I'm only going to be in there for a minute. I'm pretty tired myself."

Sensing something was wrong, seriously wrong, Audrey quickly inserted, "I hope you'll be in there long enough for me to get her supper tray. She wasn't finished with it when they came for it earlier."

"Certainly," Marshall said as he bent to unlock the door.

While his back was to them, Audrey turned to Seth and silently mouthed the question, "What's wrong?"

Her eyes grew round as saucers when Seth's response was to pat his vest pocket and shape the words, "My watch is in there." All color drained from her face.

"What's the matter with this lock?" Marshall muttered while he tried to work it back and forth. "I can't seem to get it to connect with the tumbler."

"Here, allow me," Seth offered again, relieved when this time Marshall stepped back to let him try, knowing that if the man had tried to twist the key in the other direction, he'd realized the door was unlocked.

"Maybe we should try the other door," Marshall stated, frowning while Seth bent forward to work with the lock.

"No, that won't be necessary," Seth assured him. "I think I've got it. Ah, there. I felt it give." He reached to give the knob a turn, then pushed the door open.

Audrey rushed immediately inside. Her gaze scanned the floor when she entered. Seth pretended to stumble forward into Marshall's way, blocking him from the door for a moment.

"I'm sorry," he muttered, looking chagrined while he straightened, then stepped awkwardly back out of the way. "I guess I got off balance."

Marshall waited until he was sure the oversized buffoon was not going to stumble again, before moving forward to follow Audrey inside.

Having spotted Seth's watch near a cheval dresser only a few feet from the bed, Audrey hurried across the room and kicked it with the side of her foot, sending it scooting under the bed and out of everyone's sight. She winced when it clattered against the far wall, hoping Marshall would not notice.

Rachel sat up in her bed, her covers pulled to her shoulders, staring curiously at her with tear-dampened, red-rimmed eyes. "Who are you?"

"Audrey," she responded with a cheerfulness she did not actually feel, aware their present predicament was just as much Rachel's fault for having called Seth into her room as it was her brother's for having gone. "Audrey Stoane."

Rachel's eyes widened. "Seth's sister?" But before Audrey could answer, Marshall had entered and was on his way across the room.

Immediately, Audrey grabbed up the dinner tray, and after taking time to replace a water glass that had been set off to the side, she headed back toward the hall.

"Rachel, you've been crying," Marshall said, his voice filled with concern while he hurried to his daughter's bedside.

Reaching up to wipe away any last remnants of her tears, Rachel nodded, then turned her face away. Though she had used tears as a weapon against her father on many occasions, this time she felt ashamed, for these were true tears . . . a result of her shameful behavior.

"I'm sorry," Marshall said, taking her quickly into his arms and making her face him. "I had no idea missing the theater would hurt you this much. I only meant to teach you a lesson. I never intended to make you cry."

Just as Audrey neared the door, she glanced up, wanting to catch her brother's attention and assure him she'd taken care of the watch. When she did, she was surprised to see such a pained expression on Seth's face when he stepped back deeper into the hallway, away from the door. Glancing briefly back at Rachel, she wondered if the young woman's tears had anything to do with her brother's remorse. Her insides crawled with fear. There was something Seth was not telling her, something dreadful; but she waited until she had closed the door behind her and had stepped away from Rachel's room before asking what he knew about her tears.

"She loves me," he answered quietly.

"She what?" Audrey asked, unable to believe she'd heard him correctly.

"Right after I got rid of that spider for her, she just up and told me that she loves me."

"Because you got rid of a spider?"

Seth shrugged, not sure if that had anything to do with it or not. "She says she's attracted to me for some reason," he finally told her, embarrassed to have to admit such a thing to his own sister. "And when I tried to discourage her, great big tears started to form in her eyes. For some reason, that girl really thinks she's in love with me."

"That's absurd! She doesn't even know you."

"I pointed that out to her, but she didn't seem to think it mattered much." His face drew into a perplexed frown. Nothing like this had ever happened to him. "She's infatuated with the way I look." Most women were afraid of him.

Audrey's eyebrows arched with disbelief. "What else did she say?"

"Just that she loves me. And she wanted to know what my feelings were for her."

"Which are?"

"I explained to her that I was not ready to fall in love, and even if I was ready for something like that, it couldn't be with her. I tried to get her to see that we are from two different worlds and a relationship between us just wouldn't work out, but she didn't want to hear that. I think I may have broke her heart. I think those tears are because of me."

"Nonsense," Audrey told him, knowing what a big, tender heart her young brother possessed. "She's just too used to getting whom and what she wants, then when she discovered she couldn't add you to her collection of ogling admirers, she decided to see if tears might help change your mind."

"Do you really think so?"

"I *know* so," Audrey stated, thinking Rachel very much like her older brother, Landon. It didn't matter to the girl how uncomfortable she made someone else's life, just as long as she got what she wanted. "Just be careful

101

not to let her get to your heart. Try to stay away from her whenever possible."

"I plan to," Seth admitted, nodding agreeably. "As far away as I can." Because he knew that what had happened between them tonight could very well happen a second time.

For reasons he had yet to understand, there was a weak spot somewhere inside him that only Rachel could reach. And if she'd reached it once, she could surely reach it again and again.

By the time Audrey had finished telling Seth about his watch and had vowed to return to Rachel's room sometime the following morning to retrieve it for him, she was ready to go on to her room, determined to take her own advice. Thinking that if she simply avoided Landon whenever possible and ignored him when he became impossible to avoid, thereby refusing to let him get anywhere near her heart, she would be safe enough. Still, despite such firm resolve, she hurried past his rooms and into her own, aware of how impossible the man could be to ignore at times.

When she entered the room, she glanced quickly around the dimly lit area to make certain no one was lurking in the shadows, before closing the door and latching it shut.

Safe at last! she thought as she turned toward the armoire, eager to get into a comfortable gown and climb between the cool satin sheets on her bed. It was when she neared the armoire that she noticed something lying on the smooth, pale yellow surface of her bed.

Stepping closer, she was surprised to discover a single long-stemmed red rose resting on her pillow. Beside it lay a folded piece of white paper.

Frowning with uncertainty, she lifted the folded paper from her pillow and carefully opened it, hesitant to read the words inside.

When she did, Audrey discovered the message was brief but to the point, making her insides coil with instant apprehension.

Sleep well, dear one, for tomorrow may prove to be a very trying day.

Later in the night, while she lay in bed thinking about the different ways to interpret the note, Audrey did anything but sleep well. Instead, she tossed restlessly, wondering what Landon had meant. Just what did he have in mind for her that next day? Whatever it was, he'd clearly indicated she'd find it anything but restful. She wondered if it might have something to do with the police. After all, he was constantly bringing them up in conversation. Did he suspect her? And if that wasn't enough to worry about, what of Seth's watch? It still lay condemningly in the shadows beneath Rachel's bed, where eventually it would be found. If only Rachel hadn't called Seth into her room to get rid of that spider!

Frustrated by her inability to sleep, she wondered why the two younger Steeds felt it so necessary to complicate other people's lives so. Did it give them some strange sense of power to be able to turn someone else's world inside out? Were their own lives so boring that they found great sport in forcing their attentions on others?

Perhaps it was some sort of game played among the wealthy to see how uncomfortable they could make life for those less fortunate. Or perhaps it was an easy way of building their self-esteem from time to time. But, whatever the reason, it was clear Landon had singled her out as his next official conquest. He'd admitted as much in the dining room. What she failed to understand was why, especially after she'd made her own feelings in the matter so perfectly clear. She had no intention of becoming his plaything, no matter how incredibly handsome or how extremely rich he was. Money might be important to her, but then so was her pride.

She would have her wealth in time, of that she was certain; but she would earn it through the use of her own wit and resourcefulness, and not as a reward for personal services rendered. Even when she and Seth had been starving in the streets of New Orleans in the years shortly following their parents' deaths, she had never once considered prostitution in any form. And she had no intention of resorting to it now—no matter how generous the reward. Landon Steed would simply have to find his pleasures elsewhere.

She had more important matters to think about—if only she could push these plaguing thoughts of the man completely aside.

Audrey was not the only one unable to sleep that night. Across the hall, Landon lay in the darkness, his hands locked behind his head, staring at the shadows above his bed. Pleasurably, he contemplated how to best pursue the elusive Audrey Stoane. His blood stirred, hot and fast, when he imagined what the eventual conquest would be like, finally having Audrey's silken body beneath his, eager to do his bidding.

Though he suspected she was a virgin, and he did not normally pursue women with so little experience, he was determined to conquer this one. There was just something about her that intrigued him, making him want her more than he'd wanted any woman in quite some time. Maybe it was those cautious dark brown eyes that lured him to her, or possibly it was the thought of what her long brown hair would look like undone from its pins and allowed to flow freely down her back, for he was certain her hair would prove to be both luxuriously long and sinfully thick—the sort of hair a man could get lost in. The thought of what it might look like cascading wildly over her soft, bare shoulders while she held her arms out to him drove him wild with anticipation, making him more determined than ever to have her.

He still found it hard to believe that she'd actually had the audacity to smash that plate over his head, though he'd deserved it. She had more daring than he'd ever before seen in a woman. Most women were too much in awe of his wealth and far too eager to please him for that same reason to ever do anything as outrageous. But not Audrey. She was a woman with fire, with spirit. The trick was going to be to find a way to bend her will to his without breaking that spirit, but how?

The realization that she intended to make their coming together as difficult as possible did not really bother him, for he thrived on challenge—as long as she did not try to make his winning *impossible* to achieve. He smiled as he thought about how sweet such a victory would be. For what had started out as a lark, a game to see how skittish he could make her, had somewhere along the way taken a sharp turn.

He thought of the great pleasure he found in taunting her, in watching her grow increasingly nervous whenever he tried to kiss her, or when he got a little too close, or simply when he mentioned his father having gone to the police. He wondered about that for a moment. She did seem terribly on edge whenever he mentioned his father going to the police. Why was that? Was she really that concerned for her brother? Didn't she know that Seth was capable of taking care of himself . . . almost as capable as she seemed to be of taking care of herself? How he wished that she weren't. How he'd love the chance to come to her aid, to be her knight in shining armour.

After having touched her silken skin and having sampled the unexpected potency of her kiss, he longed to have more. He had to have more. He wanted her, body and soul, and he very well planned to have her—body and soul. But first, he had to find a way to wear down her resistance. He'd try forcefulness first, but if that didn't work, he'd try the opposite approach. Either way, he planned to have her.

With that pleasurable thought in mind, he rolled over onto his side and finally drifted off to sleep.

chapter seven

Audrey was already dressed when the knock sounded at her door early that following morning. Since there was little she could do about Landon's continued brash behavior, other than to try her best to avoid him, she had decided to do something about her other problem—Seth's watch under Rachel's bed.

Though Audrey personally did not believe Seth had done anything really wrong except to be foolish in entering that bedroom alone, she was certain Marshall would think the worst of the situation. She could not chance losing her job before she'd gotten from it what she needed. She especially hated the thought of losing it over something as innocent as Seth's having rescued the terrified young woman from a spider.

Determined to find a way to get inside Rachel's room, and at a time when the young woman would be all alone, Audrey had decided that her best chance would be to volunteer to carry her breakfast upstairs, which meant she'd need to be in the kitchen when the time came. Therefore, she'd crawled out of bed at the first signs of daylight, since she couldn't sleep, anyway, and had gotten dressed.

Thinking the early morning knock at her door might mean Seth had come bearing good news concerning his watch, hoping he'd already found a way to get it back on his own without anyone else being the wiser, Audrey hurried to the door and opened it. Her breath caught in her throat when she found that instead of her big brother, she now faced the last man on earth she wanted to see, especially now.

"What do you want?" she asked sharply, aware Landon had moved forward to block the doorway with his wide shoulders. She frowned, knowing she would have dearly enjoyed closing the door in his arrogantly handsome face.

"It's tomorrow," he answered simply, brows raised in a meaningful gesture. His pale blue eyes sparkled with infuriating delight while he watched her expression turn instantly wary.

Audrey felt chills of foreboding run up and down her arms as she stood staring awkwardly up at him. She tried her best to think of a clever retort that would be sure to put him in his place, but for the life of her, nothing came to mind. It was unlike her to let such an opportunity slip by unchallenged.

"May I come in?" he asked, when all she did was continue to stare at him, her beautiful chin thrust forward at a mutinous angle.

"No," she answered, even as he pushed his way past her. She turned to watch him with an expression that revealed both her outrage and disbelief. "How dare you enter my bedroom like this."

"Like what?" he asked, his voice light with false innocence when he turned back to look at her. His blood raced through a rapidly pulsating heart when he noticed how beautiful she was even this early in the morning.

"Like you own the place," she retorted angrily.

"I do," he replied, grinning. "Or at least my father does. Or weren't you aware of that fact?"

Audrey drew in a deep, exasperated breath and held it a moment before slowly releasing it. She did not want him to see how deeply he affected her. "What do you want?"

"I already told you. I want *you*. Don't you remember?

Yesterday, in the dining room."

Narrowing her eyes into a menacing glare, Audrey tapped her slippered foot impatiently while she considered a suitable retort for such insufferable behavior. "And I believe I have already *clearly* indicated that you cannot have me. What, pray tell, does it take to get through to someone like you?"

"Odd, I was about to ask you the same question," he told her. Undaunted, he reached his arm up above her head and quickly pushed the door closed with a loud, nerve-shattering clatter.

Afraid she was about to become wedged between his strong body and the closed door, Audrey quickly moved away, circling to the opposite side of the room.

Landon watched with open fascination when she stepped into the bright morning sunlight that slanted through her bedroom window. The golden rays cast shimmering highlights through her dark hair and brought a radiant glow to her creamy white skin. How he wished she would wear her hair down in long, loose curls rather than piled into such a confining twist atop her head. His fingers itched to undo the pins and let the hair fall luxuriously over her shoulders. He smiled at such an intriguing thought.

When Audrey turned to make certain Landon had not followed her across the room, she noticed his blue eyes boldly surveying her body, an unnerving habit that made her feel as if she'd suddenly been stripped naked before him. Swallowing back the tumbling emotions that tormented her, she took another cautious step away from him. "Will you please simply tell me why you are here?"

Rather than answer her plea to know more about his intentions, Landon decided a demonstration would be more in order. Slowly, he moved toward her, his eyes studying her startled reaction, his expression amused.

Audrey lifted her chin and met his searching gaze with haughty defiance, reminded, as he slowly came closer, just how exceedingly tall he was. Though not quite the

108

height of her brother, he was a good nine inches taller than she and undoubtedly far stronger. But she refused to let any of that intimidate her, including the fact that he was nearly as broad across the shoulders as Seth and just as superbly fit.

Dark gray trousers molded against a pair of powerfully lean thighs while his legs moved with slow, steady strides in her direction. His stark white summer shirt, which had been left unbuttoned at the throat, clung precariously to well-rounded muscles along his upper arms and shoulders. If there were ever a man who had dressed for the sole purpose of ravishing the help, this man had undoubtedly matched him well. With his thick brown hair brushed back and his face cleanly shaven, he looked exquisite. Audrey's heartbeat sped with growing anticipation.

"Well?" she asked, amazed that her voice had sounded strong and clear when her insides were in such a frantic uproar.

"Well, what?" he queried, observing Audrey with frank interest when he came to a stop only a few inches from where she stood.

"Well, why are you here?" she responded, studying the firm lines of his face, bathed now in golden sunlight. Reluctantly, she noted again how truly handsome a man he was, despite his unrelenting arrogance and his extremely aggressive nature, neither of which were to her liking.

Landon's mouth curved into a sensuous half smile as he boldly dropped his gaze to the soft curve of her pink lips. "I thought by now my intentions would be extremely clear."

"Now, see here, Mr. Steed. I don't know why you seem so intent on pursuing me like this, especially after I've already told you I'm not at all interested in such things," she began, only to have her words cut short by his deep, demanding voice.

"Call me Landon," he cautioned her, his eyes lifting back to hers.

"Call you Landon?" she asked with obvious disbelief. "Just be glad I don't call you what I'd dearly love to call you," she shot back, her brow arched with obvious meaning.

Landon laughed appreciatively. "Now, that wasn't a very nice thing to say."

"It could have been worse," she informed him, suddenly finding his deep laughter contagious, infuriated with herself for wanting to laugh with him. It took all the inner restraint she had to keep her expression grim. "Much worse."

"No doubt," he chuckled. "I shudder to think how much worse."

Still battling a desire to laugh along with him, Audrey tilted her head at an angle, oddly attracted by the double set of dimples that had formed in his cheeks near his mouth. "Behave in a more gentlemanly fashion, and you may never have to find out how much worse."

"Ah, but that's asking too much of me," he countered, then happily admitted. "For, you see, I have come to steal another kiss from you that could hardly be termed *gentlemanly*." His face drew into an instantly wary, yet still clearly amused exprerssion when his gaze quickly scanned the room. "You don't happen to have any plates hidden around here, do you?"

Audrey's cheeks burned as she considered what she'd do if she did indeed have a good supply of plates within reach. Only this time, she'd prefer the dishes to be made of something a little sturdier than Marshall's delicate porcelain china; a good grade of stoneware would be nice. "I'd have thought you would have learned your lesson during that last fouled attempt to force your attentions on me."

"I was too busy studying the teacher to pay attention to my lessons," he quipped, then quickly pulled her into his arms. His abdomen tightened from the sheer intensity of the aching desire he felt for her.

Audrey drew a sharp breath with which she intended

110

to voice her startled outrage, only to have her angry words so badly muffled they came out as nothing more than an aching moan in the warm depths of his mouth.

Aware any attempt to chastise him for his bold behavior was pointless at the moment, she immediately stiffened against his embrace and again pretended complete boredom, remembering how well that had worked the last time. Patiently, she waited for the kiss to abate; but when he did not immediately pull away, as expected, she began to worry that her lack of response no longer mattered to him. Apparently nothing did, as long as he got what he wanted.

She decided the time had come to show her resistance, only to discover he had no intention whatsoever of yielding to her demands. Instead of letting go, his arms tightened around her, drawing her closer, pressing her soft, pliable curves intimately against his lean, hard frame.

Frightened by her inability to make him stop, she tried to turn her head to the side in an effort to free her lips enough to do at least verbal battle; but no matter which direction she moved or how far she twisted her neck, his mouth followed, relentless in its pursuit. Finally, she gave up the futile struggle, aware she needed to think the situation through. There had to be a way to make him stop—make him *want* to stop.

Gradually, while she continued to think, a tremor of misty warmth began to gather somewhere near the base of her stomach. The gentle, soothing heat filled her lower body, then spread slowly through her bloodstream, leaving no part of her untouched as it attempted to rob her of her senses. She struggled to fight off the unfamiliar sensations, but to her growing horror, she could not stop their overpowering effect. Her body grew more and more compliant as the heat continued to build inside her, urging her to give in to her awakening needs, to surrender to the languid stirring of warmth, to explore these new feelings to their fullest. But that response was

111

all wrong! A man whose arrogance was beyond belief had just forced an unwanted kiss on her, and suddenly, she'd started to enjoy it? Where was the reasoning in that?

More than ever, she wished Landon would tire of his stolen kiss and pull away; but he showed no signs of lessening his ardor. Instead, the kiss became increasingly stronger, and the sensations he'd stirred to life grew far more intense. She'd already done all she could to stay in full control of her senses, yet it wasn't enough.

The melting warmth that had entered her body with such languorous ease had spread until she'd begun to feel a little light-headed. Her firm resolve not to be affected by his kiss slowly gave way to the thick, sensual fog, making it that much harder to concentrate on anything but the reverberating sound of her own frantic heartbeat.

Audrey did not understand everything that was happening inside her, never having been so deeply affected by any man's kiss, but she knew enough to realize the danger. She tried again to fight the unknown sensations.

Determined to ignore the funny little tremors he'd stirred to life, she attempted to concentrate on something else—anything else. Anything but the wondrous feel of his mouth hungrily caressing hers, or the feel of his strong, hard body pressed shamelessly against hers. Yet, nothing came to mind. Nothing to rescue her from this madness.

Landon, aware her resistance was gradually weakening, strengthened his hold as he gently brushed his tongue across her lips, urging her to part them. When she did, he quickly slipped his tongue into the soft depths of her mouth. Never had he tasted such sweetness. His whole body ached with his need for more.

Though she'd heard of this type of kiss, Audrey had not expected him to actually enter her mouth with the tip of his tongue, for no man had ever tried anything like that before. When the velvety surface first touched the sensitive areas of her inner mouth, an alarming jolt shot through to her brain, breaking through the warm, sensual haze that had surrounded and controlled her. Again, she tried to pull away. But the arms that had so quickly captured her in such a bold, intimate embrace continued to hold her firmly in place, pressing her ever harder against his body.

Though she'd have thought it impossible, the kiss suddenly deepened more. His mouth became increasingly more demanding in an effort to draw her full attention, while one of his hands moved slowly from the curve of her lower back around to her midriff, then slid boldly upward until it gently cupped the outer curve of her breast.

Outraged that he would dare try such a thing, much less hope to get away with it, Audrey drew on an inner strength she was no longer certain she possessed and somehow managed to shove him away from her, though not quite far enough to assure a complete escape.

Gasping for air, in a hopeless effort to get enough breath to calm her furiously beating heart, she glared at him. Her eyes remained dark with an unfulfilled passion she did not understand, while her blood raged hot, rampant trails through her body.

"How dare you!" she shouted, her voice barely more than a growling whisper. At that same moment, she lifted her hand to strike his handsome face as hard as she could. Her rage reached unbearable proportions when his hand shot out and caught her arm just inches from the wrist, then held it securely away from his face.

Landon frowned darkly, eyeing her open hand with clear warning. "That was not quite the reaction I'd hoped for," he commented as he used the grip he had on her arm to again pull her against him.

"Don't you dare!" she cried, trying desperately to yank her arm free from his grasp, only to find herself locked in yet another ardent embrace. His mouth again descended against hers, silencing any further verbal protests.

113

Not at all ready to admit defeat, Landon put everything he had into this next kiss as he again molded his lips to hers, pressing her body even more intimately against his, determined to have a proper reaction from her yet.

Finally, as he stroked the curve of her back with strong, practiced hands and continued to fit his mouth hungrily against hers, darting the tip of his tongue inside just far enough to reach the sensitive inner surfaces, he sensed her body relax. Gradually, she allowed herself to explore one brief moment of pleasure.

Though Audrey clearly sensed the danger, aware this man's kiss was far different from anything she had ever experienced, she couldn't help but give herself to the tingling feelings his touch had aroused. And the moment her own hand moved up to timidly touch the powerful muscles in his neck, she knew she was in serious trouble; but there seemed to be nothing she could do about it. An unfamiliar hunger had developed deep inside her body, an emotional awakening so strong and so unbelievably overwhelming that it rendered her momentarily helpless —made her want to be helpless. Yet that went against everything she'd ever believed about herself. She was supposed to be above such passion.

Still, the warm, gentle tide that had claimed her without any forewarning continued to roll effortlessly through her, bathing her with yet more beckoning sensations. It possessed her with a power beyond belief, urging her to give in totally to her newly aroused needs, weakening her desire to escape while replacing it with a totally new desire—the desire to explore these foreign sensations to their fullest.

Although her strong, moralistic upbringing dictated that she make at least one more attempt to free herself, before it was too late, her body now rebelled against the idea, willing her not to pull away at all. Her body wanted her to lean forward instead and learn more about the strange, magical pleasure found in his kiss and in his touch.

Even when his hands came to rest on the soft curve of her hips, another one of those areas no gentleman would dare touch, she was unable to do the right thing and push him away. His mouth was too maddeningly sweet, too alarmingly hungry, and when the kiss deepened further still, she lost all desire to push him away and instead felt an absurd need to pull him closer.

Again his tongue dipped intimately into her mouth, teasing the velvety softness of her own tongue while his thumbs gently stroked the sensitive area above her hips. Liquid fire spilled through her, setting her heart aflame as it sent out a heat so sensual, so all-consuming that it melted any last resistance that might have eventually given her the strength to stop him.

Landon had cast his dark spell over her and she was lost to its wondrous magic. Her legs felt too weak to hold her. She leaned against him for support, gasping when one of his hands then left the soft curve of her hips and began moving upward, gently stroking its way toward her breast.

Though terrified of the intense effect he had over her, she remained helpless to stop him. Whatever he planned to do to her, she could not fight him. She was too unaccustomed to the intense passions he'd aroused in her to know *how* to fight them, and she was becoming less and less certain they *should* be fought.

Landon moaned with pleasure when he realized he had finally found the response in her that he wanted. He sensed she was still hesitant, still unsure of all that was happening to her; yet when he reached the outer curve of her breast, he was relieved to discover that this time she offered no resistance. When her only noticeable reaction was to gasp for air, he felt certain she was his to do with as he pleased.

It was not until his hand moved to take in the entire breast that Audrey's sanity returned. The sudden feel of his palm as it struck the sensitive peak of her breast, coupled with the fact that his other hand had moved to undo the fasteners at the back of her dress, made her realize just how far she'd allowed him to carry his masterful plan to seduce her. The reality of what was happening crashed down around her with startling clarity. Pushing with all her might, she managed to break free and quickly stepped out of his reach.

"If you don't leave this room right now, I will be forced to tell your father all about this," she warned him breathlessly, leaning back against the edge of her dresser while she struggled to get better control of her senses.

"Tell him what?" Landon asked, lifting one brow lazily. Except for the rapid rise and fall of his chest, he appeared totally unaffected by what had just happened between them. "Perhaps you plan to tell him how eagerly you let me come into your bedroom, where I suddenly decided to take advantage of you and steal a little kiss. Is that what you intend to say?"

"I didn't *let* you come in!" she exclaimed, then bit back the pain that resulted from his casual reference to their *little* kiss. It had been far from a *little* kiss to her. "I didn't *let* you do anything."

"Didn't you?" He asked, delighted by her outrage. It pleased him to know that she did not permit men to take such liberties with her. That meant he would be her first, and if he had it his way, he'd be her *only*. The thought of another man touching her in the exact same way he planned to touch her made him seethe with undeniable jealousy. As far as he was concerned, she was already his. No other man would ever touch her.

This sudden feeling of possessiveness surprised even him, so much so that he almost didn't hear her next comment.

"You know very well I did not let you into my room. You barged in here uninvited. And if you don't leave right now, I'll—I'll—" For the life of her, she could not think of a threat worthy enough or quite frightening enough to send him on his way.

"You'll what?" he asked, clearly interested in her next

116

plan of action while he took a cautious step in her direction.

"I'll tell Seth about how you—you've so thoroughly compromised my honor and I'll have him call you out. You won't stand a chance against someone like him."

"Is that what I've done? Compromised your honor?" he asked, unconcerned by such a threat.

"You know it is."

Landon grinned that insufferable, lazy half grin of his. "I never knew that a compromise could be so enjoyable. I should try compromising more often."

"Get out!" she shouted suddenly, having had as much of his impossible behavior as she could tolerate. "Get out, get out, get *out!*"

"I'd rather stay," he told her frankly. Then, suddenly, his eyes lit with an idea. "I know. . . . Why don't we *compromise* instead?"

Audrey gasped, tossing her shoulders back with righteous indignation. "How dare you. If I were a man, you'd never speak to me like that."

"If you were a man, I'd have no desire to," he quipped, his eyes widening when she spun about in search for something to throw at him. Quickly, her hand alighted on a small porcelain vase. Well remembering the lack of respect she had for fine porcelain, the time had come to make amends. "All right, all right, I get the message. I'm going. I'm going."

Audrey looked at him doubtfully, for he'd yet to make a move toward the door. "When?"

"Right now," he vowed, glancing at where her hand still lay atop the delicate French vase. "Before you do something we'll both regret."

"Good," she responded, but continued to watch him warily as he edged his way toward the door. If he was up to some new trick, she wanted to be ready to defend herself. She tensed, her fingers curling around the golden rim of the vase, when he paused in the doorway and looked back at her.

117

"I'm leaving now, just like I said I would," he told her gallantly just seconds before that familiar grin flickered across his face. "But, since we seem to make such little progress in this room, next time, why don't you come to my room and compromise *my* honor for a change?"

"Impossible. You have no honor!"

"I hadn't thought of that," he said, frowning thoughtfully. "Looks like I'll just have to continue coming here." Then, before she could fling another angry retort or his father's expensive French vase, he ducked artfully out of sight.

chapter eight

Getting Seth's watch back had proved far easier than Audrey had dared hope. When she'd ventured downstairs with plans to volunteer to take Rachel's breakfast tray up to her, she'd discovered that the young woman was no longer confined to her rooms. Instead, she was downstairs dining at the main table with the rest of her family, leaving her rooms conveniently vacant.

Though eager to hurry back upstairs and get the watch while everyone was still busy eating, Audrey did not want to do anything that might appear in any way suspicious. She went on into the kitchen and ate a few bites of her own breakfast before returning upstairs to her room, much like she had the day before. Only today, she detoured into Rachel's rooms, where she quickly located the watch and hurried back out happily undetected.

Once she reached the safety of the hallway, she paused long enough to wind the watch and see if it still worked. Because the watch had once belonged to their father, given to him by their grandfather only a month before the old man's death, Seth was especially fond of it. After the rap it had taken the day before, she was afraid she'd damaged it—damaged the only thing they had left of their parents or their grandparents. To her relief, though, the watch bore no grudges for having been sorely mistreated and ticked contentedly in her palm.

Smiling as she closed the watch and turned in the direction of her room, she was startled to find Everett standing in the doorway to Marshall's bedroom, staring curiously first at her, then at the open door behind her. Audrey felt certain he was suspicious of the reason she'd paused right outside Rachel's bedroom door but, at the same time, remembered that the old man had not been in that doorway when she'd first come out. She'd been careful to glance in all directions before actually moving out into the hallway. All the old butler could possibly have were his own suspicions, which didn't bother Audrey very much because she did indeed have the evidence back and that was what mattered the most.

Later, while Seth prepared to accompany Marshall during his morning appointments, Audrey pretended to give her brother a fond good-bye hug and carefully slipped the treasured timepiece into his coat pocket. When he reached inside and discovered what she'd done, relief washed over him. Audrey knew, without having to hear the words, that he would be eternally grateful to her for what she'd done. But, then, what was a sister for if not to help get a brother out of a sticky situation? She knew he'd have done the same for her—and might have to yet.

If one thing could be said of Landon Steed, it was that he was persistent. During the next few days, he tried several times to catch Audrey alone. Twice, he'd approached her room late at night, only to discover she'd had the aforethought to invite Seth to visit with her for a while before going to bed.

Having glimpsed him in the hall, Audrey took great pleasure in thwarting such obvious attempts to be alone with her and decided to make her nightly visits with her brother a regular part of her routine, because not only did it drive Landon to absolute distraction, but it also allowed her to keep up with the different events happening in Seth's life.

But Landon was not so easily daunted. Shortly after he'd discovered he would not be able to catch her alone whenever she returned to her room after work, he decided to try capturing her in the hallway on her way downstairs before work.

Having already questioned Kelly, careful not to make his intentions seem obvious, he'd learned that Audrey usually appeared in the kitchen a few minutes before noon. At ten minutes to the hour, figuring she'd never come out of her room if she knew he lay in wait, he positioned himself in the stretch of hallway nearest the stairs. Eventually, he heard Audrey's soft footsteps in the distant hallway and he prepared to do his worst; but, to Landon's disgruntlement, his sister chose the exact same moment to come out into the hall on her way downstairs.

Audrey had to smile when she turned the corner and found Landon standing in the hallway with his hands shoved into his pockets, discussing the weather with his sister. Clearly, it had upset him to have stayed home from his regular duties in hopes of catching her alone at last, only to end up in a conversation with his sister about the unusually cool temperature outside.

Still, Audrey knew it was only a matter of time before he caught her off somewhere by herself, and such a thought terrified her to the point that her insides ached constantly. But even so, she found perverse pleasure in the fact that he kept trying—and failing.

It was a week later before Landon was afforded his first real opportunity to catch her out in the hallway alone. When Kelly asked Audrey to take the tea tray she'd just prepared into the library for Marshall, since Wednesday was Everett's night off, Audrey's first thought had been of Landon.

Until now, she'd been very careful never to be alone whenever she left a room, knowing Landon could be anywhere. Even so, she felt she would be safe enough during her walk to the library, since the tea she was to

121

serve was piping hot; but, at the same time, she knew she would be at his mercy on the return trip, because she'd have nothing in her hands with which to threaten him. Her only hope was that he'd already gone upstairs to bed, or that he was in the library too involved in some important conversation with his father to excuse himself easily.

Cautiously, she left the kitchen, entering the dining room with the serving tray balanced in her hands. She cut her gaze first in one direction then another, never knowing exactly where Landon might be. The china cups rattled against their saucers when she then hurried across the room toward the hall, then on toward the library, eager to serve the tea and get back to the kitchen.

When she neared the library door, she slowed her pace, feeling very much like a thief in the night while she cautiously looked from right to left, then turned to glance back behind her, still watching for Landon.

Afraid he might pop right out of the shadows and grab her, she listened carefully for any sound that might alert her to his whereabouts and was surprised to hear Marshall's voice so clearly from inside the library. Though she was still out in the hall several yards away, she heard his words distinctly. Turning toward the sound, she noticed that someone had carelessly failed to pull the hall door all the way closed. There was at least a two-inch gap.

"There's no doubt about it," Marshall was saying, chuckling aloud with glee. "They are feeling bearish, all right."

"They'd have to to be selling short the way they are," James added happily. "And when Monday finally does get here, Martin and Mack will find themselves in quite a bind."

"Isn't it amazing what a few accidents can do to the price of railroad stock?" Marshall retorted, still chuckling.

"Prices have been dropping steadily ever since," James agreed.

122

"Ah, yes, we've undoubtedly got them both right where we want them," Marshall chortled. "They'll be ruined within the week."

"And, in the process, you'll make a small fortune," came the ready response from a male voice Audrey didn't recognize. Though it was not Landon's voice, it had the same deep, rich qualities and his speech sounded just as strong and precise. Obviously a man of authority. Curiously, she stepped closer.

"You're right about that. As long as everything continues to go according to plan, I expect to make plenty," Marshall agreed. "You just keep buying up that stock for me a little at a time so no one becomes suspicious, and when the time finally comes for them to fulfill that agreement, there won't be a single share of Buffalo and Bradford left on the market. I'll already have it all. They'll wish they'd never heard my name."

Audrey had guessed by the tone of their voices that what she'd overheard was pretty important, but when the three men fell into uncomfortable silence the second she'd tapped at the door then opened it, she realized just *how* important that conversation had been.

"Your tea, sir," she said politely as she pushed the door wide and stepped inside. Without giving the other occupants in the room any notice, she crossed the floor and set the tray in the corner of Marshall's desk. "Would you like for me to serve now?"

"No, leave it. I'll help myself later," Marshall responded impatiently, obviously eager to have her out of the room so they could resume their private conversation.

"What about your guest, sir?" she asked in her most pleasant southern accent, nodding politely toward the young man sitting coatless in a nearby chair. With his vest unbuttoned and his shirtsleeves rolled up above his elbows, he looked very much at home. He also appeared to be about the same age as Landon, and though not nearly as handsome, there was something appealing about him.

123

Perhaps it was his all-consuming smile, which made his green eyes sparkle with sheer gaiety. But when Audrey remembered the conversation she'd overheard just moments earlier and realized the sort of thing that had obviously made him so happy, she shuddered inside.

Keeping a polite smile on her face, she turned back to Marshall. "Would you like for me to serve your guest before I go?"

"Who, him? He's no guest. That's my broker . . . Roderick Desmon," Marshall informed her quickly. "He doesn't even like tea."

"Then, shall I pour him a brandy?" she asked, wanting to seem interested solely in doing her best.

"Roderick doesn't touch liquor when he's discussing business matters. I'm sure he'll have something later."

"You're attending to business at this late hour?" she asked, hoping they would not guess that she'd overheard them and already knew without a doubt that they'd been discussing business—and that it had sounded like dirty business, indeed. "Why, it's after eight o'clock."

"You'll find I do business at all hours—whenever something important comes up that needs my immediate attention. And as it turns out, something important came up tonight." Marshall exchanged a meaningful glance with Roderick and James, then pursed his lips into a pleased smile. "That's how I manage to stay on top of things the way I do."

"Well, then, if you are certain you'll have no further need of my services, I'll be on my way. There's still work to be done in the kitchen," she commented, smiling brightly, though her mind was already at work with everything she'd seen and heard, trying to discover a way to use such information for her own good.

"Pleased to meet you, Mr. Desmon," she said with a polite nod before she left the room, committing his name to memory while she carefully pulled the door closed behind her.

Still trying to make better sense of what she'd learned

124

thus far, Audrey paused outside the door to see if she could still hear the three men inside. But with the door now firmly closed, all she could make out were a trio of deep, muffled voices, the tone of which let her know that they had indeed resumed their earlier conversation and still found great pleasure in the fact that Marshall was about to make a small fortune and, in the process, two men with the names of Martin and Mack would be ruined.

Aware Seth had not been inside the room with the others, Audrey wondered where he'd gone off to and what he might know about the strange conversation she'd overheard. But she was gravely disappointed to discover that her brother had already retired for the night. That meant he was still being sent out of the room whenever Marshall held any important business discussions. Whether Marshall wanted to talk with Roderick Desmon, his broker, or Melville Cross, his banker, or even Gene Haught, his mysterious messenger, Seth was usually asked to step outside and wait until the discussions were over. And tonight, because it was so late, Marshall had told Seth he could go on up to bed.

Audrey had hoped that, as Marshall came to know her brother better, he would learn to trust him like everyone else did and would eventually allow him to stay in the room whenever important financial discussions were being held. It was through Seth that she hoped to learn something about Marshall's many prosperous business dealings.

Disappointed but not yet ready to give up, she asked Seth what he thought "selling short" meant, hoping he'd learned at least that much during casual conversations in the carriage or during some of the short walks to and from different meetings. She was not at all pleased to hear his teasing suggestion that it had something to do with midgets.

Determined as ever to make sense of what she'd overheard, knowing she'd have to understand it fully before she could possibly hope to make any use of it,

Audrey's next thought was Landon. He'd know what "selling short" meant and exactly how that might bring about someone's ruin or, better yet, another man's fortune. But she also knew she'd have to be careful with how she went about asking such questions. She didn't want to make him overly suspicious about the reason she wanted to know, aware that if Landon happened to be a part of the business deal Marshall had just been discussing, he might figure out that she'd somehow overheard things she shouldn't, and that would put her job in jeopardy. She'd be out on her ear before the sun came up. No, she had to bring the topic up in a way that he'd never connect the two.

Bravely, Audrey left Seth's room and headed straight to Landon's door. Gathering her courage about her like a well-worn cloak, she knocked lightly on the gleaming wood surface and waited for him to respond.

Inside, she'd become a twisting mass of jagged nerves, aware Landon would probably misconstrue her reason for suddenly wanting to talk with him, especially after having tried to avoid him for so long. She also worried that he might be angry with her for having made his pursuit of her next to impossible. She'd have to judge his mood carefully.

"Well, well, well," Landon said, clearly surprised to open his bedroom door and find Audrey standing before him, still in uniform, her hands folded meekly in front of her instead of curled into small, determined fists at her sides. "What have we here?"

Aware that the next few minutes were going to be nerve-racking, but still determined to have the information she sought, Audrey forced a congenial smile to her lips. "I'd like to talk with you for a moment if you don't mind."

"No, by all means, come in," he said, gesturing with a wide sweep of his hand for her to enter his room.

Though relieved to find him still dressed, Audrey's first instinct was to take a step back and suggest they hold their discussion out in the hallway. But she was afraid someone might come along and overhear them in much the same manner she'd overheard Marshall barely an hour earlier, so she reluctantly agreed to step inside his room. "All right, but only for a moment."

Landon's eyebrows arched questioningly as he moved back, allowing her into his bedroom. Clearly, he'd expected her to refuse his generous offer of hospitality and now wondered what could possibly have caused such a complete turnabout in her decision to avoid him at all costs.

"What's this all about?" he asked, his expression wary while he slowly closed the door behind her. He studied her face with a raised brow, as if trying to detect signs of madness. "For over a week now you've avoided me like I had the plague. Why are you suddenly so willing to be alone with me—and in my own bedroom, yet?"

Audrey did not like the accusing tone in his voice and quickly sought to say something to alter any suspicions he might have. "I've been thinking," she said in a soft, sultry voice, glancing up at him coquettishly.

Landon's shoulders cocked back in instant readiness, as if that alone were enough to warrant trouble. "Thinking? About what?"

"About us." She continued to smile sweetly, aware she had yet to allay his suspicions. "To tell you the truth, I'm tired of playing cat and mouse with you in the hallways. It's very distracting. I'm here to ask for a truce of some sort between us. Instead of having to avoid you like I have, I'd prefer for us to be friends."

"But that's not what I'd like for us to be," Landon replied quickly. His gaze dipped boldly to the well-rounded curves that so aptly filled out her uniform, before it slowly worked its way back up to her beautiful face. He felt his desire for her surge through his body, making him just as aware of her as ever, if not more so.

Audrey felt her cheeks grow hot, having noticed where his gaze had briefly fallen. "Yes, I know what *you'd* like

127

for us to be," she said, trying her best to control her anger. "But can't we come to some sort of compromise instead?"

Landon's eyebrows shot up at the mention of the word *compromise*. A glimmer of something Audrey could not quite identify sparkled from the blue depths of his eyes. "But I thought you were against compromising situations."

"That's not what I meant!" she said flatly, but afraid they were about to end up at odds again—before she'd learned what she needed to know—she quickly amended, "What I meant by a compromise is that I think we should try to meet each other halfway. Instead of one of us having to give in to the other's demands totally, can't we compromise between the two and just become close friends instead?"

"How close?" Landon asked, stepping toward her, suddenly interested in the direction of this conversation. He was willing to get just as close as she'd let him.

Not that close, she thought, moving farther into his elegantly furnished bedroom, wanting to put as much distance between them as possible. "Landon, I don't think you understand."

"Ah, but I think *you* do," he quipped, and continued to head in her direction with long, easy strides, much like a lone wolf stalking its prey. The thought of taking her into his arms again filled him with longing.

"Landon, I came here wanting to have a nice, friendly conversation and nothing more. But, if that is beyond your capabilities, then I'm afraid I'll have to leave."

At the mention of leaving, Landon stopped just inches short of his goal, which was to devour her with kisses until there was nothing left of her firm resolve to keep him at bay. Quirking his mouth into a perplexed frown, he studied his different options as they occurred to him and realized that if he wanted to make any real progress with her, he'd have to slow down some. For now, he'd let her do things her way.

"Okay." He gestured toward a large gray and blue Grecian couch that fit nicely into the overall scheme of his spacious bedroom. He struggled to control the desire that pounded through his body like a team of wild horses, wondering how much longer he could stand having her this close and yet still not touch her. How his fingers itched to take down her hair and show her just what being a woman was all about. "What would you like to talk about?"

Though greatly relieved that he'd agreed so readily to a simple conversation, Audrey's stomach remained tied in painful knots when she stepped over to the silk-covered couch and sank uneasily into its softness. Her heart jumped when he wasted no time joining her on the cushioned seat, but she tried not to let her nervousness show.

"Oh, nothing in particular." She hoped to sound as if she'd had no real purpose. "Just as long as it doesn't have anything to do with kitchen work. I get so tired of hearing about the care of pots and pans or how to carve a turkey so that the meat stays together. By the end of the day, I'm so tired of listening to that sort of thing that I long to discuss anything else."

"We could talk about the weather, I guess," Landon suggested, not really knowing what was a safe topic to discuss with a woman like Audrey. Though he didn't want to bore her with the mundane, he definitely wanted to be sure they talked about something that would allow him to stay on this unexpected good side of her. "I was outside earlier this evening and it looks like we might be in for some more rain."

"I hope it doesn't rain tomorrow," she commented, trying to look ahead in their conversation to a way of bringing the subject of "selling short" to light.

"Oh, that's right. Tomorrow is your day off. Yes, it would be a shame if it rained all day and ruined your chance to get out."

"Especially since I want to take some of my money

129

with me tomorrow and invest it."

"Invest it?" Landon asked, clearly surprised that a woman would be concerned with something like that. He thought women had only one notion when it came to money, and that was to see how fast they could spend it.

"Yes, I'd like to invest some of my money, preferably in stocks. I understand there are large profits to be made by owning stocks. But, then, I know so little about the stock market."

"As long as you pick a reputable broker, you don't really have to know much about the market at all. But, then, I guess it's hard to know if you've picked a reputable broker unless you know enough about the stock market to figure out if he's cheating you." He reached up to stroke the strong lines of his jaw as he thought more about that.

"Could you teach me something about the stock market?" she asked, and for the first time since she'd first sat down, she looked at him. He was far closer than she'd have liked, but there was no room on the opposite side that would allow more distance between them. As it was, she sat pressed against the delicately scrolled arm.

"What do you want to know?" he asked, studying her with a peculiar expression. A woman interested in any phase of economics was quite a novelty.

She hesitated, worried that she didn't know enough to ask intelligent questions. The last thing she wanted was for Landon to think she was just another empty-headed female. "Things like what it means to buy on margin and to sell short."

Landon studied her expression a moment longer and realized she was serious. Though he wasn't sure she should risk her hard-earned dollars on the market, especially as unstable as it had been during the past few months, he could see no reason for her not to understand the terminology. "A margin is sort of like a deposit which is given to a broker before any big purchases can be made. It insures the broker against any personal losses."

130

When she did not show signs of fully comprehending, he explained further, "Once an investor has shown himself to be a responsible person, he is allowed certain privileges when working with his broker. Simply by paying a small percentage down, usually about ten percent, he can deal in larger amounts of stock than he normally might. This up-front money which has been paid toward the purchase of the stock he wants is called a margin. About all it really does is protect the broker against any loss should the stock fall in value instead of gain, because once the stock starts to decline in value, the investor is required to sell out immediately and take the loss, or give up his margin to the broker. If he decides to ride out the decline, hoping it will eventually turn around and go back up, he must increase the margin he's put up so the broker still won't have to worry about risking any of his own money, because if his client does not come up with the necessary money, he will be forced to. But until you've established yourself as a reputable businessman—or businesswoman—you won't be offered such privileges."

"What about selling short?" Audrey asked, nodding to indicate she understood everything thus far. "What does that mean?"

"I'm afraid that gets a little complicated to explain. Besides, I seriously doubt you'll ever become involved enough in the stock market to have to worry about selling short. Just stay with the more established securities and leave any wild speculation to those who can afford such risks."

"Still, I'd like to know what it means," she prompted, not about to let it go at that.

"If you are really serious about learning all there is to know about the stock market, why not read up on it? Father and I have several books on the subject downstairs in the library. I can loan them to you if you'd like." Then, in afterthought, he added, "If you have trouble understanding them, I'll be glad to help by

131

reading some of the more difficult passages to you."

"I can read." She tossed her shoulders back in a defensive manner, her folded hands curling down around each other until they formed one giant fist in her lap. "I may not have had much opportunity to go to school, but I learned to read and write on my own. I read the newspaper daily."

"I didn't mean to imply that you couldn't read. I only meant to imply that some of the passages in the books I've mentioned might be a little too technical for a layman such as yourself. If you have a problem comprehending some of the more complicated areas discussed, I'd be glad to help out."

Though Audrey would much rather have her answers concerning the stock market immediately, she realized it would be better to accept the loan of the books with the same obvious generosity they were offered. "I'd appreciate any help you can offer. I'd really like to learn all I can before I invest any money."

"Good. I'll go on downstairs and get those books for you. Though I don't think you'll be ready to make your first investments by tomorrow, like you'd hoped, you might want to get started reading about it tonight."

"I'd appreciate it, but your father is having some sort of meeting in the library at the moment," Audrey said, afraid Landon might say something to Marshall about his reason for wanting the books. Though it would be hard for Marshall to know exactly why she wanted to learn something about the stock market, she didn't want to chance tipping him off.

"It'll just take me a minute or two to get the books. I know right where they are," he assured her as he stood up to leave the room. "I'll bring them to your room as soon as I locate them. We can get started on them tonight."

chapter nine

By the time Landon knocked on Audrey's door carrying the books he'd promised her, it was after ten o'clock and she had decided against letting him into her bedroom. Not only was she uncomfortable with the idea of being alone with him in her bedroom again, knowing the undeniable effect that had on her, but she also felt she could concentrate better on what she needed to learn from his books by studying them by herself.

"Thank you for bringing me the books," she said with a cordial smile, barely opening the door wide enough to accept them from him. "I'll be very careful with them."

"But I thought you might like to go over a few pages tonight," he responded, aware she had no intention of opening the door even an inch wider, yet hoping to convince her somehow to change her mind.

"It's late. I think it would be best for us both if I read them on my own." Her determined expression let him know the decision was final. "I think I will be able to pay much closer attention to what I'm reading if you return to your room while I stay safely tucked away in mine."

"Well, if you are sure . . ." Landon stated hesitantly as he handed the books to her one at a time.

Though disappointed to discover he would not be allowed to be her private tutor after all, he was pleased to know his presence obviously made her uncomfortable enough to want him completely out of the room while she studied. He'd been curious to find out just how much of the reading she could understand on her own and, at the same time, eager to be the one to explain the things she couldn't quite reason out. But he wisely decided not to try and pressure her into letting him stay.

He knew it would be better to wait until she came to him asking to have something explained, which he felt certain she would eventually have to do. Then his help would seem less like something forced on her and more like a favor—something she might be generously grateful for. His blood stirred at the thought of how she might be willing to show that gratitude.

"I am sure," she answered, still smiling sweetly while she accepted the books. "Very sure."

"Then I guess there's not much more I can do to help besides show you where I think you should start your reading."

Hoping to delay their parting for as long as he could, he took back the thickest book of the three he'd brought, and opened it to a group of pages he'd located and marked with a piece of paper while on his way upstairs.

"This was the economics book I used during my first year in college," he told her as he pointed to the pages. "There are several chapters devoted to the stock market, which better define a lot of the basic terminology that you'll come across again and again in your reading. This book also explains, in fairly simple terms, how the stock market works. By starting with this one, I think you'll be able to better understand the other books, which are a little more complicated in nature. By the time you've read all three, you should have a pretty good understanding of the stock market. Enough so you should be able to choose the safer investments."

Audrey glanced down at the chapters he'd indicated, eager to get started with her reading. "Thank you."

Landon frowned, still not ready to leave but unable to think of any other reason to linger at her door. Having waited over a week to be this close to her again, he hated to see it end so quickly. "When you come across something you want explained in better detail, don't hesitate to come ask me about it."

"I won't," she assured him, though she doubted she'd have to. Having glanced at the pages, she saw nothing beyond her comprehension. "Good night."

"Even if it seems late," he continued, in an attempt to add even a few extra seconds to their time together, "I usually relax by reading for an hour or two before going to sleep, so don't worry about waking me with questions. I'll gladly do all I can to explain what you need to know in terms that might be easier to understand than what you'll find in some parts of those books."

"I doubt that will be necessary," she told him, her back arched proudly, annoyed that he still questioned her ability to comprehend anything complicated . . . no doubt because she'd had the grim misfortune to have been born a woman. What was it about men that made them think they were the only creatures on earth born with any degree of intelligence? "But I will keep your offer in mind."

Still reluctant to leave but unable to find yet another reason to stay, Landon shifted his weight restlessly from one leg to the other. "I guess I'll see you in the morning then."

"True, I'll probably want to talk over a few of the things I've read before I decide exactly how I should invest my money."

Landon frowned, knowing she would not be ready to invest by the following morning. The stock market was not something one could expect to learn overnight. "That might be rushing it."

"It might be, but I happen to be in a very big hurry to be rich," she stated honestly, then reached for the edge of the door, ready to close it. The sooner she could get away from his disturbing presence, the sooner she could concentrate on the books that were balanced in the crook

135

of her arm.

"Good night," she stated firmly, making her intention quite clear.

"Good night," he mumbled, watching helplessly while her door slowly closed in his face.

Shortly after midnight, Audrey had finished the chapters in the first of the three books that had been devoted to the stock market, and she reached immediately for the next. By four o'clock, she'd read all three. Though she'd had to read a few of the passages more than once to fully comprehend what was being said, she'd come away with a much better understanding of the stock market as a whole. And at last, she knew what selling short meant and saw how it could easily ruin anyone who dealt in it too heavily.

When making a stock deal, an investor occasionally prearranged a large sale of stock he didn't yet own for a certain price and on a specific date, anticipating the value of the stock to go down before then, which would mean a larger margin of profit because he wouldn't actually purchase the stock he'd promised for resale until the last possible moment. But, if the stock should go up and he found he had to buy it at a higher price than he had anticipated, the seller would still be obligated to hold to his part of the bargain and sell the agreed-upon amount of stock to the buyer at the agreed-upon price and on the agreed-upon date, in which case he could suffer an unsurmountable loss of capital.

In Buffalo and Bradford's case—the railroad she'd overheard Marshall, James, and Roderick Desmon discuss earlier—a recent rash of accidents had obviously caused Martin and Mack to anticipate a drastic drop in the value of their stock. Judging by what she'd heard, the two men, Martin and Mack, must have agreed to sell a sizable amount of the railroad's stock at a preset price to Marshall, for sometime Monday morning. But, with

Marshall buying up all the stock himself ahead of time, slowly through his broker so it wouldn't be easily noticed, there wouldn't be any stock for Martin and Mack to buy at any price.

Stock manipulation! Marshall was clearly out to ruin Martin and Mack, whoever they were, and make a tidy profit in the process. And if that was really what the old man intended to do, there had to be a way for yet another trader to step in, using the information she now had, to outwit them all. If only she could get her hands on several thousand dollars, she was certain she could make a killing. Her days of being "dirt poor" would be over at last.

The thought of that made Audrey's heart leap with anticipation, because with money to give her the respect and the power she'd always wanted, she would no longer have to bend to anyone else's will. She could forever give up such menial jobs as being some rich woman's seamstress or some rich man's housekeeper. She would have her own seamstresses, her own housekeepers. For once, she would be the one in charge.

As children, she and Seth had always been looked down upon and made cruel sport of simply because their family had been so poor. The four of them had been forced to live near the edge of an insect-infested swamp in southern Louisiana, in a small one-room hut made from tree branches, scrap lumber, and thrown-away pieces of tin. They'd been so poor that her father had been killed while trying to steal a chicken to feed his family, back when Audrey was barely fourteen. What had made the situation worse was knowing that her father was an honest, hardworking man. Stealing the chicken had been a reckless act of desperation on her father's part. He'd taken the chicken solely because her mother was slowly dying of starvation and he'd wanted somehow to provide her with the food necessary to keep her alive.

It had been cheaper for the plantation owners and local businesses to work their slaves rather than to hire laborers, making jobs impossible to find for those without any real education or special skills. No jobs meant no money, which in turn meant no food.

The only handouts to be had in those days had come from the slaves themselves, who'd needed what precious little they had for their own families. Yet occasionally, the more prominent blacks shared a chunk of dried bread or a slab of pork that was about to turn rancid, anyway, with the poor whites.

After their mother did eventually die from starvation, only weeks after their father was killed while stealing the chicken, Audrey and Seth were forced to try and make it on their own. Times became so hard for the two that many times they'd had to go out into the streets of New Orleans and beg for scraps just to survive. On occasion, there was a job to be found for one of them, but it was usually something like cleaning out someone's stables or opening up a clogged sewage pipe, jobs even the Negroes rebelled against because of the long hours and the low pay.

During the Civil War, which were Audrey's teenage years, the work they were able to find many times included strong elements of danger, such as helping the blockade runners make contact with the people who'd financed them, by carrying messages back and forth, or by helping to load boats with dangerous cargo. These type of jobs had varied from time to time and had become more frequent during the height of the war, but the pay was never much better than what could be earned unplugging someone's sewage or cleaning out someone's stables. Still, with Audrey's keen wit and her unrelenting determination to survive, along with Seth's obvious brawn, they'd both managed to stay alive. But that had never been enough.

Audrey had always wanted more than the day-to-day existence they'd suffered throughout their lives. It was the whole reason she'd decided to make the move to New York, having heard wondrous tales of the vast fortunes to be had in the city.

It took over a year to save the money they'd needed to get there and then find a room to stay in until they could locate jobs, but as soon as Audrey felt they had saved enough, they packed up their meager belongings and headed north to seek their fortunes.

Having had experience as a seamstress, Audrey had found a job at Miss Nadine's Dress Shop almost immediately, earning higher wages than she ever had before. Barely a week later, Seth had also located a job at one of the larger warehouses near the docks. But their new jobs were not what they'd hoped them to be. They included working twelve to fourteen hours a day, six days a week. And for what? The living expenses in New York City had proved to be far higher than she ever would have imagined. Again, she and Seth had found themselves barely surviving.

Audrey had been quick to tire of living like a caged animal, always being criticized for every move made, constantly being told what to do. Rarely had she seen the light of day, except for the few rays of sun that made it through a stained window in the dingy back room of the fancy dressmaker's shop where she worked. Having seen firsthand the extravagant clothes the rich ladies wore and having watched the way someone was always doting on them, she knew she wanted just such a life for herself—and for Seth. She'd become obsessed with the idea of wealth.

And now, suddenly, she had her chance. If only she could get her hands on some money.

Though she knew it could not be much, she wondered if Seth had saved any of the wages he'd earned during those first two weeks working for the Steeds. Because it had been their first real opportunity to splurge on even the slightest of luxuries, they'd both decided to take their first two paychecks and buy whatever struck their fancies. Her only hope was that Seth had not spent all sixty dollars yet.

Eager to approach her brother for whatever money he might still have, Audrey slipped out of bed early the following morning, combed her hair into a simple twist high at the back of her neck, then quickly dressed in one of her nicest dresses, a garment she'd made for herself from the scraps that had been tossed away at Nadine's.

Originally, Audrey had planned to spend the twelve dollars she'd saved thus far on fancy new clothes, but she quickly tucked the full amount into her pocket, eager to spend every cent of it on Buffalo and Bradford stock. For now, new dresses, a new hat, and shiny new boots would have to wait.

Audrey hurried out of her room and down the hall, frowning when moments later she noticed that Seth's door was open. That meant he'd already gone downstairs to begin his day, as had Marshall. But because it was barely past sunup, she felt certain they hadn't left the house yet. At this early hour, the only places open for business were the food markets, and Kelly was in charge of taking care of any and all food purchases.

Scampering downstairs, hoping to find Seth still in the kitchen eating his breakfast, Audrey heard a pair of voices in the distance. Deep voices. Male voices. Coming from the library.

Thinking that might be where she'd find Seth, she immediately changed directions, heading toward the library instead.

"Aye, Cap'n," she heard a loud, brawny-voiced man say as she hurried along the marble hallway toward the open door near the back portion of the house. "All four accidents went off without a hitch."

"I know, and I also want you to know how pleased I am with your work," Marshall responded. "Because of what you've done in these past few weeks, the stock has now dropped to four dollars a share, which makes it that much easier for me to buy up every available piece of paper."

"I 'ope you 'ave a buyer for all that stock. I'd 'ate to

140

think of you 'aving to sit on it for very long."

"Oh, I do have a buyer. That's what's so wonderful about this whole scam. Vanderbilt needs that railroad in order to piece together two of his own lines. Which is why I'm so pleased by the way things have turned out. And to show you just how pleased I am, I happen to have a little something extra here for you."

Audrey froze, still several yards from the door, listening to the conversation in utter disbelief.

"I was 'oping you might 'ave a little somethin' extra for me," came a hearty response. "Wot with all I 'ad to go through to get the job done. It warn't easy."

Audrey's mouth dropped open as the full implication of what she'd just heard hit her.

"Close the door and I'll get it for you," Marshall told the man just before his heavy footsteps were heard deep within the room.

Seconds later, the door clattered shut and Audrey wasn't able to hear any more of the conversation between the two men. But she'd already heard enough. More than enough. Marshall was manipulating more than just stocks. He'd paid to have Buffalo and Bradford suddenly besieged with accidents.

More anxious than ever to get her hands on whatever money she could, and aware Seth never would have been allowed to listen to what she'd just overheard, Audrey spun back around and headed for the kitchen again. There, she found her brother and several other men lingering over breakfast, laughing about something Seth had just said.

"Good morning," she called out cheerfully when she first entered the kitchen.

"Good morning," Seth responded. His brows arched with surprise to see his sister up and about so early on her first full day off. "What brings you in here at this hour?"

"Breakfast," she lied, bending forward to take one of the plates and filling it with a mound of scrambled eggs and a small slice of ham. Then, knowing it was not customary for the women to sit at the table until the men had finished, she carried her plate to the counter and began to eat her food there. She waited until Seth had stood up to leave before hurrying to set her half-empty plate near the sink and following him out.

"What's up?" he asked, pausing in the hallway so they could talk, aware now that she'd been waiting to speak with him alone.

"I need some money," she stated bluntly, seeing no reason to mince words. "How much do you have left from your last pay?"

"Almost sixteen dollars, why?" Suddenly, he felt guilty over the new pair of boots he'd bought.

"I've been studying the stock market and have decided I want to invest," she told him honestly. "But all I have at the moment is twelve dollars."

"Do you think you know enough to make a good choice?" he asked, not doubting her ability to comprehend, but only how much time she'd had to learn everything she might need to know.

"Yes, I do," she stated confidently, looking directly at him so he could see how very strongly she believed in what she was about to do. "I know all I need to know."

That's all Seth needed to hear. Quickly, he reached into his pocket and pulled out his wallet. "Then invest it all," he said, handing the whole thing to her. "If anyone can make it big on the stock market, it's you."

Tears burned at the outer corners of her eyes from having witnessed such a strong display of confidence. Blinking back the hot moisture, she put her hand out and accepted the money. "Thank you, Seth."

"No need to thank me. It's the least I can do after what you did for me, getting my watch back." He shuddered at the memory of that day.

"Have you had any more trouble with Rachel?" she asked, having temporarily forgotten about the girl's unprompted declaration of love for her brother.

Seth shifted his weight awkwardly. "No. I've been

staying clear of her whenever I can." What he failed to mention was how often that had proved impossible because she was always finding a reason to speak with her father. Nor did he mention that he was finding it harder and harder to sleep nights because he could not seem to get her out of his mind.

"Good, that's really the best thing to do," Audrey agreed, tucking the wallet into her skirt pocket. Frowning again, she tried to figure out some way to come up with even more money. She knew she'd stumbled upon the sort of opportunity that came along only once in a lifetime. It made her sick to realize that all she had to invest at the moment was twenty-eight dollars. At four dollars a share, that would buy only seven shares. What she really needed was to get her hands on a very large sum of money, a couple of thousand maybe, but she also knew that was impossible. No one she knew had that kind of money—except Landon. Her heart careened wildly at the thought. Maybe he could be convinced to loan her the money.

Hastily bidding her brother good-bye, Audrey hurried back upstairs, hoping to speak with Landon before he left his room. Though the thought of being alone with him still made her insides tumble frantically, she didn't want to take the chance of anyone accidentally overhearing her asking him for the loan, especially Marshall's overstuffed butler, Everett, who was making it increasingly clear that he disapproved of her.

It seemed like an eternity before Audrey finally reached Landon's door. Knowing the housekeepers might already be at work upstairs, she knocked very lightly, so as not to alert them to her actions. Then, as if it wasn't disturbing enough to have to be alone with him again, when he finally did answer the door, he was dressed in only a pair of black stockings and a close-fitted pair of light gray trousers. Having been caught during his morning shave, he had yet to put on his boots or a shirt. His broad, deeply tanned shoulders drew her immediate

143

notice. How strong and intimidating he looked.

"I wondered who might be knocking at my door at such an early hour," Landon said, dabbing lightly with a damp towel at the remnants of soap still clinging to his neck.

"I—I wanted to talk with you," she stated, so addled by the sight of the dark, springy hair covering his well-muscled chest that she'd almost forgotten her reason for coming.

"About the stock market? How much did you get read?"

"All of it."

Landon's eyebrows arched. "And what didn't you understand?"

Annoyed that he still doubted her ability to comprehend such things, she pulled her gaze away from the soft pattern of body hair sweeping across his chest and looked him boldly in the eye. "Nothing. I understood it fully."

Landon's expression darkened, for that was not at all what he'd wanted to hear. "Then what are you doing here?"

"I want to borrow some money," she stated with a determined toss of her head.

"So you can invest in the market?" His brow notched with concern as he studied the determined slant of her jaw.

Being as honest as she dared under the circumstances, Audrey explained, keeping her voice low, "Yes, I've done all the studying I think I need to do. I'm ready to invest. My only problem is that I would like to invest more than what I happen to have at the moment."

"I'm not so sure that's wise," he commented, wiping the sides of his face with the damp towel once more before setting it aside. "Come on in and let's discuss this further."

Nodding hesitantly, Audrey decided to accept his offer and entered his room. Her gaze was automatically drawn to the rumpled covers on the bed, and she suddenly could not stop the unbidden image of what he must look like asleep there. She felt her cheeks grow fiery red before she was able to tear her gaze away and get her wayward thoughts back to the matter at hand.

Taking a deep breath to steady her racing heart, she turned her shoulder to the bed and continued with her explanation.

"I want it understood that if you let me have the money I need, it will only be a loan," she said, getting her thoughts back under control. "I'll not only pay the money back, but with reasonable interest and within a month."

"But why should I bother with loaning you any money, especially after the cold treatment you've been giving me lately? Why would I want to help someone who has made it perfectly clear she doesn't even like me?"

"It's not that I don't like you," she admitted shyly as her gaze unwittingly returned to his chest. Her cheeks blushed with embarrassment as she wondered what it might feel like to reach out and touch the dark, springy hair that grew there. Suddenly, she snatched her gaze back up and fastened it to his while she finished her comment. "It's just that I don't know what to do with you about half the time."

"Care for a few suggestions?" His eyes sparkled with the thoughts that came immediately to mind.

"No, all I want from you at the moment is a loan," she answered firmly.

"How much of a loan are we talking about?" he asked, stepping over to his dresser and picking up his wallet, obviously ready to take out whatever amount.

"Two thousand dollars," she answered boldly.

The wallet slipped out of his hand, missing the dresser and falling to the floor as he turned to stare at her. His eyes were wide with disbelief. "Two thousand—?"

"—dollars. To be paid back with reasonable interest within thirty days," she told him, sounding surprisingly calm and businesslike.

145

Landon studied the determined forward thrust of her chin, noticing for what was not the first time that morning how incredibly beautiful she looked dressed in pale pink. "You certainly must feel confident in this sudden decision you've made to play the market, especially after having read only the three books."

"I am confident . . . quite confident."

Landon couldn't help but smile. "Then why not ask for four thousand? Why limit yourself to two?" Suddenly, he saw it as a chance to have her indebted to him for quite some time.

Audrey's eyes widened at the thought of so much money. "Would you be willing to loan me a full four thousand?"

"Yes," he answered simply. "I trust you." Having retrieved his wallet from the floor, he tossed it carelessly onto the dresser. "Of course, I don't carry that much money on me. I'll have to write out a bank draft, but that shouldn't cause you any concern. You can cash my draft at any bank in this city."

Suddenly, it felt as if all the air had been sucked out of the room. Audrey struggled for breath. "For four thousand dollars?"

With no further hesitation, Landon crossed the room to a small writing desk near the window. "Unless you feel you need more."

"No, no, four thousand will be plenty," she gasped, still unable to believe her good fortune. She watched, half dazed, as he sat down and began to write.

Minutes later, he stood again and handed her the paper he'd just filled out. "Of course, this is only a loan, to be paid back within one month."

"And with reasonable interest," she added in a choked voice, swallowing back her excitement as she accepted the check.

"Yes, of course, but we can talk about that sort of interest later. Right now, my interest is in which stock you feel so confident about buying that you're willing to risk the next thirteen years of your wages."

"Actually, I plan to buy railroad stock," she answered vaguely. "I understand that is where some of the largest returns are to be made at the moment."

"That's true. There's money to be made in railroads; but at the same time, you need to consider that there is money to be lost. Just be careful to stay on top of what's happening out there," he warned. "There are no absolutes in the stock market."

"I'll be careful," she promised, staring down at the draft in her hand with open amazement. Four thousand dollars! Just like that. And with so few questions asked. She lifted her gaze to his. "Thank you for having such faith in me."

Landon shrugged, then bent forward to kiss her lightly on the cheek in an almost brotherly fashion. "You are quite welcome, my dear."

Audrey's insides quivered with excitement, partly because of the gentle affection displayed in his kiss and partly because he'd believed in her enough to loan her such an exorbitant amount of money. But, then, four thousand dollars might not seem like such an exorbitant sum to someone like Landon, who had millions to play with.

"And I want you to know that I fully intend to pay every cent of it back within the month, if not sooner," she told him. Her mind whirled at such a frantic pace that she could hardly keep her thoughts gathered about her when she turned to leave.

"I know you will," he said in a strangely soft voice, watching while she left the room, the bank draft pressed close to her heart. Not only did he believe that she would indeed pay back the entire loan, but he also felt confident she would pay it on time and with full interest—though she had yet to discover just what sort of interest he had in mind.

Landon smiled as he thought more about what had just happened.

Audrey was an ambitious woman; he'd known that from the start. And she was a determined woman. With a combination like that, he had no doubt that she'd go far. One day in the not too distant future, Audrey Stoane would be very rich; and with money to back her, she'd become more powerful than any woman he knew. She would wear the fine silks and frilly satins a body like hers deserved, and she would make men like him cower to her every whim—or at least she would try. His smile broadened as he slowly closed the door to finish getting dressed.

That four thousand was for an investment, all right— an investment into his own future. He could hardly wait to reap the benefits.

chapter ten

"I don't know what ya did to turn her head so, but ya are all Rachel ever talks about anymore," Kelly said as she handed Seth a wet cloth to wipe his hands. "Maybe it's because ya are so tall and more than a little on the handsome side. Or maybe it's those gentle brown eyes ya've been blessed with. Whatever it is, she's taken to ya in a bad way. It doesn't matter what I go in her room to do. Somehow, she manages to turn the topic of our conversation around to include ya. She's always a-wantin' to know what ya've been up to and what sort of things ya like to talk about."

"What can I do to stop that?" he wanted to know, somewhat embarrassed to hear that he was more than a little on the handsome side when he knew he wasn't, but eager for any advice Kelly might give. "I've got to do something, before her father starts getting suspicious of the reason she's always asking so many questions about me."

Though Kelly had never mentioned having come upstairs the night he'd gone into Rachel's bedroom, Seth was certain she knew about it. And because of what he felt so sure she already knew—or at least had guessed yet had kept secret—he was willing to discuss the situation with her whenever he felt certain they were alone.

"I don't know what can be done. I've said all I can to discourage her foolishness, but nothing I bring up seems to do any good. And I'm afraid if she keeps at it, she's not only goin' to alert her father to what she's feelin' about you, but she's goin' to do or say somethin' to drive that rich fiancé of hers away. Then where will she be?"

Seth's expression darkened. Though he knew he could never be the man for Rachel, he hated the thought of someone with a name like Preston Windthorst having such an important part in her life. Rachel needed a man with more personal substance than anyone named Preston Windthorst could possibly have. "Maybe it would be better if she did end up driving this Windthorst fellow away. If she doesn't love him any more than she seems to, maybe she should find herself someone altogether new. Someone who could share her vital spirit for life."

Kelly nodded while she considered that, lifting an eyebrow at the adoration she'd detected in his voice. "But until she gets over this silly infatuation she has for ya, she's not about to start lookin' for someone else. Ya have to do somethin' to let her know ya are not interested in her—at least not that way. Doesn't she know ya would be a-riskin' yer job if ya were to show any interest in her at all?"

"Of course she knows," he responded quickly, his scowl darkening. "But that doesn't seem to matter to her."

"No, it wouldn't," Kelly agreed. "Never havin' had to worry about money, she doesn't really realize that other people do. She doesn't understand that jobs like ours are not at all easy to come by. She's like a small child who has found somethin' new to play with, and she'll continue to want to play with it until she either breaks it or finally grows tired of it. I guess what ya need to be doin' is findin' a way to make her grow tired of ya."

"Sounds easy enough. Any suggestions?" he asked, his tone flat.

"Not offhand, no. But ya be thinkin' about it. She's a pretty little miss. Ya'll need to do somethin' to discourage her before she lures ya into doin' somethin' that might be puttin' yer job in danger."

Seth cut his gaze at her, aware that had already happened. Daily, he waited to hear if their brief moment of indiscretion had caused Rachel to be with child. The mere thought of having to ruin her life by marrying her made his insides crawl. "I appreciate your concern. I really do. I just don't know what to do about the situation."

"Ya're a good man," Kelly said, smiling as she accepted the wet cloth back and tossed it carelessly into the dirty clothes hamper near the back door. "I'd hate to be seein' ya lose yer job over the careless whims of a foolish little rich girl."

"Me, too," he said, nodding that he fully agreed as he turned to leave the room. His thoughts were once again focused on the one person he'd tried all day not to think about—Rachel.

Audrey was in awe of the continuous flurry of activity surrounding her as she carefully made her way along the crowded sidewalks of Wall Street, trying to decide which of the many brokerages to entrust with her precious four thousand dollars. Never had she seen such a bustling nucleus of disorder. Bank messengers hurried in all directions with their leather bags clutched tightly to their chests, bumping now and then into the throng of office boys and secretaries with their arms full of yellow envelopes, as well as the hodgepodge of curb brokers with their pockets stuffed full of assorted papers.

Detectives, with shiny badges worn outside their coats for all to see, stood on almost every corner, hoping to assure a modicum of safety to the others, while overhead a thick web of telegraph wires clicked with important notices of the ever-changing prices on Wall Street.

Horses whinnied, cabbies cursed, and traders shouted back and forth at one another, all of which added to the strong feeling of excitement and expectation that filled the air.

"Can I help you?" a particularly seedy-looking man in a patched gray and white suit called out after having watched Audrey stare curiously, for several minutes, at the many buildings around her. When she did not immediately respond to his query, he swept his hat off his head, frowned at a messenger who'd accidentally bumped into him, then bowed politely. "Yankee J. Jackson at your service. What can I do for you?"

"I—I'm looking for a broker," she admitted hesitantly, eyeing him with uncertainty.

"What luck. I'm a broker. The best on the curb," he informed her, again offering a deep bow as his gaze fell heavily on her purse. "What can I help you with, m'lady?"

Aware of the keen interest he had in her purse, she tightened her hold. "I'm afraid you don't understand. I'm looking for a particular person. A Mr. Roderick Desmon." Though she had no intention of approaching Marshall's own broker with her purchase, knowing that would foolishly alert them both to her intentions, his was the only name she knew.

The man in the gray and white suit stiffened, then pointed to a large brownstone building across the street. "You'll find Desmon in one of those offices over there. Third floor."

"Thank you," she said, then hurried away. Rather than alert the man to the fact she'd lied, she cautiously crossed the busy street, then entered the building, leaving much of the bustling noise behind her.

Lured by the cool corridors and the contrasting quiet, Audrey stepped further into the building.

On the wall, not far from the entrance, she noticed a tall plaque that announced whose offices were to be found in the building and on what floor. Deciding that

152

anyone who could afford to work in such a fancy building had to be reputable, she studied the many choices now presented to her, avoiding any that were listed on the same floor as Roderick Desmon. Though she didn't think he'd actually remember her if he happened to see her, she did not want to take any chances. Finally, she made her choice and headed for the wide carpeted stairs in the center of the main hall, her purse clutched firmly to her breast.

"May I help you?" a pretty young woman in a fashionable green and yellow dress asked as Audrey entered the spacious offices of Rutledge and Sons.

"I'm here to see a broker," she said, allowing her gaze to quickly scan the room, noting first the expensive furniture, then the elegant artwork hanging from the walls.

"May I ask which one?" the receptionist wanted to know, eyeing Audrey speculatively, obviously not impressed with what she saw.

"Rutledge," she answered quickly, having already forgotten the first names that had been listed downstairs.

"Which Rutledge might that be?" the woman asked, glancing tiredly at her well-groomed fingernails. "We do have three to choose from."

"I don't care. Whichever one is free at the moment."

"I see," she said, sighing heavily and with great effort. "Am I to assume you've never done business here before?"

Audrey did not care for the woman's tiresome attitude and chose not to hide that fact. "Yes, I think that might be a safe assumption. Now, may I please see one of the brokers?" She paused for effect before casually adding, "Before I decide to take my four thousand dollars elsewhere."

Suddenly, life came to the woman's fashionably clad feet as she rose from her chair and hurried into the nearest office. When she returned to the waiting area, there was what could easily be referred to as a pleasantly placed smile on her face. "Mr. Rutledge will see you now."

"And which Rutledge might that be?" Audrey responded with a casual lift of her brow and a haughty fling of her head, imitating the woman's earlier disinterested disposition. "There *are* three, you know."

"Edison," she answered quickly, her dark green eyes narrowing at the intended jibe. "Andrew and Tony are busy at the moment."

"Thank you." Then, with all the arrogance of a queen before her court, Audrey turned and entered the room the receptionist had just indicated.

Twenty minutes later, she left that same room the proud owner of one thousand thirty-seven shares of Buffalo and Bradford stock. Though the broker had tried his best to convince her to diversify, she'd remained adamant that she wanted every cent she had put into the tiny, accident-prone railroad.

Rather than lose his commission, the broker eventually agreed to make the purchase for her and had told her to return later that same day for the papers that would prove her ownership.

That afternoon, Audrey picked up the certificates and hid them in her room where no one could find them. Eagerly, she awaited Monday morning, when her "worthless" stock would suddenly become very valuable indeed.

When Seth entered his bedroom late that night, he was surprised and a little disconcerted to discover that a long-haired, blue-eyed white cat with five little fuzzy-headed kittens had made themselves quite comfortable on his bed. Rather than disturb them, not sure how the mother cat might take to his trying to move any of them, he turned right around and went downstairs in search of Kelly. But because it was so late and everyone else had already gone to bed, he eventually had to return to his room without help.

Not totally pleased with the idea of sharing his bed with this feline family of six, he left his door open, in hopes the mother cat would become annoyed by the intrusion and decide to exit on her own. When that didn't occur, he walked over and sat down on the edge of his bed, studying his options as he now saw them. Without really realizing it, he began to gently stroke the cat, being careful not to disrupt the kittens' hungry quest for supper while he wondered what to do about the unwanted visitors.

"It's not that I don't like cats," he said as his inner thoughts surfaced into actual words. "It's just that there's barely enough room for me in this bed. You are simply going to have to find somewhere else to feed those young'uns. I'm afraid this room is to be strictly off limits."

"Even to me?" came a soft, careful response.

It took Seth a moment to realize the cat had not been the one to speak those words, but when he did, he came off the bed with a startled gasp, stumbling off balance. "What are you doing up so late?"

"I couldn't sleep," Rachel answered from just outside his door, glancing first in one direction then the other, before suddenly stepping into his room. Before he was able to voice any clear objection, she'd turned and quietly closed his door. "But, then, that's not entirely true."

"It's not?"

"No. The truth is, I've been waiting for you to come upstairs for the night. I need to talk to you." She kept her voice barely above a whisper.

Fear seized Seth's heart. He was afraid of what she'd come to tell him. Two weeks had passed since they'd shared their moment of reckless passion. Was that enough time for her to know if she was with child or not? "Rachel, I don't think it is a very good idea for us to do any talking in my bedroom, especially when your father's

155

room is right next to mine. Why don't I meet you downstairs, or even out in the garden. Anywhere but here."

"Because I'm not so sure you'd come. I'm not stupid, Seth. I know you've been avoiding me."

The tears that filled her eyes tore at his heart. He could not help but take her into his arms. "I only do that because each time we run into each other, I'm reminded of that night—and what we did. It's hard on me to see you, knowing how you feel and also knowing that we can never mean anything to each other. The simple fact is, we are from two different worlds."

"I don't see why that should matter." She pressed her cheek against his chest, savoring the warmth and security she found in his gentle embrace. "I love you. That's all that really matters."

"But it's all wrong for you to say you love me," he said, hoping to reason with her. "Can't you understand that I could never give you the sort of things you're used to having? I could never be the sort of man a woman like you should have for a husband. There's no possible way I could ever fit into your world, and eventually you would resent me if I tried to fit you into mine."

"No I wouldn't," she said, glancing up at him, her blue eyes full of hope and tears. Her long hair cascaded over the pleated shoulders of her white nightdress and fell in a soft array of shimmering gold curls down her back. "I love you too much ever to resent you. Please, Seth, please tell me that you love me, too. I have to know that you at least care for me."

Seth felt his resistance weakening as he lifted his hand to stroke her hair gently. "To tell you the truth, it doesn't matter whether I love you or not."

"Oh, yes it does," she said, interrupting whatever he was about to say. "It matters very, very much. Oh, Seth, don't you see? You are the only man who can ever make me happy."

"That's not true."

156

"Yes it is. I know it is." Her arms slipped around him, hugging him closer.

"Please, Rachel, don't," he pleaded, and wished he could find the strength to push her away but knew already that he had no intention of doing so. There was just something about her that lured him away from all practical thought.

"Don't you understand?" she asked, tilting her head back enough so she could gaze up into his soft brown eyes. "I want to marry you, Seth. I want you to be my husband."

"That's impossible. *We* are impossible. We could never be happy."

"Yes we could," she argued softly, then swallowed hard when she noticed that his mouth had already begun a slow descent toward hers. Eagerly, she awaited his kiss. "Seth, I want you more than life itself."

"Don't say that," he groaned, still wishing with all his heart to find the strength he needed to pull away from her but already aware that his desire to kiss her was too great. Suddenly, his job did not seem so important. Nor did the fact that Marshall would never forgive his daughter if he knew she'd come to Seth willingly. All that seemed important at the moment was that Rachel was indeed in his room, her head tilted back, her lips parted for his kiss. *Rachel.*

The kiss that followed was maddeningly sweet, growing stronger by gentle degrees as the realization hit that neither of them intended to pull away. What was about to happen between them was something they both wanted. Though he'd tried to keep his senses about him for as long as he could, Seth was deeply lost to whatever magic Rachel had used. He'd fallen easy prey to his own passions.

Hungrily, he devoured her kisses as he eagerly pressed her body to his. How tiny and delicate she felt in his arms. He actually feared breaking her. But at the same time, he could not bring himself to lessen his embrace.

Nor did she want him to.

With a desire she could not deny, Rachel leaned against him, encouraging him to take the kiss one step further. Her arms tightened instinctively around his neck when his tongue darted into the soft recesses of her mouth, carefully teasing the sensitive inner edges he found there. She was aware of the moment his hands began an uncharted course along the gentle slope of her spine, seeking and exploring every curve and contour his fingers encountered, from her soft, feminine shoulders to her delicately rounded hips. Though she was barely five feet tall and had the innocent eyes of a child, Rachel was every inch a woman.

Eagerly, her hands loosened their grip around his neck as she allowed herself the same sort of freedom he had allowed himself, starting with the firm muscles across his back, then traveling down to the lean, taut muscles of his masculine hips. How amazingly strong he felt. Like a true giant from days of old. Her heart soared at the thought of having her very own gentle giant—her very own Seth.

Even through his clothing, she could feel the warmth of his skin and the power of his muscles as they moved wondrously beneath her fingertips. Her desire intensified. How different his body was from hers. She marveled at that difference and wondered at God's mastery. Heavenly feelings rose up inside her, making her want to praise God for having brought Seth to her, for having given her the opportunity to know what real love was. She savored the tantalizing sensations as they rippled through her, teasing first her spine, then her arms and legs, and finally her fingertips and toes, until they returned to circle through her all over again.

Seth, too, was beset with a passion so strong, so powerful, he could not deny its force. His heart pounded with such fierceness that he could feel it pulsating in his chest, along his neck, and at his temples. Desire spread through him like hot vapors, driving him to do things he knew were wrong but could no longer help. Though every

158

fiber in his being warned of the very real dangers they both toyed with, his heart refused to take heed. He continued to lavish kisses on her sweet mouth, then dipped lower to rain more kisses along the slender column of her throat, pausing to tease the hollows above her delicate collarbone with the tip of his tongue.

"Rachel, this is wrong. All wrong," he breathed aloud. There was little conviction in his voice as his words fell warmly against her arching throat. "Push me away. Please push me away. Make me stop."

"I can't," she answered in a tiny voice as she plunged her fingers into the soft thickness of his hair, her shallow breaths coming in short, rapid bursts.

"Please, Rachel," he continued to plead while he kissed her throat again and again. "I can't stop without your help."

"Don't stop. Don't ever stop. Seth, I love you so much."

It was her declaration of love that finally brought Seth's senses crashing back to reality. Pressing his eyes closed, he sank weakly to his knees and, with tears burning the backs of his eyelids, ordered her to get out.

Clutching her nightdress, which had come open in the fracas, Rachel sobbed aloud her shame and quickly fled the room, leaving Seth feeling painfully alone and empty.

It was scarcely ten o'clock when Roderick Desmon arrived at the house, his face as pale as a corpse. Though Landon had an appointment with his own broker at eleven, he hadn't bothered to leave the house yet and was sitting in the library talking with his father when Roderick arrived. James, too, was there, awaiting the good news, though he expected it to be several hours yet.

Having told Everett he didn't need a personal escort, Roderick paused outside the library door, hoping to gather his courage before he cautiously pushed the door open and entered the room. Once inside, he ran his tongue over his lower lip, looking from one man to the next, waiting for someone to speak. He had no desire to be the first.

"Well, let's have it, man," Marshall said, unwilling to wait another minute to hear his news. Misinterpreting Roderick's unwillingness to speak, he sat forward in his chair. "If you are worried about saying anything in front of Landon, don't be."

"I can always leave," Landon suggested, studying the worried expression that had formed deep lines across Roderick's face. He shifted forward in his chair with every intention of getting up to give them their privacy.

"That's not necessary," Marshall insisted, obviously eager for Landon to be there when the news broke. He then turned back to face Roderick. "Go ahead and tell me whatever you've come to tell me. Did you get the last few thousand shares of that stock purchased in time?"

Roderick's back stiffened as he prepared for the worst. "I'm afraid someone beat me to them."

"What!" Marshall shouted, coming immediately out of his chair, his arms tensing at his sides. "Who bought them? Why?"

"I can only *guess* why, but I did manage to find out who."

"Then out with it! Who on earth bought that stock?"

"The stocks were purchased through the Rutledge brokerage by—" He hesitated, anticipating what Marshall's reaction would be.

"By *whom?*"

"I was told her name was Miss Stoane. Miss *Audrey* Stoane."

Landon's eyes widened, but he remained wisely silent while he watched his father's anger explode.

"Audrey Stoane! Seth's sister? One of my own housekeepers?"

"I can only assume it is the same Audrey Stoane, though I suppose there could be others." Roderick's

160

Adam's apple bobbed when he then tried to swallow but couldn't.

"Why? How? When?" The questions burst from Marshall with stark clarity. "Where is she?" Turning to James, who had sat rigid in his chair, he shouted, "Find her! Get her in here. Seth, too."

When James did not immediately move to do as he'd been told, Marshall cried out at the very top of his booming voice, "Now, dammit!"

That was all the motivation James needed. Instantly, he was on his feet, out the door, and headed for the stairs.

chapter eleven

Though Audrey's room was near the back of the house, she had left her windows open and had heard Roderick's carriage clatter into the drive shortly after ten. Figuring the time had come at last, she sat patiently waiting to be summoned downstairs. She tried not to think about how angry Marshall would be, or what he might do to her in a moment of pure rage. Instead, she focused her thoughts on the greatly increased value of her stock.

She tried to guess who might offer her the best price— Martin and Mack, Vanderbilt, or Marshall himself. But whomever she eventually sold to—and at this point it really didn't matter much to her—she felt certain she could at the very least double the original investment before she was through. She just wished that whatever was about to happen would go ahead and happen. She was ready to get the whole thing behind her.

When the knock at her door finally came, she glanced nervously about her room. Aware Marshall was not about to let her stay in his house after what she'd done, she had already packed what few belongings she'd brought with her and, therefore, would be ready to leave within the hour. Her only regret was that her recent actions would no doubt cause her brother to lose his job, too. But, then, with the four to six thousand she planned to make on the deal, they could live quite comfortably for several years without having to worry about work at all.

"Coming," she called out in a cheery voice when the knock at her door sounded a second time. Quickly, she straightened her skirts, then headed toward the door. She paused just long enough to take a long, deep breath before actually putting her hand out and turning the knob. She was not surprised to find that Marshall had sent James to get her. After all, it was not the sort of thing Marshall would do for himself, and Seth would have been a poor choice considering the circumstances.

"You are wanted downstairs," James said quietly as he stepped back to allow her to come out into the hall. Audrey knew by the way his hands fidgeted at his sides that he was extremely worried over what was about to happen. "Mr. Steed asked for me to tell you that he wants to see you in the library."

"Thank you," she said with amazing calm as she turned and walked casually down the hall. Though her heart beat with painful force beneath her breast, she was determined not to show her fear. She intended to face her accuser bravely and would remain outwardly composed in the wake of whatever he had to say to her.

All too soon, they had arrived at the library door. When they stepped inside, the first thing she noticed was the drawn look of confusion on her brother's face. Her heart went out to him because he was still clearly in the dark as to the reason for Marshall's anger.

And was Marshall ever angry. Blue veins stood out in stark contrast to the reddened skin along his usually lily-white neck as he paced restlessly about the room, muttering what thankfully proved to be unintelligible remarks. Roderick Desmon floundered helplessly at his side while Landon stood across the room, leaning against Marshall's desk and watching the proceedings with what appeared to be only mild interest.

"There you are!" Marshall shouted when he glanced up to find Audrey standing proudly across the room. "How dare you! How dare both of you!"

163

"How dare us what?" she asked bravely.

"How dare you try to step in and take over part of my stock deal," he shouted, advancing toward her with long, determined strides. "You've been out to cheat me all along, haven't you? That's why you bought all those shares, wasn't it? To rob me behind my own back. Just how'd you find out about it? Have you been snooping around my desk whenever I was gone or possibly while I slept? I demand to know how you got into my private papers! Did you steal the key? Or did you simply jimmy the lock?"

When Marshall finally broke his tirade of angry questions and accusations long enough to take a desperately needed breath, Audrey calmly answered. "I did not break into your desk. I simply overheard a conversation between you and Mr. Desmon, and proceeded to put two and two together. Nothing more."

"Nothing more!" he responded, his voice strained with fury. "You bought over a thousand shares of the stock I need to bring Martin and Mack to their knees, and you calmly stand there and tell me you've done *nothing more.*" He then glimpsed Seth standing awkwardly near the door and immediately turned his anger on him. "And you! How could you do this to me after I gave you such a good job . . . after I was willing to put my life in your hands?"

"Sir, I—I—" Seth stammered, bewildered by all that was happening.

"He didn't do anything," Audrey informed him, crossing her arms more as a way of steadying her quivering heart than in defiance. "He didn't even know about it."

Seth's confused gaze went from Marshall to his sister, his eyes searching hers for a clue as to what was going on.

"I bought those stocks entirely on my own."

"How? How'd you ever get the money to make a purchase like that? Someone had to have put you up to it. Someone had to back you with the money you needed. I

164

want to know who."

"I borrowed the money," she said, glancing for the first time at Landon, who still calmly watched the proceedings from across the room.

"You borrowed it? From whom? Who would be foolish enough to loan you that kind of money? On what you make, it would take well over a decade to pay back a loan like that."

Audrey looked back at Marshall with unbent resolve. "I'm not at liberty to say where I got the money."

"You'd better say," Marshall growled, taking a step toward her, his hands shaking with angry intent.

Aware of the danger, though not yet certain why there was danger, Seth moved forward to intervene. "I don't know what this is all about, but you're not laying a hand on my sister."

Landon, too, had moved closer, his expression cautious. "Calm down, Father. What's done is done. There's nothing you can do that will change the facts as they are now. If you really do need that stock in order to swing a stock deal, then I think the wisest thing you could do right now would be to offer to buy Audrey's shares from her, allowing her a fair profit, of course."

"A fair profit? Why should I let her have *any* profit after she tried to cut in on me the way she did? No. What I should do is call in a policeman and have her arrested for—for—"

"For what?" Landon asked casually. "For outsmarting you in what was obviously a questionable business deal to begin with? What's the headline for that story going to look like in the newspapers? 'Marshall Steed outsmarted by a woman.' You'd never live it down. No, I think the wisest thing you could do at this point is offer to buy her out."

"No, the wisest thing I could do is fire her and her brother. Send them both packing," he told Landon, his anger not yet abated. "Next, I could use all the power I have to make sure no one ever hires either one of them ever again. They'll starve in the streets."

"Not with the money I stand to make when I sell my stocks," Audrey put in quietly, aware his power was considerable, but not enough to prevent her from selling out to the highest bidder.

Landon closed his eyes, shaking his head at her audacity. "She's right, Father. You are not the only one who will be interested in paying a decent price for those stocks. Obviously, Martin and Mack have a good reason to buy them; and, knowing you, I can easily guess what that reason is."

"And then there's Mr. Vanderbilt," Audrey pointed out, deciding the time had come to play her high card.

Marshall's eyes stretched wide. "You know about that, too?"

"Let's just say I've done my research" is all she would admit.

"Damn!" Marshall's hands pumped back and forth, forming and releasing hard fists while he considered this new bit of information. "Damn, damn, *damn!*"

"And as for Miss Stoane not finding a job," Roderick bravely put in, though from quite a safe distance across the room, "I wouldn't mind giving her a position at my brokerage. I could use someone with such a combination of cunning, guts, and wit."

"What?!" Marshall shouted, whirling about to face his broker with renewed fury. "You can't hire her. She works for me!"

"But didn't you just fire her?" Landon asked, notching his eyebrows as if trying to keep up with the order of events. "Didn't you just fire them both?"

"No, of course not!" Marshall answered swiftly. "Why would I do that?"

Audrey eyed the man, suspicious of this sudden change of heart.

"All I said was that it *could* be the wisest thing for me to do. I never actually said they were fired."

"Then, you are not firing them?" Landon asked,

166

wanting to be sure he understood.

"No, of course I'm not! I can't have them going off to work for Desmon. Not when I already have them working for me."

Landon shook his head as he tried to follow his father's unconventional sense of reasoning. When he then glanced up at Audrey's distrustful expression, he lifted his hand to his mouth in time to cover his grin. Rather than continue to be involved in the whole confusing matter, he slowly shook his head and moved calmly across the room, resting his weight against the side of his father's desk.

"And now, young lady, about that stock," Marshall said, softening his voice until he sounded quite pleasant. Even so, his expression remained darkly adamant. "Landon is right. You should indeed have a fair profit. Therefore, I'll give you twice what you paid for it."

Audrey drew in a deep breath, aware she would end up with more than four thousand dollars if she agreed. Carefully, she studied Marshall's determined glare, wondering if she dared push his anger further. Then she glanced at Landon, whose attention seemed equally divided between them both, and wondered what was going through his mind.

"I'm sorry," she finally said, amazed she'd found the courage to speak at all. "But my selling price is twenty-five thousand dollars. Firm."

The veins in Marshall's neck bulged with renewed vigor.

At the same moment, Seth's mouth dropped open and he took a cautious step back, not so sure he wanted to protect a crazy woman.

Roderick's arms fell immediately limp at his sides.

Landon's eyes closed as he lifted his hand to cover them.

And James tried to sit but somehow missed the chair.

"Your selling price is what?" Marshall growled, knowing he'd heard Audrey right but giving her the

167

opportunity to change her mind before he unleashed his anger on her.

"Twenty-five thousand dollars," she repeated, pronouncing each word distinctly. She purposely ignored the sudden weak feeling in her legs.

"How can you do this to me?" he demanded, suddenly pacing the floor like a caged animal. "After all I've done for you and your brother, how can you possibly do this to me?"

Landon tilted his head to one side. "Seems to me, she's only doing to you what you had fully intended to do to Martin and Mack," he quietly pointed out, his eyes again wide open and glimmering with mirth.

Marshall cut his gaze at his son. A tiny muscle near the back of his jaw pumped in and out while he thought about what Landon had said. "But twenty-five thousand? That's ridiculous."

"I don't know. It's either pay the twenty-five or let her take her business elsewhere," he shrugged, as if the situation were indeed as simple as that. "I'm sure she could find a buyer somewhere."

"I'll pay. I'll pay," Marshall muttered, turning to shoot one last angry glare at Audrey before heading toward his desk.

"The full twenty-five thousand?" Audrey asked cautiously.

"The full damned twenty-five thousand," he growled as he jerked his chair out and sat down.

Meanwhile, Seth helped James up off the floor and the two of them stood awkwardly near the door, exchanging disbelieving glances.

"Here," Marshall said when he'd finished filling out the draft. When Audrey did not immediately step forward to take the paper, he growled, "Either you come get this thing now, or you get the hell on out of my library."

Aware she'd pushed him to his limit, she quickly stepped forward and accepted the paper. Her hands

168

trembled with excitement when she glanced down and saw that he had indeed filled it out for the amount of twenty-five thousand dollars. She couldn't believe it. Even when she'd asked for such an outrageous amount, she'd really only expected to leave the room with ten thousand at the most. She was thrilled to know that Landon's quick interference had had a lot to do with keeping his father's temper at a controllable level. Had he not interfered, Marshall's anger might have hit explosive heights, after which he very well could have sent her away with nothing.

"Thank you," she said to Marshall, trying to sound grateful when what she mostly felt was stunned disbelief.

"You are hardly welcome," Marshall muttered as he stood to face her.

To Audrey's bewilderment, there was a glint of amusement in the old man's shrewd eyes when he carefully studied her. Then, suddenly, he threw his head back and roared with laughter.

Thinking the man had gone mad, Audrey instinctively stepped back, in the direction of her brother. Her heart slammed hard against her chest when Marshall then moved toward her, still laughing in that deep, throaty way.

"You certainly have nerves of steel," he said. Suddenly, he reached out to shake her hand, then, turning to Seth, he continued his unexpected praise. "I don't know if you are really as innocent in all this as she says you are, but I want you to be aware of what a clever but conniving sister you have. You should be proud of her."

Seth and James shifted uncomfortably as they again exchanged bewildered glances, as worried as Audrey that the old man had lost his mind. His mood change had been too abrupt to be credible. "Does this mean you're not angry with us anymore?" Seth wanted to know.

"Not at all. Business is business. And your sister clearly has a good head for it. I just hope you don't plan to quit working here right away. I still need a good bodyguard. And ever since you took over that position, no one has dared raise even a voice to me. Everyone has been just as nice as can be here lately. I like that."

"Why would I quit?" Seth wanted to know, seeing no reason to.

"Well, with the money your sister just made off me, you shouldn't have to work out of necessity, at least not for a while. You could live quite comfortably for several years to come on whatever is her share of that twenty-five thousand."

"But none of that's my money," Seth said, frowning that Marshall obviously still did not believe he'd had absolutely nothing to do with Audrey's stock purchase, conveniently forgetting the sixteen dollars he'd loaned her.

"I know it's not your money, but surely your sister plans to share some of her newfound wealth with you."

"I do indeed," Audrey put in cautiously, not yet ready to believe that Marshall's anger had proved so short-lived. She felt certain he was up to something, but she had no idea what.

"But I like working here," Seth said, not knowing what he'd do with his time if he were forced to quit. And the thought of never being able to see Rachel again caused his whole body to ache.

That being what he wanted to hear, Marshall then turned his attention to Audrey. "What about you? Do you like working here?"

"Not as a housekeeper, no," Audrey told him. "Seth may want to stay on as your bodyguard, but I have no intention of working here as a housekeeper. In fact, I have no intention of working anywhere as anything ever again." Her expression was adamant.

"My dear, you've got a lot of money there, but it won't last forever," Marshall pointed out, thinking her speech a little overdone.

"It will if I continue to invest it wisely," she told him,

jutting her chin out proudly. "Which is exactly what I plan to do."

"Good," Roderick responded, not about to let such an opportunity pass. "And if you ever get tired of dealing with old Rutledge and his two scatterbrained sons, come see me. Together, we could parlay that twenty-five thousand into a real fortune."

Marshall glanced at him with a raised brow but said nothing as he waited to hear Audrey's response.

"I'll keep that in mind," she said as she turned to leave, not about to commit herself to anyone just yet—especially not the broker of the very man she'd just duped. She paused in the doorway long enough to speak with Seth. "Stay here if that's what you want, but I'll be leaving within the hour."

"Where will you go?"

"For now, a hotel, but eventually I plan to find a house in one of the nicer neighborhoods, where I'll feel safe. I'll let you know when I find a permanent place to live."

"What about my stock?" Marshall interrupted, having overheard her plans to leave.

"The certificates are upstairs. You'll have them before I leave."

Then, with only a quick backward glance at Landon to see what his expression might be, she left. As she hurried upstairs to get her things, she wondered how he could look so pleased after having discovered she'd used the money he'd loaned her to finagle twenty-five thousand dollars out of his own father.

Roderick waited until he and Marshall were alone before asking any questions. "What I want to know is why you gave in to her so easily. You might have tried to talk her down to at least ten or fifteen thousand. Why didn't you?"

"I really don't think she would have gone for a lower amount," Marshall admitted as he sat down behind his desk and removed a long, fat cigar from his coat pocket. He stared at the dark covering speculatively for a moment, then smiled. "Besides, Vanderbilt has already offered to buy up whatever Buffalo and Bradford stock I can get my hands on, at seventy-five dollars per share."

"Seventy-five! I had no idea."

"Nor did Audrey, or I never would have gotten her shares from her as cheap as I did. By paying her just under twenty-five a share, she came away thinking she'd made a real killing, when in truth she barely put a dent into my profits. Besides, I liked her gumption," he said, gazing up at Roderick. "That girl has got a lot of spirit. A *lot* of spirit. Even so, she'd better not try anything like that ever again—at least not with me."

Roderick shook his head as he thought about it. "She sure pulled a fast one, all right. I wonder how she ever got her hands on enough money to do it."

"No telling," Marshall mused as he reached into another pocket for matches. "With a woman like that, there's just no telling how she got ahold of the money she needed. She's got a lot of determination for a woman— more than most men I know."

"That she has," Roderick agreed, smiling appreciatively while he watched Marshall light his cigar.

"And it's also why I want you to keep a close eye on her. I want to know what investments she's making at all times. If you can't get her to let you handle her investments, then put someone right there in Rutledge's office. Whatever it takes for me to know every financial move that woman makes."

"I understand," Roderick said, approving of the decision. "Consider it done."

Immediately after cashing the draft, Audrey put all but forty-five hundred dollars into an open account. She had both her and Seth's names placed on the account so either of them could draw from it whenever the need

172

arose, then took the money she'd held back and went to search for Landon.

Because she didn't want Marshall to think his own son had had a knowing part in what had occurred, aware she'd already done Landon enough disservice, Audrey decided it would be better to try to catch him away from the house.

From what Kelly had told her, she knew he frequently had late lunches at a place called Delmonico's, and seeing that it was barely ten minutes past one o'clock, she hired a cab to carry her to the corner of Twenty-fifth Street and Fifth Avenue, where she approached the luxurious restaurant with caution.

Because her attire did not match that of the other young ladies who entered the establishment, and knowing that most places did not allow unescorted women, Audrey was not surprised when she was turned away barely moments after stepping inside the door, but not before she was able to glimpse the many patrons inside as she hurriedly searched for Landon.

To her relief, she'd spotted him seated beside a gaily painted wall near the front and had tried to catch his attention by tiptoeing and waving her hand as she was being escorted back out onto the street. But Landon, who'd sat with his back to her, had never glanced up; yet the beautiful young lady seated at his table did, and she had frowned with shocking disapproval.

Not knowing if Landon and his beautiful companion would leave through the front door or by way of the Broadway entrance, Audrey waited anxiously for them to appear through the front. After half an hour, fearing that they had indeed slipped out through the back, she tried again to enter the establishment, barely in time to see that they were already leaving out the back.

Quickly taking her leave, much to the relief of the harried doorman, she raced around the building as quickly as her booted feet would allow, clutching her handbag. She bumped her way through the crowded sidewalk in her haste. By the time she'd rounded the corner and had spotted Landon and his lovely female companion stepping into a large, open-air carriage, she was too out of breath to call to them and expect to be heard. Yet, within seconds they would be gone.

Making a desperate lunge forward, she managed to catch hold of Landon's coat sleeve just as he was about to settle down onto the seat, catching him off guard and toppling him sideways.

"What the—?" he growled as he picked himself up off the carriage floor, glancing up to see who dared accost him in public. His eyes registered total disbelief when he discovered Audrey standing at the side of the carriage, her hand pressed hard against her heaving chest, perspiration dotting her brow. "Audrey! What are you doing here?"

"I . . . have . . . something . . . for . . . you," she said, forcing the words out between needed gulps of air as she patted her handbag in a meaningful gesture. She'd purposely been vague about what it was she had for him, aware he might not want it to become common knowledge that he'd loaned her so much money, much less why she'd wanted that money.

"I'm sure he's not interested in anything *you* might have for him, my dear," the woman at his side said, clearly upset by Audrey's outlandish behavior.

"Oh, but I am," Landon put in as he quickly swung back out onto the street. Turning to the driver, he handed over his gloves and hat. "Please see that Olivia arrives home safely, then take my things on to the house. I'll catch a cab home later, after I've tended to some unfinished business."

"Business?" Olivia asked, glaring down at Audrey with obvious disdain. "What business could you possibly have with someone like her?"

"Unfinished business," Landon reiterated. "Nothing for you to concern yourself with. You go on home and get out of the hot sun. I'll see you tonight."

Audrey, who had yet to catch her breath, watched with

174

growing ire as the beautiful woman with perfectly sculptured black curls and huge green eyes leaned forward and ran her gloved hand lightly along the strong curve of Landon's cheek. "I'll be counting the hours." Then, before she had fully sat back in her seat again, the carriage lunged forward, sending her backward with a sharp jolt.

"Who's that?" Audrey asked when she'd recovered her breath enough to finally speak.

"A friend" was all Landon was willing to tell her as he quickly offered his arm. "Am I to gather that you have come to repay a certain loan?"

"Yes. I have the full amount right here," she said, patting her handbag yet again, pleased that he had yet to display any anger toward her for what she'd done to his father.

"In cash?" he asked, frowning instantly as his gaze darted quickly about them. "Don't tell me you have the full twenty-five thousand on you. Are you insane?"

"Probably," she answered agreeably. "But not enough to do something quite that silly. All I have with me is the money to repay your loan."

"That's foolish enough. What if someone were to rob you? There's no way to recover cash."

"Now, Landon," she said in a condescending tone, as if suddenly having to deal with a small child. "Look at me."

Landon willingly obliged, letting his gaze linger along her more feminine curves.

Audrey tried not to let his bold perusal bother her. "Notice the way I am dressed. Why would anyone in his right mind want to rob someone dressed like this, when there are so many other women walking around wearing expensively tailored gowns and elaborate ropes of jewelry."

"Oh, fine," Landon quipped. "And what about me? What's to keep them from trying to rob me once you've handed it to me?"

"I don't plan to give the money to you right out here in

175

the street."

"Then where?"

She thought about that. "If it will make you feel any better, I have a room at the Victoria Hotel. I can give the money to you there."

"It would indeed make me feel better," he said, turning around to signal for a cab. But it was not so much because he was particularly afraid of being robbed, for robbers usually picked on those who looked vulnerable. Instead, he saw this as an opportunity to be alone with her when he told her exactly what it was he had to tell her.

chapter twelve

"Since it's so extremely improper for you to be here," Audrey said in a precise, businesslike manner while gesturing to the small hotel room they'd just entered, "I think we should try to settle our business very quickly. The first thing we need to discuss, of course, is the rate of interest. Although the going rate for short-term loans at most banks is four percent, because of the circumstances, I'm quite willing to go as high as ten percent. Therefore, in addition to the four thousand you originally loaned me, I am prepared to give you an additional four hundred dollars, though I've kept your money barely four days." Quickly, she opened her handbag and dipped her hand inside, ready to give him the money so she could get him out of her room. It made her very skittish to be alone with him like this, knowing only too well what the man was capable of. Just the memory of his powerful kiss made her feel all funny inside.

"Whoa, wait a minute," Landon said, stepping toward her. "Who said anything about wanting the interest in money?"

Audrey's eyes narrowed with confusion, then stretched wide with sudden understanding as she brought the yellow envelope the bank had given her out of the handbag. Her heart jumped wild with panic when she noticed the dark, determined look in his eyes. She'd seen that same look before, just moments before he'd kissed her that last time.

Quickly, she countered his unexpected advance by taking several careful steps backward. Worried about the true nature of his intentions, she glanced around for something to take up as a weapon but found nothing readily available.

"What else is there but money?" she asked hesitantly. "I have nothing else of value."

"I'm not so sure about that," he commented with a pronounced lift of his dark brow. He continued to move toward her with one slow, easy step after another. "Let's just say *my* interest does not have anything to do with obtaining more money."

"If not money, then what?" She felt tiny bumps of icy apprehension form beneath the sensitive skin along her neck and arms while she continued to move cautiously away from him.

When Landon's answer was merely to glance suggestively down at her soft, rounded body, she became instantly enraged, but at the same moment somewhat intrigued at his daring. "Surely, you are not serious."

"Oh, but I am. Very serious." He continued to move toward her with languid ease.

"Landon, I'm warning you," she stammered, her eyes locked with his. Her throat tightened painfully while panic continued to set in. "Stop right where you are. Don't you dare take another step in this direction."

When Landon finally did stop, he was only a few feet from her, just out of reach but not quite far enough away to assure Audrey a safe escape. "Don't tell me you plan to renege on the loan?"

"No, I most assuredly do not," she said, waving the bank envelope in front of her so he could clearly see. "I have more than enough right here to repay your loan."

"You have more than enough, all right," he said, grinning that infuriating half grin of his as again his

178

hungry gaze dipped roguishly downward.

"That's not at all what I mean! I have more than enough money right here in this envelope to repay your loan. All four thousand four hundred."

"But all you owe me in the way of cash is the original four thousand."

"No, there's the interest, too."

"I told you, I don't intend to take my interest in cash."

"Well, that's too bad, because cash is all that I'm offering."

"Ah, but cash is not what I'm accepting. When you agreed to pay interest on my loan, you never specified that it was to be cash," he pointed out to her, his expression filled with amusement.

"And you never specified that it was not," she quickly countered. His presence was so overwhelming that Audrey forgot to look when she took yet another step backward, and she stumbled awkwardly over a badly placed easy chair. She caught her balance in time to keep from falling to the floor, but the incident served to further stimulate an already overpowering heartbeat.

"That's because you never actually asked what my specifications were," he responded simply.

Audrey's hand tightened around the envelope, crumpling it and the money inside. "Only because I trusted you to be fair about it."

"Trusted me?" Landon shook his head with sympathetic slowness, though that show of sympathy did not quite reach the sparkling depths of his pale blue eyes. "That's something you never should have done. You should never trust *anyone* in a business deal. Always ask to have everything spelled out in advance. Sign a contract if you have to, but never leave anything to chance."

Audrey swallowed audibly as his gaze dipped provocatively to the tiny white buttons between her breasts. A playful smile curved at his lips.

"Landon, don't you dare touch me." Quickly, she

179

stepped behind the chair, hoping to use it as a protective shield.

Lazily, his questioning gaze rose to meet hers. "Oh, don't think I plan to collect my interest today. No, I'll be satisfied with merely getting the principal back today. I'll wait to collect my interest at a later date, when I feel the time is right."

"The time will never be right for that," she said, crumpling the envelope even worse. The fingers of her other hand dug deep trenches into the pleated back of the tall upholstered chair. "I think it would be a wise decision on your part to go ahead and accept the four hundred dollars I'm offering you, because I have no intention of letting you have *anything* else in its stead." Having said that, she quickly pulled the cash out of the rumpled envelope, put back the amount that would leave forty-four hundred dollars in her hand, then thrust it into his grasp.

Calmly, Landon counted out the four thousand and tossed the remaining four hundred aside. "I told you, I'm not interested in more money. I already have all the money I need."

Audrey's legs ached as a cold feeling of doom settled in over her. Quietly, she watched him tuck the four thousand into his coat pocket. Intrigued that he dared behave so boldly with her, yet at the same time terrified that he might actually try to collect what he obviously felt his due, she crossed her arms defiantly over her breasts and spoke in a low, determined voice, "I want you to get out of my room. Right now. And I don't want you ever to come back here. You may as well get it through your head that I will never, ever pay you the sort of interest you've just indicated."

"Oh, you'll pay, all right," he remarked confidently as he turned to leave. He paused in the doorway to offer her a friendly salute and a devilish smile. "When the time comes, you'll pay."

*   *   *

Audrey tried to keep her mind off of Landon's parting words and the eerie feelings they'd caused, by spending the remainder of the day looking at houses. Though she did not want to spend very much of her money on a place to live, she did want a house she could be proud of and she wanted one in a well-established, respectable neighborhood, where it would be safe for a woman to walk the streets alone.

The small six-room brick house she finally decided upon was moderately priced, already partially furnished, and just large enough to allow Seth a room of his own should he ever decide to move in with her, though she couldn't see that happening anytime soon. Despite Seth's unwillingness to admit his inner feelings to her, she suspected that one of the real reasons he seemed so eager to stay on in Marshall's employ had something to do with that pretty daughter of his, Rachel. Something had to be keeping him there. She'd tried several times to convince him to come live with her for a while, yet he'd remained adamant about staying where he was.

Audrey just hoped that she'd judged the situation all wrong, because if it were true that he'd remained behind because of a growing interest in the pretty little golden-haired Rachel, she felt certain her brother was headed for his first very real heartbreak—and she knew only too well how devastating a broken heart could be.

That's why she'd selected a house large enough to accommodate her big brother should he eventually come to his senses and decide to move in with her.

By Thursday morning, Audrey had finalized the purchase of her new house and was ready to move in. It took an entire day to put up the new curtains she'd bought and to arrange the furniture. By Friday, she was ready for her first shopping trip to buy new clothes.

Her obvious choice was Miss Nadine's Dress Shop, where she had her former employer doting on her hand and foot. Before she'd left, she had gone as far as to ask the woman to wash the dingy windows in the back room where most of the sewing was done, claiming she didn't want to worry about the girls missing a stitch due to lack of sufficient light.

Audrey had come away from that episode at the dress shop feeling very good inside. So good, that when she happened across Kelly while on her way home, she eagerly filled her in about her progress to date. Before the two parted, she gave Kelly her new address and asked her to stop by and visit with her from time to time.

On Friday, Audrey had her first visitor. To her surprise, that visitor was not Kelly Meagan after all. It was Rachel Steed.

"Please, come in," Audrey said, her tone questioning when she opened the door to allow her unexpected guest to enter. She wondered how Rachel had known where to find her, then realized Kelly must have told her. But then she wondered why Rachel would bother remembering the address. They had barely spoken during those two and a half weeks she'd worked at the Steeds. They'd never really had much reason to. Nor did they have any real reason to speak now. "I'm afraid all I have to offer you is a cup of tea. I was really not expecting to entertain guests quite so soon."

"That's not why I came," Rachel said. She kept her gaze averted while she stepped inside.

"Why did you come?" Audrey wanted to know as she escorted the young woman into her small but pleasantly decorated parlor.

"I want you to talk to Seth for me," she answered, her words rushing out with broken emotion.

When Rachel looked at her then, Audrey saw that she had been crying. It felt like cold acid had spilled into her bloodstream when she wondered what Seth had done to cause this tearful outburst. Was he pestering the poor girl now that she'd teased him with words of love? Or had he become so angry that he'd said hurtful things to her in order to get her off his back? Either way, she'd do what she could to bring Seth back in line.

"What is it you want me to say to him?" she asked, her

182

voice soothing. Gently, she put her arm around the young woman and guided her to a nearby chair. Audrey waited until Rachel had settled comfortably before removing her arm from around her shoulders, all the while listening for her answer.

"I want you to convince him to marry me," she told her, much to Audrey's surprise.

"But why?" Her gaze went fearfully to Rachel's middle as she remembered an evening not so long ago when she'd witnessed her brother slipping quietly out of the young woman's bedroom. Suddenly, she, too, felt the need to sit down, and Audrey sank heavily into the nearest chair, set only a foot from Rachel's.

"Because—because I love him," Rachel admitted, much to Audrey's relief, yet obvious consternation.

"You what?" Audrey studied Rachel's tearful expression and realized the pretty young woman truly believed that she loved Seth. But how could that be? Seth was not at all the sort of man Rachel should be in love with.

As if she'd read her thoughts, Rachel reached forward, taking Audrey's hands into hers. "I do love him. And I think he loves me, too. He's just too stubborn-headed to admit it. In fact, he's being so stubborn about it all that I can't even get him to talk to me anymore. Whenever he sees me coming, he turns away. It's breaking my heart. Please, Audrey, talk to him for me. Convince him that I'm not a child. I'm old enough to know how I feel. Try to make him understand that we could be happy together if he'd just give us a chance. The big oaf has got some silly notion that we are all wrong for each other, just because my family has money and he doesn't. Try to make him understand that's a lot of foolishness. We *are* made for each other. I just know we are."

"I'm not too sure I want to get involved in this," Audrey said. "This is the sort of thing you two should work out on your own."

"But how can we when I can't even get him to talk to me? He's so afraid of what my father might think were he to happen upon us while we're talking, that he avoids me. He won't even look at me when Father's in the room, yet I catch him glancing my way when Father's gone." The tears that had been gathering finally spilled over and left tiny wet trails down her pale cheeks.

Audrey felt a sudden rush of tenderness toward the younger woman, for she, too, had once believed herself in love and well remembered the pain associated with affairs of the heart. It was one reason she had vowed never to fall in love with anyone ever again. "I still think this is something the two of you should discuss between yourselves. What if I arranged for the two of you to talk here, in my house? Then Seth wouldn't have to worry about your father finding out and you both could openly discuss whatever it is you need to discuss."

"Would you?" she asked, her blue eyes shining with sudden hope. "Would you really arrange for the two of us to talk, here where Father would never know?"

"As long as you agree to abide by whatever decisions Seth reaches during that talk. If, after you two have talked, he still feels you are not the right person for him, you must promise to leave him alone." If there were even the remotest of possibilities that a meeting between the two might finally bring an end to Rachel's foolishness, she would gladly do whatever it took to get them together. "I'll speak with Seth about it, find out when he can get enough time off to come for a visit, then I will get word to you."

"Thank you. Thank you so very much," Rachel sobbed, then leaned forward and threw her arms around Audrey. "I'll never forget you for this. Ever."

With no real opportunity to speak personally with Seth other than to go directly to the Steed house at a time she knew he'd be there, Audrey stopped by early the following morning and caught her brother while he was still eating breakfast.

184

Although Seth did not seem too pleased with her sudden decision that he meet privately with Rachel at her house, he understood her reasoning and did not refuse. After finding out from Marshall what afternoon would be convenient for him to visit his sister, he agreed to be at Audrey's house sometime late Monday afternoon. He also agreed to see to it that Rachel knew of the plans.

After Audrey spent that entire Monday morning at Rutledge and Sons, going over several possible investments for the thirteen thousand dollars she still had left, she devoted the afternoon to preparing for her first official dinner party in her new home. Having decided to include a nice supper for her guests, thinking their talk might set better on a full stomach, she stopped at the market on her way home and bought everything she would need to cook a large pork roast, since that was one of Seth's favorites, and four different kinds of vegetables. And because she knew she would not have time to prepare all that and a yeast bread, too, she bought what she would need for a quick batch of biscuits.

She'd just climbed down out of the cab, her arms laden with her purchases, when she noticed a fancy black carriage parked in her drive.

Thinking Rachel must have arrived early, eager to see Seth, she quickly paid the driver, then hurried up the narrow walk to greet her guest. When she stepped inside the wide portico, which was partially enclosed by thick walls of dark green ivy that grew along the latticed trellises, she was startled to discover her guest was not Rachel after all. Her heart stalled in mid-beat, causing her a moment of panic, when instead she found herself face to face with Landon. Again.

"How did you find me?" she asked when it finally occurred to her that she should speak. She wondered if Kelly had taken it upon herself to tell the whole world her new address.

"Find you? I wasn't aware you were hiding from anyone," he commented, his voice deep and teasing. His eyes sparkled with something Audrey didn't dare define. "I'm not."

"Then there's no reason Kelly shouldn't have told me, is there?"

So it had been Kelly. Audrey took a deep breath. "Do you mind telling me what you are doing here?" she asked, her words abrupt.

Her blood turned to ice water when it first occurred to her that he might somehow have found out about the meeting planned between Rachel and Seth. And, if that were the case, she felt certain he'd be upset with her, too, for interfering in matters she shouldn't. If Landon's views were anything at all like his father's, he would be *far* from pleased to learn that tonight's little rendezvous was mostly her idea. Her stomach churned with strong, fearful anticipation while she waited to hear his answer.

Landon chose to ignore her question. Instead, he glanced down at all the packages in her arms, one from which fresh green carrot tops and several crisp cabbage leaves protruded. His expression darkened. "Having guests tonight?"

"Seth is coming for dinner," she admitted, carefully studying his reaction, trying to decide whether he already knew that much. "Why do you ask?"

"To be perfectly honest, I'd hoped to collect part of that *interest* you owe me," he said, arching his eyebrows suggestively as his gaze dipped briefly downward.

"That's fine. I have the money inside," she said with special emphasis on the word *money*, while she slipped her hand into her pocketbook in an awkward attempt to find her key. To her relief, her fingers struck the tiny metal object almost immediately.

Landon sighed heavily. "We've been all through that. Money is not what I want from you."

"But money is all you will ever get from me," she informed him, trying to juggle the packages enough to unlock her front door without dropping anything.

Taking her key from her hand, he bent forward and

unlocked the door for her, his expression questioning. "Why do you even bother locking the front door when you've left several large windows open around back?"

"What were you doing behind my house?" she wanted to know, aware he had absolutely no business there.

"When you didn't answer my knock right away, I figured you might be purposely avoiding me," he admitted, glancing down while he struggled to get the key out of the lock. Pursing his lips firmly together, he tugged and twisted with growing determination while he continued to explain his reason for exploring her house. "I don't take very kindly to the possibility I'm still being ignored."

"So, what did you plan to do? Break my back door down?"

"Not after I noticed the windows had been left so conveniently open. Fact is, I'd decided to give you one more opportunity to open the front door, then I was going to return to the back and go on inside to see if you were really gone."

"But that's against the law. I could have had you arrested."

"A risk I was willing to take." Finally, the key came loose, catching him momentarily off guard. He stumbled backward, brushing their shoulders together, causing her to jump with sudden alarm. Landon quizzically noted her odd reaction. "You'll find there are several risks I'm willing to take when it comes to you," he added as he politely stepped forward and opened the door for her.

While she passed through the narrow doorway with her arms still full of packages, he leaned forward so her shoulder had to brush against his again, delighted by the disturbed expression that darkened her beautiful face. He was getting to her. Whether she was willing to admit it or not, he was definitely getting to her.

"I don't know what it is exactly, but you fascinate me," he admitted while he followed her inside. "You have from the very first."

187

Deciding their conversation had taken a very dangerous turn, when there was enough danger in the mere fact that they were alone in her house, Audrey tried to think of what she might say to change the topic back to something a little more on the safe side. She hurried through to the kitchen, where she could finally set down her packages. Then, suddenly, Audrey remembered the pretty young woman that had been with him the previous week at Delmonico's, and she asked, "I wonder what your friend Olivia would think if she knew how very much I fascinated you?"

"Olivia? Knowing her, she'd probably wonder the same thing I'm already wondering myself," he said, grinning, quite aware that would pique Audrey's interest.

Wishing she knew how to ignore such leading remarks, Audrey exhaled sharply, then asked, "And just what might that be?"

"She'd wonder just exactly when it was I lost control over my own mind. You see, ever since I met you, I've had one hell of a time keeping my attention on anyone or anything else. You do have a way of getting into a man's thoughts and staying there."

"I find that rather hard to believe," she scoffed, certain he'd said that in hopes of breaking down her resistance. "You seemed to have had very little trouble keeping your lurid thoughts as well as your probing gaze trained on your pretty lady friend last week at Delmonico's."

"Do I detect a tone of jealousy?" he asked. He studied her harsh, jerky movements as she turned a shoulder to him and abruptly began to put her purchases away.

"I should say not. Why should I be jealous of Olivia?"

"That's a good question. Why should you, when you are obviously twice the woman she'll ever be? That's why I wanted to take you out to dinner tonight. I'm enthralled by you enough to want to spend more of my time with you. But if you are expecting company, maybe it would be better if I simply joined you here?" he suggested hopefully.

Audrey's heart froze at the thought of what would happen if Landon were still there when Rachel arrived. She dared not risk such a thing. "No, Landon, this is to be a private little supper between brother and sister."

"Can't it be postponed?" he asked, reaching out to run his finger lightly along the soft curve of her cheek.

"No, it can't," she answered, jerking her gaze to his as a disturbing array of tingling shivers rippled through her. "Seth can only get certain nights off."

"What about tomorrow night?" he asked.

"No. Marshall's going to some fancy banquet and wants Seth there to keep an eye on him," she answered, misunderstanding his question.

"I didn't mean Seth, I meant you. What about going out with me tomorrow night? I'd take you someplace special so you could wear one of those beautiful new dresses you bought."

"How do you know I bought new dresses?" she asked, perplexed to learn he had so much information about her.

"Kelly told me she saw you coming out of a dress shop carrying several large packages," he shrugged. "So, how about it? Have supper with me tomorrow night. We can go to the Fifth Avenue Hotel. I'll call for you shortly after seven." When Audrey didn't respond right away, he quickly folded his arms and added, "I'm not leaving here until you've promised to go out with me. If not tomorrow night, then another night. Whenever you want."

"But why?" she asked, afraid he was serious about staying. How would she ever explain that her guest list for that evening included Rachel? "Why are you so adamant that I go out with you?"

"Why shouldn't I be?"

"It just seems a little odd to me. After all, I'm not exactly the sort of woman you are used to being seen

189

with. I was your father's housekeeper, for heaven's sake. Men of your high position don't normally allow themselves to be seen publicly escorting their father's housekeepers to dinner."

"I already told you. You fascinate me. Besides, you don't work for Father anymore, so that problem—if it ever was a problem—is already resolved." He paused, waiting for a response. When none came, he lifted his eyebrows and asked, "So, how about it?"

"How about what?"

He let out a long, audible sigh. "Supper tomorrow night."

Remembering his threat to stay until she finally said yes, she reluctantly agreed. "Under one condition."

"What's that?" he asked, instantly wary.

"That the evening does go against this interest you say I owe you."

"Done," he said, grinning instantly. "I'll call for you at seven." Then, to seal their bargain, he bent forward and pressed his lips gently against her forehead. The unexpected kiss sent a wild scattering of warmth through her body, setting her heart a-thudding like some schoolgirl's.

"I'll be ready," she said, though she wasn't sure that were even possible. How could any woman ever be truly ready for someone as handsome, as wealthy, and as self-assured as Landon Steed? With widely mixed emotions, she watched him leave through the back door, wondering why she'd finally agreed to go out with him when the thought of it terrified her.

"If you two will excuse me, I have dishes to wash," Audrey said, wanting to give Seth and Rachel a chance to talk alone. Throughout supper, the two had babbled endlessly about everything but what was foremost on their minds. She realized they would have to be alone before they could openly discuss any delicate matters of

190

the heart.

Pushing her chair back from the table, Rachel glanced at her as if her words had come as quite a surprise. "You have no housekeeper?"

"Not yet," she answered, smiling inwardly at Rachel's wide-eyed disbelief. "After I bought this house, a few new dresses, and several other items I had to have before I could move in, I immediately put the rest of my money back into the stock market. Maybe after I've made enough to feel more confident about my financial situation, I might hire someone to help me with the cooking and with keeping the house in order. Until then, I'm all there is. If I don't wash these dishes, then the poor things just won't get washed."

Seth waited until Audrey had left the room with a tall stack of dirty dishes, before turning to face Rachel. "And if you were to marry someone like me, you'd have to do the same thing. We certainly couldn't afford a full-time housekeeper on what I earn, even though your father does pay me a very generous salary."

"But in five and a half months, I'll be twenty-one and then I'll have money of my own," she tried to explain. "And I'll also have Mother's jewelry, which is worth hundreds of thousands of dollars."

"I don't want your money. And I don't want you to have to sell off your mother's jewelry. Don't you see? I don't want to live like that. I don't want you to live like that."

"Well, you just may have to," Rachel said, setting her chin at a stubborn angle when she looked at him.

Seth felt a sharp stab of pain when he glanced down at her still-narrow waistline. "Why? Are you . . . with child?"

"No," she admitted, clearly disappointed. "But that doesn't change the fact that I love you. Nor does it change the fact that you love me."

"I never said anything like that," he cautioned her.

"You didn't have to. I could tell from the way you sent

191

me out of your bedroom the other night. I never saw anyone so angry. But you weren't really angry with me for coming to your room, were you? You were angry with yourself for having taken advantage of my being there . . . because you love me." She studied the pained expression on his face. "Can you deny it? Can you deny that you love me?"

"No," he admitted honestly, turning his gaze downward until he saw nothing but the shadows beneath the dining table.

Tears filled Rachel's eyes while she stood and reached out to him. "Oh, Seth, love is not something you should be ashamed of. It's something to be proud of. In fact, I wish you would take me into your arms right now and show me just how much you do love me."

"Here? In my sister's house?" He stood, but not to go into her arms. Instead, he kept his arms planted firmly at his sides and tried to figure out what had brought on her sudden desire to be held. Everything was happening too quickly. He needed time to think.

"If not here, then anywhere you say," she whispered, making her intentions perfectly clear. She wanted more than simply to be held. Her eyes were wide with innocent devotion when she slowly stepped forward and slid her arms around him. Tilting her head back, her lips parted, she clearly yearned for his kiss.

"I can't," he replied in a weak voice, his world crumbling in around him. "I can't take that sort of chance again."

"What chance? The chance that you might actually enjoy making love to me? The chance that you might decide you enjoy it enough to want to marry me?"

"It's not that. I can't take the chance that you might end up with child . . . my child. You don't know how I've worried about that these past three weeks. If you were to come up with child, your reputation would be ruined forever. Your father would banish you from the family."

"No he wouldn't. Oh, he'd be angry with me for quite some time, but he'd never completely banish me from the family. He loves me too much ever to do that."

"You can't be sure what he'd do if you were to disgrace him like that. Racing a horse through Central Park is one thing, but coming up unmarried and with child is something else all together. What if he did indeed get so angry that he banished you from the family forever? You have to consider that a possibility."

"I'd have a new family to help me over the sorrow . . . my very own family. I'd have you. And I'd have your son."

"Son?" he asked and, despite himself, was becoming intrigued by the idea of it. His blood stirred at the thought of having Rachel for his wife, raising his children and warming his bed for the rest of his life. But that was impossible. Once she'd discovered what life would be like with him, she'd no longer want to warm his bed and she'd probably take his children away from him to raise alone in some secluded spot where she could no longer be branded for her sins. "What makes you think it would be a son?"

"Because you deserve a son," she answered proudly. "You deserve to have a little boy who looks and acts just like you. Of course, eventually, I'd like to have a little girl who looks something like me."

Seth closed his eyes and shook his head, trying to push the tempting images from his mind. "It would never work out for us. You could never be happy living the sort of life you'd have to live with me."

"You keep telling me what will and won't make me happy," Rachel said, and for the first time there was anger in her voice. "How can you possibly know better than I what will and won't make me happy?"

Seth's eyes opened wide, surprised by the sudden change in her voice.

"You have no idea what emotions lie inside me," she went on, tilting her head back so she could look him directly in the eye. "You have never bothered to ask me anything about myself. And, that brings us to another thing. I'm getting pretty tired of being the only one to do all the asking around here."

Seth's mouth parted, but no words came out while he stared down at her, too stunned by her outburst to speak.

"I've had just about enough of your self-pity, Seth Stoane. Either you kiss me right now, and kiss me hard, or—"

Rachel never had to finish her sentence because Seth's mouth came crashing down on hers at that instant with a bursting passion. Hungrily, he pulled her against him and devoured the pure sweetness of her kiss, knowing already that she was right. He did love her—and he'd risk anything to have her.

chapter thirteen

The unexpected clatter of a large metal tray as it crashed to the floor startled the two lovers apart. Gasping for air, they turned toward the sound and found Audrey standing just inside the doorway, staring at them with openmouthed astonishment.

"I . . . we . . . I can explain," Seth said, swallowing hard as he quickly straightened his coat and took a tentative step forward.

"What's to explain?" she asked, quickly recovering from the shock of having found them in such a passionate embrace. Kneeling, she picked up the tray she'd brought to carry the rest of the dishes back into the kitchen. "I gather, by what I just witnessed, that you two have managed to get a few of your problems worked out."

"I . . . uh . . . I guess so," Seth answered awkwardly, glancing at Rachel just long enough to notice the high color in her cheeks as she took several self-conscious swipes at her rumpled skirts.

"I'm glad you're getting your problems resolved at last." She just hoped they were not developing a whole new set of problems in the process, by creating what appeared to her to be an impossible situation. Seth was right. He could never provide for Rachel in the manner in which she was accustomed. Nor would Marshall ever accept, with open arms, a person as unrefined and uneducated as Seth into his family.

If anything, were Marshall to discover the deep infatuation his daughter had for Seth, he would do whatever he could to be sure she never saw him again. And the first logical thing he would do would be to fire Seth and get him out of his house. Then he would undoubtedly use both his wealth and power to be sure Seth never found another job in the city.

By the time her father was finally through with him, Seth would either be forced to try and live off whatever Audrey could make through her investments, which would probably be enough but would never set well with him, or he would have to move somewhere else to make a living. Somewhere far enough away from Rachel to keep Marshall from wanting to cause further trouble. The smartest thing would be to stop any real relationship from ever developing between the two.

But aware the two lovers were beyond such reasoning, for love had a strange way of distancing the mind from the stark edges of reality, Audrey decided to keep her opinions to herself while she quickly gathered the remaining dishes from the table, then left the room again. When she returned twenty minutes later, she found that Seth and Rachel had moved into the parlor and were sitting quietly on the couch, holding hands and discussing the many possibilities for the future, dismal though some of them were.

Because Rachel had chosen not to come in her own carriage for fear her driver might talk, she'd arrived in a hired cab and had requested that same cab return for her promptly at nine.

By the time the cab arrived, she and Seth had talked about their options—or lack of them—and had decided to start meeting at Audrey's house whenever they could.

Audrey listened quietly to their plans, thinking they really should ask for her opinion since it was her house they planned to use for their clandestine meetings, but she remained wisely silent. She did not want to alienate

196

her brother in any way and knew that until he came to his senses on his own, she would indeed risk doing just that if she attempted to point out any of the bleaker realities of their situation.

That night, after Rachel and Seth had left, Audrey found it impossible to drift off to sleep. She was troubled by the hopelessness of her brother's situation. Marshall would be furious if he ever discovered the two were meeting on the sly. What's more, Landon would be furious—and not just with Rachel and Seth, but with *her*, too, for having had a part in bringing them together. After all, Rachel was destined to marry a man of far better means than Seth, and neither Marshall nor Landon would stand peacefully by and allow anything less to become of her future. They would both do whatever it took to separate the two.

Though Landon did not fully approve of Preston Windthorst as Rachel's choice for a husband, Audrey knew he would approve even less of Seth Stoane, simply because he was not one of them. Seth was definitely headed for a heartbreak. So was Rachel. And all Audrey could do was stand helplessly by and try to be there for her brother when it was over. She just hoped someone would be there for Rachel, too, when the time finally came.

Audrey awoke to the pungent smell of summer rain, followed almost immediately by an earsplitting crack of thunder. For the fifth time in seven days, it stormed, filling the streets and her cellar with an unusual amount of water.

Though already tired from so few hours of sleep, she spent the day carrying heavy pails of the dank-smelling seepage outside and dumping it off the back porch into the yard, unaware that was the area from where the water had come to begin with.

By the time the rain had slowed to a steady drizzle and

197

progress was finally being made in the cellar, the afternoon was nearly gone and Audrey had totally forgotten her promise to go out with Landon. It was when she reached into the kitchen cooler to pull out a small wedge of cheese and an apple, in an effort to appease her growing hunger and restore what she could of her drained energy, that she remembered her engagement for the evening. A quick glance at the clock let her know it was already six-thirty. Barely time to take a hurried bath and get dressed, much less do anything with her hair.

Panic set in at the thought of being only partially dressed when Landon arrived at seven. Remembering his professed willingness to enter her house uninvited if she ever failed to answer the door right away, she hurried to partially fill the tub installed in a small alcove near the back of the kitchen, then peeled off her damp clothing, which she tossed onto the floor in a wadded heap. There was no time for a long, leisurely bath. No time to worry about hot water. The very moment she sat down, she snatched up the soap and sponge. Hurriedly, she lathered her skin, rinsing immediately with cold water. Then, having forgotten to get a towel from the linen chest in the back hall, she ran naked and still wet through the house to her bedroom.

As she entered the room, she heard a carriage pull into her drive and knew she was doomed. Landon had taken it upon himself to arrive early.

Rather than take any chances—like having him suddenly decide to enter the house through her bedroom window should she not answer his knock right away— she quickly threw on her robe, overlapping the front as far as possible, then tied it securely in place. She took just enough time to take all the pins from her hair, then run a quick brush through it, before bravely going to the door to let him in.

"Coming," she called out, having entered the main hallway only seconds after she'd heard his knock. Fully aware he would try to make some quip about the fact she had come to the door in her dressing robe, she paused in the entrance hall long enough to gather enough courage to face him. Finally, she placed a pleasant smile on her face, opened the door, and let him enter.

"As you can see, I'm not quite ready," she explained as she tugged self-consciously on the scalloped ends of her sash. She bent her knees slightly so the hem would reach the floor and hide the fact that she wore no shoes, afraid he might wonder what else she did not have on.

Landon's eyes widened while an appreciative grin stretched across his face, forming deep, curving dimples on either side of his generous mouth. It was the first time he'd seen her with her hair down, and he liked the way it draped with soft, caressable waves over her shoulders, falling beyond the small of her back.

"You look plenty ready to me," he offered with a light chuckle as he slowly removed his hat.

"Lan-don," she said, clear warning in her voice, too tired from all the work she'd done to put up with such antics at the moment.

"Just stating the facts as I see them, madam," he responded, and shrugged as a look of pure innocence lifted his dark eyebrows away from his pale blue eyes.

Momentarily dazed by the allure of his handsome smile, Audrey drew in a long, unsteady breath before lifting her hand and pointing it determinedly toward the nearest doorway. "If you'd care to wait in the parlor, you are welcome to. I have to return to my bedroom and finish dressing. It'll be just a few minutes more."

Landon glanced in the direction of the parlor and frowned as he considered her suggestion. "Are you sure you want me to wait in there all alone? I could be of much more help to you in the bedroom."

"I don't need any help in the bedroom," she quickly countered, lifting a well-shaped brow to denote another clear warning.

199

"I'll just bet you don't," he muttered, glancing at her speculatively, the corner of his mouth twitching until it finally gave way to another full, dimpled grin. Unable to resist the temptation, his gaze dipped down to where the edges of the robe overlapped just inches above her breasts, to where her soft, ivory skin beckoned his touch. Suddenly, he found it extremely difficult to keep his hands to himself. His imagination raced onward, uncontrolled, while he tried to visualize what the silken robe hid from his view. "Even so, I'd like to volunteer my services just in case you happen to get back there and find you do need help."

"How noble," she muttered, keeping any further comment to herself, not about to give him the opportunity to come out with yet another of his bold witticisms. Lifting her arm higher, still pointing determinedly toward the parlor door, she spoke in clear, precise tones. "You may either wait for me in there, where you can be comfortable, or outside in the rain. I really don't care which. But I don't intend to stand out here in this robe another minute."

"Oh, really?" He looked at her with renewed interest and began counting back from sixty.

Rather than give him the satisfaction of seeing her agitation, she turned and stalked quietly toward her bedroom. She paused outside the door to be absolutely certain he hadn't attempted to follow her, before hurriedly disappearing from his sight.

Immediately, she bolted her door, then closed and latched all four of the windows in her room before getting dressed in the elegant pink and white silk gown she'd bought five days earlier at Nadine's. Once dressed, Audrey reopened her windows to let a breeze back into the room, then sat down before the tall oval mirror and arranged her hair into a simple but becoming twist just above her neck, shaping several tiny finger-curls at the hairline nearest her temples.

All the while, she listened for any noises that might

200

alert her to the fact Landon was up to his usual pranks. Though she had securely bolted her bedroom door and hadn't opened the windows quite wide enough to allow him to enter her bedroom from the outside, she'd heard several curious noises near the front of the house and had a definite feeling he was up to something.

When she stepped out of the bedroom minutes later and passed through the main hall, she found out exactly what that something was.

"The streets are a mess," Landon began his explanation the moment he'd noticed a movement in the doorway. But when he glanced up from the candle he'd been about to light to get a better look at her, the beautiful image in the doorway caused him to suddenly lose his train of thought right in the middle of his well-planned speech.

It took several seconds to recover from the beautiful sight before him, for he'd never seen a woman quite as exquisite as Audrey. Finally, he remembered what he'd been about to say before she had temporarily stolen his breath away. "Ah . . . and rather than worry about you getting your lovely new dress all muddy, I decided to have our dinner catered here, which is why I came so early. I wanted to help them get everything ready."

Audrey stepped cautiously into the dining room, stunned by the elaborate table setting before her.

Silver appointments, tapered candles, crystal goblets, and tiny pink, yellow, and white floral arrangements lay in perfect array atop a beautiful silk and lace white tablecloth. Rose-tinted china gleamed with delicate silver inlays and had been positioned at opposite sides of the table, the matching side pieces set in their proper places.

On a small cart nearby, she noticed several large, gleaming silver domes set atop elaborate silver trays on yet another silk and lace cloth. At the far side of this serving cart stood two immaculate waiters dressed in black formal attire.

One of the waiters came forward when she neared the

table and presented her with a single red rose decorated with delicate pink, yellow, and white ribbons. "For you, *mademoiselle*," he said with a thick French accent, then promptly pulled back her chair and waited for her to be seated.

"*Merci*," she responded, smiling despite the many misgivings that still fluttered about inside her like a swarm of lost butterflies.

Landon looked at her, clearly surprised by her response, but said nothing.

"You speak French?" the waiter asked while he helped her with her napkin, pleased that she knew his native language.

"*Un peu*," she admitted. "I learned just enough in New Orleans to get by."

Landon's curious expression relaxed as he settled into the chair opposite hers. "Of course. I should have guessed."

Immediately, the two men served the dinners, then stood attentively off to one side. Cautiously, Audrey picked her fork off the table and began eating, hoping Landon had not chosen one of the odd delicacies the French were famous for, like *escargots* perhaps. The thought of anyone purposely eating snails sent sickly shivers through her.

"Is your meal all right?" Landon asked, worried when she'd failed to comment on either the taste or the preparation of her food. "It is cooked well enough, isn't it?"

"Oh, yes, it's fine," she said, smiling pleasantly while she placed another small bite into her mouth. She decided it would be best not to know just what it was she was eating. Though it clearly wasn't beef, pork, chicken, or anything else to which she was accustomed, Audrey still felt she'd be a lot better off thinking that it was possibly cubed mutton or something else a little more conventional in nature.

"You're angry with me," he concluded when, after several attempts to draw her into a cheerful conversation, she continued quietly contemplating her food. "You were expecting to be taken out to an elegant restaurant so you could show off your beautiful new gown, and I ruined it for you."

"This is fine," she assured him, still a little overwhelmed by it all . . . too overwhelmed yet to think of a reason to be angry, though now that he'd mentioned it, she was certain there should be. Then it occurred to her what that reason was: He'd made the arrangements to eat there at her house so he would not have to be seen in public with her. Though he'd proclaimed it didn't matter to him what station in life she'd come from, it obviously did matter enough for Landon to find ways to avoid being seen with her. Suddenly, she felt ill.

Landon watched her expression darken and shook his head. "No, it's not fine. This is not at all what I promised you, and I'm sorry. I should have realized. Tell you what. I'll make it up to you tomorrow night. I'll take you anywhere you want. We can go to the Fifth Avenue Hotel like we'd planned tonight, or we can go somewhere even fancier than that. The Emerald Club, perhaps. Anywhere your heart desires."

Audrey studied the sincerity in his blue eyes and decided she'd jumped to an entirely wrong conclusion. Maybe he *had* chosen to have their meal catered for the simple reason that he didn't want her to ruin her new gown. Or maybe it was just his way of assuring they'd be alone for their first evening together.

Audrey's eyes widened as that last thought sent chills of awareness through her, because except for the two nameless waiters who stood off to one side and would be reluctant to do *anything* to upset Landon, they were very much alone—a situation Landon would no doubt try to take full advantage of before the evening was over.

"So, where do you want to go tomorrow?" Landon

asked, ready to pin her down to definite plans.

Audrey thought about it a moment before answering, "Delmonico's."

She'd feel great pleasure upon entering that establishment on Landon's arm, knowing that no one in his right mind would dare turn her away then. "Yes, I'd like to eat at Delmonico's."

Landon nodded and smiled, having suspected her reasons. "Then, Delmonico's it is. But because I do have a late afternoon meeting with my broker, I'll have to come by for you a little later than I did tonight. Shall I plan to pick you up around eight?" He grinned as a thought occurred to him. "Maybe by pushing my arrival time up over a full hour you can manage to be ready when I get here." His grin widened further still. "On second thought, maybe I should forget the meeting with my broker and plan to arrive a little after six, so I can help."

"I'm not usually late like that," she declared, in ready defense of herself. "It's just that I forgot you were coming. It was after six before I finally remembered."

"Looking that forward to my coming, were you?" Landon asked, looking terribly crushed.

Audrey smiled at how her words must have sounded. "It had nothing to do with you. My cellar flooded from all the recent rains and I was too busy bailing it out a bucketful at a time to think about anything else. In fact, there's still almost a foot of water down there. I'll probably have to spend half the day tomorrow bailing out the rest, then scraping and sweeping the mud off the planked floors. Then I'll have to try and find out how all that water is getting in."

"Tell you what. Why don't I send Baxter over to have a look at it tomorrow?"

"Your father's handyman?"

"Sure. If it can be repaired, Baxter is the man to figure out the best way of going about it. I'll stop by on my way to see my broker and find out how he's coming along."

"There's no need for that," Audrey said quickly,

thinking it was disturbing enough to know she'd already made plans for the following evening with him. She did not need to worry about seeing him that afternoon, too.

Landon would not be swayed. "I'll come by to hear what he has to suggest. Expect me about mid-afternoon."

"But there's no reason for you to go to such trouble. If Baxter can repair the leak, I'll have him get right to it. Besides, he's not the type to have to be prodded all the time in order to get any work out of him."

Landon shrugged. He fully agreed that Baxter would do whatever he was told and to the best of his ability, but he still wanted an excuse to come by and see Audrey earlier than the following evening. Now that she was no longer in the house with him, where he could happen upon her at will, he found he missed her dreadfully. Far more than he should. Still, he couldn't seem to do anything about it. Somehow, she'd implanted her image in his brain until she'd become a very real part of him. He thought of her constantly. "I have to be out this direction anyway. Like I already told you, I have an appointment with my broker. I need to make sure he's all set to buy up the stock I told him I wanted."

"Oh? And what stock is that?" she asked, wondering what sort of investments interested him. Although she knew Marshall bought both common and preferred stocks, mainly in railroads, coal, and iron, she wasn't sure what sort of investments appealed to Landon. Suddenly, she was aware of how very little she did know about him.

Landon glanced at her, surprised. He was still not used to having a woman show any real interest in the stock market. "I've decided to diversify," he said, watching her closely while he spoke. "There's a new shipping company starting up, and after having investigated the planning, to make sure this wasn't going to be some bubble operation, and finding out just how sound the business end of it really was, I've decided to buy a large portion of their stock. Wilson, my broker, is supposed to do everything he can to get me in on the initial buy, which should happen sometime day after tomorrow."

Landon watched as her eyes brightened with interest, and he decided to drop the name of the company casually so Audrey could make a profit along with him should she, too, decide to diversify. "I told him that the very second Atlantic Export hits that exchange floor, to buy until I had at least ten percent of the stock offered."

"Do you expect a quick profit?"

"I expect a steady profit."

Audrey nodded thoughtfully, eagerly committing the name of the company to memory, already having decided both Baxter and her flooded cellar could wait. First thing come morning, she would head for her own broker and find out which of her present investments could be quickly diverted to allow her to purchase as much of Atlantic Export as possible. If Landon was that sure there was a profit to be made, then she, too, wanted to be in on it from the very beginning.

Suddenly, Audrey began eating her meal with vigor, her appetite and waning energy fully returned. Soon, she was through and sat back pleasantly full, watching while Landon slowly finished the last of his meal.

Something inside her stirred to life while she studied him from so close. In the golden glow of the candles, he appeared even more attractive, though she never would have thought that possible. The soft moving shadows gave his face an added strength. When he glanced up and discovered she was staring curiously at him, his eyes widened, and for the first time ever, she sensed a moment of vulnerability. She supposed his finding her gaze so intently upon him caught him temporarily off guard, allowing her a glimpse of a different Landon, a more susceptible Landon.

Suddenly, she lost the dark image she'd come to associate with him—that of an arrogant aristocrat whose sole purpose in life was to have his way in all matters, not caring whom he hurt. Somehow, sitting there in her house before the soft glow of candlelight, he was different. Before, his bold exterior had seemed as solid as rock, impossible to penetrate. Yet something about the vulnerability she'd just glimpsed made her realize he was a deeply sensitive person, capable of being hurt like anyone else. The thought that Landon bore such true, human qualities stunned her.

"Finished?" he asked. When he glanced at her plate, he was surprised to find nothing left there but her fork, napkin, salt spoon, and butter knife.

Audrey nodded while she watched him place the last bite of food into his mouth. There was something about the way his tongue and lips seemed to caress his food as he slipped it off his fork, then slowly chewed it, that totally unnerved her. She could not pull her gaze away from the sensual movements.

"Then, may I assume that you enjoyed your meal?" he asked, starting to feel uncomfortable at her close scrutiny. Before, he'd barely managed to get her to meet his gaze. Now, she stared at him as if he were some oddity.

"Yes, it was delicious," she admitted, though she still had no idea what she'd eaten.

"And the service?"

Audrey glanced at the two waiters, who pretended not to listen, and she smiled, knowing full well they hung on to every word. "The service was excellent." She noticed that their shoulders straightened a tad, though their gazes remained locked on the far wall.

"And the company?" Landon asked, pressing for a compliment. "What did you think of the company?"

"The company was quite enjoyable," she admitted, and tried not to be affected by his little-boy eagerness to hear a small word of approval. "The entire meal was very enjoyable. Just don't let such high praise go to your head. I'd hate to know I was in some way responsible for feeding that monstrous ego of yours," she said, staring at him with a deadpan expression, though amusement glittered from the dark depths of her brown eyes.

Landon tried to look offended by that last remark but he burst out laughing instead. Even when she insulted him it felt like a compliment. "Then, would you care for dessert? We have a choice of fresh strawberry pie or peach cobbler."

Though ordinarily Audrey would have jumped at the chance to have fresh strawberry pie, her stomach rebelled at the thought of eating anything else when she was already so painfully full. "No thank you."

Turning to the waiters, he placed his napkin on the table near the edge of his plate and offered a cordial smile. "Just leave the desserts. We'll have them later. After you've gathered up your belongings, you may leave."

Audrey felt her insides burst with a sudden flurry of activity, aware in a very few minutes they would be alone.

"Why don't we go back into the parlor where we can be more comfortable?" Landon suggested, his tone casual as he pushed his chair away from the table and stood. "I'm sure they can manage in here without us."

Audrey tried to think of a reason to stay, eager to put off the inevitable. She considered eating one of the desserts after all, but knew that as nervous as her stomach was now, she'd never be able to keep anything else down.

Next, she considered offering to help the waiters pack their things but knew that would be preposterous. Finally, she accepted the fact that she had no logical excuse to remain in the dining room and agreed to join Landon in the parlor. Rising hesitantly from the table, she watched Landon circle around and take her arm. His touch sent a shower of electrified tingles up her arm, through her shoulder, and down into her roiling stomach.

While being escorted from the room, she noticed again how very tall he was, a fact that both intrigued and worried her. For with such height usually came great strength, and Landon was nearly as tall as Seth and just as broad across the shoulders, though decidedly leaner at the waist and hips. His strong, sturdy build, coupled with the fact that his skin was so bronzed in comparison to the stark white of his dinner shirt, made her think of a man who made his living in the outdoors, not of a wealthy industrialist who spent most of his day tucked away in different meetings.

Finally, she had to ask, "How does a man like you manage to stay so fit?"

"A man like me?" Landon asked, thinking that an odd statement. "And what sort of man am I?"

"Well . . . you're wealthy. Wealthy enough to hire others to do whatever heavy work there is to be done. Wealthy enough to afford covered carriages and personal attendants with umbrellas. So, why is it your skin looks so dark from the sun, as if you'd spent many hours outdoors, and why aren't you"—she hesitated, hoping to find a delicate way to state her question—"*soft*, like most other wealthy people?"

"For one thing, my skin tans easily; for another, I enjoy the outdoors. I enjoy letting the top down on the carriage and basking in the sun. As for not being soft," he paused, eyeing her with amusement, "I'm very glad you noticed."

Audrey felt the color rise to her cheeks. As they entered the parlor, she tried to think of something to change their topic of conversation before he found a way to embarrass her further, but she couldn't come up with anything that didn't sound forced. Finally, she pulled away from his disturbing touch and suggested they have another glass of wine. Though they had had a generous portion with their meal, she felt another glassful was in order. Anything to keep their hands occupied.

"Yes, another glass of wine would be nice," he agreed. "Would you like for me to return to the dining room and get it?"

Although she had an unopened bottle of wine in the cabinet just across the room, she decided that would be a way to have a moment alone to better catch her breath and calm her frayed nerves. Ever since he'd suggested that the waiters leave, she'd been on edge, worried about his intentions. "Yes, please."

Landon returned all too quickly with a small decanter of wine and two delicately stemmed glasses, and promptly set them on one of the small sofa tables. "Since the waiters were about ready to leave and I didn't want to make them stay any later just so we could finish with the glasses, I bought them. That way, we can have our wine and our privacy, too."

"I have glasses," she assured him, thinking his actions rather extravagant, but then she remembered that extravagance was a way of life for Landon.

"Shall I pour?" he asked, though he'd already begun to fill the glasses with the dark liquid.

For lack of anything else to do, Audrey sat down on the edge of the nearest couch and accepted the glass from him.

Though wine had never been her favorite drink, the idea had originated with her, so Audrey quietly put the glass to her lips and sipped. Her heart burst with growing apprehension when Landon then sat down beside her and slowly sipped from his own glass. Several minutes of awkward silence followed, broken only when the chime of her new case clock sounded in the hall.

The hour was past what she'd realized. "Nine o'clock," she announced unnecessarily. "It's getting late."

"Is that your way of hinting that it's time for me to leave?" he asked, setting down his now-empty glass on a nearby table and turning to face her.

"Well, I am tired from having had to haul all that water from the cellar," Audrey said. She glanced at him, then turned quickly away, her heart fluttering wildly. There was that look again. That look that meant he intended to kiss her. She tried to think of something she might do to prevent it from happening, aware the waiters had already gone and there would be no one to come to her aid should he try to take the kiss too far. Quickly, she stood and took several steps toward the door. "I really do need my rest."

Landon was clearly disappointed when he, too, stood and followed her across the room. It bothered him to see that she was still so afraid of him. "Then I guess I'll go ahead and kiss you good night and be on my way."

Audrey turned to argue that he had no good night kiss coming, but he was much closer than she'd anticipated. She was swept into an intimate embrace far too quickly to protest. His mouth had found hers instantly. And just as instantly, she was overpowered by a warm tide of swirling sensations, the same sort of spinning sensations that had caused her to lose grasp of her sanity before. Aware of the danger, she tried to tear herself away from his embrace before it was too late, but he'd anticipated the move and held firm.

Her sensed reeled and her heart pounded hard against her chest. Again, she was reminded that no other kiss affected her quite like Landon's. She feared where the kiss might lead. The feel of his lips fiercely caressing hers and of her breasts firmly pressed against such a hard, muscular chest sent a need coursing through to the very core of her, a need so strong and so basic that it startled her. She was threatened by its very intensity yet, at the same time, lured by its languid warmth. Suddenly, she felt vulnerable, very vulnerable, and that was not something she wanted to feel.

The last time she'd allowed herself to be vulnerable where a man was concerned, she had ended up with a badly broken heart. Audrey didn't want that to happen to her ever again. She thought back several years, to New Orleans and her first and only real love. Although she'd never been able to interest Robert Akard in quite the same way he'd interested her, which had never been enough to have actually had the pleasure of experiencing either his kiss or his loving embrace, she'd still been devotedly in love with him. Enough so that she had been devastated when he'd chosen someone else over her, someone older and with more experience in life. The pain of that rejection had become a lasting part of her. And it was a pain she never again wanted to experience.

Again, Audrey tried to pull away, only this time she found his grip had weakened and she was able to break free.

"I think you'd better leave now," she said, her tone adamant as she tried to regain control of her rapid heartbeat.

"I think you are right," he whispered, his voice deeper than usual as he drew in several long, unsteady breaths. "I'll see you tomorrow."

He gazed down at her a moment longer, making Audrey fear that, despite his words, he intended to kiss her again. Her heart froze with renewed apprehension. She was not so sure she'd be able to pull herself away a second time. But, in the end, he turned to leave.

Finding her legs were far sturdier than they felt, Audrey walked with him to the door. While she watched him climb into his awaiting carriage, then slowly disappear into the foggy darkness, she fought an odd desire to call him back. Though she had truly feared a second kiss from him, it disappointed her to know that he hadn't at least tried to take it. She shook her head as she thought more about that, realizing Landon had aroused too many unfamiliar emotions in her far too quickly. Turning back, she reached up to touch her lips where a tingling warmth still lingered. She realized she would need to be more careful of him in the future or she might chance actually falling in love with the man. And that would never do.

The last thing she needed at this stage in her life was to have to nurse another broken heart.

chapter fourteen

Roderick laid the report on Marshall's desk.

"You'll find that over the past two days, she's had one of Rutledge's sons busy transferring several thousand dollars worth of her holdings in the B & D Railroad to that new shipping company that Landon was telling you about just last Wednesday," he stated, though it was all in the four-page report he'd just set before him.

"I wonder how she ever found out enough about that new company to want to make such a large investment?" Marshall muttered with a disgusted shake of his head.

"My guess is from Landon himself," Roderick stated, then explained unnecessarily, "After all, we've both heard the rumor that the two were seen dining together at Delmonico's just night before last. If what we heard is true, they shared a long, leisurely supper right out in plain sight of everyone. And just yesterday afternoon, Olivia herself complained that she hasn't seen Landon since the picnic on Sunday. Said he's been too *busy* to stop by even for a short visit. Seems pretty obvious that Audrey Stoane has somehow managed to lure Landon into paying calls on her so she can wheedle this sort of information out of him. That way she can make these lucrative stock purchases without having to do any research concerning their validity."

"I agree. I just wonder what Landon's getting in

return," Marshall grumbled, though he'd already decided what that something must be. "What that conniving woman won't do to turn a dollar!"

"And turning them she is. In the past week alone, our Miss Stoane has brought her holdings up twenty percent. And judging from the way the price of Atlantic Exports is climbing, she's apt to make another twenty percent by the weekend. By next week, she'll have turned that thirteen thousand she reinvested into nearly twenty thousand dollars. No doubt about it. That girl may be from the South, but she sure has the luck of the Irish in her somewhere."

"And the face and body of a Greek goddess," Marshall added, nodding that he fully agreed. "And with a combination like that, Audrey Stoane will be a very wealthy woman in no time at all. I just wish she'd leave Landon alone, find someone else to get her information from . . . before Olivia finds out about them."

"Before Olivia finds out about whom?" Landon asked as he entered the room unannounced, having found the door partially open.

"About the foolish way you've been behaving here lately," Marshall snapped, leaning back in his chair and staring up at his son with open annoyance. "If you don't start being a little more discreet with your little dalliance, these ugly rumors about you and that conniving little Audrey Stoane are going to reach Olivia's ears eventually. What's she to think when she learns that you've been spending so much time with someone else when you should be spending any extra time you have with her?"

"What's she to think? Possibly, that I've become very, very interested in that someone else."

Aware Landon had a view of everything on his desk, Marshall quickly shuffled a few papers to hide the report Roderick had just handed him. "*Exactly*. You are taking a terrible risk by allowing yourself to be seen out in public with that fool woman. Olivia will be furious to learn that you've been so indiscreet."

214

"Audrey is anything but a fool," Landon corrected him. His jawline hardened as he glanced at Roderick, who had taken several steps away from the desk as if in fear of what might happen between father and son. Landon then looked back at his father. "And to tell you the truth, I really don't care what Olivia thinks."

"You don't mean that," Marshall thundered, angry that his son could be so careless with his words. "Do I need to remind you of the fact that you and Olivia are expected to be married eventually? In fact, your wedding plans are long overdue."

"That may be what you and her father, Thomas Arlington, expect, but I've never indicated to anyone that I have any real intention of marrying Olivia," Landon reminded him. "Olivia and I have known each other since childhood, and because of that, we are very close friends—most of the time—but that's all we are and all we have ever been."

"You are much more than friends," Marshall insisted. "You have been seeing her exclusively for over a year now."

"Olivia and I have enjoyed each other's company for several years, and the only reason I've been enjoying her company exclusively in the past year is because no one else has interested me. Therefore, whenever I needed a lady companion, I usually invited Olivia, and when she was in need of a male escort, she called upon me. That has now changed. I have now found someone else who interests me more—a lot more."

"But Olivia would make the perfect wife for you. She's not only extremely beautiful, but her family is one of the wealthiest in this entire United States. She's cultured and refined—a real blue blood with all the right connections. You couldn't ask for a better match."

"Ah, but I prefer red blood," Landon said, smiling as he thought of the hot, fiery red blood that flowed through Audrey. It pleased him that he'd made so much progress over the past few days, to the point where she now

215

responded favorably to his kisses. Yet, even so, whenever he tried to carry the kiss a step too far, she turned into a real tigress, fighting him tooth and nail. That was not something Landon was used to. After all, *most* women tended to do whatever they could to please him, but he liked the way Audrey fought him just the same. What he liked even more was the thought of finally getting beyond whatever fear held her back and being the only man ever to discover the true passion that was hidden beneath.

"Are you blind?" Marshall asked, shaking his head with disbelief. "Have you forgotten what that young woman did to me? Doesn't that tell you something about her? Can't you see how she's just out to get her hands on your money?"

"Quite the contrary. Audrey is not after my money at all. She is out to get her hands on her *own* money," Landon defended her proudly, because it was something he truly admired about her. In fact, she was the first woman he'd met who *hadn't* been interested in getting her hands on some of his money. She had never hinted, like most women did, for some expensive little gift to prove his affection.

Marshall rolled his gaze heavenward, as if unable to believe Landon could be so dense, before looking him in the eye again. "But, don't you see? She is using you to get that money."

"Only because I want her to. I've been purposely dropping tidbits of information to help her make sound financial decisions. She's still new to the investment game, and I don't want her to lose her shirt on some high-risk investment before she ever really gets started." Landon paused to think about that, then grinned privately when the image that had come to mind of Audrey losing her shirt had actually proved rather interesting.

"Why don't you just pay her for her services instead?" Marshall hurled back. "That way, she wouldn't have to worry about risking anything on the market at all."

216

Landon's blue eyes narrowed. While he studied his father with an expression of pure disgust, Roderick took several more steps back, grimacing in preparation for the explosive tirade that was sure to follow.

"This conversation has ended," Landon stated in a surprisingly calm voice, then turned abruptly on his booted heel and stalked out of the room, leaving his father sputtering angrily at an empty doorway and Roderick still holding his breath.

Preston Windthorst paced about the front parlor like a caged animal. For the past several days, Rachel had refused to see him, claiming to have taken to her bed with a violent headache, yet he'd heard how just yesterday she'd somehow found the ability to go shopping with two of her friends and had even had lunch at The Season's. It seemed clear enough now that she'd been creating excuses not to see him and he was determined to find out why.

"I'm sorry, sir," Everett said as he entered the parlor door to confront the young man whose agitation was obvious, "but Miss Rachel says she does not feel up to visitors at the moment."

"The hell she doesn't," Preston snapped, then pushed past the elderly butler and headed immediately for the stairs. "I don't care if she has a headache or not, she is going to see me."

"But, sir, you can't go up there," Everett called after him, shocked at the young man's behavior. "It's not proper."

"I don't give a damn if it's proper or not. I'm tired of playing all these ridiculous games. Rachel has some explaining to do, and it damn well better be good."

"But, sir, you mustn't—" Everett tried again, hurrying to follow. "Miss Rachel is not properly attired."

When it seemed clear that Preston Windthorst had no intention of heeding any of his protests, Everett turned around to alert his boss to what had happened, certain that if anyone would know how to calm young Windthorst, it would be Marshall Steed.

"That's just too bad," Preston shouted back as he topped the stairs, unaware Everett had already turned to go get help. He never looked back as he headed straight for Rachel's closed doors. Pounding hard with a flawless white hand, he cried out his demands, not caring who overheard. "Rachel, open this door! Now! Before I break it down!"

When there came no immediate response from within, Preston took several steps back and kicked the door with the two-inch heel of his black Hessian boot. There was a loud, resounding crack, but the door did not give way to the angry force. He tried again, but his only accomplishment was to badly rumple the fitted lines of his new summer-weight walking suit. The door had refused to open. "Damn it, Rachel, let me in!"

"Go away! I don't feel up to having visitors," Rachel finally called out to him, fearing he might indeed break her door if she didn't find a way to make him stop. "I'll speak with you tomorrow if I'm feeling any better."

"No, you will speak with me now," Preston insisted, then made a wild lunge at the door, slamming his shoulder against it as hard as he could. This time the door gave way to the sudden pressure and burst open with a loud, splintering crack. Rachel and Emma both screamed in response.

By the time Preston had burst victoriously into her bedroom, finding Rachel huddled beneath her bedcovers and Emma standing nearby with her hand pressed firmly to her pounding chest, heavy footsteps were heard clamoring up the stairs.

"What's the meaning of this?" Marshall asked in an angry voice when he entered the room moments later, glimpsing the damage done to Rachel's door as he passed through.

"I've come to see Rachel," Preston answered simply,

218

his green eyes narrowed with angry intent. "I've been trying to see her for several days now, but she keeps sending word down that she's not feeling up to visitors."

"I know. She's been suffering from severe headaches," Marshall told him in a calming voice. "She hasn't felt up to seeing anyone."

Preston spun around to face him with such suddenness that his short-cropped blond hair fell forward over his forehead in wild disarray. Rachel's eyes widened apprehensively. It really was not like Preston to look so unkempt.

"Yet," Preston spouted, waving a pointed finger for emphasis, "she felt well enough yesterday to join Patricia and Carla in a lively afternoon of shopping."

"Is that true?" Marshall asked. He gazed at his daughter with stunned disbelief. "Did you go shopping yesterday?"

"I was starting to feel much better," Rachel explained as she stared down at her bedcovers, unable to look up at her father. "In fact, I was completely over my headache for several hours; but then yesterday evening, shortly after I'd returned home, my headache suddenly came back. By the time Preston had stopped by at seven, I was again in severe pain." She twisted her forehead as if to demonstrate the true devastation of her pain. "I still am."

Marshall studied her for a moment, a curious mixture of doubt and hopeful belief filling his face when he turned to look at Preston. "She has been suffering from severe headaches for several days now. The doctor has given her powders that do help a little but don't seem to ease the pain for long."

"She doesn't look like she's in too much pain to me," Preston muttered, stepping forward toward the bed. "There's a high color in her cheeks and not a hair out of place."

Rachel cowered beneath her covers, pulling her sheet higher until it met with the tiny cleft in her delicate chin, her eyes wide with growing apprehension. The high color Preston had spoken of quickly left her cheeks.

"And if she is in so much pain that she feels she must refuse visitors, why is it she's fully dressed?" he asked, and suddenly snatched the covers from her hand, gracefully jerking them back to reveal a lovely pink and white summer dress.

"Rachel!" Marshall responded, his expression confused as he, too, stepped forward. "What's the meaning of this?"

"I—I—" she stammered helplessly, knowing that if she spoke the truth, her father would be furious with her, but that if she lied, she'd simply prolong the inevitable. Yet, when she watched the anger slowly building in Marshall's harsh expression, she decided the healthiest thing for everyone at that moment was to lie—and to lie well. "I had hoped to overcome this thing by getting dressed and coming on downstairs for lunch, but while Emma was helping me get ready, the pain became far too severe and I was forced to lie back down."

All eyes cut to Emma for verification, but she was suddenly too busy picking tiny pieces of lint off her dark gray skirt to take part in their conversation.

Rachel quickly continued. "Then when Everett came upstairs only moments later and told Emma that Preston was downstairs waiting to see me, the thought of walking down those stairs was too much to bear. Besides, I didn't really want him to see me, knowing how I must look."

Having said that, she reached up and ran her fingers through her hair in such a way that it was left tousled on one side. "If I look even half as poorly as I feel, I must be a fright."

Preston's eyes remained narrowed, doubt clearly etched on his handsome face. "If you were finally starting to feel better yesterday afternoon, why didn't you send word to me so I could come right away? You know I've been wanting to see you."

Rachel blinked back any guilty feelings while she tried

to think of a reasonable answer. Her blue eyes lit brightly when an idea occurred to her. "Because I thought the headache was finally gone for good, and I knew you intended to stop by for a visit that evening, anyway. I thought, why ruin your plans by having you come rushing right over when we would have that entire evening to ourselves? Besides, I wanted to find something new to wear, something pretty enough to make you forget how very much I've had to neglect you lately. How was I supposed to know that my relief was only temporary?" She drew her face into an indignant frown as she tossed her shoulders back and lifted her chin. "You do believe me, don't you?"

"To tell you the truth, I don't know what to believe," Preston muttered, raking his hand through his hair. His gaze shifted back and forth between Marshall, Rachel, and Emma. "All I know is that here it is Friday afternoon and I haven't been able to see you even once since last weekend."

"That's because her headache started late Monday evening," Marshall quickly supplied. "It came on suddenly while she was out shopping with Carla. When she came home just a little after nine, her eyes were red and watery, and her head was throbbing with this peculiar pain."

"Shopping with Carla?" Preston asked, his suspicions renewed. "I spoke with Carla just a little while ago and she never mentioned having gone shopping with Rachel last Monday."

"They go shopping together so often I suppose it never crossed her mind to mention it," Marshall said, hoping to dismiss the young man's obvious doubts. "But I well remember that Rachel went out shopping with her last Monday evening and came back looking pale and weak. She went immediately to her room, complaining of a terrible headache. I was afraid she was coming down with something dreadful and called the doctor right away. He said it probably was the result of something she'd eaten

221

and gave us the medication to help ease her discomfort."

"If you don't believe Father, you can stop by Dr. Lindley's office and ask him yourself," Rachel put in, jutting her chin forward as if she found his continued display of doubt offensive. "Or you can ask Emma about my illness, or better yet go downstairs and ask Kelly, since she's been the one to bring my medication to me every three hours."

What she did not suggest, though, was that he ask Carla about their supposed shopping trip last Monday, because although her friend agreed not to volunteer any information that would indicate they had never been together that day, she had refused to lie for her. Carla had gone as far as to ask not to be told whom Rachel was secretly meeting so she would not feel obligated to tell.

"I just might do that," Preston said, thrusting his own chin out to match the stubborn angle of hers. Then he noticed Rachel's eyes widen and her tense expression lessen ever so slightly. He turned to see what had caught her attention. It puzzled him to find nothing more interesting than Marshall's new bodyguard standing in the doorway, glancing curiously at the broken door frame while obviously waiting to speak with his boss about something. And behind him, tiptoeing in an effort to peer over the bodyguard's massive shoulder, was Everett, his eyes round with concern.

"For now, I'll give you the benefit of the doubt," he continued, turning back to face her. "But if this headache of yours lingers much longer, I'll send my own doctor over here to examine you. After all, the Grand Cotillion is next week and I don't care to have to go to it without you. I want to be sure you are over this strange illness by then." Having said that, he turned briskly away. When he passed Marshall, he nodded briefly. "I'll send someone over to repair the door as soon as I can."

"No need," Marshall answered, then hurried to follow Preston out of the room. "If I can ever find out where Baxter has gotten off to, I'll have him repair it."

"Then I'll send a check to pay for the damages," he insisted, his voice fading as he and Marshall descended the stairs together. "It's the least I can do."

Seth stayed behind long enough to look questioningly toward Rachel, who responded by merely shaking her head—a silent exchange that did not go unnoticed by either Everett or Emma.

Landon stopped by shortly after three to see how Baxter and his two helpers were progressing with the repairs to Audrey's cellar, and also to invite her to the Grand Cotillion, which was always the largest social event of the year.

He had first considered asking Audrey after that brief but pointed conversation he'd had with his father that morning; but when Olivia had confronted him out on the street the way she had, also demanding that he stop seeing Audrey, threatening to not only ruin his already questionable reputation but Audrey's as well, Landon had made up his mind. He was determined to make good use of his invitation to attend the most prestigious ball of the year and he fully intended to have Audrey at his side.

At first he'd felt no interest in even going, for the Grand Cotillion had always proved to be such a tiresome event, but after having had been told twice now to stop seeing Audrey, he was suddenly very eager to attend. He was ready to let the entire city know how he felt about Audrey. Let them raise their eyebrows if they wanted, but he saw no reason to hide his interest in her.

"How's it coming?" he asked as he closed the front gate and entered the yard, already having noticed Audrey standing beneath the shade of a large elm while watching Baxter and the two workmen pack fresh cement into a large rectangular hole they'd carefully carved out along the base of the house.

"Think we found her problem," Baxter offered,

unaware Landon had intended his question for Audrey. "There was a narrow crack in the cellar wall that was letting all that water seep in. I've reinforced the wall as best I could inside and am now sealing off that leak on the outside with a thick outer wall of plaster and cement. After all this dries, I really don't think she'll have to worry about any more water in the cellar, at least not any more than most folks get. We should be done here in another couple of hours."

"Good. I think Father has a job for you. Rachel's door is in need of repairs."

"Repairs?" Baxter asked, straightening his back and pushing his sweat-soaked captain's hat back on his balding head. "What happened to it?"

"Someone broke it in. Split the door frame in two places."

Audrey's eyes widened. She wondered if Seth had had anything to do with the broken door. "Split the door frame? Who would do something like that?"

"Her fiancé. You remember I told you how she's been suffering from a series of terrible headaches lately, so much so that she's refused to have any visitors? Well, the way I understand it, Preston had somehow jumped to the conclusion that she was neglecting him on purpose, though I really couldn't blame her if it were true. Windthorst is about the least interesting person I know. Anyway, suspicious of Rachel's repeated refusals to see him, Preston took it upon himself to march right up our stairs unannounced. Then he knocked her door open with his shoulder, demanding that she see him or else."

"Windthorst did that?" Baxter interrupted, clearly not believing he'd heard him right.

Landon grinned that lazy grin of his, revealing two rows of even white teeth, while he slowly shook his head. "To tell you the truth, I didn't think he had it in him, either. I can just imagine how sore that skinny shoulder of his is going to be come morning. He'll probably still be nursing the thing next Friday."

"Is there something special about next Friday?" Audrey asked.

"The Grand Summer Cotillion," he reminded her. "Remember? It's to be held in the ballroom of the Fifth Avenue Hotel next week."

Audrey's heart skipped a beat while she nodded that she did indeed remember having read something about it. It would have been difficult not to have read at least *something*, what with all the different stories associated with the upcoming ball filling the many society magazines. How she longed for Landon to choose her to be his companion for the grand event but, at the same moment, knew she was hoping for the impossible.

Landon would want to take Olivia Arlington to something like that. Though Audrey had no way of knowing for certain if he was still seeing Olivia, she had no reason to believe they weren't still what the society pages liked to call "an item." There were nights when Landon did not come to see her, nights he could be spending with Olivia.

But then, what if he was still seeing Olivia? Audrey had certainly placed no personal demands on him; she had no right to. Landon was free to see whomever he wanted. And he was just as free to take whomever he wanted to the Grand Summer Cotillion. Still, she wished it could be her.

Her thoughts wandered next to the dress she would buy if only he'd ask her to be his companion for the evening. It would be the grandest gown ever made, carefully stitched and dripping with spangles. She would make Landon proud to have her at his side. If only he would ask her.

When Landon cleared his throat to recapture her drifting attention, she quickly came out of her ridiculous daydreams and returned to the starkness of reality. Landon had probably already asked Olivia. After all,

225

Olivia was the sort of woman he'd want at his side during such a truly grand event. The thought of it made her ache inside.

"Now, I know it's not something you can decide immediately," Landon said, frowning that she had shown no response at all to his invitation. "But I'd like to know your answer as soon as possible so I can make the proper arrangements."

Audrey hated to admit that she'd been so lost in her frivolous daydreams that she had not heard a thing he'd said. "What arrangements?"

"I'd want to make sure my driver would be available to drive us. I'd want to order a corsage to match your gown." Landon shrugged. "You know, that sort of thing."

Audrey's heart froze, afraid to believe what his words indicated. "You want to take me to the Cotillion?"

"That's the main reason I asked," he said, puzzled that she had yet to grasp the intention of his invitation. Or was she stalling because she didn't know how to refuse him without hurting his feelings? "I realize it gives you barely a week to get ready, and I apologize for that; but I really hadn't thought much about the ball until today. I've had a lot on my mind lately." When she still did not respond, he quickly added, "I know it may seem like I'm rushing you, but I'd really like your answer sometime today if at all possible."

Audrey was not easily fooled. She realized that the real reason Landon's invitation had come at the last minute like this was because, for some inconceivable reason, Olivia had decided not to attend the Cotillion this year. Or, what seemed even more inconceivable, that she'd decided to attend with someone else. Yet, for some reason, none of that mattered. All that really mattered was that Landon had indeed asked her to go, and even if she were his second choice, it was better than not being chosen at all, and she had no intention of refusing him.

Her heart raced wildly with anticipation, aware this was exactly what she'd wanted. All she had to do was accept.

"I'd love to go," she said.

Her voice had sounded amazingly calm for someone who could barely catch her breath. Her heart thudded firmly against her breast as she next wondered if she had time to make it to Nadine's Dress Shop before closing time. Aware a week was hardly enough time to have a gown made, much less a gown as grand as she wanted to wear to the Grand Summer Cotillion, she was eager to make her selections. Spotting his carriage along the curbside in front of her house, she asked, her eyes bright with excitement, "Would you mind giving me a ride to Nadine's Dress Shop? I'll need her to get started on my gown right away."

"I'll do better than that. Not only will I take you, but I'll wait for you to finish, then bring you back."

"No need to do that," she said, though pleased he'd offered. "I know you have that business meeting tonight, and it might take me a while to choose the design I want."

Afraid his presence outside the door might hurry her at a time she did not want to be rushed, Landon agreed to leave her there—with the stipulation she take a cab back and not try to walk that distance as she usually did.

Knowing it would be nearly dark by the time she'd made all the necessary selections, everything from what lace she'd like to what color ribbons, she readily agreed.

Quickly, she changed into a more presentable dress than the one she'd had on and, less than twenty minutes later, entered Nadine's Dress Shop eager to look through her most exclusive pattern books.

Smiling as she settled comfortably onto one of the three emerald silk settees in the small parlor near the front of the elite dress shop, Audrey stated, with a rather haughty toss of her head, "I'm here to order an evening gown to wear to the Grand Summer Cotillion." When Nadine's eyes widened as if to protest the fact that the Cotillion was only a week away, she quickly added, "Of

227

course, money is of little concern."

Nadine's harried expression relaxed as her demurely painted lips stretched into a pleased curve. "Yes, of course. Would you care to glance through a few of my pattern books while I get my order pad?"

Two hours later, Audrey had made her final selections and promised to return on Tuesday for the first fitting of what promised to be the grandest ball gown ever made.

chapter fifteen

Even though it had been Seth's idea for Rachel to agree to go to the Cotillion with Preston, knowing it would raise too many complicated questions if she suddenly refused, he still hated the thought of his beautiful Rachel being swept across the dance floor in someone else's arms. Though he understood that it was still too soon for them to allow their feelings for one another to be known, it was becoming increasingly harder for him to keep those feelings buried inside. If it weren't for the trouble it would cause Rachel, he would gladly shout aloud his feelings for her from the very top of the tallest building in New York and be done with it. But he couldn't . . . not yet.

Glumly, he shrugged into the black silk with velvet trim evening jacket that was a part of the formal outfit Marshall had ordered especially for him to wear that night. How Seth dreaded the next several hours, though his duties for the evening were to be simple enough. He was to try to stay as close to Marshall as possible and keep an eye out for any impending danger, because the man had obviously managed to cultivate an unknown number of business enemies over the past several years. The two hoodlums who had tried to kidnap him just five weeks earlier were still at large, having eluded the police entirely. It was Marshall's theory that they were just lying low, waiting for a second opportunity—a second opportunity Seth was not about to give them.

But, despite the possible danger, Seth knew his attention would be constantly drawn to the dance floor, where he expected to find Rachel and Preston enjoying the gay music and bright lights throughout the evening. Since the pair was officially engaged, Rachel would be expected to share the majority of her dances with Preston. Seth's heart ached with a misery he'd not expected when he finally stepped out into the hall and walked over to Marshall's door to wait for him to come out.

While he waited, he heard Everett's light footsteps on the stairway and watched as the rigid little man hurried to Rachel's door. After knocking lightly exactly three times, which was his custom, he announced in a loud, crisp voice that Preston Windthorst had arrived and awaited her in the front parlor. Everett was such a stickler for what he considered the proper protocol for a butler.

"Tell him I'll be down in just a few minutes," came Rachel's muffled reply from within her room.

Seth was pleased to hear no eager anticipation in her voice and smiled inwardly as he watched Everett turn briskly around and head back the way he'd come. He felt a moment of discomfort though when, just as the spry little butler was about to descend the stairs, he turned and gave Seth a questioning look.

It was the same sort of look he'd given him several times over the past few days, a look that made Seth wonder if Everett suspected something was amiss. His stomach hardened into a tight, painful knot at the thought, because if Everett suspected, then it wouldn't be long before Marshall suspected, and once her father's suspicions had been aroused, Rachel's life would surely become a living hell.

Swallowing hard, he shook the odd feeling of impending doom and turned back to watch Rachel's door. He hoped she would come on out so he could catch a glimpse of her before Marshall appeared and whisked him away.

To his delight, the two opened their doors and entered the hall from opposite directions at precisely the same moment. After several complimentary exchanges between father and daughter, Seth was then allowed to escort them both downstairs. He followed a half step behind Marshall, where he would not be that easily noticed, and cast several meaningful glances in Rachel's direction to let her know that he, too, approved of her gown. It thrilled him to have his silent messages met with timid glances of her own. His heart soared as her gaze locked with his momentarily, then darted away. A knowing smile tugged at her lips. He still found it difficult to believe that anyone as enchanting as Rachel could actually care for him.

His blood stirred while he watched her walk ever so gracefully at her father's side. Dressed in a fluid gown of pure white silk, with tiny rows of pink ribbons twisted in and about her wide, flounced hem and around her narrow waistline, she reminded him of a beautiful angel. A long strand of tiny shell-pink pearls lay at her ivory throat. Another strand had been carefully woven into her honey-gold hair, which had been piled into a glorious arrangement of soft curls.

It took all the self-restraint he possessed not to reach forward and sweep her into his arms right then. How he yearned to claim her for his own . . . to sample the sweetness of her lips . . . to touch the softness of her skin. He ached to hold her with a longing so severe, he was not certain he could bear the crushing pain much longer. Then when they entered the front parlor and Preston crossed the room to press a brief kiss upon her temple, it felt to Seth as if someone had stepped forward and kicked him in the stomach.

In the end, he had to look away.

*   *   *

Audrey did not care to speculate why her insides remained all aflutter while she waited for Landon to arrive. She'd spent part of the morning and most of the afternoon getting ready, and despite the fact she could not detect anything wrong with either her gown or her hair, it felt as if something was still amiss. Something about her appearance was not quite what it should be—or could be. She wanted to look absolutely perfect for Landon that night and had done all she could to attain that goal; but something just didn't feel right.

For the twentieth time, she returned to the large mirror at the far end of the hall and tried to locate the problem. And for the twentieth time, she found nothing noticeably wrong in her reflection. Her gown was flawless, exactly what she'd envisioned: a fawn-colored brilliantine that gathered with a sash at the waist, then flowed gracefully to the floor in wide, even flounces. Though the neckline was moderate in cut, the close fit of the bodice itself revealed the perfect shape of her breasts and was spattered with thousands of glittering silver flecks, as was the material several inches above the hemline.

Tiny tear-shaped diamonds dangled from the delicate lobes of her ears and others rested at the base of her throat, twinkling with elegance, though the earrings would hardly be noticed beneath the elaborate array of dark curls she'd arranged atop her head.

While she studied her reflection further, she found no hair out of place, no fallen eyelashes on her cheek, and nary a wrinkle in her gown, yet still she felt lacking, as if something were terribly wrong with her appearance that she simply could not see. Though she stared at perfection, what she saw was anything but.

Moments later, when Landon arrived looking quite debonair in his three-piece formal attire, he quelled her odd feelings of inadequacy by the leisurely way he allowed his gaze to rove admiringly down the length of her gown, then back up again. With a sparkle of obvious approval in his pale blue eyes, he turned and offered his arm, smiling as he proudly proclaimed that she'd be by far the most alluring woman at the ball.

Thinking he'd overstated her appearance, her first inclination had been to argue with him. But, too afraid she might actually win the argument and thus dispel any shred of confidence his wonderful praise had given her, she wisely chose to remain silent while she walked with him out to the carriage. Once there, he brought forth the largest white orchid she'd ever seen, gaily decorated with silver sequins and tiny strips of silver brocade.

"It's beautiful," she gasped as she offered her arm and allowed him to secure the decoration to the gathered hem of her puffed sleeve, which fell several inches above her wrist. Knowing it would have no aroma, she lifted the flower to her cheek and felt its delicate softness instead. "It is absolutely beautiful."

"I'm afraid it pales in comparison to your beauty," he said. His gaze rose to meet with hers, letting her know that he had been sincere in his compliment.

A disturbing wave of vibrating warmth spilled through her. She found it impossible to take her gaze from his and waited for him to look away. For a moment she thought he was going to kiss her, and she waited breathlessly for him to lean forward. But after gazing at her for several seconds more, he stepped back to help her into the carriage.

Only after she'd settled onto the soft leather seat was she able to bring her reeling senses back under control.

"I am looking forward to seeing everyones' reactions when I enter that ballroom with you on my arm. I have no doubt at all that you will be the hit of the ball," he said proudly, smiling as he settled in beside her. His expression darkened though when his next thought was to caution her. "Just don't let all the attention I'm sure you'll receive tonight go to your head. Just you remember who it was you came with. And make certain you reserve both your first and your final dance for me."

233

"But I don't plan to dance with anyone else," she protested, having no desire to dance with total strangers and aware there was very little chance she'd know many of the men there. Tonight would be her first real opportunity to meet any of the "right" people . . . people she'd always longed to associate with. A heavy jolt of apprehension shot through her at the mere thought of meeting New York's finest. The added thought of having to dance with any of them terrified her.

"I'm afraid you'll have no choice. As beautiful as you are, the men will flock to your heels the moment you enter that ballroom, begging for a place on your dance card."

Audrey twisted her lips into a perplexed frown. "What happens if I simply tell them no?"

"They won't let you. They'll plague you and plead with you until you finally give in. And I really can't say that I blame them," he chuckled. "I'm guilty of no less."

Audrey looked at him with surprise and laughed. The laughter eased some of her apprehension, allowing her to lean back against the tufted carriage seat and wonder if the Grand Summer Cotillion would be anything like she'd dreamed it to be.

For the first half hour after their arrival at the elaborately decorated Fifth Avenue Hotel and before the music was scheduled to begin, Landon proudly escorted Audrey from group to group, introducing her to everyone he knew. And, like Landon had so well predicted, Audrey was in great demand. The men flocked to her side, eager for a chance to catch her attention. Every available male he introduced her to immediately asked for a place on her dance card—and even a few who were considered not so readily available.

Before long, Audrey's card was filled with names, some of them disturbingly well-known. By the time she tucked her folded card into her sleeve to indicate she had no more dances available, she'd added some very prominent names such as Vanderbilt, Gould, Stewart, and Kilburn . . . the true giants of the investment world. She was in awe that men like that had asked to dance with her. Men she'd never had the privilege to meet before that night were treating her as if they'd known her all their lives.

She was overwhelmed by the sheer prominence of many of the people she'd met thus far, some known throughout the world for their financial wizardry. So overwhelmed was Audrey that she did not at first notice the many whispers being passed behind raised hands. Nor did she notice the curious gazes directed at her from all about the room, and certainly not the murderous gaze that bore through her from the grand stairway where Olivia Arlington had just entered on the arm of her prestigious father, Thomas K. Arlington.

Dressed in a bright emerald-green gown, which was cut exceptionally low to reveal an ample amount of rounded womanly flesh, and adorned with a spectacular display of diamonds and emeralds draped low from her neck, ears, and wrists, Olivia might have looked very much like a true fairy princess, if it weren't for the hard, angry expression that shot royal daggers through both Audrey and Landon.

The whispers in the room rose to a steady murmur. Everyone eventually turned to watch the proceedings with noted expectation. Thomas, too, had spotted Landon across the room and his eyebrows shot skyward when he then noticed the beautiful young woman laughing at his side. When he turned to immediately glance about the room, as if in search of someone who might tell him the identity of this young woman, he glimpsed the harsh expression on his daughter's face.

At that moment, a soft strand of music drifted through the room, overriding the low din of voices and making it apparent to everyone that the dancing was about to begin. The dance floor filled quickly with those eager to start the festivities.

"I believe the first dance is mine," Landon said as he

took Audrey by the wrist and led her out onto the floor.

Within seconds, the first waltz had begun and Audrey was swept immediately into his strong arms. As she'd expected, Landon danced with an easy grace, moving smoothly across the polished floor, his hand pressed intimately at her lower back.

"I think it would prove much better for your reputation if you were to remove your hand from the small of my back and place it at my shoulder where it belongs," she said, glancing pointedly at him while he continued to twirl her around and around.

That lazy grin of his stretched easily across his face, shaping two fascinating dimples near the outer corners of his curved mouth. "How nice that you are so concerned for my reputation."

His teasing response made her laugh. "Okay, maybe it is my own reputation that concerns me. After all, if you continue to hold me in the shameful manner in which you are holding me now, your friends just might start to talk."

"I'm afraid it is too late to worry about that. The talk has already begun," he said, little concerned. "In fact, the place is all abuzz with conversations about us."

"Is it?" she asked, glancing around at the crowded room while he continued to twirl her gracefully around the floor. It was true; most eyes were upon them. Then, suddenly, she understood why they'd drawn such interest. "Because you brought me instead of Olivia?"

Landon's eyebrows arched with troubled concern, his expression dark with sudden caution. "And what do you know about Olivia?"

"Only what little I've read in the society pages," she admitted, wondering why he suddenly seemed so tense. "Plus, I'm aware she was the beautiful woman with you at Delmonico's that day I paid you your money. Remember? I know that was her because I heard you call her name when you told your driver to take her home." Glancing around again, letting her gaze sweep the hundreds of beautiful women at the ball but finding none that she recognized, she asked, "Is she here?"

"Yes," he answered, his voice low, as if he feared their conversation might be overheard.

Audrey's brow drew into a pretty frown. "But I don't understand. Why didn't she come with you?"

"Because I didn't ask her," he answered simply.

"But why? I thought you two were supposed to be practically engaged," she asked, but no sooner had she voiced the question than she knew the answer. For some reason, Landon was out to make Olivia jealous. A cold, sickly feeling bore down on her like a leaden weight when she realized she was being used. Had all their evenings together been a ruse to make Olivia jealous?

"I'll explain it to you exactly like I explained it to her," he said, his tone deadly serious. "Olivia is a very close friend. She always has been. We grew up knowing each other, and as a result, we have a lot in common. But that's about as far as our relationship goes. We've never been anything more than good friends. And despite any rumors you may have heard, I have never once considered asking her to be my wife. In fact, until recently, I hadn't considered ever marrying *anyone*."

"Until recently?" she asked, finding little sense in what he'd told her. "But if you are finally considering marriage, like you just said, then why try to convince me that the two of you are just friends?"

"Because Olivia is not the sort of woman I'd ever want for my wife," he answered honestly. His gaze bore deeply into hers, as if trying to deliver an unspoken message.

Just then, the last strains of the waltz fell away, and the men swiftly released their partners to go in search of the next beautiful lady who'd promised a dance. Landon held Audrey a moment longer than might be considered proper by most, staring silently at her upturned face; but he released her willingly when George Kilburn, an older gentleman who owned one of the largest stockyards in

237

the North, appeared at her side to claim his dance.

For the next two hours, Audrey rarely caught sight of Landon, but not for lack of trying. After the confusing conversation they'd had, she could give her full attention to no one else.

Occasionally, they would pass one another on the crowded dance floor, but even that proved rare. Dance after dance, with dance partner after dance partner, Audrey tried to sustain pleasant conversation, but her thoughts continued to dwell on what Landon had been about to say. Could he possibly have meant that the woman who had interested him enough to consider marriage was her? Or was there yet someone else who'd turned his head? Maybe it wasn't Olivia he sought to make jealous after all.

And if there was someone else, was he off dancing with her or perhaps out in the torch-lit courtyard, walking arm in arm while gazing into a star-filled sky and enjoying a private conversation together? The thought of that made her insides hurt while she continued to keep a constant watch for him, eager to discover whom he was with.

To her growing confusion, he was almost always with an older woman, some even old enough to be his own mother. Only twice during those first two hours did she notice him dancing with anyone younger, and both times it was with his sister, Rachel. Not once did she see him dance with Olivia.

By the time the orchestra had left the stage to go out into the courtyard for a breath of fresh air, having played two straight hours with only enough delay between songs to allow the regular change of partners, Seth was in a dismal mood. He'd been forced to stand idly by, watching from a distance while Preston and Rachel danced again and again. Rarely were the two apart. Occasionally, she'd set aside a dance for Landon or her father, but most of her dances were with Preston. He was forever at her side. The only consolation to the whole miserable evening was that Rachel had not smiled once since she arrived. She was clearly as unhappy as he was.

Whenever their gazes met across the room, which they had again and again, Rachel had sent Seth clear messages of regret. She was not with the man she wanted. And it was that comforting thought that had helped Seth get through those first two torturous hours. He hoped it would be enough to get him through the rest of the evening.

After several of the dancers left the ballroom for a moment's respite out in the small courtyard and others had lined up for cool refreshment around the many punch bowls, Seth searched the crowd for another glimpse of Rachel—something he seemed accustomed to doing. It surprised him to find her standing with a small circle of friends off to one side because, for the first time that evening, Preston was nowhere to be found.

"Would you like for me to get you a cup of punch?" Seth asked Marshall barely seconds after he'd returned from the dance floor. He was eager for a reason to walk past Rachel while Preston was still away and give her a knowing glance or brush her shoulder, to show her how deeply he shared her misery.

"Oh, yes, that's a wonderful idea," Marshall said, taking his handkerchief out of his pocket and dabbing at the perspiration that had collected on his cheeks and brow. Glancing at the high ceilings, he muttered, "Those new four-bladed ceiling fans may be all the rage, but they just aren't helping keep this room cool."

Seth looked up. He hadn't noticed the large white ceiling fans. Nor had he noticed the intricate design of the hand-carved ceiling. Fact was, he hadn't noticed much of anything about the grand ballroom, which was reputed to be one of the finest in all the United States. His attention had been too centered on Rachel and Preston to give anything else much notice. Nothing else

239

mattered. Not even Marshall's foul mood, which had befallen him only minutes after their arrival.

"When you get that punch for me, bring it out into the courtyard, because that's where you'll find me. I've got to get a breath of cool air," he said, scowling as he gently fanned the lapels of his coat to let a bit of air circulate through his hot, damp clothing.

While Seth turned to go to the refreshment table nearest Rachel, Marshall spun about and headed toward the four wide double doors that led to the gardens outside.

Pausing a few feet away in pretense of letting someone pass, Seth turned to give Rachel an inconspicuous glance, pleased that although she continued to speak with her friends, her gaze had followed him across the room. Aware none of her friends had yet to notice him, he winked at her, then continued on past. His dark mood temporarily lifted. While he waited in line to get the punch he'd promised Marshall, Seth halfheartedly listened to some of the conversation around him while he continued to cast admiring glances in Rachel's direction.

"Did you see how quickly he appeared at her side after the music stopped?" a tall red-haired girl asked of her short brunette friend while she dabbed lightly at her slender neck with a small lace handkerchief. "I've never seen anyone maneuver through a crowd like that."

"Well, he's been watching her every little move all evening," the brunette answered with a light shrug, as if it hadn't surprised her in the least.

"So has Olivia Arlington," the redhead added with a giggle.

"As have most of the people here," the brunette was quick to put in. "You included."

"I'm just waiting to see what happens. Has anyone found out who she is yet?"

"No, but Richard tried to convince me that she was Landon's father's housekeeper," the brunette answered, frowning with annoyance as she spread her silk and lace

240

MORE PASSION AND ADVENTURE AWAIT... YOUR TRIP TO A BIG ADVENTUROUS WORLD BEGINS WHEN YOU ACCEPT YOUR FIRST 4 NOVELS ABSOLUTELY *FREE* (AN $18.00 VALUE)

Accept your Free gift and start to experience more of the passion and adventure you like in a historical romance novel. Each Zebra novel is filled with proud men, spirited women and tempestuous love that you'll remember long after you turn the last page.

Zebra Historical Romances are the finest novels of their kind. They are written by authors who really know how to weave tales of romance and adventure in the historical settings you love. You'll feel like you've actually gone back in time with the thrilling stories that each Zebra novel offers.

GET YOUR FREE GIFT WITH THE START OF YOUR HOME SUBSCRIPTION

Our readers tell us that these books sell out very fast in book stores and often they miss the newest titles. So Zebra has made arrangements for you to receive the four newest novels published each month.

You'll be guaranteed that you'll never miss a title, and home delivery is so convenient. And to show you just how easy it is to get Zebra Historical Romances, we'll send you your first 4 books absolutely FREE! Our gift to you just for trying our home subscription service.

BIG SAVINGS AND FREE HOME DELIVERY

Each month, you'll receive the four newest titles as soon as they are published. You'll probably receive them even before the bookstores do. What's more, you may preview these exciting novels free for 10 days. If you like them as much as we think you will, just pay the low preferred subscriber's price of just $3.75 each. *You'll save $3.00 each month off the publisher's price.* AND, your savings are even greater because there are never any shipping, handling or other hidden charges—FREE Home Delivery. Of course you can return any shipment within 10 days for full credit, no questions asked. There is no minimum number of books you must buy.

4 FREE BOOKS

TO GET YOUR 4 FREE BOOKS WORTH $18.00 — MAIL IN THE FREE BOOK CERTIFICATE T O D A Y

Fill in the Free Book Certificate below, and we'll send your FREE BOOKS to you as soon as we receive it.

If the certificate is missing below, write to: Zebra Home Subscription Service, Inc., P.O. Box 5214, 120 Brighton Road, Clifton, New Jersey 07015-5214.

FREE BOOK CERTIFICATE

4 FREE BOOKS

ZEBRA HOME SUBSCRIPTION SERVICE, INC.

YES! Please start my subscription to Zebra Historical Romances and send me my first 4 books absolutely FREE. I understand that each month I may preview four new Zebra Historical Romances free for 10 days. If I'm not satisfied with them, I may return the four books within 10 days and owe nothing. Otherwise, I will pay the low preferred subscriber's price of just $3.75 each; a total of $15.00, *a savings off the publisher's price of $3.00.* I may return any shipment and I may cancel this subscription at any time. There is no obligation to buy any shipment and there are no shipping, handling or other hidden charges. Regardless of what I decide, the four free books are mine to keep.

NAME

ADDRESS _____ APT _____

CITY _____ STATE _____ ZIP _____

( )
TELEPHONE

SIGNATURE _____
(if under 18, parent or guardian must sign)

fan and began to work it to its best advantage. "He said he got that from someone who knows the Steeds personally. Of course, we both know that can't be true. Why would someone as important as Landon Steed bring his father's housekeeper to an event like this? My, how rumors do get started."

Seth's eyes widened at the mention of Landon's name. He'd been so engrossed with his forlorn thoughts of Rachel and with keeping her in his sight at all times that he'd not taken the time to notice any of the other guests. Twisting his dark eyebrows into a puzzled frown, he wondered whom Landon had brought to the ball and why it was causing such an uproar. Cocking an ear, he listened to the conversation with deeper interest.

"I wonder what dear Olivia has had to say about this pretty new lady friend of his?" the redhead asked, rising up on her toes to look over her friend's shoulder at where dining tables had been set up across the far side of the room. "Poor little thing. I noticed she's hardly danced at all tonight. Keeps pressing at her temple as if she has a headache." Then in a lower voice, "Probably plans to make an early night of it, don't you think?"

Seth followed the direction of her gaze and noticed a group of elegantly dressed people seated around one of the larger tables, none of whom seemed to be having a very good time. It was the same group of people to whom Marshall had spoken with earlier.

Studying them from a distance, he decided the beautiful young woman seated at the table must be this Olivia Arlington the two girls had mentioned. He wondered why that name sounded so familiar. It was when he glanced back down at the two conversing girls that he remembered. He'd heard Marshall mention the name earlier, and if Seth recalled the conversation correctly, Olivia Arlington was the only unmarried daughter of one of Marshall's most revered friends. And, judging from the talk going on around him, she was also a very close friend of Landon's—or at least she had been

241

until tonight.

By then, the brunette had also turned to look at Olivia. "Just goes to show that money can't buy everything. Hmm, I wonder if *she* knows who Landon's new lady friend is," she mused in a pleased but spiteful tone. "I'll just bet she does. By now, I imagine she knows all there is to know about her—and then some." When she turned to look back at the redhead, her expression was amused. "Shirley, dear, if you are really so eager to know this woman's name and find out just where it is she came from, why don't you sashay over there and ask Olivia herself."

"I value my life too much," the redhead answered with a giggle. "But don't you wish you could be a fly flittering around that table right now? Can you imagine the conversation you'd overhear?"

"Judging by those stony expressions, yes, I can." The brunette nodded agreeably, then glanced up unexpectantly and noticed Seth was looking down at her, his expression speculative. Mistaking the reason for his obvious interest, her eyes brightened while she brought her fan in front of her pretty face and fluttered it coquettishly before her.

Aware he'd been caught staring, Seth swiftly glanced away, still trying to digest everything he'd just heard. Clearly this Olivia was not at all pleased with the fact that Landon had brought a strange woman to the ball, which led Seth to assume that the unhappy Miss Arlington must want him for herself. As he reached forward to accept a cup of punch from one of the young stewards behind the serving table, he turned to see if he could catch a glimpse of Landon and see for himself what his controversial guest looked like. He had a feeling she would prove to be a real beauty, but then one would expect someone like Landon to have nothing less at his side.

When Seth did not see him anywhere inside, he decided he and his lady friend must have stepped outside, as Rachel probably had, for she, too, was no longer in sight. Passing through the doors that led into the courtyard, he spotted Rachel immediately; but to his dismay, Preston had returned to her side and the two of them had joined Marshall out near the fountains. His heart felt heavy as lead when he strode across the bricked area, knowing he'd have to stand silently by while he again listened to Preston go on and on about himself—a habit that Seth found increasingly annoying.

"I agree with your father," Preston was saying to Rachel when Seth came near enough to hear, but his words came as no real surprise since Preston was constantly agreeing with Marshall and rarely ever agreed with anything Rachel had to say. "Your brother showed very poor judgment in bringing Audrey Stoane here."

Seth's eyes widened at the mention of his sister's name. He almost dropped Marshall's punch before he could hand it over.

"Not if Audrey is the one he prefers to be with," Rachel argued in a calm voice, jutting her chin forward to emphasize that she meant what she'd said. "Why should Landon be forced to endure someone else's company when he's obviously more interested in Audrey?"

"The only thing he's interested in is her bed," Preston put in, glaring angrily at her for having come to Audrey's defense so readily. "Your father is right. There is a time and a place for everything, and the Summer Cotillion is not the place to bring one's trollop, especially when one's own fiancée is in attendance."

Seth stiffened, his anger rising to an immediate boil. Rachel's startled gaze flew from Preston's annoyed grimace to Seth's rigid face. Then, upon seeing the black fury raging in his eyes, she hurried to intervene. "Preston, take me home."

"But why? The evening is still young," he noted, glancing up into the cloudless night sky as if he hadn't a care in the world.

"Because I do not intend to stand here and listen to you talk like that about Audrey Stoane, especially not in front of her own brother. Take me home."

Preston drew in a long, irritated breath, glanced only briefly at Seth, then crossed his arms defiantly as he cocked his head to one side. "Look here, young lady. I will say what I please, and I'll say it where I please and when I please."

"Fine, but you won't be saying it around me. I've had more than enough of your pompous ravings. I'm leaving," Rachel said with a determined toss of her head, then, to show that she meant it, she spun immediately about and marched briskly away.

Preston's eyes widened with disbelief while Marshall hurried after his daughter. "Rachel, come back here. You are making a spectacle of yourself!"

Rachel never bothered to look back and within seconds she'd disappeared into the crowd. Marshall, too.

Having been given strict orders to try and keep his boss clearly within sight that evening, Seth immediately followed, while Preston tried his best to look unconcerned.

chapter sixteen

"Sorry, gentlemen, but the last dance has been promised to me," Landon said as he reached into the circle of men and drew Audrey safely out of their midst. "And I am here to claim what's mine."

He lifted an eyebrow in warning to still the mumbled complaints as he led her away from them, to a less crowded area on the dance floor.

"I wondered if you were still here," Audrey teased, pleased to feel Landon's strong hand on her elbow. She smiled as the warmth of his touch moved through her body, but the smile slowly gave way to a soft yawn. Until now, she hadn't really realized how tired she was. Her feet ached from having danced so many dances without pause, and her head spun crazily when she tried to remember the names and faces of everyone she'd met or talked with in so short a time. "I was starting to think you'd left without me."

Landon glanced away, his face rigid with emotion while he waited for the final melody to begin. "I was outside having a talk with my father."

"Oh," Audrey responded quietly, wondering what the two had spoken about. She hadn't seen Landon look this grim in quite some time.

The music started and Audrey went willingly into his arms. As he stepped in perfect three-quarter time, she noticed that he did not move across the floor with quite the same vigor he'd shown earlier. Though he still danced eloquently, something was lacking in his movements. She wondered if this present lack of enthusiasm was because he'd simply danced too many dances in a night's time, like she had, or if it had something to do with what he and his father had discussed outside.

"It's been a long night," she commented, hoping to draw him into a conversation that might give her some insight as to the reason for his suddenly dour mood.

"You might be interested to know that Rachel left early," Landon said, as if he hadn't heard her comment yet was eager to start a conversation of his own.

"Oh? And why would I be interested to know that?" she asked. She hoped to keep the conversation alive, at least until she discovered why he was in such a dark mood.

"Because she left with your brother."

An icy tendril of apprehension coiled around her stomach. She wondered what could have brought about such an incident and worried about the repercussions that would surely follow. How could Seth have done something so foolish? "Why would she leave with Seth?"

Landon didn't look at her. Instead, his attention rested on the thinning crowds around them. Much of the older group had already gone. Only the younger couples and a few of the true diehards remained. "Appears she and Preston had some sort of a disagreement a few hours ago and she decided to leave without him. Rather than allow her to travel alone on a night when most men have had a little too much to drink and are apt to have muddled senses, Father ordered your brother to see her safely home in his carriage. But he also told him to report back here as soon as he had done that. Odd thing was, Seth was gone for well over an hour."

"I wonder what took him so long," Audrey said, thinking Seth should have shown better sense than that.

With the Steed house only several blocks away, he should have returned within twenty minutes.

"So does Father," Landon put in, glancing down at her for the first time. When his gaze met hers, some of the anger that had been building inside of him melted away. The harsh lines around his mouth slowly disappeared. What was there about her that made everything else seem so insignificant? "He also wonders what became of Preston, who left about that same time."

Audrey's eyes widened with concern for her brother, suddenly relieved that Seth had returned after all. "Is that what you and your father talked about?"

"Partly," Landon said, and the harsh lines instantly returned, making her wonder again about the full content of their conversation.

His jaw flexed spasmodically for a moment before he added, "He's curious to know what happened. All Seth will tell him is that Rachel refused to go straight home and demanded the driver take them for a short ride through the park first. To calm her nerves, I think."

Audrey closed her eyes for a moment. A sharp, sickly feeling pressed down on her. She could easily imagine what had happened between Seth and Rachel on a moonlit ride through the park. She only hoped the driver had shown the proper restraint and had kept his eyes on the road ahead and not on his two passengers. "What else did you and your father talk about?"

Landon hesitated before answering truthfully. "You."

"Me?"

"He thinks that you somehow tricked me into bringing you here tonight."

"What?" Audrey asked, startled that anyone had come to such a conclusion. "Why would he think that?"

"Why does that man think any of the things he thinks?" Landon responded bitterly. His shoulders and arms tensed visibly, though he continued to dance with the same ease and agile grace as before. "In this case, it just doesn't suit him to believe the truth."

247

"Which is?" she prompted, ready to hear that herself.

The first traces of a smile tugged at the corners of his mouth while he considered his answer. "Let's just say my father and I don't see things in quite the same way. He would prefer I focused all my attentions on Olivia. In fact, he went as far as to demand outright that I stop seeing you all together and then ordered me to find Olivia, who'd left well over an hour ago. He wants me to apologize to her for my outrageous behavior—before it's too late."

"And what did you say to that?" she asked, though she wasn't too sure she wanted to know.

"I explained how there were certain conditions that would have to exist before I would even consider apologizing to *anyone* for having brought you here tonight."

Aware he was using her as some sort of leverage against his own father, Audrey glanced away, no longer able to meet his probing gaze. "Oh? And what might that be?"

"Had to do with the weather conditions in hell," he admitted. A pleased grin stretched full width across his face. "The chances of which are slim, to say the least."

Audrey looked back at him with surprise. "And what did he say to that?"

Landon shook his head and shrugged, as if to indicate it mattered little, though the angry glint in his steel-blue eyes told a different story. "It doesn't bear repeating."

Audrey stared at him, astonished that he had come so readily to her defense when it had meant going against a member of his own family. That was not at all what she would have expected, even had she been there.

Landon pulled his gaze away from hers and drew her closer as the music began to build slowly to its third and final crescendo. The waltz was nearing the end, and for the first time that night, Audrey wished the music would go on forever. Suddenly, she no longer felt tired. Instead, a strange, giddy exhilaration filled her senses. It grew stronger when his arms slowly tightened around her. For

248

once, Audrey decided not to try and analyze the powerful physical response she had to him. She refused to worry that she might have come one step closer to falling in love with Landon at a time in her life when she definitely did not need that to complicate matters. Nor did she stop to wonder why she suddenly didn't care.

Instead of worrying about her private emotions getting in the way of her long-awaited chance to be rich in her own right, she closed her eyes and concentrated on the entrancing beat of the music, allowing the soft rhythm to gently seduce her. The touch of his strong, manly arms holding her a bit too close thrilled her, as did the rippling movement of his stout shoulder muscles beneath her fingertips. For one brief moment, she let down all her defenses and drifted willingly in a hazy cloud of languid warmth.

All too soon the song ended, and Audrey was forced to open her eyes again and rejoin the real world. Reluctantly, they pulled apart.

Disappointed that the magical moment had not lasted any longer, Audrey turned and allowed Landon to escort her toward the front door. Her senses still soared as she thought of the strong, virile man at her side, making it seem as if she were still caught up in a light, swirling sea of clouds. Oddly, she wished she would never have to come down.

When they neared the crowd that had gathered near the front exit, a young man Audrey remembered only by the name of Douglas paused to talk with Landon.

With a wide, off-centered grin, from having had far too much to drink, he nudged Landon good-naturedly in the ribs and spoke in a loud whisper, as if what he had to say should be considered confidential—yet not too much so. "It worked like a scharm, old boy," he said with a drunken drawl. "I never shaw Olivia look so jealoush."

Landon glanced at him, startled by his comments. "What worked like a charm?"

"Ahh, you know, the ploy to make her mad e'nuff to

want to marry you," Douglas said with a conspiratory wink. "It shure as hell worked."

His words, slurred though they were, rang sharply in Audrey's ears when she looked from Douglas's glazed eyes to Landon's wide-eyed expression. The pain was immediate. Her initial suspicion had been correct: Landon *had* used her to make Olivia jealous! What a fool she'd been to have believed otherwise.

Tears of humiliation burned her eyes when she turned and hurried away from them, eager to be alone before either of them could witness her shame.

"Audrey, wait," Landon called out as he pushed Douglas out of his way and hurried after her.

Audrey heard him but never looked back. Moving blindly, she shouldered her way through the milling crowd. Her direction didn't matter, just as long as it was away from Landon. She did not want to listen to anything he had to say. She'd heard enough of his lies.

"Audrey!"

His voice sounded closer. Though she still did not bother to look back, certain one glimpse of his face would be her emotional undoing, she knew he had closed the distance between them. Her heart hammered wildly while she continued to push her way through the crowds lingering in the lobby, her gaze focused on the front door. To her rising frustration, no one seemed willing to let her pass. A few attempted to engage her in friendly conversation instead. She did what she could to evade them, but before she could make it through to the outside, she felt Landon's hand close over her shoulder.

Aware all eyes were upon them, he slowly but carefully guided her on through the door. With his grip still firmly on her shoulder, he forced a smile and spoke in a surprisingly cheerful voice. "Slow down. You actually lost me there for a minute."

"Did I?" she asked, mocking his cheerful tone as she glanced back at him with a tight-lipped smile of her own. Her gaze dropped intentionally to where his hand still held her shoulder in a tight, painful grip. "How careless of me."

Landon swallowed hard when he noted the dark mixture of hurt and anger that glowered from her huge brown eyes. No longer caring what those around them thought or what sort of rumors might result, he bent forward, placing his face near hers, his expression grim. "We have to talk."

"Save your sugary words for Olivia," she said in an icy tone. Her nostrils flared with anger when she looked at him then. "I've already had my fill."

A dozen mouths flew open in startled response. Eager silence surrounded them. Aware of the unwanted attention they'd drawn, Landon cut those who dared to stare at them a devil's glare, sending all but the very bravest scurrying on their way.

"Audrey, since I am the one who brought you, I will be the one to take you home," he said, his voice low with warning. He then motioned down the street toward his carriage. "Let's go."

Her first inclination was to argue, but common sense quickly intervened. She knew that if she refused to go with him, she'd have to find another way home, and with all the cabs already filled to capacity, in all likelihood she'd have to walk. Aware what the streets of New York were like at such a late hour, she knew what a truly poor choice walking would be.

Reluctantly yet wisely, she allowed Landon to guide her toward his carriage, and once there, she climbed immediately inside and sat down, but refused to lean back and be comfortable. Instead, she sat rigidly on the edge of the dark leather seat, her arms firmly crossed when he climbed in beside her.

"I don't know where Douglas got the idea that I brought you tonight because I wanted to make Olivia jealous," he said only moments after the driver had the carriage under way. He saw no reason not to get right to the heart of the matter. "Making Olivia jealous was

251

probably the furthest thing from my mind."

"Then why did you bring me?" she asked, turning to face him, though he was barely more than a well-defined shadow in the dark confines of the carriage.

"If anything, I wanted to show her once and for all that I am not as interested in her as she and everyone else seem to think."

"Oh, and that's supposed to make me feel better?" she asked, her anger rising immediately. "Either way, you used me."

Landon sighed with exasperation. "Not as much as you think. Though it's true I wanted to prove something to Olivia, the main reason I invited you to the Cotillion tonight was because I wanted to be with you. I happen to enjoy your company. You aren't like other women. You don't primp and preen and bat your eyelashes as if suddenly trying to take flight. Nor do you have to be told how pretty you are all the time."

Audrey's eyes narrowed. She wasn't sure if he'd dealt her a compliment or an insult. After all, most men flocked to women who primped and preened and batted their eyelashes.

When the dim glow from a nearby street lamp rolled across Audrey's grim expression, Landon could tell he had not made any real progress toward soothing her anger. He tried a different approach. "Besides, you have a lot more sense than most women."

"And coming from someone who obviously holds women in such high regard, that must surely be a compliment," she said, her voice dripping with sarcasm, eager to make him feel even a portion of the pain and anger she felt.

Landon let out a slow, barely controlled breath, then asked, "Exactly what is it you want me to say? That I'm sorry? Okay, I'm sorry."

"For what?" she asked, wanting clarification.

Landon tossed up his hands, provoked that she hadn't let it go at that. "Hell if I know. I can't very well claim to

252

be sorry for having used you, because I don't think that I did. And I can't very well say that I'm sorry I brought you tonight, because until a few minutes ago, I had a very enjoyable time." He tapped his foot impatiently for a moment while he considered the situation further. "Just what is it I'm supposed to be sorry for?"

Audrey thought about that for a moment. Somewhere along the way she, too, had lost track of what had made her so angry.

"Well?" he prompted, ready to get on with it.

"I'm thinking," she muttered. Her face twisted into a perplexed frown.

Landon's eyes widened with realization. "Don't tell me you've forgotten, too?"

Audrey looked at him with a puzzled expression. "I'm not really sure. Maybe if we went over everything carefully. Just what was it that started this whole argument?"

"What argument?" Landon asked, then broke out laughing as he put his arm around her and pulled her close. For the remainder of the trip neither bothered to speak, but both continuously burst into brief bouts of laughter while the carriage slowly closed the distance to her house.

By the time they stepped up onto her porch, Audrey was feeling so lighthearted and gay that she truly hated to see the evening end. When Landon hinted that he'd like to come in for a little while to talk, her inner defenses did not signal their usual warning. Instead, she allowed him to unlock her door for her and they both went inside.

"Would you care for a glass of wine or a cup of tea?" she asked, lighting a lamp in the front parlor. When she turned to face him again, she was startled to find him standing quite close, his eyes dark with a passion that frightened yet at the same time intrigued her.

"Landon, I—" She paused, trying desperately to remember whatever it was she had been about to say, when his lips slowly and deliberately descended on hers.

Staring dazedly at him, Audrey did not turn away. She could not. Though she knew it was wrong, she was as eager for the kiss as he. Slowly, she tilted her head back and closed her eyes, ready for the powerful onslaught of emotions she knew would envelop her . . . that always enveloped her whenever Landon kissed her.

A low, almost indiscernible growl emitted from deep within Landon's throat as he pulled her body hard against his and pressed his mouth hungrily to hers. All night, he'd fought the overwhelming desire to kiss her, to hold her close. He was like a man starved and he supped eagerly.

When their mouths finally broke apart, only minutes later, they were both short of breath and their lips slightly swollen, an indication of the true and overwhelming power of their desire for one another. Their eyes met for a long moment, then slowly, Landon lowered his lips to hers again. Each kiss grew longer and more powerful than the last as their passion began to build to a force beyond their control.

Landon continued to hold her body pressed firmly against his, his hands roaming freely over her back and shoulders. Then, suddenly, he dipped his hands first to caress her ribcage, then moved forward and upward to gently cup the underside of her breast. Audrey felt her first real inkling of panic, but the dizzying sensations that had so quickly overwhelmed her had left her too weak to pull away. Instead, she leaned against him and allowed him the freedom to explore her breast.

In her passion-dazed state of mind, Audrey parted her lips and he dipped the tip of his tongue into her mouth, gently probing its sensitive inner edges. She pressed her body closer, accepting the pleasure his kiss offered, yielding to her own burning desire, allowing her hungry body to thrill to his touch and enjoy the womanly passions he had aroused in her. While her body burned ever hotter with desire, her thoughts drifted beyond the kiss, onto the wonder of what it must be like to be made

254

love to by a man like Landon—so gentle, yet so demanding.

Their kisses deepened, and his explorations of her body became more and more intimate, causing her mind to send out one more faint alarm. But again the message went unheeded. As his thumb caressed the tip of her breast through the soft fabric of her gown, she felt shock wave after shock wave of desire pulsate through her. The burning heat that resulted settled in the deepest part of her being, and at that moment, she wanted him more than she'd ever wanted a man.

Timidly, she lifted her own hands from where they had remained at her sides and began to gently explore the hard, muscular curves of his body, marveling at how strong and virile he felt. Meanwhile, Landon had worked with the buttons at the back of her dress until he had the garment loosened enough to slip his hand inside.

Fire shot through her when he touched her breast again. This time, there was no fabric in his way, nothing to dull the sensations. Gently, he teased the nipple until she was so overpowered by a roiling sensual heat that she could hardly remain standing. The pleasure that came from his touch was slowly drugging her senses.

"Audrey, I want you," he murmured as he pulled away to gaze into her dark, passion-filled eyes. He carefully studied her reaction while he gently tugged at her clothing, eager to hold her beautiful body naked in his arms.

When Audrey's only response was to moan softly, he bent forward to reclaim her lips in another hungry kiss and deftly removed her clothing. He dropped her garments to the floor one at a time, until she stood before him in her camisole and bloomers, leaning heavily against him. He slipped his hand into the silky thin garment and cupped her breast again, heightening the passion that already raged inside her.

Audrey's blood raced furiously, making her feel more vibrant, more alive than she had ever felt before. Her pulses pounded with such astounding force that every part of her body throbbed. Lost in a wild state of delirium, she yielded eagerly, instinctively, to his masterful touch. She was so very lost to her heightened desires that she was only vaguely aware when he had begun to take off his own clothing. It was not until he bent to lift her into his arms that she realized he was naked.

Frightened of the unknown, she did not protest when he headed for her bedroom, nor did she try to stop him when he gently laid her on the bed and slowly pulled the tiny silken sashes that held her camisole in place. By the time he had removed the last of her garments, her desire had risen to consume every inch of her.

When he then lay down beside her and pulled her body against his, she ached with a need to somehow be closer to him. She pressed her body harder against his while his mouth lowered to claim hers yet again.

Aroused to the point of madness, she closed her eyes and moaned softly while Landon's hands continued to work their magic, first on one breast, then the other. Though somewhere in the very back regions of her mind, she knew this was wrong, that this was exactly what she had wanted to avoid, she was lost to the bittersweet torment of his touch.

When Landon broke away from their kiss, his breaths came in deep, halting gasps. Gazing down at her beautiful body, he could not resist sampling the ample feast before him. Slowly, masterfully, he made a nipping, teasing trail down the ivory slope of her neck, then across the tempting curve of her collarbone, making his way to her breast. He teased the straining peak lightly with the tip of his tongue before closing his mouth around it and savoring the feel and taste of it.

Audrey cried out softly with both pleasure and alarm. With every stroke of his skillful hand and with each caress of his hungry tongue, her need to be fulfilled rose higher. She tossed her head restlessly on the pillow, wondering when he would bring an end to this burning torment, when suddenly he rose above her, then slowly lowered himself and entered her. Carefully, he eased through the barrier that proved he was her first, then with smooth, lithe movements, Landon brought their wildest longings, their deepest needs, to the ultimate height. When release finally came for Audrey, it was so wondrous, so deeply shattering, that she gasped aloud the love she suddenly felt for Landon.

Only a moment later, the same shuddering release came for Landon, leaving him gasping for breath. When he collapsed beside her, he was so overcome by his love for Audrey that he wrapped his arms around her and held her close, wanting to stay like that forever. But then, suddenly, she pulled away from him and asked him to leave.

"What's wrong?" he asked, confused by this sudden change in her emotions.

"That should never have happened," she said, turning away from him so he could not see how angry she was with herself—angry and disappointed that she had not had enough restraint to stop it from happening. "And I can assure you it will never happen again." After all, she had her future to think about, and being Landon Steed's mistress was not at all a part of her plans.

When Landon let himself out he was deeply hurt, but he was not about to give up. Not after finding out exactly how much he really did love her.

It was nearly three in the morning when Seth entered his bedroom. After having spent almost an hour trying yet again to explain to Marshall why Rachel had not wanted to go home right away, all he had on his mind was sleep. The last thing he expected was to find Preston Windthorst sitting on the side of his bed waiting for him.

"What are you doing here? I thought you left," he said as he tugged off his coat and tossed it aside.

"I'm waiting for you, obviously," Preston told him.

Slowly, he pushed himself off the bed, then crossed the room to stand only a few feet away from Seth, his feet apart and his legs braced. "I wanted to have a word with you before you went to sleep."

"I said all I got to say while we were downstairs," Seth told Preston, and moved to step around him, unwilling to listen to any more of his accusing remarks.

"Don't you walk away from me," Preston retorted. Angrily, he reached out to grab Seth by the arm. "I still have a few things I want to say to you. Things I think are better said in private."

Seth jerked his arm free and spun about to face him. His brow lowered into a menacing glower. "And just what is it you have to say to me that couldn't wait until morning?"

Preston's eyes glittered with uncontained fury, but his voice came out remarkably controlled. "First of all, I wanted to tell you to stay away from Rachel."

"Stay away from her?" One eyebrow rose curiously.

"Don't think I haven't noticed the pathetic way you look at her, like some poor little pup eager for even a scrap of her attention."

"I have no idea what you are talking about," Seth responded with a firm shake of his head, not willing to believe he'd been so obvious.

"The hell you don't," Preston spouted, raising his voice in anger, yet still somehow managing to keep it down to not much more than a harsh whisper. "I've kept my eyes open and I've seen the way you go sniffing after her like some ill-bred mongrel in heat. I want it stopped."

"I think you're imagining things. Either that, or you've had far too much to drink and it's affected your senses."

"The hell I have. And I suppose next you will try to convince me that I have also imagined the way she looks back at you? Tell me, are you by any chance behind all these headaches she's suddenly been suffering from? Are you why she's suddenly so disinterested in seeing me?

258

Because if you are, and I find out that you are, you'll go down so hard and so fast you won't know what hit you."

"You'd resort to physical violence?" Seth asked, finding that hard to believe. Preston did not seem the type to pit raw strength against raw strength.

"I wouldn't have to," he muttered. His eyes narrowed with intent. "There are easier and far more lasting ways to bring you down. Therefore, I think it would be in your best interest to stay as far away from Rachel as you possibly can, so she can finally come back to her senses."

Though Seth knew Preston had spoken the truth—that he could indeed bring him crashing down without as much as raising a hand—he was too angry to care. Curling his lips against gritted teeth, he leaned toward Preston, hoping to intimidate him with his sheer size. "I wasn't aware she'd ever left her senses."

"Don't press me," he warned, straightening his shoulders in an effort to better confront Seth's enormous height.

"And don't you threaten me," Seth told him, also straightening, to show him that there was no contest when it came to sheer brawn.

"Just stay away from her and I won't have to," Preston responded, thrusting his chin out bravely, though for the first time he seemed concerned with the fact they were very much alone. He glanced toward the partially opened door, as if gauging the best possible route for an escape should it suddenly prove necessary. "Besides, you aren't even the sort of man a woman like Rachel needs."

Aware he had the advantage, at least for now, Seth took an intimidating step forward, expanding his chest to full width for added effect. "At least I am a man. Maybe that's why she's so attracted to me."

"She may be temporarily infatuated by your size and possibly by your ruggedness, but believe me, that sort of thing doesn't last very long."

"Doesn't it?" Seth asked calmly, though he had no idea what this word *infatuated* meant, nor did he like the sound of it.

"No, it doesn't. And if Marshall ever found out that you've been trying to seduce his daughter behind his back, he'd have your head. He's already angry enough because your sister is doing all she can to ruin Landon's life. If he found out that you were out to ruin Rachel's life, too, he'd destroy you both. He'd see to it that neither one of you was ever able to set foot in New York again."

"I can't say I'm all that fond of New York, anyway," Seth shot back, not about to let him strike a chord. "Too much *filth* in the streets." He let Preston know his meaning by glancing at him with an expression filled with disgust.

"Just make sure you don't become a part of the filth that fills our streets," Preston said in a parting shot. "Because if you don't leave Rachel alone, that's where you'll end up—groveling with the rest of the filth."

Seth's massive hands curled into fists, but before he could make use of them, Preston turned and walked out of the room, leaving Seth so angry and confused he couldn't sleep.

Audrey smoothed her hair with the palm of her hand, then cast a last critical look at her mint-green summer dress before she slipped her bonnet into place and headed for the door.

After Landon had left, she'd finally managed to push aside the beckoning images of their lovemaking and the deep shame she had felt when she realized how easily she had given in to her own passion. Though she had made a foolish mistake—one she would undoubtedly regret for the rest of her life—she had managed to drag her thoughts away and focus them on what she had learned during the Cotillion. She had spent several predawn hours sorting through the many different investment ideas she'd discussed that evening with several of Wall Street's most successful investors. As a result, Audrey was able to temporarily forget her shame over what she had allowed to happen between Landon and her, and she was now very eager to speak with her broker about the investments that had interested her the most.

As she reached for the knob, there came a sharp knock from outside that at first startled and frightened her. Thinking Landon had dropped by for an early morning visit, she hesitated to open the door. After last night, she was not ready to face him. Finally, she gathered her courage and swung the door wide, calling out a pleasant greeting, but was surprised when instead of Landon's smiling face she was confronted with Olivia's dark scowl.

"What do you want?" Audrey asked. Her stomach clenched with intense apprehension while she waited for an answer.

"We need to talk." Olivia spoke sharply before she abruptly pushed her way through the door. Once inside, she glimpsed at the surroundings with obvious disdain, then headed toward the front parlor.

Audrey was left with no choice but to follow. "What do you want to talk to me about?"

"Landon, of course. What else could we possibly have in common?" Her gaze swept the room with cold disinterest. "I'm here to make you an offer."

"You're what?" Audrey asked, unaware she had anything worth offering, and even if she did, what it could possibly have to do with Landon.

"I said, I'm here to make you an offer," Olivia repeated, then turned to face Audrey squarely. "I understand you have quite an appetite for money. And, as it so happens, I have more than one person could ever possibly spend."

Audrey did not say anything. She merely narrowed her eyes and waited for Olivia to continue.

"I also understand from very reliable sources that the only real reason you've been leading Landon on the way you have is because you are hoping to get your hands on some of his money. I want that stopped immediately, because as long as you keep trying to lure him away like you do, I don't get to see as much of him."

Audrey felt a sharp ache. She didn't think Landon was seeing Olivia anymore. Though she'd had no real reason to believe otherwise, she'd assumed he was spending what little spare time he had visiting her. And judging from the way he'd talked about Olivia last night, she'd assumed he had completely washed his hands of her. But obviously, that was not the case.

"Therefore," Olivia continued in a very businesslike manner, not allowing Audrey to dwell on any thought for very long, "I'm willing to pay you to leave him alone."

Audrey's eyebrows rose with interest. "And just how much do you think Landon is worth?"

"I'll pay you five hundred thousand dollars to leave the city for good. Of course, I'd have to insist that you not tell Landon why you suddenly decided to go, nor would I want you to mention to him anything about your eventual destination. All you can tell him—if you do decide to tell him anything at all—is that you will not be returning and that you do not want him to try and find you."

Audrey could tell by the tone in Olivia's voice and by the way the woman's green eyes bore into her that she was deadly serious. "Five hundred thousand?" Audrey couldn't imagine having so much money.

"More if you need it," Olivia responded. "I'd be willing to pay as high as six hundred thousand if you were to be gone by Monday morning."

In two days? That was asking the impossible. But, then, she didn't plan to accept her ridiculous offer, anyway. She studied the determination in Olivia's strong features for a moment before asking, "And what if I say no?"

"Why would you?" Olivia glanced around again at her surroundings, as if finding the room repugnant.

"Well, for one thing, I happen to enjoy Landon's company," she said, amazed at the truth in those words. She did enjoy Landon's company—tremendously. Even after last night's episode, and despite her earlier fear that she might not be able to face him, she truly did want to see him again. Not only was he handsome and far more charming than any man she'd ever known, but he treated her with respect—something she'd yearned for all her life. He might not always agree with her opinions, but he'd accepted the fact that she had them, and he allowed her to express her views openly—no matter how they differed from his.

As odd as it seemed, he was always interested in hearing what she had to say about things—even in matters usually considered too complex for women to grasp. Whenever they went out together, or even while just sitting in her parlor sipping a chilled lemonade, they found plenty of time to talk. Often, they discussed topics as complicated as the downturn in world economics and as controversial as national politics, and even though they didn't always agree, each listened to what the other had to say. As hard as it was for Audrey to believe, Landon treated her as an equal. That was something she refused to give up.

Olivia shook her head with annoyance, ready to get on with negotiations. "You seem to be a fairly intelligent woman. Surely you can see the advantages I'm offering you. Not only will you be assured instant wealth, but you can turn right around and focus your attentions on some other wealthy gentleman; just do it in some other city."

"But what if I say no?" Audrey persisted, curious to find out how far Olivia was willing to go with such foolishness.

Olivia's green eyes narrowed into angry slits. "Then I'd be forced to take a different sort of approach to the problem."

Audrey felt her resentment flare, aware she was about to be threatened. "Such as?"

"Such as making your life as miserable as it deserves to be," Olivia answered, smiling sweetly. "Besides raking your name through the mud until everyone who is anyone knows exactly what sort of manipulative little tramp you really are, I could and I would proceed to ruin you financially. And I'd ruin Landon, too. I'm not sure if you are aware of it, but my family has far more money than Landon's, and therefore we have more power and better connections, which I'm proud to say allow us to do whatever we please. Power and connections I would gladly use against you both."

Audrey ignored the painful knot of dread twisting in the pit of her stomach as she shot Olivia a venomous glare. "Your power and your connections don't frighten me," she lied. "And your money doesn't interest me. Nor do your threats. The only thing that interests me at the moment is getting you out of my house." She then pointed in the direction of her front door. "I will not tolerate such childish threats in my own home. Get out!"

"That will be my pleasure," Olivia said with a haughty toss of her perfectly shaped black curls while she again surveyed the room with disgust. "Besides, I think you need some time alone to better consider the sort of future you want to have. The choices are simple. You can either become over half a million dollars richer, or be forever poor. The offer stands as made. The decision, my dear, is entirely yours. Don't decide foolishly." Then, brushing lightly at her silk skirts with her gloved hands, as if worried something from the room might have contaminated the fine fabric, she added, "When you've come to your senses, let me know. I'll have a bank draft waiting for you."

"Don't hold your breath," Audrey muttered, watching with open disgust while Olivia swept gracefully from the room. Then, when she heard her dainty footsteps pass through the front door, she called out in a voice loud enough to be heard outside, "No, on second thought, *do* hold your breath. In fact, hold it until you burst!"

She then went to the window and watched with seething anger while a liveried driver helped her unwanted visitor into an elaborately designed European carriage.

Though infuriated beyond belief, Audrey was none-theless impressed that meek little Olivia Arlington, who hadn't had the courage to speak to either of them at the hotel the night before, had suddenly shown such unexpected bravado.

While she paced restlessly about the room, trying to decide if there was any way to get even with Olivia for all the cruel things she'd said about her, Audrey struck upon the most obvious answer. Despite the sudden, frighten-ing turn their relationship had taken the night before, she would find more time to be with Landon, encouraging him to take her places where Olivia would be certain to see them together. Though it might not have crossed Landon's mind to try to make Olivia jealous by taking Audrey to prominent places such as the theater or perhaps even the opera, it was definitely crossing Audrey's mind. How wondrously satisfying it would be to happen upon Olivia and her friends while casually hang-ing onto Landon's arm in some important public place.

Determined as ever to cower to no one, especially not to someone who'd tried to bend her with money, Audrey decided to fight back the only way she knew how, and that was with everything she had.

Eager to meet the challenge, she tried to figure out where she should have Landon take her first, then decided on Booth's Theatre—where she'd wear the grandest theater gown ever to grace its elaborate halls. Before she was through, she'd prove to everyone that she was every bit as good as Olivia Arlington, if not better.

Without stopping to consider that she was about to use Landon in much the same manner she'd accused him of using her earlier, she quickly decided to put off the early morning visit with her broker and headed straight for Nadine's Dress Shop instead. It was time to expand her wardrobe considerably. Before she was through, she'd have Landon eating out of her hand and Olivia Arlington wishing she'd never even heard her name.

265

chapter seventeen

Since it would be virtually impossible to project the image she wanted to project—that of a lady truly worthy of Landon's attention—without a proper lady's maid doting over her while she shopped or while she went about her daily business in the city, Audrey set out immediately to hire both a lady's maid and a house-keeper.

If she wanted everyone to continue thinking of her in the proper light, then she'd have to do whatever it took to meet their standards, and having rough, work-worn hands did not fit the mold. Therefore, she would have to stop doing all her own work, both inside the house and outside in the yard. She would have to start letting someone else do that sort of thing for her. Though she had no idea what she would do then to help pass the time of day, she realized major adjustments had to be made in her life-style if she wanted to impress the right people. And, suddenly, impressing the right people had become even more important than ever.

By the end of the week following the Summer Cotillion, Audrey had the first two of her elegant new gowns, which she was assured were the latest of European fashion, and she had Roberta Givens to help her into them. Roberta was not much older than Audrey, but she came with all the appropriate references. She'd been a lady's maid to a real countess for three years and, before that, a laundress for Alvin Z. Stewart, an extremely influential businessman who lived only a few blocks from Marshall Steed.

Though Roberta was not yet twenty-nine, she came across as very knowledgeable in what was and was not expected of a lady's maid, and had taken over Audrey's personal care with a flourish.

And since a lady's maid, Audrey soon discovered, was not expected to straighten more than the lady's private bedchamber or her bathing room, Audrey was quick to employ Leslie Feldman, a housekeeper who also came with several letters of recommendation and gave the clear impression that although she was rail thin in stature and pale as a ghost, there was nothing she couldn't or wouldn't do.

The two women took to arguing with each other immediately about whose duty it should be to do what, yet together they did whatever was required of them and did it without complaining directly to Audrey.

Between the two combative domestics and Walter Zimmerman, the gardner she had hired to landscape and care for her yard two days out of each week, there was nothing left for Audrey to do but concentrate on her investments—which she knew she'd better do to the best of her ability if she planned to pay for her elaborate new life-style.

That Saturday, when Landon came by to take her to the theater as planned, he was given his first dose of the new Audrey. Though he loved her latest gown and especially appreciated the low-cut bodice that hugged her sumptuous curves, he was not too fond of the idea of having Roberta along just to keep up with her summer cloak and her fan. Because, unlike his driver, who was expected to stay with the carriage, he knew Roberta would remain at Audrey's beck and call throughout the evening until she'd made a blamed nuisance of herself, something all lady's maids seemed to do.

While he escorted Audrey to the carriage, knowing that Roberta followed only a few steps behind, he wondered about her newly adopted life-style. Although he'd expected there to be changes in her life as her different investments took hold, allowing her to afford better, he hadn't expected there to be that much change this soon.

He was flabbergasted by how truly regal she looked with her diamond-studded hair piled high in a fashionable array of brown curls and wearing a new peach-colored silk gown that flowed gracefully over her body in soft, shimmering swirls. He felt it a pity she had not been born to royalty, for tonight she looked so extraordinarily beautiful that she could easily put any real princess to shame.

Audrey had noticed the way Landon kept staring at her, as if he could not believe what he saw, and that pleased her very much. She just hoped that everyone received the changes she'd made with as much open-mouthed enthusiasm. She wanted talk of her evening with Landon to travel through all the right circles, and she wanted it to travel quickly. It would especially delight her if one of the society magazines decided to mention something of their evening together. Then the whole world would know about her accomplishments thus far.

What annoyed her enormously was knowing that, by now, Olivia had no doubt reached the wrong conclusion, thinking her brief visit early that past Saturday had done exactly what it was supposed to. By now, Olivia probably believed she'd frightened Audrey into silent submission with her angry threats of retaliation. After all, what else should Olivia think when she and Landon had not been seen out anywhere in public since?

But all that was soon to change.

Smiling contentedly, Audrey settled into the carriage. She could hardly wait for the news of their evening together to reach Olivia's ears. It had taken all the self-restraint she had to wait until her new gowns were ready,

268

so their next appearance in public could have the very best possible effect.

Yet now that she sat at his side, dressed once again in the finest silk and with her very own lady's maid seated across from her, eagerly anticipating her every move, she felt the wait would prove worth it. What would make their evening absolutely perfect would be for Olivia to see them herself, though Audrey knew that would be asking Fate for too much. Still she hoped. Because tonight she was making her statement to Olivia and to the rest of the world. Whenever faced with angry, hate-filled threats, she would fight back in every way she could.

Audrey Stoane would cower to no one. She never had, not even in the worst of times; and she had no intention of doing so now.

News of their evening together did indeed travel quickly. By Sunday noon, not only had Olivia heard of it, but Marshall had, too. That same afternoon, he confronted Landon again. Angrily, he demanded that his son get his priorities straight. He wanted Landon to promise to stop seeing that worthless, conniving Audrey Stoane and to go immediately to Olivia's side, take her by the hand, and beg for her forgiveness. But, as had happened the last time Marshall had made such suggestions, Landon refused even to listen to his reasoning and had walked out during the middle of yet another heated discussion.

Angered that his son could be so blind, Marshall decided to take an entirely different approach to the problem. That afternoon, while his son was busy overseeing the repairs to his carriage, which had broken an axle shortly after he'd left Audrey's house in the early hours of the morning, Marshall paid Audrey a little visit of his own.

Thinking along the same lines as Olivia had, he'd entered her house shortly after noon with every expectation of buying her off. Foreseeing no problems, he waited until the two of them were seated comfortably in the front parlor before casually pitching out his offer.

"All you have to do," he explained briefly, "is give Landon a quick brush-off, and I'll see to it that two hundred thousand dollars are immediately transferred to your personal account, to do with as you please. Then, for as long as you continue to avoid his company, I'll give you five thousand more each month. And I'll keep adding that monthly five thousand to your account for at least three years . . . more if Landon has yet to marry."

Audrey had expected something like that when she'd first opened her door and found him standing so cocksure of himself on her doorstep. Her first instinct had been to close the door politely in his face, and she'd come very close to doing just that; but in the end, curiosity had taken over and she'd invited him inside to hear him out. She was eager to find out what he thought might be a fair price for his son.

"I guess you don't place quite the same value on the situation as Olivia does," Audrey said, smiling while she lifted her orangeade to her lips and quietly sipped the cool liquid. She noticed that Marshall's orangeade had gone untouched, indicating that he'd never intended for this to be a social call.

"You've spoken with Olivia?" he asked, surprised. He quickly leaned forward in his chair, clearly interested that the two had exchanged words. "When was this?"

"She came by just last weekend to present a similar proposal," Audrey admitted, showing neither pleasure nor displeasure while she sipped again from the tall, frosted glass. "Only real difference between her visit and yours is that she wanted me to move completely out of the city and offered me five hundred thousand to help with that move . . . six hundred thousand if I could have been gone within just two days."

Marshall's eyebrows arched with surprise. "She offered you over half-a-million dollars to leave New York

270

and you refused?"

"Exactly like I intend to refuse you."

"Don't be foolish. Take her money and get out while you still can. Hell, take my money, too. In fact, I'll up my offer to match hers, so you can leave this city with more than a million dollars. Surely, Landon can't be worth that sort of money to you."

Audrey could not believe that Marshall had so easily placed a monetary value on his own son. "I don't have any real need for that sort of money just yet. Besides, if my investments continue to do as well as they have in the past few weeks, I'll eventually have that much money, anyway—and I will have gotten it on my own."

"Don't feed me that garbage. I am aware that in just over a month's time, you have more than tripled the value of your stock investments, but that's because you happened to hit a particularly lucrative stock at just the right moment. You can't always expect to do so well. Besides, I'm not as blind as you seem to think. I can see right through you. It would take years to amass such a fortune, and you have no real desire to wait quite that long to be rich."

"I don't?"

"No. You're hoping to marry a very wealthy man and, by doing so, live the rest of your life in luxury without having to go to all the trouble of earning it yourself. That's why you've been leading Landon on the way you have. But I'm here to point out to you that there are other men . . . men who are even wealthier than Landon and would jump at the chance to marry a beautiful young woman like you. Think about it. You could end up with all the money Olivia and I have offered you and a rich husband, too."

Audrey's spine stiffened as she set her glass aside and stared at him with calm dignity. "You have overstayed your welcome. I really think you should leave now."

"Not until I have an answer from you." He leaned back into the easy chair, laced his hands together, and

271

rested them casually over his middle as if to show that he had no intention of leaving.

"I really don't think you want to hear my answer," she cautioned him. "It will only upset you."

Marshall drew in a long breath, held it for a moment, then slowly released it. "Don't be a fool. You are being offered the chance of a lifetime. A chance to be quite wealthy by most standards. An opportunity that could allow you to buy a house ten times as large as this one and have ten times the servants awaiting your slightest command."

"I prefer to call them domestics," she answered haughtily, for no reason other than to perturb him further. "And I'm quite satisfied with the two that I have."

"In a tiny house like this, you don't need more than two," he nodded agreeably. He looked about the room as if he found the six-room house barely adequate for one person's needs. "But you are not the type of person to stay satisfied with such a simple life. I've seen your type before, and you won't be truly happy until you have a really grand house with at least a dozen serv—domestics waiting on you hand and foot."

"And one day I will have them, but on my own terms and by my own merits."

"Don't try to convince me that you have any real principles, young lady. After all, I happen to know firsthand how you happened to get that start."

Audrey felt a sharp pang of apprehension. She wondered if that meant he'd somehow learned about Landon's involvement, innocent though it was. She hated the thought of her friend being falsely accused of something he had no knowledge of. Her stomach tightened in response.

Marshall could tell by her serious expression that he'd managed to strike some sort of nerve. He continued his verbal assault without hesitation. "You would still be working as my housekeeper, cleaning up after my family

272

and even cleaning up after Rachel's fur-brained cat if you hadn't figured out a way to eavesdrop on my private business meetings and then made very cunning use of what you'd managed to overhear. I just wish I knew where you got that original four thousand, because I have a feeling if I knew that, I'd also know who tried to kidnap me and has since been sending me angry, unsigned letters. You are part of a conspiracy against me, aren't you?"

Audrey's eyes widened at the mention of the correspondence, for she had no idea he'd been receiving such letters. Her first thought was for her brother's safety. Her next thought was for Landon's safety. If Marshall was in danger, then those around him were in danger, too. "What sort of letters?"

Marshall snorted. "Chances are it's the same person who loaned you the money. Someone out to undermine me in any way he can."

"I can assure you that the person who loaned me the money is in no way connected with any threatening letters," she told him, knowing Landon would have nothing to gain by harassing his own father in such a way.

"How'd you know the letters were in any way threatening?" Marshall demanded to know, his murky blue eyes narrowing with distrust.

"Why, you just said—"

"What I said was that they were angry, unsigned letters. I didn't say anything about them being threatening. Just how'd you know that?" he asked. His eyebrows rose high into his forehead when he added, in a low, accusing voice, "Unless possibly *you've* been sending me those letters."

"No, of course I haven't," she insisted.

Marshall's eyes narrowed. "Let's hope not. Because if you are in any way responsible for those horrible letters and I can find a way to prove that you are, I won't have to bother paying you off to get rid of you. I can simply have you arrested instead. I won't have to worry about what you're up to anymore if you're locked securely away in some prison." A smile touched his face, as if he'd struck upon an idea worth pursuing.

Aware she was not the innocent she pretended to be, having orchestrated the fake kidnapping the way she had, Audrey felt her body grow icy cold with deep pricklings of fear. Though it had been nearly seven weeks since that incident and the two men she'd hired hadn't been seen in New York by either her or the police since then, Audrey still worried that they might return, make a few foolish comments, and she would eventually be found out. It especially worried her now that she'd discovered just how powerful a man Marshall Steed really was. "But I haven't written you any letters."

"Well, somebody has," he pointed out with a contemplative nod. The tiny streaks of silver in his otherwise brown hair caught the light from the window when he tilted his head to one side and looked at Audrey, as if truly seeing her for the first time. "And until I find out differently, I plan to keep you high on the list of prime suspects. I may even have you investigated; whatever it takes to prove you are indeed the one harassing me through these anonymous letters. That is, unless you were to decide to take me and Olivia up on our more-than-generous offers and leave town. Because if that were the case, then I'd probably be less inclined to find you guilty of any crime. I sure wouldn't want to turn right around and have you brought back here just to stand trial, not after having worked so hard to get rid of you. So maybe you'd like to reconsider taking us up on our offers."

Audrey's spine stiffened at his implication. It sounded like blackmail: Either leave town or face being falsely accused of someone else's crime. "I did not write those letters. And I see no reason why I should have to sit here in my own home and listen to you try and intimidate me like this. I have politely suggested that you leave, but since you have chosen to completely ignore such a

274

suggestion, I will now *demand* that you get out of my house."

"Or you'll what?" he challenged, clearly believing she had no way to reinforce such demands.

"Well, sir," she drawled, sounding every bit the southern lady, "for starters, I'll tell that handsome young son of yours all about your little visit here. I'm sure he'd find it most interesting to learn how you decided to take it upon yourself to go behind his back like you have in a very real effort to buy me off. And while I have his attention, I might even mention Olivia's unfriendly little visit. I really do think he would find it most disturbing to learn that she, like you, has taken it upon herself to manage his life for him."

She batted her eyelashes in an overly sweet, coquettish manner, hoping to infuriate him more. "And just think how pleased he will then be to know that I had a chance to leave the city with over a million dollars in cash but chose to throw it all away just so I could stay and be with him. By the time I got through with all I'd have to tell him, your son would be so angry with you and with Olivia that he'd probably refuse to ever speak with either of you again."

Marshall's eyes glittered with dark fury. "Don't threaten me."

"Don't give me reason to," she responded quickly, dropping the demure act, her steely gaze just as determined as his.

Marshall studied her with quiet, seething anger. Blue veins protruded from his neck while he worked his jaw muscles in and out. Then, without offering another argument, he stood and nodded briskly, snatching his hat up off the table where he'd laid it when he first entered. "Since you have no butler, I suppose it'll be up to me to see myself out."

Aware that had been a parting shot, Audrey leaned casually back in her chair and responded with a droll wave of her hand, "I realize it will be a hardship for you,

275

but do try not to get lost."

Then, as if to dismiss him entirely, she turned her shoulder to him, reached with little enthusiasm for her drink, and took another slow, leisurely sip. Audrey pretended not to notice when he jerked his rumpled hat down over his head and stalked out of the room. But she couldn't help but flinch when he slammed the front door with such angry force that all the pictures in the house rattled against the walls.

More determined than ever to prove to everyone that she was just as worthy of Landon's attention as anyone else, and having had her small house insulted twice, Audrey began searching for a larger one the next day. She wanted to find a home that was not only larger, but was located in a far more prominent neighborhood. Though the smarter choice at the moment might have been to leave the money she'd need for the new house invested in the shipping company, where it could continue to grow at its present high rate, she viewed a larger, more prestigious house as an investment of a different kind, one that might pay off in gains other than financial. One that would afford her the respect of everyone—even Marshall, to some degree.

By the end of that same week, she'd located the perfect house. It was a two-story brownstone only a half block off Fifth Avenue, with a yard large enough that it could be considered *grounds*. Because she liked Walter Zimmerman's work and wanted to keep him on, Audrey quickly upgraded his working title from that of being her gardener to that of being her groundskeeper, and she asked that he come at least three times a week instead of two, to keep her gardens in immaculate repair.

Unlike her previous move from the Steeds' house, which she'd been able to accomplish in less than an hour, when the time came to pack up everything and move it to her new house, Audrey hired professional movers, knowing that was what the wealthy always did.

In just under two days, she was completely moved out of the old house and had been comfortably installed in her elegant new home. And because the new house was almost three times as large as the last house, she spent another two days selecting new furniture to help fill the vacant rooms, then immediately hired another house-keeper, Hilari McCurdy. She even started shopping around for a horse and carriage, though it would mean having to hire a driver.

Her investment in the new, larger house began to show its benefits right away, because as early as that following week, several ladies from the neighborhood stopped by to introduce themselves and visit with her. She also received an invitation to tea with Mrs. Abcott, the wife of the department store magnate. Yet, even so, most of her neighbors, male as well as female, continued to keep a cautious distance from her, as if not quite certain what to think of a woman who had come upon such wealth all on her own.

Landon was pleased with her new house, not because it was so large, but because it was much closer to his own neighborhood and that made it more convenient for him to stop by for short visits during the middle of the week, when time was not so readily available. Weekends were no longer enough to sustain him, and even when he had managed to stop by for a few brief visits during the week, it left him wanting to see her even more.

Soon, it became all too apparent that he had fallen deeply in love with Audrey. And there was nothing he could do to stop himself. There was nothing he *wanted* to do to stop it. He liked feeling the way he did about her. Audrey was everything he had ever wanted in a woman: beauty, grace, and intelligence. If only there were a way to make her care as much for him as he cared for her, then his happiness would be complete.

But he'd already tried everything he knew to break the cold, steellike barriers she'd so carefully thrown up around her heart, but nothing seemed to work. For two months now he'd wined her and dined her, and had also given her several stock tips that had resulted in terrific gains on the market. Yet no matter what he did to win her heart, she remained strangely aloof.

He could not understand the contradictions in her. She allowed him to call on her as often as he liked and even allowed him to hold her hand in public, which normally was considered an admission of strong personal interest; yet whenever he kissed her, she responded only to a certain point, then, as if she'd suddenly remembered her vow never to allow him to become intimate with her again, she quickly pulled away and asked him to leave. It was as if she were afraid of him, afraid because of what had happened that one night when they'd allowed their emotions to take control of them.

Frustrated but unwilling to give up his quest to win her heart, Landon appeared at her door at every given opportunity. Gossip that often included how frequently his carriage appeared outside her house spread through the neighborhood like wildfire, causing all manner of speculation about their unusual relationship. Yet thus far, Audrey had not seemed too terribly annoyed by the gossip and allowed him to continue to call on her whenever he wanted. Which was something he did more and more, until at times he wondered if he spent more time at her house than at his own. Some days, all he could think about was visiting Audrey, seeing her beautiful face, hearing her delightful laughter.

"I finished my last meeting a little early," Landon said, as if it were necessary for him to explain his not-so-uncommon early arrival. While she held the door open for him and he quietly stepped inside, he purposely failed to mention that the only reason his meeting was over early was because he'd called an unexpected halt to the proceedings. His broker had not been very pleased with his sudden decision to leave, because they still had had several reports to go over together.

"I'm glad," Audrey responded cheerfully, having come to expect it.

While Landon waited for her to close the door, he glanced curiously at the bright smile stretched happily across her face. Something was up. He studied her expression closely while he finished his well-rehearsed explanation for having called on her that early. "And rather than go back home and wait around for twenty minutes or so, I thought I'd come on over and wait here while you finished getting dressed."

"But I'm already dressed," she commented, gesturing to her lovely lemon silk gown with a wide sweep of her hand. Her eyes sparkled with delight.

Landon could not help but smile, too, while he continued to study the sheer joy bursting from her face. "What's gotten into you? You look like the proverbial cat who ate the canary."

"I just got back from a visit with my broker barely an hour ago," she explained excitedly.

"And?"

"And he told me that those two shipping companies you suggested I invest in have both more than doubled in value—and in barely a week. It's uncanny the way you seem to know which stocks are about to take off and which are ready to take the plunge."

"I do my homework," he admitted, pleased that she had taken his advice and invested in the companies.

"That you do," she agreed happily, then tossed her arms around him in an exuberant embrace. "I can't believe how lucky I am to have you as a friend."

Not one to ignore such a grand opportunity, Landon rested his hands at her waist and held her near. Gazing down into her upturned face, he responded to her warm praise in the only manner he saw fit. He agreed with her wholeheartedly. "And I am just as lucky to have you for my friend."

"I'm serious," she protested, unable to believe he could honestly think himself lucky for such an insignificant thing, especially when she had done nothing for him except cause unnecessary gossip. "Landon, because of you, many of my lifelong dreams are finally coming true."

Landon did not like the uneasy feeling that settled over him. A dull ache centered in the pit of his stomach. He had a strong hunch that if he were to ask her straight out about those lifelong dreams of hers, he'd discover they had nothing at all to do with having finally found the right man or with falling in love. Suddenly, his father's warnings came back to haunt him. Was Audrey leading him on *just* for the financial advice he could give her? Was her only goal in life to be wealthy? Would nothing else make her happy?

He studied her bright, eager expression, trying to read her deepest thoughts. Though he dreaded the answer, he had to ask the question. "Oh? And what lifelong dreams might those be?"

"To be rich," she answered honestly, unaware that was the very answer Landon had hoped not to hear. "I've always wanted to live in a grand house like this, wear nothing but the latest in ladies' fashions, and eat only the freshest and most expensive foods—food that someone *else* had prepared for *me*. I realize you don't know much about my past. That's because I hate to talk about it. I hate to even think about it. My family was poor—very poor." She just could not bring herself to say "dirt poor." "We were so poor that even the local slaves looked down on us. And after my parents died, Seth and I many times had to beg in the streets just to get enough food to stay alive. But no more."

Audrey's eyes lit with a dark passion Landon had never seen before.

"Now, thanks to your help and my determination, I am wealthy enough to afford all these luxuries, and getting wealthier by the day." She threw back her head and laughed, knowing how her latest stock market gains were going to drive Marshall crazy. "At this moment, I haven't

280

a care in the world. And I have you to thank for it."

Her exuberance became too much for her. Overwhelmed by the unbridled emotions bursting inside of her like tiny bubbles rising to the surface, she leaned forward and kissed him. And not just a friendly little peck on the cheek like she might give her brother. Instead, she wrapped her arms firmly around his neck and pressed her mouth hard against his with all the unrestrained passion she possessed.

Taken aback, Landon's eyes widened until they looked as though they might pop. His first inclination had been to try and catch his hat before it hit the floor, but he decided to let it go. He could look for it later. He was not about to let this unexpected opportunity pass him by. Eagerly, he fastened his arms around her and drew her body hard against his.

Audrey was too full of joy to worry about right and wrong at the moment, or about the fact that her legs suddenly felt like melted rubber and her pulses pounded through her body at an alarming rate. Nor did she worry about any complications falling in love with Landon might cause for her. For once, the future seemed of little significance. With her most glorious dreams finally coming true, all she wanted to do was share the extreme pleasure she felt at that moment and not worry about the painful heartaches that might lie ahead.

She offered no resistance at all when his tongue coaxed her lips apart. Instead, she received him willingly. Her ecstatic feelings of joy grew tenfold when he then entered her mouth with the tip of his tongue and gently teased the sensitive inner contours. His hands moved to the small of her back and pressed her closer.

Too consumed with happiness to think of anything else, she gave herself up to the overwhelming feeling of fulfillment that his sudden kiss had brought her. Instead of pulling away, which she otherwise would have done before now, she eagerly accepted his ardent embrace, aware of the intimate way their bodies touched and just

281

as aware of where the sensations building rapidly inside of her could lead.

Too happy to care what the consequences might be, Audrey pressed closer. Her skin tingled with growing awareness while her senses floundered endlessly in a warm, churning sea of emotion.

Overwhelmed by her eager response, Landon's arms tightened their hold around her, molding her firmly to him. He willed himself to go slow. He'd longed for this moment for far too long and didn't want to do anything that might frighten her. But his hands refused to accept any such cautionary demands and roamed hungrily over the soft curves of her body, exploring all the places he'd yearned to touch, rediscovering every intimate detail.

To his bewilderment, she still did not pull away. Instead, she responded in kind, by letting her palms roam freely over the rounded muscles of his shoulders and along the firm planes of his back and hips. A low, guttural growl welled deep in his throat when he realized she was just as eager as he was.

Eagerly, he continued to explore the soft curves of her hips and waist, then the delicate bones of her ribcage, moving eagerly higher until he cupped her breast with his hand. Even through the silky layers of fabric, he felt her nipple respond instantly to his touch and it made him long to remove every stitch of clothing from her body, made him long to see with his eye the wondrous treasure his hand had found.

Desire raged through him. At last, she had let down her barriers again. She was willing, even eager, to share her passion with him, but something was wrong.

Although he wanted to make love to Audrey again, more than he'd ever wanted to make love to any woman, he also sensed that the timing was all wrong. Though he wanted to believe that she was responding to his every touch for all the right reasons, the thought that she might not be nagged at him. He knew there was a very real possibility she was responding more to the fact that the latest stock tip he'd given her had paid off royally than to any true feelings she had developed for him. If that was the case, making love to her right now would be a mistake. He needed to be sure why she wanted him so she would not regret what they'd done after it was over, like last time, because if that happened, he knew this time he might lose her forever.

Still, he hesitated pulling away.

It was that hesitation that brought Audrey to her senses at last. Aware of how very close she had come to allowing her excitement to override her good sense, she jerked back, shocked by the overwhelming power of her own basic desire. Emotions she'd promised never to fall victim to again continued to rage through her body, making her feel all weak and helpless inside.

When she glanced up into his eyes then, Landon's heart went out to her in a strong rush of tenderness. It hurt to see such a painful look of confusion on her face. But then his heart leaped with sudden joy when he realized that meant she *had* felt something. Something more than mere passion. Something so powerful, so all-consuming, that it had frightened as well as confused her. It was then he felt certain that she was as much in love with him as he was with her. She just didn't know it yet.

What an amazing revelation that was.

He wondered how long it would be before she realized the feelings she had for him. A smile spread slowly across his face when he thought forward to the day she would realize her emotions and openly declare her love for him, for he was now certain it was only a matter of time.

Next, he wondered what, if anything, he could do to hurry along her admission of love. There was something holding her back, something blinding her to her own true feelings, but what?

chapter eighteen

That night, Audrey was far too upset with herself to sleep. The memory of the passionate kiss she'd so wantonly bestowed on Landon came back to haunt her again and again. She still could not believe she had allowed herself to become that carried away by her own momentary excitement and wondered what Landon thought of her now.

After having initiated such a shamefully immoral kiss, during which she'd allowed him certain liberties she'd sworn she would never again allow him, he had become oddly silent. Undoubtedly, he'd started having second thoughts about her. What was worse, he'd stayed like that for the rest of the evening.

All through dinner, she'd caught him looking across at her with the strangest expression, as if he suddenly saw her in a whole new light. Though she'd wondered what sort of thoughts were traveling through his mind, at the same time, she was glad not to know, certain she never could have borne the humiliation.

Turning over onto her back to stare hopelessly into the dark shadows over her bed, she moaned aloud her misery. Why had he stayed that quiet? After having been so adamant about curtailing their relationship, had her bold behavior shocked him so deeply that he could no longer think of anything to say? Did it shock him to the point he would never be able to open up to her and enjoy her company again?

Probably. It had certainly shocked her. Shocked her to the point that she'd found it impossible to meet his gaze after that. And now, while she lay in bed thinking about what a terribly brazen thing she'd done, especially when coupled with the fact that she had once before allowed her emotions to run free, she wondered if she would ever be able to look him directly in the eye again.

Shame flooded her when she realized what his opinion of her must be now, for she had initiated that kiss and everything that had followed. He was the one who had brought an end to their moment of passion, probably because she was no longer the woman he thought her to be. Tears sprang to her eyes, blurring the shadows overhead. After what had happened tonight, she wasn't sure he would ever return. Even if he did, would it be because he still enjoyed her company, or because he expected to make even further progress toward seducing her? Did he now think it was only a matter of time before he took her to bed?

Her heart ached with misery. Just when she'd finally convinced Landon that there was no room in their relationship for that sort of intimacy ever again, she'd done something so blatantly foolish as to throw herself at him like that—and for no explainable reason other than she'd felt driven to thank him in some way for all he'd done for her.

Why couldn't she have simply placed that kiss on his cheek like she'd originally planned? It would have been the proper thing to do. Why had she been compelled to kiss him on the mouth instead? It just didn't make sense. It wasn't like her to be that impulsive. She was more the type to think things through before acting on them.

Now she'd ruined everything. Not only would it be harder to convince him she was not interested in continuing an intimate relationship, but it was going to be harder to convince herself. Because, for one brief moment, when his hand had cupped her breast, causing that unexplainable fire to rage uncontrolled through her veins, she'd longed for him to take the kiss further. She'd wanted him to make love to her again, to know once more what it meant to be a real woman. Shame overwhelmed her again when she felt her blood stir hotly inside her just from the memory of his intimate touch.

To Audrey's relief, when Landon stopped by the following afternoon, he treated her no differently than he had before she'd kissed him. Though she really wasn't sure how she'd expected him to act toward her, he entered her house with his usual heart-stopping smile already in place and asked if she'd like to join him for dinner. He'd managed to hurry through his afternoon appointments so they could have time to dine at their leisure.

All through the evening, she kept waiting for him to make some brash comment about their kiss or about what he hoped to accomplish after they returned to her house. But, to her relief, he seemed interested only in discussing business, especially his latest investment, which had already proved quite profitable after being on the trading floor just half a day.

"You might want to think about getting in on it," he told her while he set his soup bowl aside and cleared space for his dinner. He'd planned to mention it to her the night before, but that unexpected kiss had destroyed his ability to think straight. "It concerns a new kind of passenger ship that will provide more than the usual basic services. It will cater to the passenger's every whim. There will be croquet courts, badminton courts, billiard rooms, gaming rooms, and *two* main dining rooms—both as elegant as any restaurant here in New York. One dining room will even have a stage for entertainment of various kinds and will be large enough to use as a ballroom, too. There are even plans to provide dove hunting for the men and afternoon tea for the ladies. And the cabins will be designed with the utmost of luxury in mind."

He moved his wide hands to emphasize his words. "Every one of the passenger cabins will be larger than what you would find on most ships. That's because these ships will be designed with smaller cargo holds. After all, they don't plan to carry much cargo other than what the passengers carry with them." He paused to think about that. "I guess you could say this ship's real cargo will be the passengers themselves."

"Have you seen the plans for this ship?"

"I have," he admitted with growing excitement, and pressed his hands down on the table in front of him as he leaned forward. "Not only will the cabins be half again as large as most, but they will be furnished with elaborate sitting room suites, compact writing desks that will be built right into the walls, and they will also offer larger-than-usual berths. I know it sounds a bit frivolous, but I think it's an idea whose time has come."

"Sort of like a floating resort," Audrey commented, not really certain people would be willing to pay the money such a trip would undoubtedly cost. To make up for all the wasted space, the ship would have to charge twice the usual rate.

"Exactly like a floating resort. Not only can the passengers look forward to the time they plan to spend abroad, but they can also look forward to the time spent getting there. There will be more to keep the passengers occupied than idle conversation and waiting for their daily meals to be served."

A glimmer of excitement lit Audrey's eyes as her mind quickly explored the possibilities. A ship like that was starting to make sense. "I guess for people who can afford such luxuries, it will become *the* way to travel."

Landon felt a little apprehensive when he noticed the abrupt change in her attitude. Before she had been in such a grim mood that he'd feared she'd never smile again, yet now she was bubbling over with excitement. Clearly, the enchanting smile lingering at her lips had been the direct result of yet another promising investment. A second cold inkling of uncertainty settled over him when she then reached out to cover his hands with her own. Until now, she had avoided touching him. Now, suddenly, she had taken the initiative again. The saddest part was that she didn't even seem aware of it.

"Tell me a little more about this new luxury passenger ship," she said, watching him eagerly.

Heat radiated from where her fingers curled down over his, making it hard for him to think. "The company that is planning to build the ship will be run by a man known to me only as Cunard. Though I know little about the man personally, I do know enough to believe he can pull it off. He's got quite a reputation for his inventive imagination. Something that really interests me is how he plans to build this modern-day luxury ship out of steel instead of wrought iron, which should make the vessel not only sturdier, but much lighter and able to travel much faster. He's even thinking about installing electric engines instead of steam, or maybe a combination of both."

"How long until such a ship is ready to sail?"

"Three, maybe four years. It's still in the planning stages, but they've already started to sell stock in the company."

"And you are sure this will be a good investment?" she asked, eager for his reassurance. She hated the thought of pulling some of her money away from her other investments, which were all doing so well, in order to become a part of this new venture.

"I am. Enough that I invested over six hundred thousand this afternoon." Again, he felt a nagging ache in the pit of his stomach while he watched her eagerly digest everything he had to say. It hurt to know that her bright, hopeful smile had nothing at all to do with him, only with the information he'd just provided.

"Long-term or short?"

"For now, look at it as short-term. But if there are no major setbacks lurking ahead, no contractual delays, I believe it'll be the sort of investment that can and will pay off handsomely for several years. It'll just take close watching, is all."

Audrey was convinced. "I'll go down to Wall Street first thing in the morning and have Rutledge buy as many shares for me as I can afford," she stated happily, but then frowned when she thought about it more. "I wonder which of my present stocks I should give up in order to free the capital I'll need?"

"Sell off a little of each," Landon suggested, wishing now, for some unexplainable reason, that he'd kept his big mouth shut. It was then that he realized he was jealous. Jealous of her deep love for the stock market. Jealous of the fact that the possibility of making another profitable investment could cause her more excitement and more happiness than he personally had ever had. Yet she was in love with him, too. He was certain of it. She was just too blinded by her desire to be rich and powerful to realize it.

"What's that?" Seth asked as he lowered himself into his favorite chair and waited for Audrey to hand him his usual glass of brandy. Though he would have preferred a stout shot of whiskey, Audrey liked for him to drink brandy because it was more popular among the rich, and she still fantasized about the two of them one day fitting in socially with the upper class.

"Brandy," she answered, preparing to get testy if he dared complain, for she had paid over eighteen dollars to get this particular brand. It was supposed to be one of the finest available.

"No, not the drink. What's with the rumpled letter on the table?" He nodded in the direction of what appeared to be a wadded-up piece of very expensive stationery lying beside an opened envelope. "Who was that from?"

Audrey offered a perverse smile, pleased with the knowledge that she'd elicited so much anger from Olivia to cause her to write such a scathing letter. "Oh, that," she answered, as if it were something of little significance. "That's just a letter from someone who doesn't agree with the way I've been spending so much of my time lately."

Seth's eyebrows rose with interest. "But you don't do anything anymore except sit around here reading while giving your housekeepers orders, or sometimes taking a daily stroll over to your broker's. Every now and then you go have a new gown made up to impress Landon, but even that is rare here lately. Who could possibly find fault with any of that?"

"Olivia Arlington," she stated matter-of-factly, trying not to show even a trace of the anger Olivia's unexpected letter had caused.

Seth recognized the name immediately, remembering she'd been one of Landon's former lady friends. "Olivia Arlington? What did she want? To threaten to come over here and scratch your eyes out if you didn't stop seeing so much of Landon?"

"Not exactly. She wasn't quite as obvious in her threats as that."

Seth studied the hard lines around his sister's mouth. "But she did make threats of some kind, didn't she?" It was a statement more than a question.

"There were definite undertones," Audrey admitted. "Mostly, what she wanted was to remind me of a conversation we'd had earlier."

"What conversation? You never told me that you two had had words."

"Because it wasn't that important."

Seth glanced back at the rumpled letter. "I guess she doesn't much care for the idea of the two of you getting married someday. The way I heard tell of it, until you came along, Olivia thought she had Landon all ready to propose to her. I can see why she'd be upset."

"Married?" Audrey sputtered. "What makes you think Landon and I would ever consider getting married?"

"Well, for one thing, he's been spending more and more of his time with you. And, too, I've seen the way you look whenever you talk about him. It's the sort of look that eventually leads to getting married."

"That's nonsense," she insisted. "I couldn't marry Landon even if I wanted to."

"Why not?"

Audrey thought about that for a moment. There was a wide range of answers to that question, but she didn't know which one made the most sense. "If I were to marry Landon—though I really can't believe he'd ever ask me—but if I were to agree to be his wife, everyone would think I tricked him into it. Most people already believe that the only reason I've been spending so much of my time with Landon is because I'm secretly after his money. Marrying him would make it look like they had been right all along." Audrey's expression darkened. She was far too proud to let everyone think she was so manipulative.

"Well, if you aren't hoping for marriage and you're not after any of his money, then what are you after? Why *do* you spend so much of your time with him?"

"About all I'm really after at the moment is his advice. And his friendship. If you must know, Landon treats me nicer than anyone I've ever known—except maybe for you. He always listens to what I have to say about things and respects my opinions, even when he doesn't quite agree with them. Besides, he's not even interested in me romantically."

"But what if he was. What if he did ask you to marry him?" Seth wanted to know, not ready to let the subject drop. He was curious about his sister's relationship with Landon Steed . . . always had been. "What would you do then?"

"I'd have to tell him no," she answered simply, though deep inside, the thought of having to refuse him hurt far

291

more than it should. The ache pinching at her stomach made it feel as if she had suddenly been bound by a tight, cutting rope. "If I married Landon now, not only would his father and everyone else he knows believe that I was marrying him for the life of luxury he could easily provide for me, but eventually Landon himself might start to believe it, too. He'd think I used him as an easy way of getting what I wanted, and I couldn't bear that. No. I have to prove that I can make it on my own first."

Seth studied her suddenly sad expression, wishing he could do something to ease her pain. "But what if you do make it on your own? What if you somehow manage to become filthy rich all by your little lonesome? Then what? Would you then agree to marry him if he asked you?"

Reluctantly, Audrey turned her thoughts to the prospect of what it might be like to be Landon's wife, improbable though that was. She was surprised that her pulse pounded with such deep longing. The thought of one day becoming such a permanent part of Landon's life and at long last being able to explore the feelings she felt for him was intriguing, to say the least. But at the same moment, she knew she was dreaming the impossible. Though she had tried her best, she had never been accepted by his friends. She was too different from them. Her background was too different. Landon would never want to marry such a complete social misfit. His wife should be someone far more acceptable to all his rich friends—a true social flower.

The thought that Olivia fit into that category made her insides ache even worse.

"Well, answer the question," Seth prodded, tired of being ignored. "What would you do if after you did make it rich on your own Landon then asked you to marry him?"

"What a ridiculous question."

"So, give me a ridiculous answer," he told her, not about to let her evade the question entirely. His sister's happiness meant too much to him.

"I don't know what I'd do. And I doubt I'll ever have a chance to find out," she said, trying to convince him of his foolishness. Then she quickly changed the subject before he could come up with any more such ridiculous questions. "It's almost eleven. When do you think Rachel will arrive?"

Seth glanced at the clock. "Hard to say. Earlier, I heard her tell her father she planned to meet her friend Carla at some fancy restaurant just before eleven; but, of course, she don't have no real intention of spending her day shopping with her friend. Not when I've finally managed to get my first day off in over two weeks. I figure it'll take her a few minutes to catch a cab after her driver lets her off somewhere near that restaurant. She should be here soon." His eyes glittered brightly with the thought of spending a few uninterrupted hours in the company of his lady love.

"Has Preston said anything more about the two of you?"

The change in Seth's expression was frightening. His eyebrows dropped low over cautiously narrowed eyes while he pressed his lips back against hard, gritted teeth. "He's been keeping a close eye on the two of us whenever he's at the house, which is most of the time these days. He can't seem to get the message that Rachel is no longer interested in his company. He probably thinks it's some kind of phase she's going through that will pass in time."

"And have you given him any more reason to wonder if the reason she's going through this phase is because she's really interested in you . . . that the two of you are interested in each other?"

"Evidently not. Though he's always watching me as if he's just waiting for me to make some sort of terrible mistake—something that he can use to get me fired—he hasn't actually done or said anything to make Marshall suspicious of me. At least not yet." His gaze rose to meet with hers.

"I still think you are playing with fire," Audrey cautioned him. "I think you both are."

"I know, but what choice do we have? If Marshall ever did find out how much we love each other, he'd see to it that I never got to see her again. I couldn't bear that."

"So you settle for sneaking around like a couple of school children, meeting on the sly."

Seth stared glumly at the brandy glass he held but had yet to put to his lips. "We have to. Until she can figure out a way for us to be together forever, we have to continue to sneak around like we do."

"Why don't you just marry her and be done with it?" Audrey asked, thinking that would be the obvious solution now that she was convinced they did indeed love each other. "If you can't bear to live without her, why not do something about it?"

"Because if she gets married before she's twenty-one to anyone other than a man of her father's choosing, she will be cut off without a penny. Though she says she's willing to risk that, I can't let her chance it."

He looked at Audrey again, his eyes full of uncertainty. "It could be she's right about her father, that eventually he'd come to his senses and forgive her for having married me, but what about all the misery she'd have to go through before that happened? And what if it never happened? What if she was cast out of her family forever and never allowed to touch the money that's been set aside in trust for her? You know as well as I do that on what little I'm able to make, even if I *was* lucky enough to get another bodyguard job that pays so well, Rachel would have to go without a lot of the luxuries she's used to having. I sure couldn't afford to pay for a passel of servants, nor could I afford to buy her a new gown every week. She'd be lucky to get a new gown once a year. I'm afraid she'd start to resent me if I made her live like that."

Audrey sat down on the arm of her brother's chair and patted his cheek reassuringly. Her heart ached right

294

along with his. "If you are worried about money, don't be. I've got over sixty thousand dollars now in stocks and bonds, and you already know I am more than willing to share part of that with you. It might not allow you to afford *all* the luxuries she's used to having, but I can at least buy you a nice house and pay for a reliable housekeeper to help her with the work."

Tears glistened in Seth's eyes when he looked away. "I can't ask you to do that."

"It would be my wedding present," she said, leaning forward so she could look into his downturned eyes. "And it's something I'd want to do no matter whom you married."

"It wouldn't be right."

"Why not?" she asked, starting to get angry at his constant refusals. For two months now, she'd tried to share part of her newfound wealth with him, and for two months, he'd flatly refused. She was starting to believe there was a very fine line between what most people called male pride and what others referred to as plain old stubbornness. "Look at everything you've done for me since our folks died. Why, more than once, you've saved my life."

"I have not."

"Yes you have. If you hadn't pushed me into the water the night that boat we were helping to load caught fire, I'd be dead for sure. Once those flames hit the cargo hold where all the guns and ammunition were stored, that thing blew up like an overloaded cannon. There was nothing left of her but a sea of broken boards and torn canvas."

"Don't remind me," Seth groaned, not wanting to remember how close to death they'd really come. And for what? A two-dollar gold piece they were never able to collect because the man who'd hired them had not reacted as quickly.

"And then there was the time that gator got me by the leg. If you hadn't jumped right on his back and used that

295

rope to pull the top of his mouth back in order to free me, I very well could have lost my leg. As it is, I still have scars." She lifted her skirt to allow him to see the two jagged discolorations on her right leg.

Seth glanced at the faded scars, then chuckled. "I never did figure out why that gator didn't spit you out on his own." He turned to face her again, his earlier grim mood temporarily forgotten. "You know, we both have led pretty colorful lives through the years."

"That depends on what you mean by *colorful*," she muttered, not quite as amused by the hard life they'd been forced to endure as he was. It was that "colorful" life that had turned her bitter and made her so determined to be rich one day. "If by colorful you mean black and blue or blistery red, then yes, I guess we have led quite colorful lives," she finally admitted.

"Don't forget to mention the colors grimy black and dusty gray," he commented, still chuckling at some of the memories he'd evoked.

"Those colors described *you* more so than me," she commented with a cautioning raise of her brow. "As you will no doubt recall, I was far more prone to taking regular baths than you were."

"If by *regular* you mean every other Saturday, I guess you were," he said, chuckling louder, when all Audrey could do was gasp aloud her outrage and pop him playfully across his forehead with the flat of her palm.

She certainly couldn't deny the accusation. After all, during the years they'd been forced to live out along the edge of the swamp, then later in the dirty back streets of New Orleans, baths had been hard to come by. Even a used bath had cost plenty. Most of the time, she had been forced to do her washing with plain water stolen from a horse trough or that had caught in some water-tight receptacle during a rain.

Audrey narrowed her eyes while she tried to think of a good retort to her brother's good-natured teasing, but a loud knock sounded at the back door before she could quite decide what to say. Aware it was probably Rachel coming in the back way so she could not be seen from the street, Audrey remained seated while her brother rose from his chair and hurried to greet her.

Knowing Seth and Rachel would treasure any time alone, Audrey left the room before their return. She went to the kitchen, where Leslie and Hilari were busy putting up the tomatoes that they'd bought at the market that morning, while Roberta watched. Audrey instructed all three of the women to stay out of the front parlor for as long as her brother was there. And she ordered them not to admit to anyone that he was there should someone come to the door and ask for him. They were not to mention *either* of her guests to anyone.

As soon as she'd seen to it that her brother would have complete privacy, she paused in the hall doorway to tell him good-bye, then closed the door, gathered up her handbag and gloves, then left the house and headed for her broker's office.

Due to a growing labor dispute that had arisen suddenly and had already caused several workers to band together in protest, Landon had advised her to pull out whatever money she'd invested in the luxury ship venture, at least for now. Knowing that time was of the essence in a situation like this, she intended to get it done before proceeding with any of her other errands. Not having the time for a leisurely stroll, especially now that she lived even farther away from Wall Street, she hailed a cab and had him drive her there.

"Good morning, Miss Stoane," the receptionist said in a cheery voice the moment she'd glanced up to find Audrey standing only a few feet from her desk. "I'll tell Mr. Rutledge that you are here."

Audrey did not bother to return the cheery greeting while she waited to be escorted into her broker's office. She still found the abrupt change in the woman's attitude a little annoying, aware it was the fact she had money that had made all the difference, not anything she'd personally done or said.

"You can go in now, Miss Stoane," she said, standing back to give her plenty of room to pass. "He's eager to see you."

"Thank you," Audrey muttered, though she had no idea why she'd bothered. People like Anne Taylor didn't deserve such common courtesies.

"I'm glad you stopped by." Andrew said. A smile lit his face as he rose immediately from his chair and walked around to the side of his desk. He waited until his receptionist had left the room before explaining the reason for his pleased expression. "I was just thinking about you."

"How nice," she responded with a pleasant smile, thinking his words nothing more than the usual social amenity.

"No, really, I was," he told her, waving his hands excitedly for emphasis. "I have something I'd like to mention to you."

"About my stocks?" she asked, thinking he was about to warn her away from the passenger ship venture.

"No, not your present stocks. It concerns something else entirely." He then lowered his voice, as if wanting to keep his words in the strictest of confidence. "I've just this hour gotten wind of something that is sure to make some lucky soul a *lot* of money."

Audrey's eyes widened with interest. "And what might that be?"

Andrew cautiously cut his gaze toward the open door, then walked quietly across the room and closed it. He waited until he was certain they would not be overheard, before explaining, "It has to do with a particular railroad that is having a few operational problems at the moment. The price of its stock is now extremely low. But I have it on good authority that its present troubles are only temporary and that the stock is soon to be worth ten times as much as it is worth now. Probably even more than that."

"What's the risk?"

"Minimal."

Audrey's eyes widened further. How could that be? There was something he was not telling her. "If it's really such a good deal, why are you telling *me* about it? Why not one of your more established clients?"

Andrew shrugged, as if he didn't quite understand the answer to that himself. "There's just something about your tenacity and your dogged determination that intrigues me. It has from the very first day I met you."

Audrey felt compelled to blush and did so, but without looking away. "Tell me more." When she realized he might misinterpret that as a request for more of his generous compliments, she quickly added, "About this railroad."

"What it amounts to is this: There's a tiny railroad called the C & A that runs on only eleven miles of track along a narrow valley of the Allegheny Mountains. Right now that railroad can be bought for practically nothing."

"*Practically?*" she asked, finding that hard to believe. Most railroads, even smaller ones, cost in the millions.

"When you consider what the person who purchases that stock stands to make in the end, it *is* practically nothing."

"How much is *practically?*" She wanted definite amounts.

"To buy up all the shares that are on the market right now, which amounts to almost ninety percent of the entire railroad, it would only cost about six hundred thousand dollars."

Audrey felt the air rush out of her lungs. "Six hundred thousand? Why are you even bothering to tell me about it. You know I don't have that kind of money."

"Because if you bought it on margin, you'd only need . . . oh . . . say, about fifty-five to sixty thousand dollars."

Audrey's face twisted into a puzzled frown. She had never before been offered the chance to buy on margin.

The thought of trying something so risky was frightening, but at the same time intriguing. Had she really reached the point in her rapidly rising financial status to be allowed such privileges as to buy stock on margin? What a heady feeling that caused. "Even at fifty-five or sixty thousand, it would take nearly everything I have."

"I know, but just think, in a very few months that fifty-five or sixty-thousand-dollar investment should bring in a profit of at least five to six hundred thousand. Probably more. When all is said and done, you could very well be worth nearly a million dollars. But then again, you don't have to buy up *all* the shares, though the more you can get your hands on, the better."

"And you say the risk is minimal?" she asked again, still thinking it was a little too good to be true. "Just what is it about this railroad that makes it such a good deal? You mentioned accidents. What kind of business is it doing?"

"Right now, it's down to making only one run a week. But that is about to change. In the very near future, there will be trains running constantly through there, because that little railroad is about to become vital to the two big mining companies that have just moved into that valley."

"Mining companies?" He had her full attention again.

"Yes, they are after the iron deposits that were recently discovered just a few miles south of that railroad and the coal deposits that are just to the northwest. Here, sit down and I'll tell you all about it."

Audrey quickly took the chair offered, eager to know more.

Andrew, too, sat down before going into further detail, "That railroad has the good fortune of being in the right place at the right time. Because of how rugged the terrain is in that area, there is only one plausible route for a main track to be built from the mining sites on through to Lake Erie, and the C & A sits right smack dab in the middle of it. In fact, at the moment, the C & A is the end of the line for that area. And if they want to extend it on across toward that lake, they're first going to want to buy it."

"Lake Erie? Why would they want a track that goes all the way to Lake Erie?"

"Because it would be far more economical to send the coal and the heavy pigs of iron by flat barge to the coast than it would to route it down through the lower part of the state, back up to Harrisburg, then across New Jersey and on up to New York Harbor, where the best prices are to be had. And, because it is wiser to own or at least have a controlling interest in whatever mode of transportation is to be used, both of those companies are going to be jumping at the chance to buy out that little railroad so they can complete the passage to the lake. And with two companies like that bidding against each other, there's no telling how high the price of that stock will go. Therefore, whoever happens to own most of the stock in that little railroad when the time comes could hold firm and eventually get whatever price she wanted."

The fact he'd used a feminine pronoun made it obvious he intended for her to be the one to buy the stock.

"I still don't understand why you are telling *me* about this and not one of your better customers."

"Are you at all interested?" he asked, ready to get on with it.

"I'm not sure. If it fell through, if for some reason, they decided to bypass that little railroad, I'd lose my margin. I'd lose almost everything I have."

"But, if it does go through—and there's no reason it shouldn't—you'll end up with enough money to make you a very wealthy woman."

Wealthy enough to at last make her worthy of Landon and his friends? she wondered, but quickly pushed the thought aside. "I still want to know why you've chosen me to be the lucky one. It just doesn't make sense that you would choose a newcomer like me over the rest."

chapter nineteen

"To tell you the truth, I did mention it to someone else, but that person wasn't really interested in making any drastic changes in the present status of his investments. There for a moment, he acted as if he just might be tempted but, in the end, decided to let the opportunity pass. In fact, he had just walked out of my office, which left me sitting here wondering who might be willing to chance such a large investment on so short notice, when I thought of you. Then, barely a few seconds later, you showed up, almost as if Fate had brought you to me."

Audrey was not so sure Fate had ever had her best interests at heart. "If it's such a great investment, then why don't you put money into it yourself?"

"I would if I had any," he admitted with a forlorn sigh. "But I don't happen to have that kind of money. I have a wife and six children to take care of. I barely make enough these days for us to get by."

"But what about your brother or your father? Why aren't they taking advantage of this?"

"My mother is in very poor health right now and all my father's money is going to doctors and hospitals at the moment. And my brother is little better off than I am, with a wife and four children to support. Although it might be possible for him to purchase a few shares, he can't possibly buy enough to take any real advantage of the situation. But you can. You have plenty of capital to buy controlling interest and, thereby, take full advantage of this. Which means through you, I am apt to make quite a penny myself in commission, even after I let my brother and father have their share. And then when you turn around and reinvest the money you make, which I figure you're likely to do, my family will make even more. So, you see, by getting you or one of our other clients to jump in on this before someone else does, we stand to come out ahead, too, and at a time when we need to come out ahead."

Well, that certainly made sense. But, still, something was not quite right about the whole situation. "If this railroad is so important, then why haven't the companies who are planning to mine that area bought it for themselves? If they really do need that track like you say they do, why haven't they already done something about it?"

"Best I can figure and the best my source can figure, they are too busy securing what land they'll need for their mines right now to worry about any possible transportation problems just yet."

"What are the two companies involved? Who owns them?" She wanted to make sure they were financially solid organizations that would not have to fold before ever seeing their exalted plans complete.

"The iron ore operation is a part of Carnegie Iron Works, which is owned by Andrew Carnegie. The coal operation is a part of Steed Enterprises. Marshall Steed heads that. He also has other interests in that same area, a little further to the Southwest."

"Marshall Steed?" The thought of having something Marshall Steed would eventually need interested her almost as much as the unusually high amount of profit she stood to make. After that unfriendly little visit in which he had tried to buy her off, she'd wondered what she could do to better even things between them. The thought of selling the railroad to him at a greatly inflated price pleased her immensely.

But, still, something bothered her. Simply put, it was just too good to be true. She needed more time to check out the C & A Railroad, to see if it really did lie along the only possible route for a railroad track to be built from that mining area on across to Lake Erie. "Tell you what. I'll let you know my decision first thing in the morning. Before the exchange opens."

"But that may be too late. Someone else could get wind of this and buy up that stock this afternoon, right out from under our noses," he said, trying to convince her of the urgency. "In fact, it could be selling right now for all I know."

The misery he felt at the thought of such a loss was evident by his pensive expression when he glanced back over his shoulder to the small windowed room where the noisy ticker tape machine was kept and a jittery little man sat watching the fluctuations in the market with a notepad in hand. At that very moment, news of a large purchase of C & A stock could be coming across the wire.

Though the high-speed, clattering noise caused a strong feeling of urgency to surge through her, she refused to jump headlong into something she had not investigated thoroughly, especially if she was going to have to buy it on margin. She was well aware that if it fell through, she could very easily lose her margin money and have absolutely nothing to show for her trouble, because as soon as the loss had exceeded the margin amount, if she did not come up with more margin money to continue holding it, the stock would immediately revert back to her broker and be his to sell for whatever he could get out of it.

"I'm afraid that's a chance I'll have to take. I'm not about to go into this blind, but I also don't expect you to hold off until I have had time to consider it. Therefore, if before I can get word to you to either buy or let it ride, you happen to find someone else who wants to buy it,

I'll certainly understand. There will be no hard feelings."

Andy sighed heavily. "I guess that's fair enough. Just don't take too long. Time is important here, and I really do think you are going to find out that this is the deal of a lifetime. Just the sort of thing to put you on your way to the top."

Aware he spoke the truth about one thing, that time was indeed of the essence, Audrey went straight to find out what she could about this railroad.

Her first stop was the library, where she studied maps and railroad construction at length. Her second stop was the office of the *New York Times*. Through the records she was able to locate concerning the railroad and the two companies Andy had mentioned, she was pleased to discover that everything checked. Both companies were obviously planning very large mining operations in that area. In fact, Carnegie Iron had just that morning acquired the titles they needed to a very large section of land only a few miles south of the railroad and were finalizing negotiations for more. Being that far into the acquisition of the land, surely they would look toward their different transportation needs next. Her heart raced with growing anticipation. If she did want that railroad, time was rapidly running out.

Still, she could not get over the feeling that something was not on the level. It was still too good to be true.

When she left the newspaper office, she went directly to the Steed house, hoping to find Landon home. Though she knew she risked running into Marshall, a most unpleasant prospect indeed, she had to find out what Landon knew about the railroad and about his father's operations in that area.

As the cab she'd hired neared the house, still over a block away, she noticed Landon's carriage pull out of the front gate into the street, headed in the opposite direction. Leaning forward with the sudden fear that she was about to miss him all together, she shouted to her driver, "Catch that carriage. That's the man I wanted to see."

The cabbie was quick to pop his whip high over his horses's ears. "Eeeigh!" The cab lurched forward at top speed.

Though several carriages had moved to take up the space between them, the cabbie proved to be very adept at getting around the slower traffic and, within a very few blocks, had pulled up beside Landon's carriage and slowed to an equal pace.

"Landon, I have to talk to you," Audrey shouted to him with a wild wave of her hands when he glanced over at her. "Have your man pull over."

Landon, startled but pleased, immediately instructed his driver to find a place to stop. By the time the driver had drawn the carriage to a halt along the side of the busy residential street, Landon had already swung out of the back and was headed to the area where he expected the cab to pull to a stop.

"What's wrong?" he wanted to know, his face drawn with concern. His gaze searched hers as the cab did indeed stop in the very spot he'd predicted. "What's happened?"

Realizing she'd probably made it seem like a life-and-death situation by the frantic way she'd shouted at him, Audrey felt suddenly foolish. She'd hoped to approach him very casually.

"Nothing is really wrong. I just need to talk to you for a minute," she explained as she, too, climbed down onto the street. "Can you spare a minute or two? It won't take long."

"Do you want me to wait?" the cabbie called down to her when she began to move away, not quite certain what he was expected to do.

"No need," Landon answered in her place. "I have my carriage. I will see that she gets wherever she needs to go."

"That'll be thirty cents, then," the cabbie said, bending low in his seat and thrusting his sweaty palm toward him.

"Thirty cents?" Landon asked, startled by the high amount.

"Fifteen cents extra for having to chase you down," the cabbie explained. "That sorta thing puts a strain on my horse."

When Landon noticed Audrey pull open her handbag and begin what was a futile search for the correct change, he reached into his pocket, extracted the necessary money, and quickly pressed it into the cabbie's palm. He then motioned for her to join him in his carriage. "It's too hot to stand out here on the sidewalk. Let's go for a ride."

Eager for the privacy his carriage would offer, she quickly agreed and wasted little time climbing in and getting comfortably situated in the rear seat, wanting to be as far away from the driver as possible. Though she felt Patrick O'Mack could probably be trusted to keep whatever financial secrets he overheard to himself, she didn't dare take any unnecessary chances. He might not be as satisfied with his job as he appeared to be, and if that were indeed the case, he might not be totally opposed to selling a stock tip such as hers for whatever he could get.

"So, what is it you wanted to talk to me about that couldn't wait until tonight?" he asked after the carriage had eased out into the mainstream of traffic, creating a light breeze that ruffled his thick brown hair. A wide smile stretched across his face, forming handsome creases in both cheeks. "Or was that just a ruse to see me? Perhaps you were so eager to be with me again that you simply could not wait until tonight."

Audrey rolled her eyes heavenward, as if to ask for the strength needed to ignore such an extremely egotistical remark. "I wanted to ask your advice about something."

Landon felt instantly crestfallen, yet he tried not to show it. It hurt to know that she had sought him out simply for his advice. Though he'd been teasing when he originally made the comment, he had hoped to discover

307

that she had indeed chased him down for purely personal reasons.

"You know me," he said with a forced smile. "Always willing to hand out advice. What's up?"

Audrey didn't know how much she should tell him and how much she should keep to herself, since his own father was so strongly involved. She didn't want to put him in the awkward position of knowing about something that might eventually complicate matters for his own father and then being asked not to speak of it to anyone—especially not to Marshall.

"Well, what it really amounts to is that I have an opportunity to buy over ninety percent of a small railroad in the midwestern part of Pennsylvania, but because putting up the margin required to make the purchase will cut my other investments down to almost nothing, I'm a little hesitant. I guess what I want from you is your reassurance that I'm making a smart decision."

"Why would you want to own a railroad?" he asked, carefully studying her face while he spoke. "You've never mentioned having such aspirations before."

"That's because before today, I've never even thought about owning one. But, the way I understand it, this particular railroad is about to become very important to some very influential companies that are starting up operations close by."

"How important?"

"It happens to have been built down along the only valley that will allow those companies to complete a railroad line to Lake Erie."

"And their products are such that they will want to send them on up to the lake instead of across land by rail?" Landon asked, deeply hurt by all the secrecy. Even though he had willingly shared valuable information with her on several occasions, she obviously planned to keep the identity of this railroad from him. The reason for such secrecy was painfully obvious. Though he hated

308

to admit it because he had tried for so long to believe it was not the truth, having money was the most important thing in Audrey's life.

It was a heartbreaking revelation. Though he'd known from the very beginning that she yearned to be rich, that she wanted not only all the luxuries but also the undeniable power that accompanied being rich, until now he hadn't realized just how deep that desire ran. Apparently, she wanted wealth more than she wanted *anything* else. Including him. Which had never made a lot of sense to him, since he could easily offer her the life of luxury she sought. But, then again, he knew how important it was for her to accomplish her dream on her own.

"Yes, they are the sort of products that could be shipped by barges rather than in railcars," she assured him, careful not to mention just what those products were, for fear he might guess which railroad she was hoping to buy or that one of the companies involved belonged to his father.

"And there is no other possible way for them to get these goods up there?" he asked, wanting to find out how cautiously she'd looked at the situation.

"None that I can see."

"And neither company has yet reached the point of securing transportation for these products?"

"They are both still working on getting the land titles they need. But as soon as they have all that squared away, I think the next logical step will be to find the most economical means of getting their products to market."

Landon closed his eyes against the hollow ache throbbing deep in his chest. The truth pressed against his heart with painful clarity. Audrey's main interest in life was money—her *only* interest in life. Her desire for wealth ruled even her heart, leaving no room for anything else, not even him. What hurt even more was knowing she was deliberately keeping the names of the two companies as well as the name of the railroad a careful secret, even though she claimed she wanted his advice. She was so eager to make her fortune that she wasn't even willing to share any part of this opportunity with him. Yet, over the past several weeks, he had shared many a good opportunity with her.

In a last effort to disprove his own disheartening theory, knowing it was possible that her failure to mention the name of the railroad had been unintentional, he tried to make it easy for her to give him the information. "If you'd like, I could check this railroad out for you, make sure there is no way for those companies to route around it. It shouldn't take an hour."

"I've already done that," she assured him, aware he was hinting to be included. She looked away, unable to meet his gaze any longer. She tried to keep in mind that it was for his own good he be kept in the dark. "The mountains in that area are far too steep to make building a railroad over them feasible. And that particular valley is the only one in the area deep enough or wide enough to be of any real use."

"Then you don't want me to check into it for you?" he asked, still hanging onto a last thread of hope, giving her one last chance to share the information with him . . . not because he was in any way interested in being a part of the investment itself, but as a sign of good faith. To show that she cared enough to trust him with her secret.

"No," she answered quickly, knowing he couldn't possibly check the railroad out without being told the name of it. "I guess what I really want from you is the reassurance that I'm about to do the right thing."

"And what is that?"

"Buy myself a railroad." Her eyes widened at the sheer thought of owning an entire railroad, small though it was. She might not own it for long, but for however many weeks it took to make the negotiations to sell it, she would have title to enough stock to be legally considered the owner.

Landon sighed inwardly out of regret. He wondered

why he should care so much what she did. Any fall she might be headed for would be completely of her own doing. Her own greed would have led her to it. And until she was willing to share more information with him than she had, there was nothing he could do . . . nothing he should do. "The choice is yours. It's your money. But if everything that you've told me about the venture is correct, it sounds as if it could be a very good opportunity for you."

Still curious to find out just how large Marshall's operations were in that area, she asked, trying to sound only mildly interested, as if it were nothing more than an afterthought to their previous conversation, "Your father has several business interests in that area, doesn't he?"

"What area?" he asked, still hoping she would share some of her wondrous discovery with him.

"The Allegheny Mountains," she responded, keeping her answer very general.

Further disappointed, aware how carefully she had avoided pinpointing the location of the railroad, he answered with an unhappy nod. "Father has controlling interest in several railroads that run through the lower part of Pennsylvania. Mostly, his railroads are small and branch off of the main Pennsylvania Railroad line into outlying areas. He also has partial interest in an iron mill operation near Johnstown. And, if I'm not mistaken, I believe he has just recently become involved in some of the massive coal operations that have been developing through that area. But, then, he really doesn't talk much about his investments with me, since my interests lean more toward shipping and exports, and his interests are more industrial."

"You say he is involved in some of the coal operations there?" she asked casually, still trying to sound only vaguely interested.

"Yes, he has mentioned his coal mines several times. In fact, I think he's about to open up a new mine somewhere near Ridgeburg."

"But that's up there in the middle of nowhere," she said. Her heart raced with anticipation, aware he'd mentioned the very operation her broker had told her about just hours earlier. "How does he plan to get his coal to market?"

"I think he said something about shipping it by rail around to the Great Lakes, then carrying it by barge to the coal yards in New York. Sort of like what you were talking about before."

"But how? There are no railroads up through there."

"I guess he'll have to ship it on across through Ohio." Landon frowned. "I'm not really sure how he plans to get it there. But, then, like I already told you, we really don't discuss our investments at length with each other, except when we happen upon a really great deal that we can't resist sharing, or to brag about something that netted us quite a profit. Father is very competitive when it comes to his investments. He likes to keep quiet about what he's up to, at least until it's apparent no harm can come from the information leaking out. He became especially secretive about his business affairs right after what you did to him a couple of months back."

Audrey glanced up at him, wondering if he held that against her in some way, glad to see nothing short of amusement glimmering in his eyes.

Landon looked at her for another moment, then switched his gaze to the many people hurrying along the sidewalk. "So, is that all you wanted to talk with me about . . . this railroad you are wanting to buy?" he asked, suddenly returning to the original topic of conversation.

Audrey felt her heart go out to him. He looked so forlorn. "That, and to give you this," she said, leaning boldly forward and placing a kiss on his cheek, very near the corner of his mouth.

Landon's reaction was mixed. The skin where she had gently pressed her lips tingled from the unexpected pleasure, but the ache in his heart swelled to unbearable proportions. He noticed that the only time Audrey ever felt truly compelled to reach out and touch him in some way always came during or right after they'd discussed some lucrative business deal that was certain to bring her more wealth. Would she ever want to touch him for any reason other than gratitude? His heart filled with misery. He'd truly believed that she was starting to love him for himself, not for the advice he could offer her. Now he wasn't so sure what she felt. As he watched her settle back into her seat, smiling contentedly to herself, he realized that he might have misjudged her all together. She might not love him at all. And that hurt far more than he ever would have believed possible.

"Now, if it is not putting you to too much trouble, could you ask your driver to let me off at my broker's? I want to tell him the good news . . . that I've decided to buy that railroad after all. As much as I can get my hands on."

Landon closed his eyes for a moment, in an attempt to still the throbbing ache in his heart and to prevent any of the pain he felt from showing. Then, with his emotional world falling slowly apart, he leaned forward and shouted, in a loud voice, the address of her broker.

"Would you like for me to wait and give you a ride home?" he asked as the carriage rolled to a stop in front of the impressive brownstone building.

Remembering Rachel and Seth could still be at her house, she answered quickly . . . too quickly, "No, I might have to be here for a while. I'll just catch a cab home when I'm finished." Her heart raced with wild bursts of uncontrolled fear when she thought about what could happen if Landon ever found out about the private little rendezvous between his sister and her brother. He would be furious and would no doubt blame her for having helped the two lovers see each other instead of doing what she could to keep them apart. She couldn't bear the thought of Landon being angry with her, certain he would never understand her reasons for helping. She wasn't too sure she understood them herself.

Thinking her response had been a little abrupt, he looked at her with a puzzled frown. "You will be home in time for our dinner engagement tonight, won't you?"

"Of course. It's still early yet," she tried to convince him, though she really had no idea what time it was. "I'll see you at seven." Then, before he could ask any more questions, she alighted from the carriage and stopped briefly to wave him on before turning toward the front door. When Audrey entered the building and glanced at the wide-faced clock near the entrance, she saw that it was nearly three-thirty. Almost time for the stock exchange to close, which always happened sharply at four. Running as fast as she could, she bounded up the stairs in a most unladylike fashion and burst into Andy's office without bothering to wait for the flighty receptionist to announce her.

Within seconds, Andy had dispatched a messenger with the order to liquidate most of her present stock, especially any tied up in the passenger ship company, and to buy all the C & A stock available. The stock exchange was barely two blocks away, and barring any accidents, the messenger would be there in a matter of minutes, which usually proved a lot faster than waiting for the telegraph lines to clear.

With her heart lodged high in her throat, Audrey followed Andy into the small ticker tape room to monitor all the latest information firsthand, eager to know if the messenger had made it in time for her purchase to go through before closing.

"We only have to wait four more months, until the trust Mother had Father set up for me can officially go into effect," Rachel reminded Seth, who had slipped off into another one of his gloomy it-will-never-work-out-for-us moods. "If by my birthday I have not married

314

someone who's not of Father's choosing, and if I have managed to stay in Father's good graces in all *other* ways, I will have over a hundred thousand dollars coming to me, in addition to all of Mother's jewelry. With that, we should be able to live quite nicely for several years to come."

"Yes, but what about after that money is gone and we have to live strictly on what I make?" he asked, thinking she had not thought the situation through. "What then? You'll no longer be able to go out and spend money on a new gown whenever the whim strikes you, and you won't be able to go to the theater every time a new show opens. And we both know how you love the theater."

Rachel smiled that will-you-please-give-me-more-credit-than-that smile of hers as she leaned forward to plant a small series of teasing kisses along his neck, which with her short height was as high as she could reach without his full cooperation. "The theater is fun," she admitted between her playful kisses. "And I enjoy going. But it will never measure up to the joy I feel when I'm in your arms. When are you going to get it through that thick skull of yours that I love you? More than I love the theater. More than I love wearing expensive gowns. Even more than a quick race through Central Park. Seth, try to understand, I love you more than life itself, because until you came along, I had no idea how important my life really was."

Seth emitted a low, almost indiscernible groan from his throat. He wasted no time pulling her body hard against his, bending low to meet her lips in a passionate kiss. When their mouths finally broke apart a few minutes later, they were both short of breath and their lips slightly swollen, an indication of the true, over-whelming power of their desire for one another. "And I love you, Rachel. I just worry that I'm somehow going to ruin your life by agreeing to marry you."

"You'd be ruining my life if you didn't agree," she assured him, raising on her tiptoes in an effort to lure him into another hungry kiss.

Seth proved most obliging as he dipped down to meet her lips with his again and again. Each kiss grew longer and more powerful than the last. Soon their passions were too great to be ignored and their hands began to search out the intimate areas of each other's bodies, knowing that because there were servants in the house they dared not allow their emotions to carry them away, but unable to stay apart.

It was torture to be so close, to share such love, such passion, but be unable to do anything about it. Finally, Seth had to pull away. For an unbearably long moment, he simply looked at her, knowing she felt the same ache for him that he felt for her. How he loved her.

"Seth," Rachel said in a soft, adoring voice while she tried to be content with pressing her cheek against his. "I do love you."

Seth glanced down at her and smiled with joyous pride, but then his smile slowly dissolved into a worried frown. "I just hope you can still say that several years from now."

"As long as there's a breath in my body, the words will come easily from my lips," she said, and lifted her face for one more lingering kiss, to help her get through the long, lonely nights until they could again be together.

chapter twenty

By the time Audrey returned home, it was nearly six o'clock. In her handbag was a receipt that proved she'd put up the full amount of margin necessary to finalize the purchase of just over ninety-one percent of C & A stock, which represented all the shares that had been made available that day.

Because of a continued drop in the price of the stock during the few hours it had taken her to investigate the railroad, the amount of margin she'd had to put up in order to secure her stock had cost only a little more than fifty-two thousand dollars, which was a lot better than the fifty-five to sixty thousand she had expected to pay.

Even so, coming up with that much margin had tied up over four fifths of her total capital, which left her with barely eleven thousand in her other stocks and a little more than two thousand in the bank. Still, she was thrilled that no one else had moved in to take advantage of the situation before she had had a chance to make up her mind.

She felt as giddy as a schoolgirl on the last week of school, knowing that as soon as Marshall Steed or Andrew Carnegie finished worrying about their different land titles and mining permits, and finally started trying to secure the transportation they would need to get their products that eighty miles to Lake Erie, she would be able to sell her railroad stock at a tremendously inflated price. If everything went just right, by the end of the year she could be worth as much as a million dollars, though she might be willing to settle for a few hundred thousand less. The eventual selling price really depended on how eager the two men were to get their operations under way.

Because of how late it was when Audrey finally returned home, she had not expected for either Seth or Rachel to still be there. When she opened the back door she was surprised to find her brother seated at the kitchen table, quietly sipping a cup of hot coffee while listening to Leslie, as she stirred the stew that was to be her and Hilari's evening meal, tell him all about the time she almost got married.

"Why are you still here?" Audrey asked, glancing around to see if Rachel were there, too. "You aren't expecting supper, are you? I thought I told you that I am having dinner with Landon tonight."

"No, I'm not expecting supper," he assured her. "I'll probably go on back over to the Steeds' and have supper with the rest of the men, since I have been asked to be back in time to go with Marshall when he leaves for his nightly walk at eight. It's just that I got something I was wanting to tell you." He paused, wondering how to go about it without actually mentioning any names. He certainly didn't want to give Audrey's housekeepers something new to gossip about.

"Well, what is it?"

"I just wanted to tell you how *she* and me talked it over this afternoon, and we've decided to get married the very next day after her birthday. It won't be no formal wedding, like she's probably always figured on having; but we were sorta hoping you'd let us get married here in your house."

"Here?" she asked with surprise, then quickly took him by the arm and pulled him out of the room so they could talk without any fear of being overheard. She knew Leslie already had a pretty good idea who *she* was, and if

318

there were more to this than should be made known, she wanted it to be said in private.

"Of course, we wouldn't expect nothing fancy," Seth went on to explain as he followed her down the hall and into the front parlor. "It'll probably just be her, me, you, and a couple of her closest friends—and a preacher, of course. I don't think that any of her family is going to want to attend." He chuckled sadly over the profound understatement. "Fact is, you probably couldn't drag them here with a stout chain and team of sturdy mules. So, it's not like you'd have to do no special decorating or anything. The date being so near to Christmas and all, we wouldn't expect you to go to no trouble. Just give us a nice place to hold the ceremony. We don't want to get married in some judge's chambers."

"Christmas? When is her birthday?"

"December third. We plan to get married on the fourth. That way, by having waited until one day after her twenty-first birthday, she will have fulfilled the provisions of the trust and can then legally collect what's coming to her."

"Do you honestly think the two of you can continue sneaking around the way you have without getting caught until then?"

"We'll have to."

Audrey shook her head, her delicate brow notched with concern. "You've said it yourself: If you get caught with her, or even if Marshall starts to suspect there is something between the two of you, he'll do everything within his power to see to it that you never set eyes on her again."

"It's a chance we have to take. Although Rachel claims the money in her trust fund is not that important to her, her mother's jewelry is, and that is part of what she is supposed to receive on her birthday—that is, if she's fulfilled all the requirements of the trust."

"Exactly what are the requirements?"

"She's not supposed to have gotten married to a man

319

her father hasn't approved of or"—he hesitated to mention the other requirement, knowing how easily it could ruin everything, "or have a child conceived out of wedlock. As long as she doesn't do either of those things before her next birthday, she's supposed to get both the money and the jewelry." He sighed before he then added, "Rachel wants to be married with her mother's wedding ring."

Audrey smiled at such a sweet sentiment, nodding that she understood. She wished their mother hadn't had to sell her wedding ring, when Seth was still a baby, to buy food. She'd have loved to have it for her own wedding, even though it had been a very simple band of gold.

"Holding your wedding here will be fine with me. In fact, I love the idea," she admitted, blinking back the tears that threatened to spill at the thought of sharing in her brother's happiness. "But I want you to know right now that I plan to fill this parlor to the ceiling with flowers and bows, and there's nothing you can do to stop me. I also intend to buy you that house I promised, and that live-in housekeeper, maybe two." She could hardly wait. By December, she should have resold the stock in her railroad for quite a hefty profit and could easily afford lavishing the newlyweds with such gifts.

When Seth rose from his chair and opened his mouth to speak, Audrey expected to hear him argue with her about spending so much of her money on them. Narrowing her eyes, she placed her hands on her hips, preparing to stand her ground; but to her amazement, her brother did not argue at all. Instead, he bent over and swept her into a big bear hug.

"I love you, Sis," he admitted openly with a heavy sheen of moisture glimmering along the outer corners of his eyes. "And I want you to know that I love Rachel, too. I really do. Her and me, we may have to face some pretty tough times ahead, but I now believe with all my heart that we will somehow see those hard times through. We talked about our future for a long time this afternoon, and she's finally convinced me that she will be happy no matter what sort of house or apartment we end up with or no matter what sort of life-style we eventually have to get used to. As long as we got each other, we'll be happy."

"And that's all that matters," Audrey told him, though a heavy, sinking feeling passed over her. Would their love be enough to see them through? She wondered if that could possibly be true, or if it were just something that happened in fairy tales and English novels.

By the time Seth and Audrey had finished discussing the wedding plans, sketchy though they were, and Seth had finally left, Audrey barely had twenty minutes to take advantage of the warm bath Roberta had prepared for her and slip into one of her new evening gowns.

Because she'd discovered blue was one of Landon's favorite colors, no matter what the shade, she selected an ice-blue silk gown trimmed with narrow white ribbons of Italian lace and delicate roses shaped from starched white velvet. With only a few minutes remaining to worry about her hair, she left it like it was, piled into a simple display of dark curls, adding only a strand of blue sapphires and the pins necessary to hold it in place.

Having rushed around at a maddening rate of speed, Audrey had managed to be ready by the time Landon arrived exactly at seven. Because she had accidentally sloshed water on Roberta's uniform in her haste to get ready and there was no time for her to change into another, she decided to leave her lady's maid behind, much to Landon's relief.

During the short ride to the Fifth Avenue Hotel, where they planned to eat, Landon remained uncharacteristically silent, which left Audrey to try and come up with most of the conversation. For the first hour or so, that was not a difficult task. She told him, with far more enthusiasm than he'd wanted to hear, about the success she'd had in purchasing the stock in her new railroad just minutes before the market closed.

But after she'd exhausted that story and mentioned

that she'd managed to hold onto most of her stock in Atlantic Exports, there was not much else Audrey could think of to tell him and a thick wall of silence fell between them.

All through dinner, Landon remained withdrawn. Rarely did he initiate any of the conversation himself. Finally, Audrey had had enough and asked him what was wrong. She worried that he was still having second thoughts about her.

"What makes you think something is wrong?" he asked, gazing at her beautiful face and wishing he could find even a spark of interest for him. Though her eyes glowed with childlike excitement and her face radiated with the utmost of joy, he knew none of her happiness stemmed from the fact that she was with him. She was simply reacting to the thrill of having just bought her first railroad. Nothing more.

The ache that had been pulling at his heart all afternoon, ever since the truth had first struck him, grew to unbearable proportions, causing him to look away. He tried to feign interest in the elegantly clad couples sitting at the tables surrounding them.

"Something is too wrong," she said, studying his odd behavior. "You've hardly spoken all evening and you look a little pale. And look at your plate. I'm already finished with my meal and you've hardly eaten anything." She drew her face into a pretty frown. "Maybe you're coming down with something. If that's so, you really should go straight home and get into bed."

Aware the reason she was so eager to be rid of him was to have more time to focus on what she planned to do with the money she hoped to make on the resale of her railroad, Landon agreed, "I am feeling pretty awful. Maybe it would be best if we left now."

While signaling for the waiter to bring them their bill, he placed his napkin across the edge of his plate and took a last sip of his water to help clear away the constriction that had developed in his throat. The dull ache inside him

322

made it impossible for Landon to look at her beautiful face. Instead, he turned his attention to first his wallet and then the waitress.

Soon, they were back in the carriage and on their way across the dark streets of New York to Audrey's house. When they neared the entrance to her carriage drive, he could not resist turning to glimpse her lovely profile one last time. He had a feeling that tonight might very well be their last night together. Now that she so obviously considered herself in control of her own finances, she didn't need him anymore. She was drifting away from him. "Audrey, I want you to know that if something ever happens and you find yourself in need of help, I'll do whatever I can for you. I've never wanted anything but to be there for you."

Audrey felt that was an odd thing to say and wondered just how sick he really was. Her heart raced with sudden fear while she studied his pale face again, too afraid to speculate why he'd worded his statement quite like that. "I know. And you always have been there for me. That's why I consider you my dearest and most trusted friend."

Hearing the truth from her own lips struck Landon hard, causing him to flinch from the resulting pain. Tears burned the outer corners of his eyes. He blinked rapidly to clear them but refused to meet her probing gaze.

The only reason she'd finally agreed to let him be her friend was for the advice he'd been able to give her toward choosing profitable investments while she was still learning how to judge an investment wisely. He had never truly interested her as a man. "Just promise, that no matter what happens, you will think of me in that way . . . as your dearest friend." The constriction in his throat became even more painful when the thought crossed his mind that he'd so hoped to become more than her friend—so much more.

Again, it seemed to Audrey as if there were something he was not telling her, something dreadful. Her insides ached with sudden fear. Was Landon dying? Is that why he looked so deathly pale and so terribly forlorn. She had to know. "Landon, why does it sound as if you are trying to say good-bye to me?"

Aware he'd fallen into far too sullen a mood, he quickly brought himself out of it and produced what he hoped was a convincing smile. "Because we have arrived at your house. If I don't tell you good-bye now, I can't go home and get into bed like you suggested I do." Then, without giving her a chance to comment further, he stepped down from the carriage and held his hand out to her.

As she allowed him to escort her to the door, she tried her best to shake the icy feeling of apprehension his words had caused; but she couldn't forget the frightening implication of what he had said. While standing in the dark shadows of her porch, he closed his eyes and bent forward to place a perfunctory kiss upon her cheek, but Audrey turned her head so that his lips met her mouth instead. For some reason, she wanted a real kiss from him. Something she could hold onto after he'd gone. A kiss like he used to try and get away with before she'd finally convinced him she was not interested in such nonsense. A kiss as wonderful and as passionate as the one they'd shared just a week ago inside her house.

Landon's eyes flew open when he realized what she'd done, and for a brief moment he considered pulling away. If she was still responding to all the wondrous excitement she felt over the purchase of her new railroad and all the wealth she expected to come of it, then he didn't want any part of that kiss. Or did he?

The truth was, he was so starved for her that he would take whatever he could get for whatever reasons given. Eagerly, he slid his arms around her waist and drew her body closer. Instead of lifting her hands to push him away, like she usually did, her arms slid boldly upward to encircle his neck.

Though he knew this willing response had occurred for all the wrong reasons, he refused to bring the kiss to an

324

end. He desired her too much. Savoring the sweet taste, he dipped his tongue past her parted lips again and again, plunging timidly then retreating, coaxing Audrey to do the same. When she did move her tongue to meet with his halfway, Landon moaned and the kiss suddenly exploded. He crushed her to him like a starved man. He drew her tongue deeply into his mouth, caressing it with his own.

His hands roamed eagerly over her shoulders and back, until he finally brought them to rest on the rounded curve of her bottom. He pressed her soft body flush against his hardened frame, needing to bring her closer still. When she moaned softly with pleasure, he moved one hand around the curve of her waist to first stroke her narrow ribcage through the silken material of her gown. Then, slowly, he moved the hand upward to gently cup her breast.

Audrey gasped when his thumb came into contact with the sensitive nipple, sending a startling jolt of electricity through her body. Her skin burned from his touch, though his hand had yet to come in direct contact with her body. Inside, she was a throbbing mass of reawakening emotions . . . emotions so strong and so powerful that she was not at all sure what to do about them.

A now-familiar hunger had begun to spiral outward from some deeply private spot within her body, while a warm, gentle tide of sensations rolled effortlessly through to her soul, bathing her with a wild mixture of beckoning needs. His mouth remained maddeningly sweet though alarmingly hungry, while his hand continued to work its shocking magic on her breast. Liquid fire spilled through her veins, setting her heart and her very soul aflame, spreading a heat so sensual, so all-consuming, that it left her weak and wanting.

In the regions of her mind, she sensed that she was in very real danger of once again falling prey to the extremely volatile passions that only Landon had the ability to arouse in her. Her brain tried to warn her, insisting she pull away before she became more involved than she wanted. But her heart was sending out its own message . . . a message to hold onto him with all her might, to explore these wondrous feelings to their fullest. She could worry about the consequences later.

Standing in the dim glow of a distant street lamp, Landon pulled back long enough to gaze down into her flushed face and again glimpsed what he felt certain was a definite form of love. His breath held while he studied the passion glittering in her eyes, then his heart soared skyward with renewed hope. He had not imagined it after all. Although she might not be ready to admit it yet, even to herself, Audrey did indeed feel something for him, something very special, and if it wasn't love, then it was very close to it. He felt almost giddy with joy when he brought his mouth down to cover hers yet again.

Slipping his hand on the doorknob, he opened it and, while never breaking apart, pulled her inside the darkened hallway. He kicked the door closed again with the back of his heel. Without uttering a word, he bent low and lifted her into his arms, then quietly, so as not to alert the servants, he carried her upstairs and into her bedroom.

Audrey's brain screamed for her to demand he put her down, that he leave her house at once, but her heart refused to listen. When he gently set her on the floor beside her bed and slowly, deftly, began to unfasten her clothing, she did nothing to stop him. Instead, she leaned heavily forward in his arms, eager for his touch, eager to know the passion only Landon could arouse in her.

Soon he had removed not only all her clothes but, within seconds, had taken off all his own clothing as well. Standing naked beside the bed, he pulled her again into his arms and pressed her body hard against his own while dipping his head to take yet another heady kiss.

Audrey swooned. Each kiss grew longer and more powerful, leaving her weak yet wildly exhilarated.

Half starved for her, Landon placed his knees on the bed, then slowly lay down, pulling her on top of him. Hungrily, he kissed her mouth, then her neck, then arched his neck so he could quickly nip at the tips of her breasts.

Audrey tossed her head back and gasped aloud. Her hair came loose from its many pins and streamed down over her shoulders in a riotous mass, making her look very much like some wild goddess.

"Audrey," he muttered her name with a sigh of reverence. Holding her tight, he rolled so that he lay on top of her. Eagerly, he dipped his mouth to again sample her honeyed kisses.

Beyond reasoning the why or how Landon was able to make her need him so, Audrey plunged her fingers into the dark thickness of his hair, moaning aloud with pleasure when his lips nipped lightly at her collarbone, then moved gradually lower to claim one of her full, thrusting breasts. An electrifying jolt shot through her when his lips closed around the treasure he'd found and drew the straining peak deep into his mouth.

Though this was only the second time Audrey had given herself as a woman, she knew only too well what lay in store for her and anticipated it eagerly, for Landon meant the world to her and sharing his love was suddenly very important. Burning with desire, she arched her back, curling her fingers around his head to press his mouth harder against her breast, encouraging him to continue with his magic.

But Landon needed no such encouragement. Overwhelmed by the power of his own love, he suckled hungrily on one breast, then the other. Meanwhile, he continued to mold his body against her softness, driving himself wilder with his overwhelming need for her until he could bear the waiting no longer, nor did she want him to. There was an urgency that demanded to be met.

Gently, he moved to claim her. Audrey tossed her head restlessly from side to side, softly moaning his name when he lowered his weight to hers. Eagerly, she rose to meet him, ready to make him a part of her. A sensation of belonging washed over them both, a sensation so great it brought tears to Audrey's eyes. Slowly and carefully,

Landon moved inside her, determined to bring her to the fullest height of arousal. The aching fire inside her rose to unbearable heights, until she had to bite the tender flesh of her lower lip to keep from crying aloud with joy.

Only seconds later, release came in a glorious explosion for both of them, shaking them to their very souls. For Audrey, it was no less than astounding. To Landon, it was proof that she did love him. Despite all she'd said and done in the past, she did love him and she did enjoy making love to him. When they finally broke apart, Landon was filled with renewed hope, but when he looked down into her eyes, he found she was already having second thoughts.

Rather than stay and make her feel awkward, he decided it would be best to leave and let her think things through alone, let her come to her own conclusions as to why they had allowed their passion to get out of control yet again.

"I—I guess I'd better be going," he muttered, still breathless, as he hurried to get dressed. Keeping his back to her so she could cover herself, he added, "I—I might not be able to get away from my meeting with my broker in time to see you tomorrow, but if everything goes all right, I'll be by for you early Thursday evening. You can choose wherever you want to eat."

Though she had not expected to see him again before Thursday, already knowing about his meeting, Audrey still couldn't help but feel disappointed while she watched him hurry to leave. It hurt to think he was that eager to get away from her but, then, what reason did he have to stay? At least it was reassuring to see color back in his cheeks. He no longer looked as if he was at death's door, which was a great relief. The thought of losing Landon all together had been terrifying. It might have been part of the reason she'd been so eager to know his love again.

* * *

When the knock sounded at the door late Wednesday afternoon, Audrey's heart jumped with hopeful anticipation, thinking Landon had somehow found time to come by for a short visit after all. After pausing in front of the hall mirror to make a few quick repairs to her hair, she hurried to open the door and let him in.

Having had plenty of time to think about her feelings, she'd come to the conclusion that although she had not wanted it to happen, she was already deeply in love with Landon and there was no way to reverse that. The best she could do was to try to control her desire for him . . . to try to keep from letting him know exactly how she felt until she could find out what his feelings were toward her—though she was not too sure she would be pleased with those findings, not after having given herself freely to him twice.

Audrey wondered why Landon bothered with her at all. Even if she did finally amass a sizable fortune on her own, enough that people would not be so inclined to believe she'd fallen in love with him just because of his money, she was not so sure she and Landon could ever be really happy together. Their backgrounds were too different. *They* were too different. Having come from a poor family with no real exposure to anyone with money before now, she simply did not fit in. She was not the type of woman Landon would ever want, at least not on any permanent basis. Still, she could hope.

And she did hope. She hoped that after she'd made her fortune with the sale of her railroad, she would finally earn the respect of his friends and eventually start to fit into his life. She would be someone he could be proud of . . . someone everyone would be proud of. Money had a way of making a big difference in how people were perceived. Look at how her broker's secretary treated her now.

With that thought to sustain her, Audrey smiled as she swung open the door, eager to greet Landon. She could not help but feel bitterly disappointed when instead she

329

found a total stranger standing at her door.

A large man, probably a full two inches over six feet, with large meaty arms and a wide, sagging girth, looked down at her expectantly, then glanced past her into the house. He was dressed in a worn pair of dark gray moleskin trousers and a faded green cotton shirt, and he smelled as if he'd already worked a full day in the hot August sun. The unruly tufts of hair that shot out from beneath his rumpled, wide-rimmed hat were shaggy and dull brown, and in bad need of a good washing.

"Miss Stoane? Miss Audrey Stoane?" His gaze slowly returned to hers.

"Yes?" she asked cautiously, wondering what this man could possibly want with her.

A pleased smile stretched wide across his unshaven face as he suddenly pushed his way inside. "I 'ave a message for ya, Miss Audrey Stoane."

"A message? From whom?" she asked, tilting her head to one side and continuing to watch him cautiously. For some reason, the man's voice sounded frighteningly familiar, but she was certain she had never before seen his face. She'd remember a dark, leering face like that.

"Close the door and I'll tell ya all about it," he said, turning back to look at her again, though he continued to show an enormous interest in his surroundings.

"If you don't mind, I'd prefer to keep it open," she said, not about to close off her best means of escape, especially when she hadn't invited him to enter in the first place. A chill skittered through her when she considered what his intentions might be. "And I want you to know right now that I am not at all alone here."

The big man shrugged as if that really made him no difference. "Didn't think ya were."

"What is your message?" she asked, growing rapidly impatient with him, still unable to shake the feeling that she'd heard that voice somewhere before. "And who is it from?"

"It's from Marshall Steed," he said, glancing again at

all the elegant furnishings, as if making a mental inventory of everything of value.

Marshall Steed? Suddenly, Audrey knew where she'd heard his voice before. This was Gene Haught, the man she'd overheard talking with Marshall in the library that same morning she'd borrowed the four thousand from Landon. This was the same man who had arranged all those railroad accidents at Marshall's request, as a way of driving down the price of the stock he wanted to buy. Her insides crawled with revulsion when she realized that this sorry excuse for humanity was every bit as disgusting inside as he appeared on the outside.

"And what sort of message does Marshall Steed have for me?" she asked in a cordial tone while continuing to study the man's ugly face. Audrey refused to let her repulsed feelings show, but at the same time, she had no intention of inviting the man to tea, either. She remained very close to the open door.

"Just this," he said, but then failed to follow through with the message. Though he'd spoken to her, his gaze continued to roam about the room, making Audrey think of putting a second set of locks on all her doors and lower floor windows.

"Just what?" she prompted, ready to be rid of him.

"Mr. Steed, 'e wanted me to make sure ya understood that 'is offer still stands. 'E said ya'd know what offer 'e was talking about. I didn't ask. Didn't think I should be sticking my beak into it. 'E also said that if ya should find yourself in need of any money any time soon, to be sure and give 'is offer the consideration 'e feels it deserves. 'E even said something about upping the offer a 'undred thousand or so, to make the deal just that much more temptin'."

Audrey's anger was immediate, but somehow she managed to control it and smiled.

"How very nice of him. You be sure and thank him for me," she said in her sweetest southern drawn while she quickly shoved the huge, smelly man toward the open

331

door. "But I really don't think I'll find myself needing any of his money anytime soon. So you just tell Mr. Steed that I do appreciate his generosity, but that I am managing quite nicely on my own."

Reluctantly, Haught allowed himself to be maneuvered out the door. "Is there anything else you want me to tell 'im?" he asked, stepping awkwardly out onto the porch until he was once again on the outside looking in. His perplexed frown let her know that he had not expected such an outwardly calm reaction from her. He had hoped for something with a little more fire.

"Why, yes, there *is* something else you can tell him," she said, still smiling sweetly as she lightly gripped the outer edge of the door. "You can tell my dear friend Mr. Steed that I'd truly appreciate it if he would go straight to hell." Then, before he could react, she slammed the door in his face just as hard as she could and, as an added precaution, shoved the door bolt firmly into place.

Pressing her back against the closed door because her legs suddenly felt like they were about to give out on her, she listened carefully for the sound of retreating footsteps, afraid he might try to do something drastic to get even with her for slamming the door in his face. He looked the type not to let something like that pass easily. She held her breath when at first she heard nothing from outside. But finally, Audrey heard his loud stomping footsteps cross her front porch and she sagged with relief.

After she felt certain he'd gone, she quickly turned her thoughts to the fact that it had been Marshall who had sent the man there. She smiled inwardly as she remembered her little railroad and the outrageous price she could soon demand Marshall pay for it. She wished she could somehow be there to see his face when he finally discovered who owned that little railroad he needed so badly. Knowing how much pleasure she would get to once again have him over a financial barrel, she hoped it wouldn't take too long before he found out.

chapter twenty-one

After two weeks of patiently waiting for word to arrive that either Marshall Steed or Andrew Carnegie had finally shown an interest in purchasing her railroad stock from her, Audrey could no longer stand not knowing. She went to see her broker.

Although she had vowed to stay at home and keep a low profile until the hour of reckoning finally came, she had to find out if Andy Rutledge had any idea what the holdup might be. Both companies had had plenty of time to secure all the land rights they could possibly ever need and enough mining permits to be allowed to dig up half the state of Pennsylvania. If something had gone wrong, she had to know what. Either that, or be reassured the time was finally close at hand. The way the price of her stock had continued to drop, especially this past week, she was not sure how much longer she could afford to hold on to it.

"Good morning," Andy Rutledge said with far less enthusiasm than usual when he glanced up from the papers scattered across his desk and noticed her standing in the middle of his office, chewing nervously along the inner edge of her lower lip. He rose immediately from his chair and hurried around his desk to greet her.

"Good morning," she responded hesitantly, hoping that it would prove to be a good morning indeed. "Anne

333

was away from her desk, but I saw through the open door that you were in here alone, so I came on in."

"I'm glad you did. Please, sit down. Make yourself comfortable."

"I'm really too nervous to sit," she responded honestly. Her fidgety hands were proof of that. "I haven't had any word from you about my stock in several days. I was starting to get worried."

Andy's cordial smile fell into a grim line. "That's because until today there was no reason to send word. The truth is, I was just getting ready to dispatch a messenger to your house."

She knew from the solemn way he spoke that the message he had planned to send was not one she wanted to hear. "Why? What has happened?"

"That's just it. Nothing has happened. Carnegie has gotten all his land purchases out of the way, and as far as I know, all his government permits have been approved, yet he hasn't done a thing toward assuring his transportation needs. Neither has Old Man Steed, though I hear he's still waiting for final approval on two of his permits. I just can't understand why they are holding back like they are. It's not like either one of them to move this slowly."

Audrey felt a painful tightening in her gut. "Well, then, if nothing has really happened yet, why were you planning to send a messenger to my house?"

Andy took in a long breath, held it for a moment, then slowly released it. "The value of that stock is still dropping. There has been another accident. A major trestle collapsed, which caused the railroad to have to shut down operations all together. As a result, a thousand more shares went on the market, and because I wasn't so sure you should involve yourself any more than you already have, I passed on them. It was two days before that stock eventually sold—and for much, much less than what you paid for yours."

"Which means?" she asked, though she already knew.

"Which means I'll have to ask you for more margin money," he admitted, then quickly added, "I don't want to, but I have no choice in the matter. If you want to hold on to that stock, you are going to have to come across with more money."

"How much more money?" She reached out to hold on to the back of a nearby chair. Bravely, she waited to hear the amount. She knew that if it was over thirteen thousand, she would not be able to cover it without selling her beautiful house, which to her had become the symbol of everything she had accomplished over the past few months.

"At least another ten thousand. I realize that will leave you with barely a thousand in that shipping company you are so fond of, but if you want to hold on to the railroad, you really will have little choice, rather than to sell off most of your other stock. You have to come up with that money—today, if possible."

His words had come as no real surprise. It was a risk she had been aware of from the beginning. "And do you still think that railroad is a good investment? Do you still truly believe that either Andrew Carnegie or Marshall Steed will want to buy the C & A?"

"Yes. Nothing has changed there that I can see. That valley is still the only one they can possibly hope to use when it comes time to route a railroad across those mountains and on toward Lake Erie," he said, trying to sound convincing, though he, too, was clearly experiencing his first real doubts. "I've kept my eyes and ears open, and I know of no reason to believe anything is different. To reach the Great Lakes, they will have to either buy your preexisting railroad and extend from there, or build their own tracks over the mountains, which would be almost impossible, considering the steep terrain."

Audrey pressed her hand over her face while she thought about it more. She had a strong feeling that Marshall had something to do with the accident that had caused the price of that stock to drop even more, an action that could mean one of two things. Either he'd somehow found out she was the one who had bought that railroad and he had seen it as a way to even the score with her, or he was simply getting ready to buy it up for himself and was trying to lower the cost of the takeover. She wondered which it could be.

"Have you kept my identity a secret as I asked you to do?" she asked, hoping to be assured that he had.

"Of course. No one outside this office knows who I bought all that stock for. I made it very clear to all my employees that you don't want anyone to know you are the owner."

"How clear?"

"If anyone asks, they are under specific orders to claim they think I bought it for myself. And now that the railroad is temporarily out of operation, there's no reason to disclose your identity to anyone anyway."

"And you are certain your employees have kept the secret?" She studied his eyes to try to decide if he spoke the truth or not.

He met her gaze straight on. "They'd be risking their jobs if they didn't."

That much was reassuring, because it meant Marshall was definitely getting ready to buy that railroad—and probably very soon. "Well, if you are absolutely certain no one has yet to discover that I'm the one holding most of the stock to that railroad, then I guess it is safe to invest another ten thousand." She swallowed bravely, then nodded. "Go ahead and sell off however many shares of Atlantic Exports it takes to raise the money. I'm going to ride this thing out to the end."

"She's just invested another ten thousand in that railroad," Roderick said when he handed the weekly report over to Marshall. "She sold off all but a few hundred shares of that stock she still had in Atlantic

Exports to do it."

Marshall's brow pulled into a curious expression of disbelief and delight. He picked the report up off his desk. Quickly, he glanced over all three pages. "Are you sure?"

"That's what the man we've been paying to keep up with her told me," he answered, shrugging. "I see no reason to doubt him."

"It just seems too good to be true," Marshall commented, then slowly grinned. "That girl isn't quite as bright as I thought she was."

"You hope," Roderick said cautiously, not ready to believe Audrey didn't know what she was getting into.

Marshall's pleased grin fell abruptly into a dark scowl. "You just continue to keep me informed so I'll know when to make my move."

"You still think she'll go for your offer?"

"That girl has sampled the good life. She's not about to go back to being poor."

"I don't care what you say. I've sunk my last dollar into that railroad," Audrey said with an authoritative toss of her head, unable to believe that the last ten thousand had not lasted any longer than a week. When she'd received the message to return to Andy's office, she had honestly believed either Steed or Carnegie was finally ready to buy. She was infuriated to discover she had guessed wrong.

"But if you don't come up with some more money, I'll have to sell your stock for what I can get and you just might come out of this with absolutely nothing," he tried to reason with her.

"That's not fair. That is my railroad!"

"You only put up the margin for that railroad," Andy reminded her, his pale expression revealing the misery he felt. "And unless you put up the additional money I need to continue to hold all that stock for you, it automatically reverts back to me. I'll have to sell it for whatever I can get out of it, which, at this point, won't be much. But, then, if I do have to sell it and I am lucky enough to get enough money for that stock to earn back any of your margin for you, I'll gladly see that you get the cash."

"That's because you are required to," she muttered, not wanting it to sound as if he were doing her any favors, especially when he was the one whose worldly advice had gotten her into this predicament to begin with.

"Yes, I know I'm required to. All I'm saying is maybe I'll get lucky and find someone willing to buy it for enough so you will indeed see some of your money back."

"How likely is that?" she asked point-blank.

"Not very," he admitted glumly. "In all honesty, I doubt I can get two thousand for that railroad the way things are right now. I just don't understand why those two companies haven't attempted to buy it yet. Why would they want to hold back purchasing a railroad they so obviously will need to complete their transport to the lake? Instead of trying to buy up that stock like you'd expect, someone has continued to dump more and more of it onto the market, which is why the price keeps going down—and on what was already a practically worthless railroad. It's almost as if someone is out to get you, but then no one outside this office has any way of knowing you are even involved in the deal."

"Maybe Marshall Steed is trying to force the stock down so he can then turn around and buy it for a song," she suggested, hanging onto that last thread of hope. "I know from previous personal experience that's exactly the way he likes to operate."

"But why would he, when it's almost time for him to start moving his equipment in? Besides, the price was already so low it was practically nonexistent. It just doesn't make sense for him to wait this long before buying, any more than it makes sense for Andrew Carnegie to hold back like he is."

"You are right. It is almost as if someone is out to get me," she agreed, giving up any further reason to hope.

338

Somehow, it must have leaked out that she was the one involved in the railroad purchase. She felt sure of it. But to whom? And why would that person want to go to so much trouble to ruin her? A cold feeling of apprehension curled down around her spine. She knew of two possibilities: Marshall Steed or Olivia Arlington.

Either Marshall himself had set her up for a deliberate fall or Olivia had. Both had warned her. Both had readily admitted they would gladly ruin her if she didn't wise up and stay away from Landon. And she certainly had not done that. In fact, she and Landon were closer now than they had ever been. Her stomach twisted into hard knots when she realized her growing relationship with Landon alone would be reason enough for either Marshall or Olivia to decide to put such an elaborate scheme into action. But which one was guilty?

There was only one way to find out. She would have to confront them both. She would start with Olivia.

The Arlington mansion was one of the most imposing homes in all of New York. Grounds and all, the residence took up a full block. The house itself was built of light gray stone, stood four stories high, and was wider than most downtown office buildings. After Audrey knocked at the mammoth hand-carved front door, a liveried butler answered, then upon hearing her request to see Olivia, he escorted her into the library.

Audrey was kept waiting for several minutes in a room that was filled to capacity with an amazing assortment of leather-bound books, elegant furnishings, and elaborate chandeliers. Around the room, scattered with tasteful negligence, were several fine works of art. Everything, from the massive paintings on the wall to the intricately detailed vases and statuettes on the tables and mantels, indicated great wealth.

Though Audrey hated to admit it, she was very impressed with what she saw. Tears filled her eyes as she realized how very close she'd come to being wealthy herself. She might never have acquired this sort of wealth, but she had earned enough in just a few short months to live very comfortably for many years to come. Yet, because of either Olivia or Marshall, she was down to only a few thousand. A cold rage spilled from her heart, filling her bloodstream with anguish, while she waited for Olivia to come into the library.

Finally, she heard a rustling noise out in the hall and turned in time to watch her beautiful adversary make a grand, sweeping entrance. Though it was still early morning, Olivia was dressed in a elaborately designed black gown that appeared to Audrey more fitting for an evening out at the theater than for lounging about at home.

"I understand that you are here to speak with me," Olivia said with cautious reserve as she entered the library and quickly closed the door. "What is it you want? Are you here to finally accept my offer?"

"Hardly," Audrey muttered, eyeing her suspiciously. Obviously, Olivia knew of her need for money. "Why would you think that?"

Olivia shrugged her delicate shoulders. "I can't think of any other reason for you to be here."

"Well, there is another reason. And it has something to do with the C & A Railroad." She watched closely for Olivia's reaction.

A triumphant smile spread smoothly across her pretty face. "So, you've finally found out."

Audrey's eyes widened. She had not expected her to admit her guilt so readily. "Then, it was you."

"No, not me. But I can see why you might think I was involved, knowing how very close Landon and I are."

"Landon? What does Landon have to do with this?"

"Then you don't know. You were only guessing!"

"I asked you what Landon has to do with this."

"Why, my dear, Landon is the one who set you up. He's the one who spread those rumors that his father

340

would be needing that little railroad, so the news would reach your broker immediately. He knew his father had no plans whatsoever of buying that railroad, but he saw how someone else could be made to believe that he did. Then, after he found out you'd actually taken the bait and bought all that stock on margin, he proceeded to do all he could to drive the price of it down. He knew that would force you to have to come up with more margin and would eventually bankrupt you. And I gather by the pitiful little expression on your face that it worked."

"You are lying. Landon would never do something like that." But even as she spoke, she felt a tiny piece rip from her heart and plunge to the very pit of her soul. The pain was unbearable.

"You don't know Landon very well, do you?"

"Well enough to know he wouldn't do something like that to me," she declared, still not willing to admit it could be true.

"Then why don't you just go ask him?" Olivia suggested, clearly pleased to be the bearer of such painful information. "Ask him to his face if he wasn't the one who set you up. In fact, why don't you also ask him who keeps down-selling and repurchasing the other eight or nine percent of that stock."

Even through her smoldering rage, Audrey realized Olivia was telling her the truth. There was just something about the confidence she displayed that made the truth very clear. Pain seized her heart with a ruthless grip, tearing away more tiny pieces until she feared she would have no heart left at all. Suddenly, the room did not have sufficient air. Her lungs burned for want of oxygen. "But why? Why would he do such a thing?"

"For sport, I guess," Olivia answered with an amused smile. "And you have to admit, you did make it very easy for him. The way I understand it, after he carefully set the bait by placing those rumors in the right ears so that it would be sure to reach yours, you went right to *him* for advice about whether or not you should make the buy."

341

Olivia's laughter filled the room. "How delicious that must have been. Silly girl, you went to the very person who'd set you up to ask if you should take a daring risk or let it pass."

Audrey felt weak. Her fragile pride lay shattered in a thousand little pieces at her feet. It was true. It had to be true. How else would Olivia know that she'd gone to Landon for that advice unless he had told her? Lifting her chin, she forced her words around the painful lump that had swelled nearly beyond the limits of her throat. "Enjoy your little laugh, Olivia, because it will be the last one either of you will have at my expense."

"Don't tell me you plan to hold a grudge?" Olivia asked with disbelief. "After what you did to his father?"

"How do you know about that?" Audrey wanted to know, thinking that would be something the Steeds would have tried to keep quiet.

"Landon and I have no secrets. He tells me everything," she purred, smiling with such contentment that Audrey felt a definite urge to slap that perfect smile right off her pretty little face.

"Then perhaps you won't mind telling him something for me," Audrey said in an outwardly calm voice, trying her best to keep her last shred of dignity in place when, in fact, she felt like the biggest fool ever to walk the streets of New York.

"That depends on what you want me to tell him," Olivia answered offhandedly.

"Just tell him that I did not find any humor in what he did to me, and that some day, I will find a way to get even with him for what he's done."

"Anything else?" Olivia asked, as if that message were hardly worth relaying.

"No, that about says it all," she answered before turning to leave, knowing she had to get out of there before her legs buckled right out from under her. "Good day, Miss Arlington."

"And a good day to you, Miss Stoane," Olivia

responded in an all-too-cheerful voice. "A very good day indeed."

Audrey was furious, as much with herself as she was with Landon. Why hadn't she foreseen what a cold and lying blackheart he really was? Why hadn't she realized that he was using her for his own amusements? How could she have been so blind, especially when she'd known from the very beginning that she was not at all the sort of woman that should interest him? He had used her for what he could get.

Humiliation washed over her and tears burned her eyes as she climbed into the cab that had waited for her and ordered the man to drive.

"But where to, miss?" the cabbie asked, turning in his seat to look at her.

"I don't care!" she sobbed, no longer finding any reason to hold back her emotions. The street was too far away from the house to worry that Olivia might look out through a window and see her tears. "Just drive."

"Yes, ma'am," the cabbie responded, his eyes wide with concern. He was not used to his passengers looking so distraught. "If that's what you want, then that's what I'll do. You just call up to me when you finally make up your mind exactly where it is you want to go."

Once the tears began to fall, they poured hot, streaming rivers down her face. How could she have been such a fool? She had honestly believed Landon cared about her, when his wondrous display of kindness had been nothing more than a front he had thrown up to keep her from suspecting what he was really trying to do. Bitterly, she wondered how many of Landon's other friends knew about his elaborate prank. Were they all laughing at her the way Olivia had? Probably. It was exactly the sort of thing they would all find very amusing.

Never had Audrey known such pain. Never had she

felt so humiliated. She had believed herself in love with him and had even begun to think he might actually feel the same for her. What a fool she'd been.

Her tears continued to stream down her face and she saw no reason to try and stop them. Her heart was broken and her pride destroyed, both carelessly ground beneath the heel of Landon Steed's boot. The pain that resulted was so overwhelming she did not believe she could bear the onslaught much longer. It was too strong. But then, suddenly, the hurt reached its limit and slowly boiled over into a dark, simmering fury. Why should she allow herself to wallow in self-pity and suffer endless heartache? Sure she'd been injured by what he had done, badly injured, but not to the point it had left her totally helpless. There was still some fight left in her. There had to be.

"Driver?" she called up to the man whose pensive face looked as if he were in some way participating in her misery.

"Yes, ma'am?"

"Take me back to where you originally picked me up, over on Wall Street near the Exchange," she said, strictly on impulse. "I have a little unfinished business I need to take care of." She reached into her handbag to find a handkerchief to wipe away all traces of her bitter tears.

The cabbie's expression lifted. "Yes, ma'am. Right away, ma'am."

At precisely ten minutes after eleven, Audrey re-entered the offices of Rutledge and Sons. This time, Anne Traylor was at her desk, and Audrey, feeling far less important than she had just hours before, decided to wait and be properly announced. Five minutes later, she was led back into Andy's office, where he quickly rose from his desk, clearly surprised to see her.

"I see you found out, too," he commented when he noticed the puffiness around her eyes that indicated she'd been crying.

344

"Found out what?"

"That neither Carnegie nor Steed ever had any use for that railroad. After you left, I decided to take matters into my own hands and approached the brokers for both those companies with the possibility of buying that railroad, thinking I might yet be able to salvage some of your investment. That's when I learned how neither man ever had plans to build a railroad to Lake Erie. They both had already made private arrangements with Vanderbilt to ship their products by way of the Pennsylvania Railroad. The fact that they were both so eager to build a railroad to Lake Erie had only been a rumor of some sort." He paused, watching the way Audrey had to grip the back of a chair to remain standing. "I am sorry. I am truly sorry."

Audrey took several long, deep breaths, then calmly spoke the words she had come to say. "You mentioned earlier that you doubted you could get two thousand for that railroad now. Is that still true?"

Andy nodded, his eyes filled with regret. "I'm afraid so."

"Then I'd like to buy it from you. Outright. For two thousand dollars."

"But you can't. You barely have a thousand dollars left and I'd definitely advise you keep that right where it is, in Atlantic Export stock."

"I have other resources," she said proudly, though it hurt to think of having to draw that last two thousand dollars out of the bank, especially to buy back a railroad that should by all rights already be hers. "Will you sell it to me or not?"

Andy scratched his head while he thought about it. "Well, the stock has reverted back to me, which means I am free to sell it now for whatever I can get for it."

"Then, will you sell it to me for the two thousand?"

"Actually, I'd only need a thousand and nine hundred to keep from taking any loss myself. Anything above that would have been yours anyway."

345

"Then I'll buy it for a thousand, nine."

"But why would you want to?"

"I'm not really sure," she answered honestly. "Maybe it's because I don't like finding out that I've been cheated out of something that should rightfully be mine. Or maybe I simply have a hunch that I can still make something of that little railroad. In fact, I'm determined to." More than anything, she wanted to somehow prove to Landon Steed that it had been a worthwhile investment after all.

Andy stared at her for a long moment, as if reluctant to agree to her request. Finally, he made his decision but spoke with strong reservation. "If that's what you truly want, then that railroad is yours again. All except for that other eight and a half percent that keeps getting batted around the stock exchange floor."

"I want you to buy that for me, too. Whenever any of it comes up for sale, I want you to snatch it up, but at the best price available. I'll sell off a few of the shares of Atlantic Exports I still have if I have to, in order to pay for it, but I want to own as much of that railroad as I possibly can. I don't want anyone else profiting from any improvements I might be able to make." Especially not Landon Steed.

"I'll see what I can do," he promised, slowly shaking his head, apparently worried she had completely lost her mind. "It's your money."

"What's left of it," she muttered, then forced a brave smile. "But don't look so worried. I'll come out of this on top." She was determined to.

chapteR twenty-two

"Are you absolutely certain you know what you are doing?" Wilson Eubank asked, still not sure why Landon kept selling off his stock in the C & A Railroad only to buy it back later at a much lower price. It was obvious he was attempting to push the value of the stock down but had said nothing about trying to buy it out once the price hit rock bottom, which had to be soon.

"Why must you always ask so many questions? Why can't you just do what I tell you?" Landon asked, not about to try to explain to his broker the reason he wanted to drive that stock into the ground. A man like Wilson Eubank would not understand, anyway. Wilson was all business. His mind worked only with practical logistics. He could not possibly understand such matters of the heart. Wilson would never comprehend his trying to drive the price of that stock down with hopes of making Audrey Stoane broke enough to be willing to marry him . . . even though Landon truly believed she was already in love with him and, because she was in love with him, would gradually come to realize what her feelings were. And as a result, he believed she would eventually agree to marry him for all the *right* reasons. But he also knew that might take years.

He was simply too impatient to wait that long for her to figure out what her feelings meant. Therefore, he was willing to hurry Fate along by getting her to marry him for what most people would consider a *wrong* reason— money. And as far as he could tell, money would be the only reason she would agree to marry anyone right now. Audrey had tasted the sweet life. She would not be willing to return to a struggling life of poverty for very long.

After his scheme had worked and she was broke again, he would wait until he felt certain she'd had a substantial reminder of what it was like to be poor, then he would propose to her. By that time, she would be more than willing to agree to become his wife. And once they were married, it would be no time before she realized she was indeed in love with him. Therefore, the end would eventually justify what might appear to some to be very questionable means. He felt very little guilt for having been the one to instigate the stock market rumors that would eventually bring about her ruin.

"Anything else you want me to do?" Wilson asked, knowing it was best not to argue with Landon when his mind was this set.

"No. Just make sure the price of that stock keeps going down. And see to it that my name stays out of it. I'll drop back by sometime tomorrow to find out how well you did."

"Will you be wanting to go over any of your other investments at that time?" Wilson asked. "It's been almost a week since we've done a complete review."

"No. I have too many other things on my mind right now. I'll simply have to trust you to keep an eye on my returns."

"It's just as well," Wilson muttered. "The overall outcome for last week isn't all that great once you figure in the loss you've taken on this one little railroad."

"Sometimes you have to take a few losses to make any gains," Landon assured him. "You just remember to let me know if and when any large quantity of that same stock suddenly appears on the exchange floor," he said, knowing that would indicate Audrey had finally been forced to give it up for resale.

"But you don't want me to buy it," Wilson restated, wanting to be sure he had understood correctly. "This is not to be a takeover or anything like that."

"That's right. Don't buy it. Just let me know about it," Landon assured him. Satisfied that Wilson would do just what he had been instructed to do, he plucked his hat off the track near the door and left the office.

Believing it was only a matter of days before Audrey would be forced to give up both her margin and stock, thereby leaving her broke and willing to consider marrying him, Landon did not go straight home. Instead, he stopped off at Tiffany Jewelers to look at wedding rings. When the time finally came to propose to Audrey, he wanted to be ready.

By the time Audrey left Andy's office, she was the proud but angry owner of all but a very few shares of C & A stock. She still was not sure what she would do with the railroad, but she intended to study everything she could find on railroad management until she discovered something that would help return her dormant little railroad to a once-again thriving business.

Determined to find the answers that might possibly turn the little accident-prone company around, she planned to stop by the library and take home every book she could locate on railroad management and railroad safety. But first, she wanted to tell Landon to his face exactly what she thought of him.

When a cab stopped to pick her up, she set her jaw at a determined angle and gave the driver Landon's address. With her hands clenched at her sides, she turned her attention to the crowded streets. She wished the cab would hurry and reach its destination before she had time to lose her nerve.

It was while she let her gaze wander idly over the people rushing busily about the crowded streets that she suddenly noticed Landon. He'd just come out of a jewelry store and paused to allow a trio of ladies to pass in front of him.

"Stop!" she shouted to her driver, craning her neck for fear of losing sight of him in the crowd. "Stop. I want out!"

Hurriedly, she searched her handbag for the fifteen cents the driver demanded, then took off in the direction she had last seen Landon.

Spotting his carriage still parked alongside the curb with Patrick O'Mack in the driver's seat, studying something on the far side of the street, she felt instantly relieved. Landon had not taken off yet. Audrey rushed toward the carriage, planning to wait until he returned, but when she neared the vehicle, she heard Landon call out her name.

It felt as if her heart had ceased to function when she turned toward the deep sound of his voice. All the blood had drained from her face to go to the aid of her rapidly pounding heart as she prepared to say what she had come to say.

"Audrey, what are you doing here?" he asked, hurrying toward her. A smile spread full width across his face and his blue eyes sparkled as if he were truly glad to see her.

What a master of deception he is, she thought while she waited for him to catch up to her. She decided he really should have been an actor. "I saw your carriage and thought I'd have a word with you."

"Wonderful! Do you have the time to go for a ride?"

"I think not. What I have to say won't take long and can be said right here," she told him with what she hoped sounded like cool indifference.

Landon drew back at the hurt and the anger he saw in her wide brown eyes. "What's wrong?"

"What could be wrong?" she asked, blinking against a fresh onslaught of tears, her pain still too raw, her emotions still too strained to be controlled.

"*Something* is wrong," he insisted. Taking her by the arm, he pulled her out of the main flow of pedestrian traffic and toward his carriage. His instincts told him that her sullen mood had something to do with that railroad. Either she had lost it entirely or had been warned she was about to lose it.

If she were there to ask him for the money to help her keep the railroad, he would agree to give her whatever she needed—as long as she agreed to marry him. Thinking the time was finally drawing near, he patted his pocket where the ring lay, then placed his hands gently on her cheeks and looked deeply into her tear-glistened eyes. "Something is terribly wrong. What has happened?"

"As if you don't know," she answered bitterly, twisting her face so that she freed herself of his electric touch. "I just found out what a truly conniving scoundrel you really are."

"Me?" he asked. His heart filled with sudden fear. "What did I do?"

"What didn't you do? First, you started the rumor that led me into buying that railroad, then you proceeded to do whatever it took to drive that stock down, knowing I'd hang onto it as long as I could, believing your father would eventually need to buy it."

Landon's stomach clenched. How could she know? How could she possibly have found out? Wilson had been so careful to keep his name out of it.

"You were out to break me right from the beginning, weren't you, Landon? The only reason you ever pretended to be my friend was so you'd have a better chance to get back at me for what I did to your father. Why were you so determined to hurt me? Was it because I'd gotten the money I needed to make that deal against your father from you?" She shook her head bitterly but didn't give him time to answer. "I never dreamed that the interest I'd eventually have to pay for that little loan of yours would ever end up being quite this dear. When you

351

said you did not want to take that interest in money, I had no idea you meant to do something so drastic."

"Wait a minute. You've got this all wrong." He had finally found his voice and tried to interrupt her angry tirade long enough to explain.

"Do I now?" she asked, livid with the biting rage that consumed her but, at the same time, hoping that she was indeed wrong—very wrong. "Can you deny that you were the one who started the rumor that your father planned to build a railroad from his newest mining area in the Allegheny Mountains over to Lake Erie and in doing so would have to buy that particular little railroad?"

"Well, no, I can't, but—"

Hurt beyond reason, she refused to hear any excuses. "Then, can you deny that you next caused the accident that finally put that railroad completely out of operation, and then started dumping portions of your own stock into the market as a way of continuing to drive its value down?"

"I may be guilty of dumping stock, but I had nothing to do with any accident. That was purely coincidental."

"And was it also coincidental that by driving the stock down until it was practically worthless I lost all the money you so graciously helped me earn?"

"I have a reason for that if you'd just give me a chance to explain."

"You don't deserve a chance to explain. Besides, what could you possibly have to tell me? I already know everything. I know that you've been setting me up for this fall right from the very beginning. First, you helped me to accumulate a small fortune, knowing all along that you were merely building up my confidence in you so it would be easier to snatch everything away again in the end. I also know what a big laugh you and Olivia had after you found out I'd fallen for it."

"Olivia? Is that where you got all this? Olivia?" he asked, his anger climbing. It was the same sort of anger that had caused him to tell Olivia about it in the first place, hoping to make her see that he was dead serious about wanting to marry Audrey instead of her. "Obviously, she didn't tell you everything."

"She told me enough!"

"There's more."

"I don't want to hear it," Audrey retorted, unable to believe he could be so cruel. Why must she know every painful detail?

"Well, you are going to hear it," he told her, his voice edged with impatience.

"No, I'm not," she answered, ignoring the dangerously grim set of his jaw as she spun defiantly away from him. "I refuse to listen to another word you have to say."

"Audrey!" he called out when suddenly she grabbed her skirts and broke into a run. "Audrey, come back here."

When, instead of stopping, she continued to dart in and out of the many pedestrians who hurried along the sidewalk, he made a wild dash to catch her, crashing instantly into an older woman who was carrying an armload of packages.

Quickly, he gathered up her different purchases and shoved them back at her in a haphazard heap, apologizing as he did. He then turned to resume his chase of Audrey, only to discover she was gone. He stretched up on his toes and studied the bidirectional flow of the crowd for blocks ahead, hoping to catch sight of her, but saw nothing of her lemon yellow dress or of her bright yellow bonnet. He'd lost her.

Spinning about, he hurried back to his carriage. "Patrick, did you see which way she went?"

"Which way who went?" the older Irishman wanted to know, having become so preoccupied with watching a working crew repair a large jagged hole in the street that he hadn't noticed anything else.

"Miss Stoane. Audrey. Did you see which way she went?"

"Sorry, sir, I didn't," he admitted, but cut his gaze to the crowded sidewalk to see if he might be able to spot her from his higher vantage point.

"Take off down the street," Landon told him as he swung up beside him, also wanting to take advantage of the higher seat. "I have to find her. I have to explain to her why I did what I did."

But Audrey was not to be found. After half an hour of riding along the busy streets, searching for her, Landon asked his driver to take him directly to Audrey's house, only to discover that she had not yet returned home.

Angry with himself for what he had done, and just as angry with Olivia for having twisted it around in Audrey's head, and even a little angry with Audrey for having believed it, Landon stalked back to the carriage and shouted furiously up at a very wide-eyed Patrick O'Mack, "Take me back to my brokers. I need to make some changes and fast!"

Driving as hurriedly as he dared on such a crowded street, Patrick wove in and out of traffic, almost tipping the carriage over at one point. He knew his boss was angry and did not want to do anything to turn that anger against himself. Within ten minutes, which Patrick felt certain had to be some sort of record, they arrived at Landon's broker's office. Patrick wasted no time in hopping down to jerk the door open, before Landon had a chance to rip it right off its hinges.

"I'll be right back," Landon barked as he brushed past the hapless driver. Within minutes, he had given his broker the order not to try to sell his stock after all, but rather to send a messenger right over to the Stock Exchange to put out the word that he was eager to buy up all the C & A stock he could and at a very high price.

Thinking Audrey would probably check back with her broker before the day was through to see if her stock was at all salvageable, he decided it would probably be the easiest and fastest way to let her know he was truly sorry for what he had done. By attempting to make up her loss out of his own pocket that way, he hoped she would see it for the apology he meant it to be and would therefore finally give him the chance to explain the poor reasoning behind the foolish thing he'd done. His heart had been in the right place all along; it was apparently his common sense that had taken a temporary leave of absence. He should have known something so sinister would backfire in the end.

Looking back at the situation as it had been, he realized what he should have done. Instead of trying to undermine her like that, he should have continued helping her to succeed, until she finally felt enough confidence in herself and in her new position in life to consider marrying him. Maybe if he restored that which he'd so foolishly taken away, it would give her back that damnable pride of hers, and he could then start working a whole new approach. He needed to find some way to convince her that she loved him. But first, he had to win her friendship back.

"It really is none of yer business what if anythin' is goin' on between Miss Rachel and Seth Stoane," Kelly admonished, wagging a wet finger just inches beneath Everett's thin, hawk-shaped nose before angrily plunging her hands back into the soapy water where she busily washed dishes, hoping to get them done before Cora and the new girl returned from the market with the purchases she had neglected to get earlier.

Fearing for his immaculate uniform, Everett stepped swiftly back, but he kept his head haughtily erect. "I happen to believe it is my business. As private butler to Mr. Marshall, I have certain responsibilities that should not be ignored. And if I see that something suspicious is going on between his daughter and that oversized buffoon he calls a personal bodyguard, then I think it is my duty to tell him about it."

"And what if ya're wrong about those two? What if all

this evidence ya keep talkin' about is mere coincidences? What if ya've been readin' all the signs wrong?"

"Who could misread the fox-hound looks those two keep tossing at each other when they think no one is paying them any heed?" Everett asked, puffing his chest out and tossing his bony shoulders back to show Kelly how close she had come to injuring his pompous British pride. "Surely, you must have noticed it, too. I know Emma has."

"I don't go lookin' for things that can get me into trouble. Nor that can get other people into trouble," Kelly told him, meeting his haughty gaze head-on. "And I advise ya to be doin' the same."

"Humph! I did not come in here to obtain any of your ill advice," he lied, taking an exaggerated sniff out of the air. "I just thought you might like to know what was going on."

"*I'd* sure like to know what in the hell's going on!" Marshall's booming voice filled the kitchen, causing both Kelly's and Everett's eyes to pop open wide and their mouths to go slack when they spun about to face him.

"Sir . . ." Everett stammered. All color left his face. "How long have you and Mr. Windthorst been standing there?"

"Long enough to hear you blithering some foolish thing about my daughter and Seth Stoane. Just what gives you the ridiculous idea that those two are in any way interested in each other?"

"Sir, it is not ridiculous. I feel quite certain that those two are indeed interested in each other. I've seen how they look at one another and I've also seen her—" He hesitated, knowing that the rest of what he had to say would further infuriate the two men who, at that moment, hurried across the kitchen to confront him face to face.

"You've seen her what?" Marshall demanded to know, then upon turning and seeing the angry set of Preston's jaw, he decided it might be best to wait and hold this discussion later, after the young man had left.

"I—I don't like to be telling tales, sir, but—" he said, hesitant to tell them everything, at least not while they were already so upset. If they knew Rachel had actually been seen coming out of Seth's room in the wee hours of the morning, they might become angry enough to throttle him.

"Then don't!" Marshall spouted. "I'll not have you speaking ill of my daughter. From now on, I want you to keep your petty gossip to yourself."

"Let the man talk," Preston encouraged. "Maybe it's not petty gossip. I, too, have thought something was going on between those two. I just haven't been able to prove it."

Not wanting to believe his daughter could possibly be involved with his own bodyguard, of all people, Marshall turned to face Preston with his wide shoulders arched back and his steely eyes narrowed. "Don't be preposterous, Windthorst! Why would Rachel be interested in someone like Seth Stoane? Just because she's been playing a little harder to get these days does not mean she's interested in anyone else. I think you and Everett are imagining things, and I don't want to hear any more about it." Because, he knew, if it *was* true, all he had to do to find out was to sneak into her room while she was out and pry open her diary. There was nothing Rachel would not admit in her personal journal. And until he had verifiable proof, there was little point batting around his daughter's good name.

Audrey couldn't remember it ever being so hot, not even in southern Louisiana during the height of summer. When she'd left the library with an armload of books about railroad management and safety, her first thought had been to hail a cab. But then she'd remembered she now had only a few hundred dollars in the bank and barely a thousand still invested in Atlantic Exports. She no longer felt she could afford to hire a pay coach, and since the public horse cars did not travel in the direction of her house, she immediately began the long trek on foot.

As she trudged along the sun-baked sidewalks with her load growing steadily heavier with each step she took, she was glad she'd decided not to bring Roberta with her today. Being more accustomed to the indoors and rides in covered carriages, Roberta never would have survived walking home in such relentless heat. Audrey was not too sure she, herself, would survive. She tried to keep in mind that September was less than a week away, which meant cooler days were soon to come.

By the time she finally arrived home, her pretty yellow dress was drenched with perspiration and clung to her in places like a second skin. Her hair had started to sag along the back of her neck, trapping part of the unbearable heat against her skin. Immediately upon entering the house, she dropped the books, which by then felt as if they were made of lead, on the entrance hall table and called out for Hilari to bring her a cool glass of water as she sank irritably into a nearby chair.

She had already been burning inside with barely controlled anger and now she was burning on the outside from the severe August heat. Having reached her limit of endurance for the third time that day, she tilted her head back against the chair and sobbed openly. How could life be so painful?

Even a cool bath and a change of clothes did little to lighten her spirits. And at four o'clock, when Hilari brought her a chilled glass of orangeade and a toasted slice of cinnamon bread to hold her appetite until supper, she was still too steeped in misery to care. She had reached the point in her despair that nothing seemed to matter anymore. Nothing.

358

While bathing, she had considered selling her beautiful new house and leaving New York altogether, going somewhere else to fight her way back to financial stability, some other thriving city where there were lucrative investments to be made.

Aware now that Landon and Olivia were still very much in love, still seeing each other regularly and sharing each other's secrets, she knew if she stayed in New York City, she would be forced to see them together again and again. And that was something she was sure her heart could never take. Leaving New York would be the easiest solution.

But then, she remembered Seth. She knew that he still needed her emotional support, at least until December, and she then remembered how she had promised the two they could be married in her home. Reluctantly, she decided to stay. Though she could no longer fulfill her other promise, that of buying him a nice house as a wedding present, she could indeed see to it that he had a memorable wedding, even if she had to sell some of her new jewelry or part of her new furniture to do it.

For Seth's sake, she would try to forget the bitter betrayal she'd suffered and get on with her life. First thing she knew she should do would be to look for a job to help bring in a little extra money until she could get her investments back into good shape. She remembered Roderick Desmon's offer to hire her to work in his office and wondered if she should accept that or look for something else. But either way, she had to find work. She certainly could not live off the profits of her stocks anymore.

With new found resolve, Audrey silently vowed to restore the two things Landon had taken from her with such carefree ease—her pride and her money. If only she could find a way to restore her broken heart as well.

"Ma'am?" Hilari spoke in a soft voice as she entered Audrey's bedroom, hoping to gently rouse her mistress from her reverie. "Ma'am, you have a visitor."

"Who is it?" she responded weakly, pressing her hand against her temple to ease what felt like the beginning of a headache. It was then she realized that she had not eaten all day. She reached for the cold slice of toast Hilari had brought her just minutes before.

"It's Mr. Steed, ma'am."

"Landon?" she asked. Her heart twisted with fearful anticipation. Was he there to try and force her to listen to the rest of what he'd done to her, even though she'd already told him she did not want to know all the details? Or had he possibly come to apologize?

"No, ma'am, not Landon Steed. This is Mr. Marshall Steed. He says he wants to talk to you. I led him on into the front parlor to wait until I could find out if you was up to havin' visitors or not. I know you's not been feelin' very well."

Audrey's eyes slowly widened. What could Marshall want? Was he there to find out if she was willing to take him up on his offer yet? Leave New York for half a million dollars? If that were so, then she just might do it. Especially now that it suited her needs perfectly to put Landon Steed completely out of her life. Why not take the half a million? It could certainly help her over her misery, and it would definitely solve her money problems.

"Tell him I'll just be a few minutes," she said, then hurried to her mirror to quickly rework her hair. She'd been so tired after her bath that she had gathered the thick, dark tresses into a loose twist atop her head and had left it like that. Now she wanted to look her best so Marshall would still think there was reason to worry about his son's involvement with her. That is, if he didn't already know the truth about what Landon had done. And if that were the case, she had no idea what he wanted with her, unless it was to gloat.

Barely ten minutes later, Audrey entered the parlor, where she found Marshall waiting impatiently in one of

360

the rococo easy chairs. His personal secretary, James, sat nearby. She glanced around to see if Seth might be with them but realized her brother had not come. But, then, Marshall might not want Seth to know about the bargain he may have come to make with his sister, which suited Audrey just fine, because she was not too sure she wanted her brother to know about it either.

CHAPTER TWENTY-THREE

"So, what you are trying to tell me is now that you no longer see me as any real threat to Landon, you are willing to let bygones be bygones," Audrey said, her eyebrows arched with obvious suspicion. Marshall seemed just a little too forgiving to be believed.

"And to try and convince you to take that job," Marshall admitted with a brisk nod. "The only thing I ever really had against you was the fact that I thought Landon was becoming too involved with you; I was afraid it would cause trouble between him and Olivia. But after having had a chance to talk with her personally and finding out how they'd resolved their differences weeks ago, I suddenly realized I have no reason to bear a grudge against you. If anyone should be holding any grudges around here, I guess it probably should be you, not me."

Hearing him mention Landon and Olivia hurt far more than Audrey wanted it to, but she managed to keep the pain from showing on her face. "What about the fact I manipulated that twenty-five thousand out of you a few months back?"

"Oh that?" Marshall said, laughing. "That was business. All's fair in business. I don't hold that against you. In fact, I thought you handled that very well. That's why I think you'd be perfect for what I have in mind. You just have a way about you that keeps people from becoming angry with you, and if and when they do get angry with you, they don't seem to stay that way. You are not only sharp, but you know how to handle people to your own best advantage."

"But I don't know anything about handling strikes," she protested, still thinking it an odd job for someone like her.

"Nonsense. With your cool wit and Seth's brawn, you'll have that strike ended in no time."

"Seth? Seth is to be included in this?"

"Yes. For something as important as this, I'm willing to do without him for a while," he said. In truth, he saw this as a grand opportunity to get rid of two major problems with one easy solution. After having read his daughter's diary and discovering she was the one sending him those threatening unsigned notes, to make absolutely sure he had a reason to want to keep Seth on his payroll no matter what, he was no longer afraid of going out with only James and possibly Everett to protect him. No one had made a life-threatening move against him for months now. Besides, it was far more important to keep those two separated until he could figure out the best way to solve the situation permanently. "Seth will be your show of strength."

"I don't know," she said, hesitant to agree to something she knew so little about. "You never said how much you'd be willing to pay."

"Since I figure to save myself the cost of having to hire a dozen Pinkerton men to go in there and break that strike the hard way, I'm quite willing to offer the two of you twenty thousand dollars. I'll pay you ten now, before you leave, and another ten after you've succeeded."

"But what if I don't succeed?"

"Then you two can keep the original ten thousand dollars, just as long as I know you've given it your best effort. You just won't get the second half. I'm aware it might take you weeks, even months, to accomplish this, but as long as I think you can indeed accomplish it

363

without violence—and without having to bring in any high-priced Pinkerton men—then I really don't care how long it takes you. Just as long as it doesn't take *forever*."

"What sort of bargaining power will you allow me?"

"I plan to send an extra ten thousand with you. If placed in the right hands, I think you might be able to end this strike with very little trouble at all. All you really have to do is figure out who instigated the uprising, who has the biggest influence with those workers, and slip them some of that money to change their views. If that isn't quite enough, tell them it's only a down payment. Tell them they'll get the other half when the strike is over. You also might mention the fact that I am not above sending in an entire force of Pinkerton men—who will not be nearly as nice in dealing with them as you."

Unaware that Marshall's real reason for sending her, instead of one of his own men, on this job was because he saw it as a means to get her out of town before Landon could find a way to reconcile with her, Audrey finally agreed. "Okay. I will do it as long as it is understood that I get to keep that first ten thousand dollars no matter what the outcome." She figured that with her half of that money invested in the right stocks, she would be able to get back on her feet in no time. And then, too, the trip to Pennsylvania would allow her a little time to get over her broken heart before having to see Landon again.

"Great!" Marshall said, his eyes sparkling with eager anticipation. "Only thing is, I'll want you to leave today."

"Today? It's already after four o'clock. Why so soon?"

"The sooner you can get up there and get something done, the better. I realize it will take a while to bring an end to the strike entirely, but I can't afford to have my iron mills lying idle for very long. The sooner you get started, the sooner you will be finished. I already have your first train tickets and enough money to make the different connections that will eventually get you to

Ridgeburg. I also have a list made up naming a few of the people who should prove to be the most helpful when you get up there. You and Seth are scheduled to leave for Pennsylvania promptly at six-thirty. Don't take it for granted that the train will be late."

"Six-thirty? That's only a little more than two hours away. I can't possibly be ready by then. Neither can Seth."

Aware time was of the utmost importance, because Landon and Olivia had in no way resolved their differences, and knowing his fool son would do everything he could to patch things up with Audrey, Marshall reached into his pocket and pulled out his wallet. He knew Olivia was supposed to try and stall Landon as long as possible, but he also knew his son could be pretty mule-headed at times. Time was important. He had to get Audrey on her way. "What if I add an extra two thousand to that original ten? Would that give you the added incentive to be ready in time?"

An extra two thousand? "It probably would help hurry me up a little, but I'm not so sure about Seth."

"That's already been taken care of. I told Seth all about my plans a couple of hours ago. I told him to go ahead and start packing his things in case you agreed. I really do want the two of you to be on that six-thirty train."

To Audrey's amazement, Marshall withdrew a large handful of high-denomination bills and counted out her money. "Here you go, twelve thousand. Just see to it that you are at that station in time to catch that six-thirty train."

"I'll be there," she stated positively as she accepted the train tickets and a large sealed envelope, which she was told contained a list of names she might want to contact first, together with ten thousand dollars more for bargaining.

"Oh, and since I had so little time to prepare for this and couldn't wire ahead to secure any of your other

365

train tickets for when you have to change lines," Marshall said as an afterthought, "here's an extra hundred to take care of getting those other tickets. And here's another hundred to get you back home. That should also take care of your meals while you are traveling. Is there anything I'm forgetting?" He looked at her, then at James.

"What about my accommodations? Will there be a hotel or a rooming house when I get up there?"

"No, but I've wired ahead to tell the foreman that you are coming and why. He's to make room for the two of you in the house I've provided for his use. There should be plenty of room. I had that house built with extra rooms so that I would be able to stay there whenever I visit. Is there anything else I'm forgetting?"

When neither Audrey nor James could think of anything, he smiled and returned his wallet to his coat pocket. "Then, I guess we'll get on out of here so you can start packing. I'll send a driver by shortly after six. Seth will already be with him."

While she walked with Marshall and James to the door, Audrey wondered what her brother thought of this unusual new undertaking of theirs. Was he eager to go so he could make an extra six to eleven thousand, which would certainly come in handy after he and Rachel were married? Or was he bitter because it meant he'd have to be away from Rachel for such a long time?

Audrey was quick to find out, because no sooner had the train pulled out of the station than Seth revealed exactly what his feelings were.

"I'm only going along with this because I was afraid Marshall would fire me if I didn't," he muttered, his expression rock hard when he turned in the uncomfortable bench seat to look at his sister. "That, and to keep you out of trouble."

"Keep me out of trouble?" she asked, finding that an odd thing for him to say.

"Somebody's got to help protect you." Seth nodded.

"No telling what sort of mood those strikers are going to be in, especially after they find out the real reason you've been sent there is not to hear any of their grievances, but to buy off the bosses. I think this little job you've agreed for us to do might prove to be very dangerous."

"That's probably why Marshall was willing to pay so well," she pointed out. And it was also why she'd borrowed Roberta's little derringer and had listened attentively to her instructions about how it use it. She hadn't needed Seth to tell her she was headed into a hostile situation. She'd been able to figure that much out on her own. "Just remember, we are each going to come away from this with at least six thousand dollars to spend—more if we succeed."

"I don't care nothing about that money. That's because I don't care nothing about this job that you done agreed for us to do. I don't care nothing about it at all."

"Nor do I," she admitted, expelling a short sigh. "To tell you the truth, I dread it almost as much as I dreaded running those messages out to the blockade runners back in New Orleans. But then, again, I have to try and remember that these strikers we are planning to have a talk with will probably fare a lot better with us handling the situation than if Marshall had sent someone else . . . someone who could care less about the strikers or their problems . . . someone who would probably just as soon resort to violence. At least with us, nobody is going to get hurt. For once, I think that Marshall was right."

"Right? 'Bout what?"

"A little well-placed money in the back pockets of a few of those striker bosses should bring that strike to a prompt and peaceful end. After that, all those bleeding hearts should finally get on back to work and quit trying to get a free ride out of life. According to Marshall, they are already being paid a very fair wage, and because of how little work they are putting out, they don't deserve to make any better."

What she didn't tell Seth was that she had two other reasons for wanting to go to Ridgeburg.

One was to get away from Landon. The other was that the C & A Railroad, of which she now owned over ninety-one percent outright, was in the same area they were headed. In fact, it was the only railway leading from Ridgeburg to the few communities that lay in the higher valleys off to the northeast. After she'd settled that strike, she planned to take time to get a good firsthand look at her railroad. She wanted to know more about the C & A than the fact that she now owned so many of its gilt-edged certificates. And because it was the only tangible thing she owned at the moment, besides her house, she also wanted to see if anything could be done to restore it to its original state of solvency.

Audrey was still very determined to make something of that railroad, something she could be proud of and, in the process, show Landon Steed that no matter what he did to her, she would find a way to come out ahead. It was the whole reason she'd brought all those library books with her. At nights, when she wasn't busily discussing the strike situation with the striker bosses, she planned to read every last one of those books. She felt certain that in them she'd find the key to saving her railroad. It was all she thought about while the train continued to jostle and clatter on its way toward Pennsylvania.

When they finally reached the small town where they knew they'd have to change lines one last time to complete their trip up into the higher mountains, Audrey and Seth quickly got off. Having become accustomed to these train changes after a day and a half of traveling, Seth waited on the platform to collect their baggage while Audrey went inside to find out where the station for the other train might be.

To her chagrin, she was told the station for the train that headed north up to Ridgeburg was on the opposite side of town. Since it was five o'clock in the morning, they were also told there was not much chance of hiring a wagon or a hansom to carry their things all that distance. Disgruntled that the train companies couldn't somehow agree to share the same tracks, or at least share enough track so more than one company could make use of the same station, they had to load everything in their arms and make the mile-long walk on foot.

It was after six by the time they reached the other station, and as twice before during the previous lines changes they'd been forced to make, they missed the first train out by only minutes. With little choice but to wait until noon for the next train, brother and sister piled their things into a small heap, and while Seth stood guard, Audrey went to find a place to eat. Because the only restaurant in town did not prepare food to be carried out, Audrey had to eat her meal alone, then send Seth to eat his.

While Seth was gone, Audrey pulled out one of her many library books on railroad management and began reading. The more she read, the more she realized that whoever owned the little railroad station where she was being forced to wait out her morning had not read the same book, which stated that customer courtesies were important. Not only was the station dirty, with only a few rickety chairs for a traveler's comfort, but the stationmaster was a grumpy old man who acted as if they had performed some personal crime against him by having shown up minutes after the first train had departed. She only hoped that the unkempt station was not a preface of things to come.

As it turned out, the station was really very nice when compared to the dilapidated condition of the train itself. She really was not too surprised to discover that the owner of this small, ill-kept railroad was none other than Marshall Steed himself. Knowing what a penny-pincher the old miser could be when it came to spending money on someone else's comforts, she should have expected his railroads to be in awful disrepair. Still, it was hard to believe he had allowed his railroad to deteriorate so badly.

After a six-hour perilous ride through the lower Allegheny Mountains, Audrey was happy to hear the conductor tell her that the stop at the mining encampment was next. The sooner she had her feet on firm ground again the better. She was relieved that she did not have to travel on to Ridgeburg and catch a wagon or a buggy back to the encampment, as she'd first assumed she'd have to do. She doubted she could have tolerated even another eight miles on that rickety train, riding on tracks that at times looked as if they would crumble right off the rugged mountainsides and plunge into the deep valley below.

When she glanced out the window to see what the terrain was like, as the train slowly began to lose speed, she was appalled to see that the lush green scenery from before had turned ugly and black. Everything looked charred or sooted, even the dirt, which was a dark, dingy black. As the train squealed to a slow, jerking stop, she glanced up and noticed that the sky was filled with a thick gray haze, probably smoke from the blast furnaces being kept banked, ready for when the strike came to an end.

She shook her head with disgust as she brought her gaze back down to the bleak patch of land that surrounded the train. Though winter was still months away, the trees—what there were of them—were, for the most part, bare of their leaves. What few leaves did still cling to their branches were also smudged with gray and black soot. In fact, there was so much gray and black on the trees and bushes that there was hardly any distinction between the vegetation and the ground itself. Even the tiny stream that wound through the narrow valley was a dark, murky gray.

"What a miserable place to live," Seth commented, leaning over her shoulder to get a better look.

"Isn't it, though," she agreed, already taking her white gloves off and placing them inside her handbag. This was definitely not the place to wear white.

"Well, I guess we'd better get on off," Seth added, though he was not too quick to rise to his feet.

Having already learned that this train car was not quite as tall as most, he stooped slightly to keep from banging his head while he waited for Audrey to step out into the aisle in front of him.

"I hope we can finish our business here quickly and be on our way," she commented over her shoulder then headed for the door near the front of the passenger car.

Because the door they were to use to get off was on the opposite side of the train from their seats, they were finally allowed their first view of the encampment when they stepped off the train. The view on this side seemed even worse, cluttered with crooked rows of smoke-stained company houses that were not much more than one-room hovels, clinging precariously to the tall, rugged hillside off in one direction. A train station, which was not much more than a tiny hut, and the company store stood off in the other direction, built on a large, flat area barely above the level of the tracks.

The store was the only structure of any size that Audrey noticed, until she gazed down the track toward her right. There, probably a half mile away, stood several fat metal and brick buildings, along with the tall, rounded smokestacks that represented the iron mill itself. Other than two thin pillars of smoke that rose and slowly spread across the sky, the mill was as lifeless as the encampment itself. The smell of smoke was prevalent, despite the fact it must have rained recently.

371

With dusk rapidly approaching and the temperatures dropping, the only people to be seen outside along the one muddy street that ran parallel with the train track were a few gaunt-faced men, a pair of hollow-eyed women, and one rail-thin child. All of them were slowly backing away from Audrey, as if afraid of her.

Coughing from having taken in too deep a breath of the smoke-filled air, Audrey glanced back to see what Seth's reaction was to these pitiful-looking people, and she noticed that he was as appalled as she. When she turned to look at the people again to ask them for directions to the foreman's house, they were gone.

Perplexed, Audrey glanced quickly around, first to see where they might have gone, then for sight of anything that could possibly be the foreman's house. She saw nothing that really seemed nice enough for a foreman. In fact, she saw nothing nice enough for any human being.

The houses looked as if they had been thrown together out of scrap lumber, with flaps of canvas and flour sacks for shutters. She frowned with the disgusting thought that even the poorest slaves in Louisiana had had better living quarters than these people. Even the one-room tin hut their father had built from thrown-away pieces of tin and lumber was a good step up from some of the hovels she saw before her now.

"I wonder which one it is?" Seth asked, voicing his sister's thoughts out loud while he, too, studied the dilapidated little shacks that were scattered off to their left.

"Your guess is as good as mine," she muttered, wondering why no one had come out to greet them. She realized they were over eight hours late, due to so many unavoidable delays, but surely the foreman or his wife had heard the train pull in. Why hadn't they come out to show them where to go?

It wasn't until the train had slowly pulled out, headed on toward Ridgeburg, leaving them stranded alone in the middle of all this nothingness, that Audrey finally spotted what must be the foreman's house.

She nudged Seth and pointed across the train tracks where, on the far side of the small stream and well away from both the company houses and the mill itself, there stood a tall, gray-streaked two-story Gothic-styled house. In any other surroundings, the house would have been rather pretty, and it was clear that the occupants had at least tried to do something to improve the appearance of their home. The only bright colors to be found in the entire valley sprang from the small flower box out front, with tiny bursts of yellow and orange. Apparently, the flowers had not been in bloom long enough to become dingy and gray like everything else. Even so, the house looked foreboding perched in the shadows of the mountain, with two skeletal trees standing off to one side.

Since Audrey was certain this had to be the house where they were expected to go as soon as they'd arrived, and since no one had yet bothered to come forward to greet them, they gathered up their belongings and headed toward a narrow bridge that supposedly would allow them to pass over the small stream to the other side. But when they got closer and saw the weatherworn condition of the sagging planks and the narrowness of the crossing, they had their doubts.

"Better carry these things across one at a time," Seth suggested, wisely deciding the planks would not take the strain of any excess weight.

"I think you are right," Audrey agreed, setting down everything she had in her hands except for one small valise.

While she and Seth made repeated trips across the narrow wooden bridge, Audrey had the distinct feeling they were being watched. But by whom? Taking a quick glance around at the lengthening shadows that lurked all about them, she saw no one. In fact, except for the murky water in the stream and the pillars of smoke, nothing moved, not even an animal, and she thought that was awfully strange. Where were these people's poultry? Their cows? How did they get fresh eggs or fresh milk? When she made her last trip across the flimsy boards, Audrey gave one last look around for sight of a community barn . . . someplace where the animals were kept out of the weather; but she saw nothing to indicate where that might be. She decided they must be kept farther up on the mountainside.

"That's the last of it," Seth said when he joined her on the far side of the bridge. "Let's gather it all up and get on to that house before it gets too dark to see. This seems like a very likely place to be finding snakes, if you ask me."

Knowing how afraid her brother was of snakes, she grinned and hurried to pick everything up. "I think we are too high up in the mountains for snakes."

"How do you know?"

Audrey laughed at the hopeful tone in his questioning voice. "I don't. I was just trying to reassure you," she admitted as she started toward the house, which now had a dim light glowing in the front window that indicated the foreman must probably be home.

"Thanks a lot," he mumbled, following closely at her heels while listening for sounds that would indicate they were not alone. The loud, sucking noise of his boots pulling out of the deep black muck while he followed Audrey up the wide, muddy path sounded like the hiss of a snake. By the time they'd reached the front porch, he was jittery all over.

"I sure wish Rachel was here," he muttered, thinking that if he could just see her face again, everything would be all right.

"Why? So she can protect you from the snakes? Why, if I remember right, the poor girl is deathly afraid of tiny little spiders. No telling what she'd do if she saw a snake."

"Still, I wish she was here," he said, pouting because he missed her so dreadfully.

"You'll see her again soon enough," his sister tried to reassure him, knowing the words would be of little consequence.

After they climbed the six steps and crossed to the front door, Audrey immediately noticed a pair of mud-caked boots sitting at her feet, further evidence that someone was indeed home. Setting down the valises and boxes she'd carried, she flexed her fingers until she felt the blood return to them, then curled one of her hands into a tight fist and knocked sharply at the door.

They heard padded footsteps inside, as if someone was walking around in stocking feet, then heard the door bolt slip out of place. Seconds later, they were face to face with a tall, bearded man with long, curly black hair, who appeared to be about forty years old. Standing in the doorway glaring down at them, he looked as burly as a full grown bear.

"Mr. Clifton?" she asked, extending her hand in greeting.

"Yeah, that's me. You that Miss Stoane I was told to 'spect?" he asked, his tone abrupt as he stepped forward to completely fill the doorway. He purposely ignored her hand.

"Yes, sir, I am," she said, frowning at the definite undertone of hostility she'd heard in his voice. "And this is my brother, Seth."

Because the foreman was a big man, he met Seth eye to eye and was hardly impressed with what he saw. "Well, git your boots off 'fore comin' in. No sense trackin' up the front hall with a lot of mud."

Quick to oblige, they both sat down on a wide bench and tugged off their boots, then followed their reluctant host inside. Once inside, Audrey was surprised to discover the house neat, clean, and orderly.

"There are two bedrooms upstairs. You can decide

between yourselves which of you gits which room. I don't really care," he told them gruffly, gesturing toward the stairs with a swift jerk of his hand. "You got here too late for supper, and breakfast ain't until six. Won't be much unless you happen to know how to cook. I sent my wife to stay with her folks for a while, and about all I ever learned how to fix is eggs, beans, and toast."

"Eggs and toast will be fine," Audrey assured him, thinking to get on his good side—if he had one.

"Would be if I had any eggs. And with my wife gone, I don't got no bread cooked to make no toast. So, it'll be beans for breakfast. And unless you can cook and can afford to buy food at the company store prices, it'll be beans for lunch and supper, too."

"How do you live on just beans?" Seth asked, appalled by the thought.

"Look, it's better'n what most folks around here's got," he told them harshly. His bearded jaw hardened with anger. "And where I come from, vis'tors don't go 'round bellyachin' 'bout that what's given to 'em."

"We're sorry. We didn't mean for it to sound as if we were complaining," Audrey was quick to intervene, still not understanding why this man was acting so hostile toward them, but knowing they needed him on their side.

"Well, you'd better git on upstairs and git yourselves some rest. I reckon you've got a long day ahead of you t'morrow."

"Then, Marshall told you why we were sent here?"

Jeb nodded grimly. "He told me enough. And you might as well know it right from the start: I may be what's considered a company man, but I'm sidin' with the strikers. Fact is, I'm plannin' to resign at the end of the week, just as soon as I collect my next pay so I can afford the ticket out of here. I thought you ought to know that up front. And, you also ought to know that I'm dead agin' you and what you are here to do. I plan

376

to fight you every step of the way. Now, if you don't mind, I'd like to get on to bed. Take that candle there on the table so's you can find your way, but don't you go leavin' it burnin' for very long. You'll find sheets and pill'rcases for your beds in that tall chest at the end of the hall. Good night."

Then, without bothering to see if his guests might have any questions, like where the privy might be, Jeb Clifton stalked off toward the back of the house. Seconds later, a door slammed so hard that the tremors could be felt in the floor itself.

And he was one of the four men Marshall thought would be the most helpful.

chapter twenty-four

"What do you mean she's still not home?" Landon shouted, no longer trying to hide his frustration. "Where is she?"

"I told you yesterday," Roberta answered calmly. "She and her brother took off on a short trip. She did not tell me when I should expect her back."

Landon shoved his fists into his pockets to keep from ramming them through something. "Just like that? They just packed their bags and took off?" he asked, clearly doubting the logic in that. Even as angry as Audrey had been yesterday, it did not make sense for her to run away like that. Audrey was a fighter. She had been one all of her life. "They didn't even tell you *where* they were headed?"

Roberta narrowed her eyes. He sounded as if he doubted her honesty. "Miss Stoane said she would wire me of her whereabouts in a day or two. At that time, she said she would know more about how long she'd expect to be gone. Until then, I've been left in charge of the house."

"And she didn't even give you a *clue* about where she was headed?" He rose up on the tips of his toes to look further into the house, hoping to discover that the uppity little lady's maid had lied and to see Audrey standing off to the side listening.

Roberta sighed, growing tired of all those questions. She had just gone through the same thing with Andy Rutledge. "No clues at all. All I know is that two men came by here to talk with her late yesterday afternoon while I was gone—Wednesday *is* my afternoon to do whatever I please. And I also know that as soon as the two men had left, Miss Stoane started packing for the trip. She and Hilari were still packing her things when I got home so I helped them, even though it was my afternoon off."

"And she didn't say anything about where she might be headed while you helped her pack?" he asked, taking his hands out of his pockets again and waving them about frantically.

"I already told you—nothing. And I didn't feel it was my place to come right out and ask. Not even when, half an hour after I'd gotten back from my sister's, right at six o'clock, Miss Stoane's brother arrived with a driver and a big fancy carriage to get her and her things. After that, the three of them took off in a hurry."

"And she didn't once mention a town or even a hotel where she planned to stay?"

"All I heard was something about already having the train tickets. Nothing about where those train tickets were to take them."

Landon felt his heart fall through to his stomach. That meant she was no longer in the city. "What about those two men? Do you know who they were?"

"I think I do, but I'm not at liberty to say."

Taking a deep breath to keep from reaching out and strangling the woman, he asked, "And she didn't even say how long she'd be gone?"

"Not a word." Roberta crossed her arms to show how tired she was of all his questions. "I expect to hear in a day or so."

Landon's shoulders sagged, weighted with misery. He had hurt Audrey more than he realized if his actions had caused her to pack up and run off like that. He was just glad Seth had been willing to risk angering his father by taking the time off to go with her. At least she was not traveling alone. Then, suddenly aware Seth might have mentioned something to his father about where he and Audrey were headed, he bid Roberta farewell and hurried home to see what, if anything, Seth had said to get permission to take some time off.

If he could only find out where she had gone, he would be on the very next train headed in that direction.

Though Audrey had had a hard time falling asleep, she was dead to the world when the loud whistle blast and the bone-jarring clatter of a train passing through brought her suddenly awake. Blinking with sleepy confusion at her unfamiliar surroundings, she tried to remember where she was and how on earth a train figured into it. Then, after the drone of the train slowly faded into the distance, the sound of clanking pans downstairs and the rank odor of stale smoke from outside reminded her exactly where she was and why she was there.

Hurriedly, she dressed, wisely choosing a light gray dress over her other summer pastels, and went downstairs to help Mr. Clifton warm the beans they were to have for breakfast.

"Good morning," she said cheerfully when she entered the kitchen and found Jeb standing beside a small stove, carefully stirring a large pot of beans with a long wooden spoon.

"Mornin'," came his gruff reply. "Beans'll be ready in a coupla minutes. Plates're in the cabinet beside me. Git one and sit down. Water is in that jug if you're thirsty. But don't guzzle it down. Fresh water's hard to come by and I don't feel like goin' after none."

The hair on the back of Audrey's neck bristled. She was not used to being treated this rudely. She decided to try and soothe his unreasonable mood by being extra nice to him. "If you'd like, I can finish cooking those beans for you," she said in her softest, sweetest southern drawl.

"They's already cooked. I'm just heatin' 'em up is all," he snapped back at her, not about to be taken in by her charms.

"You've already decided you don't like me," she stated the obvious, after having studied his scowl for a minute. "Why is that?"

"Because the wire I got said you was comin' here in Marshall Steed's behalf."

"So? Does that automatically make me some sort of ogre?"

"As far as I'm concerned, yes, ma'am, it does."

"Why's that?"

"Because that wire didn't mention nothin' about you wantin' to meet with the strikers and hear none of their complaints. All it said is that you was comin' to solve his problems and I was to help you in any way I could."

"But you don't plan to do that, do you?"

"I'm providin' you breakfast, ain't I?" he shot back. His heavy black brows dipped low over his brown eyes, letting her know that although he was indeed providing them with food, it was not because he wanted to. Obviously, as long as he was still working for Marshall Steed, he felt he was obligated to at least feed them.

"And I will provide our lunch," she offered, thinking that maybe a nice meal would help win him over. Before she met with the striker bosses, she needed to make at least one friend in the place. "I'll go over to the company store and buy what I need right after breakfast."

"Can't. They don't open till nine o'clock."

"Okay. I'll go as soon as they open."

He eyed her suspiciously. "Can you afford it? Food costs dearly at that place."

Seeing it as a justifiable expense, Audrey was willing to dip into the ten thousand Marshall had sent with her to pay off the striker bosses. Smiling pleasantly, she nodded, "I'm sure I can afford it."

Jeb studied her for a moment before abruptly

returning his full attention to his beans. "You do whatever you like. I reckon I'm not opposed to eatin' a decent meal for a change."

Audrey smiled, realizing that she had just won her first victory, small though it was. She decided to push her luck and go for another. "Tell me something, Jeb. Why is it you are so willing to give up your job to side with those strikers?"

Jeb's shoulders tensed, making her aware just how deeply he did feel about his decision to take the strikers' side. "Because I don't happen to think they are gittin' a fair shake 'round here. Those men risk their necks to work like starvin' dogs for a man who doesn't care a ding-dad about 'em or their families. He don't even pay those men enough to keep food on their tables, and the only doctorin' he provides is if they's to git hurt while workin' in the mill. They deserve better'n what they git."

"That's not true. Mr. Steed told me what most of these men are making. Five dollars for a twelve-hour day. And I know for a fact that it is more than a fair wage, especially when you consider how little work those men are willing to do for that."

"I can see he's already done brainwashed you. Either that, or you don't care any more about those men than he does." Jeb turned to look her in the eye. "Which is it? You been brainwashed, or are you just here to do what Mr. Steed told you to do so you can collect a handsome fee, no matter what it costs these poor men?"

"I'm here to help," she said, squirming uncomfortably in her chair.

"Then you're plannin' to see to it that these men git an honest day's wage for an honest day's work and a fair price at the company store?"

"Like I already told you, these men *are* getting a fair wage. If they're not able to afford to put food on their tables, that's because they've been squandering their earnings elsewhere. I can't help what they do with their money."

382

"There's no money to squander. Not when you consider that a five-pound sack of flour costs two dollars, and a half a pound of sugar costs twice that."

"What?" Audrey's brown eyes widened with disbelief.

Jeb nodded, as if he'd just verified his own suspicions. "I didn't think you knew the whole story. There's just some'n' about you that doesn't fit Marshall Steed's mold." He glanced at her chest, with no lewd intent whatsoever. "There is a real heart in there somewhere, ain't there?"

"A ten-cent sack of sugar costs four dollars here?" she asked, still not able to believe such a price.

"A fresh quart of milk goes for six," he told her. "But you can sometimes git it for three once it starts to go sour."

"You're not serious?"

"Oh, but I am, li'l lady. Your Mr. Steed might pay a more than fair wage, but he gits it right back by overchargin' for goods in the only store we can buy at. You'll find out when you go over there to buy up the things you need for that meal you're plannin' on cookin'. If you're thinkin' on havin' meat, you're only choices'll be salted pork roast or dried beef. But, I warn you, it's goin' to cost you nearly twenty dollars to buy a decent-sized chunk of it. Maybe more. And if you want eggs, they'll cost you a dollar apiece."

"If that's so, why buy your eggs or your meat from that store at all? Why not go in together, buy a few chickens, and supply your own eggs? Why not buy a young bull and slaughter it yourselves, and a milk cow or two to provide your own milk?"

"These people came here with cows, chickens, geese, and the like, but little by little, they've had to kill off all the animals to stay alive. Even the horses. And because it costs forty dollars to git a train ticket out of here, and the roads to Ridgeburg are almost impossible to cross by wagon even if they was to git ahold of a horse, they can't very well go anywhere else to replace their lost stock. A

383

couple of families still have a few chickens, but they keep them locked away inside their houses so's nobody can possibly git to them. They know how desperate hunger can make a man. Even an honest, God-fearin' man can be made to steal if he or his family is hungry enough."

Audrey felt a sharp tug at her heart. She thought of her own father.

Jeb stepped closer. "If only you could make Marshall Steed see that an honest day's pay along with a fair price at that store of his would git him more than an honest day's work from these men. Once they are able to afford decent food, they'd git enough of their strength back and enough of their pride back to do the job he wants them to do. As it is now, most of them're too weak to do the heavy work that's required of 'em. And that only leads to more accidents in a mill that's already unsafe to work in."

"Unsafe? Is it really that unsafe?"

"I'll say. Nothing ever gits repaired, at least not like it should. Just in the past six months alone, we've had four men killed in mill accidents, another two die of the black lung, and five others crippled or maimed for life. And I can't count how many're out there right now dyin' from bad injuries or black lung because of all the accidents and because those smokestacks ain't high enough to git the smoke on out of here like they should."

After having seen the condition of Marshall's railroad, Audrey was inclined to believe Jeb about the mill. "Would it make you feel any better about me if I promised to go down to the mill this afternoon and take a look for myself?"

"You'd actually go in?" He took a step toward her.

"That's the only way I'm going to know the truth."

Jeb hesitated. "I don't know. I don't really like the thought of that. You could git hurt."

"I'll be careful."

"That's what Garrison Taylor said, too, 'fore he climbed up to check a leaky valve," he told her with a dark, glowering expression. "We buried him three days

384

ago. Buried his wife and kids the next day."

Audrey felt a sickening chill cascade down her spine. "His wife and kids? What happened to them?"

"Knowing she could never hope to provide for those young'ns once Garrison was gone, Beth decided to take the easy way out. Rather than slowly starve to death like so many others have, she killed her two children while they slept, then took the same knife and did herself in." Tears filled Jeb's eyes, but he refused to let the emotion affect his voice. "Probably best that way. At least she and them young'ns didn't have to suffer no more." He blinked hard and looked away. "I was the one that found them. I'd gone to take them a pot of beans, knowin' they couldn't have much food left, and with my wife gone to her folks, I felt I could spare some; after all, I get paid more than most of the men around here." He heaved a heavy sigh. "I found them all over in the far corner, huddled up in the same bunk."

"I can't believe it is actually as bad as that. How could that woman give up like that? Why didn't she fight to keep those children alive?" Like she had fought to keep herself and Seth alive. Then she remembered how many times she had come close to giving up.

Jeb lifted his gaze to the ceiling, still struggling to keep his emotions under control. "I reckon all the fight had done gone out of her." Then he looked back at Audrey with renewed resolution. "But it hasn't gone out of the rest of us. The men met that same morning and decided not to go on to work. It was Beth Taylor's death that caused them to see what the future would hold for all of them if they didn't do some'n' 'bout it now."

"When can I meet with the striker bosses?" she asked, ready to find out if everything Jeb had told her was true.

"I can set it up for right after breakfast if you want."

"Yes, that will be fine. The sooner I get to the bottom of all this, the better."

Jeb studied her determined expression for a long moment, then reached for the battered hat that lay on the counter near the back door. "I'll go tell 'em to come on over in about thirty minutes. Meanwhile, you help yourself to those beans."

For the first time since arriving, Audrey saw hope in Jeb's tired brown eyes and she felt good that in some way she had brought it to him. But then, a moment later, she felt concerned that she might not be able to do anything to help even after she did find out the whole truth. Marshall had never said anything about agreeing to any improvements. She felt strongly apprehensive while she helped herself to breakfast.

Jeb proved true to his word. Thirty minutes later, Audrey saw six men headed toward the house with Jeb towering at their sides. By that time, Seth had come downstairs and, after having been told how scarce food was for these people, kept his breakfast down to one helping of beans. It was not the first time he'd gone without much food, but it had been so long since he had that his stomach protested loudly when he did not head for the stove for his usual second helping.

Since all the men arrived with mud-caked boots and Jeb felt they'd feel at a disadvantage sitting around inside talking to a woman in their stocking feet, he asked Audrey to come outside to talk with them. They let her have the long bench near the door, while they all perched on the top railing of the wooden bannister that surrounded the porch. Seth and Jeb stood off to one side.

Jeb was quick with the introductions, so quick that all Audrey had a chance to catch were the men's first names. She hoped they would not become angry with her for acting so familiar, but she hated to admit her failure to catch any last names.

"So, tell me, Cody—the name is Cody, isn't it?" she asked of the young man closest to her. When he nodded that she'd gotten it right and made no protest to her using his first name, she forged ahead. "Why is it you won't go on to work?"

"'Cause I ain't 'bout to work for no murderin'

386

cutthroat like Marshall Steed. Unless that man does some'n about that mill and about the prices at his store, I ain't doin' a lick of work for him," the young man told her. Nervously, he ran his hand through his freshly combed hair, undoing all the good his comb had done. His long hair, which had laid straight back, fell forward to cover part of his face. He was in severe need of a barber. And, when he had spoken, Audrey had noticed the pitiful condition of his teeth. They'd been a lot like her father's teeth had been. What teeth Cody still had were dingy in color and rotting on the sides—clearly the mark of a man who did not eat right. She studied his thin frame for a moment and noticed that the rope he used to hold up his oversized pants couldn't be twenty-two inches around. And Cody was a fairly tall man.

"Then you agree with Jeb. The conditions of the mill are sorely deficient."

The men looked at each other, puzzled.

"If that means the damn thing's fallin' apart, so much so that them there buildings are always full of smoke, or somethin's always falling off and hittin' us in the head, then, yep, that's exactly what I mean." He then pulled back part of his hair and pointed to a large jagged scar at the hairline near his forehead. It was at that moment Audrey noticed that Cody's right hand no longer had a thumb. "And my brother, Brandon, he's got the black lung so bad that we don't 'spect him to live out the week. His coughin' done reached the point that half what he spits up is blood."

Audrey's stomach lurched at the thought. "Can't the doctor do something for him?"

"What doctor?" another man put in. This time it was Dan who spoke, a short, wiry, soft-spoken man who looked to be about forty. "We ain't got no real doctor here. Just old Mack Caster, who knows just enough about doctorin' to clean and wrap a wound."

Audrey fell silent, too appalled by what she was hearing to speak. That's when Seth decided to ask a few questions.

"Does the company at least pay for the funerals?" he wanted to know, clearly disgusted by what he'd heard thus far.

"They supply a box and we then bury 'em up on the hill."

"What about the family? Do they get compensated for their loss in any way?"

"They git free use of their shack for the next three months, but that's hardly what you'd call compensation," Jeb put in quickly. "I can't count how many widows and kids have starved to death after their husbands died, simply because they can't afford the train ticket out of here and there's no extra food to be had for them. Charity is next to nothin' around here, because none of these families got nothin' to spare. And with no game to be had in these parts, there's no chance of them goin' out and killin' their own. And you've seen the way that smoke kills plants around here. A vegetable garden is out of the question, too."

"Why is there no game?" Seth asked, glancing around at the bleak countryside for a sign of life.

"Because the noise and the smoke from that steel mill has done drove all the wildlife away," Jeb told him. "Fact is, most of the people here are just plain sufferin' from starvation. And if they don't take a stand right now, all these people will eventually starve—that is, if they don't die of black lung first. And if I didn't have my wife waitin' on me to come and if she wasn't carryin' a child who'll be needin' a father, I'd probably stay on and starve with 'em," he said proudly. "These men don't deserve to be treated like they are. They got a right to feed their own families."

"That's what I don't understand," Audrey said, deciding to make one feeble attempt at getting these men back to work. "If their families are so close to starving, why don't they go back to work so that they can at least provide them with something?"

388

"Because even when we work, we go hungry," a man Audrey remembered only as Bill answered angrily. "At least by not going off to work, we're not working up more of an appetite. Besides, most of these men are too weak to work very long at a time, anyway."

Audrey fell silent again, remembering what a slow and gruesome death starvation really was. Her mother had suffered terribly before she had finally died. Her pain had been so great that at times she'd folded over with agony and screamed out for God to take her. Audrey's throat tightened from such heartbreaking memories, because shortly after that, her mother had caught a high fever of some sort and, in her weakened condition, had died within hours. And there had been nothing Audrey could do to help her. Nothing she could do to ease her pain.

It was then that Audrey realized exactly how sympathetic she was to these men's cause. Hunger was a horrible thing. She glanced at Seth and could tell he was just as sympathetic as she. But, then, he had been sympathetic all along. She had been the one who had come there wanting to believe they had no legitimate complaints. Not willing to believe anything different, she'd truly expected to find a bunch of bleeding hearts who enjoyed causing trouble.

"So, what you goin' to do 'bout it?" Cody asked, effectively breaking into her miserable thoughts.

"First, I plan to make a personal inspection of the mill, then I want to see what your houses look like on the inside."

The men looked at each other, some appearing hopeful, the others still clearly doubtful.

"You goin' in that mill all by yourself?" Bill asked, definitely one of the doubtful ones.

"I will if I have to; but I was hoping to get Jeb or one of you men to go with me and point out some of the worst hazards."

"I'll take you," Cody volunteered, stepping forward.

"No, I'll take her," Rade interjected, though until now

389

the older man had remained cautiously quiet. "Your foot ain't quite healed from that last accident."

"Neither is your back. I can go with her," Bill offered. "I'd kinda like to keep an eye on her, anyway."

"That's all right," Jeb quickly inserted. "I can take her." Then to Bill in particular, he added, "And I can keep as close an eye on her as anyone."

Before it was over with, Jeb had offered his arm to escort her, while all six of the striker bosses followed. Since Seth did not have his boots on yet, he agreed to catch up with them before they reached the mill.

By the time Audrey was finished with her inspection, she was thoroughly appalled by both the working and living conditions these men had been forced to endure. Everything Jeb had told her was true, and then some. The mill was in horrid disrepair—*an accident waiting to happen* was how Seth had so aptly put it. And the houses were little more than *rat traps*—a term Jeb had readily supplied, though Audrey was not too sure even a rat would be willing to go near some of the rickety shacks that had been provided for the workers' families.

But it had been the hungry expressions of the starving children that had made her feel sick to her stomach. There had been one little girl in particular who had looked up at her with wide brown eyes and asked if she could wash her clothes for a dollar. She wanted to buy her mother an egg for her birthday. The girl had reminded Audrey so much of herself at that age that she had immediately turned to Seth for a dollar, then handed it to the child.

When she next headed for the company store, which was to be the final stop in her inspection tour, she was already wondering what could be done to make Marshall Steed do right by these people. Sadly, she realized the answer to that was nothing. There was nothing anyone could do to make Marshall improve things for these poor workers and their families. Marshall was not about to give in to any of their demands. He was too stubborn to allow anyone to tell him what to do with his mill, especially his own employees, and he loved his money too much to let go any of it to help anyone but himself.

Audrey's hands curled into tight fists at her sides. Only once had she ever felt this helpless, and that was when she and Seth had been forced to watch their own mother die. What little food they had been able to provide for her had merely prolonged her death. They had not been able to prevent it.

But she refused to sit back and simply watch these people die. It was as if God were giving her a second chance to make up for having allowed her mother to die, and she would do whatever she could to save them. Problem was, all she could really do was spend the money that Marshall had sent with her to buy off the striker bosses on purchasing food for everyone instead. But she was very willing to do that.

She knew Marshall would be furious with her when she discovered what she had done, and that he would demand she repay the money she had spent, which would probably mean selling her house to do it, but she intended to spend every penny he'd sent with her on these people. Now, she wished she had brought more of her own money as well. As it was, she'd brought only enough for incidentals, never believing the price for them could be so dear.

For the first time in a long, long while, Audrey had found something more mportant than money—these people's welfare. She might be ruining her own future by helping them, might even be headed for jail if Marshall should decide to have her arrested for misusing his money, which he probably would, but she intended to follow through and spend that money to everyone else's best advantage.

When she stepped up onto the narrow platform outside the company store, the first things that caught her attention were the heavy iron bars across the windows and the fact that there were two separate doors covering the front entrance. One swung to the outside and the other swung to the inside. The store was a veritable fortress, as if it had been built to protect gold instead of supplies. Then, when she stepped inside and noticed the prices on the goods, she realized exactly how close her assessment had been. Marshall did have a veritable gold mine in the store. The prices were every bit as outrageous as Jeb had told her they'd be.

She felt a cold rage take hold of her when she considered how little that ten thousand would help. By having to divide it among all the people she had seen thus far, which included over fifty families, she knew that the money would not go far at all, not in this place. If she figured it right, she would have about thirty to thirty-five dollars to spend on each person, and at these prices, the food she could buy would not last them two weeks.

Angrily, she turned to Seth. "I'm going to Ridgeburg to buy food for these people. And I'm bringing a real doctor back with me."

Seth was already headed for the door. "I'll get the money."

To Audrey's growing frustration, by the time Seth had returned with the money, she had already discovered the train did not stop at the encampment unless notified ahead of time. And when she tried to have a wire sent to ask that the train stop for her, she was told by a very cocky old man behind the counter that the telegraph was for company use only.

"But I work for Marshall Steed," she tried to convince the man, especially after finding out that he was the only person in the entire place who knew Morse code. There were two other *company* men working in the store, but only this old man knew the secret of sending messages that others could understand. "I've been sent here in his behalf. Surely, he sent word to you about me."

"He knows you work for Marshall," Jeb put in, his expression grim. "He took the message that told me you was comin'."

"That doesn't matter," the old hunchbacked man told them, his eyes narrowing behind thick glasses. "Unless I'm sent a personal message informing me that she works for Mr. Steed, then I can't let her send a message. Company policy, you know. Could be that Mr. Steed don't want her sending no messages. And I get paid too well to go against anything Mr. Steed don't want."

Audrey turned to Jeb. "What about you? You're the foreman. That means you work directly for Marshall. You are a company man. Why can't you wire the message for me?"

"Because I had my telegraph privileges took away from me last week when I tried to send a message to a newspaper back east, telling them all about what's goin' on here."

Audrey stared at him, dumbfounded. These people had no contact with the outside world. Marshall literally had them trapped here. By not paying them enough to save up the forty-dollar ticket fare to freedom, and by not providing decent roads or even allowing them use of the telegraph, he literally had them trapped.

Her skin felt icy cold when she realized she was just as trapped as they were. Though she had the money to pay for a train ticket, unless this old man was willing to send her message to get a train to stop for her, there was no way for her to get out of there, either, except to walk. Walk over miles and miles of the most rugged terrain she had ever seen in her life.

"Why can't we make a big sign telling the next train that comes through to stop because we have an emergency?" she asked, still hoping to find a way out without any help from the stubborn old man.

"Because the train is also owned by Marshall Steed and is under orders not to stop unless instructed to do so by him or one of these here men," Jeb explained, nodding toward the small telegraph worker and his two tall, well-armed sidekicks who were standing in opposite corners nearby.

"Which I guess explains why you haven't tried to get a message out by way of one of the railroad workers whenever a train does stop. They are probably under orders not to relay messages."

"You guessed right."

"So, what do we do?" she asked, feeling more and more helpless by the minute.

"How far away is this Ridgeburg?" Seth asked.

"Seven and a half miles over some of the roughest land you'll ever see," Jeb answered. "But if you're brave enough to risk the train tunnel on foot as a shortcut, it's only a little over six and you don't have to climb nearly so high up, and you'd be less likely to get lost."

"I'll risk it," Seth told them, then to Audrey, he said, "I'll leave some of the money here so you can go ahead and buy some food for these people, even at these prices. Then, as soon as I get to Ridgeburg, I'll buy what I can get my hands on and bring it back here by train."

"But what if the train won't stop to unload all that food?" she asked fearfully. "What if they're under orders not to leave anything that hasn't either been okayed by him or one of his men?"

"I'll get that train to stop if I have to stop it myself," he vowed. "It'll probably take me a full day, maybe more, to make it to Ridgeburg, the mountains being as steep as they are. Look for me to return sometime tomorrow."

"Follow the train tracks when you can, but avoid the coal mine camp that's about a mile to the north," Jeb warned him. "Marshall Steed owns that, too. And he's got a lot more company men working there than he does here, since it's still such a new operation. If they were to find out what you were up to, they'd probably do everything they could to stop you." Suddenly, his eyes widened and he turned to look at the old man behind the counter, aware he was leaning forward, all ears. "We'll see to it no messages get sent out of here warning them." Then he glanced back at Seth. "Good luck. Even as strong and healthy as you are, you're gonna need it."

Seth hurried out of the building toward Jeb's house to get a blanket for when it got cold that night and a jug of water in case he didn't find any that was drinkable on the way.

"You know, Jeb," the old man spat out angrily. "Mr. Steed ain't a gonna like it when he finds out you're siding with the strikers like you are."

"I don't care what Mr. Steed likes," Jeb shot back. "By the time he finds out anything, I'll be out of here—if I have to walk." Knowing he'd just alienated the only man who could get the train to stop for him, he realized walking might be his only way out.

He felt guilty to know that he was one of the few men there who still had the strength to try it. Being paid three times what the others were paid, he hadn't had to suffer nearly as much. He and his wife had never been without food. And because Gordon was paid more than he was to run the store and see that the profits were shipped safely out of the valley at the same time the profits from the mill were shipped, the old man made six times what the others did and was not charged these outrageous prices. Gordon and his two henchmen got their goods at cost. Though they were forced to live in the three small rooms that had been built on behind the store right next to the animal shed, old Gordon was stockpiling quite a fortune working for Mr. Steed. A fortune he would not readily risk losing.

"And when I do finally git out of here, I'm goin' to tell every newspaper I come to exactly what's goin' on up here," Jeb added with a defiant toss of his head.

"You'll never live to tell anything," the old man hissed, narrowing his beady eyes with warning. "You're not going to ruin this for the rest of us."

Jeb's response was to reach up and yank the telegraph wires, snapping them off right out of the wall.

chapter twenty-five

"Okay. That's it. Store's closed," the old man said, coming out from around the counter with a heavy double-barrel shotgun in his hands. Gordon's two younger sidekicks also had their rifles raised and aimed at the two they'd decided would put them at the best advantage—Audrey and Jeb.

Angered beyond belief but not about to argue with a loaded shotgun, Audrey headed immediately for the door, praying the others would have the sense to follow without causing any further trouble. She waited until they were all safely outside before turning to the short hunchbacked old man who had followed her outside and stood just a few feet beyond the doorway. "But what if I have a few purchases I'd like to make?"

"You can make them in the morning," he snapped with a harsh shake of his bald head. "I'm closed for the rest of the day."

Not giving her a chance to argue with him, he waited until the two other armed men had stepped back inside, then reached for the outer door and pulled it closed with a loud bang, which was followed by the metal clank of a latch being closed. Seconds later, Audrey heard the inside door clatter shut, then she heard something heavy and metallic slide into place.

Without saying a word, Jeb walked immediately to the

side of the building, stretched up, and gave the two outside telegraph wires a good solid yank. The wires snapped in two just inches from the building. "There, now, if he's plannin' to reconnect those wires inside there so he can use that telegraph machine, he's goin' to find out he still can't get no messages through. So, if that's his intention, he'll have to come outside to repair these two wires, too." He crossed his arms defiantly, as if to say they'd also have to go through him to do it.

"But they've got guns and we don't," Audrey pointed out needlessly, though she remembered that she did have Roberta's derringer back at Jeb's house, hidden away inside her handbag. "How are we going to stop them from coming out here and making the repairs?"

"Bein' a company man, I've got a rifle, but because cartridges cost so much, I only have one bullet for it," Jeb said, then scratched his head just beneath his battered hat. "We'll just make so many breaks in those wires that they can't all be repaired, at least not in a day's time."

With a wild whoop, the other men took off toward the railroad track, where the wires ran along the side on uneven eight- to ten-foot poles. Taking sticks, boards, and long pieces of pipe, they broke the two wires—each leading off in opposite directions—in more than two dozen places before they were through.

"We might not get no message out, but now neither can they," Jeb commented to Audrey happily while he watched the men head back in their direction, obviously proud of their accomplishment.

"But what are we going to do about food?" Audrey asked, too filled with misery and future concerns to think of anything but the bad aspects of what they'd done. "Gordon has just refused to let us buy anything until tomorrow. And now that we've done this to his wires, I doubt he'll sell to us even then."

Jeb shrugged. "I can't see that we're any worse off. Since I'm the only one who has any money comin' to him and I'd already planned to use that money to git a train ticket out of here, we couldn't have bought any food, anyway. You was the only one who had the money for food. *We* still got exactly what we woulda had, anyway."

"No," Cody corrected him, grinning a wide, near-toothless grin. "Now we got us something more. Somehow we seemed to have got back some of our pride, which is somethin' we sorely been lackin' in." He chuckled. "Did you see the look on that old man's face when you tore them wires right out of his wall? He couldn't believe you done it."

Audrey had to smile, too. Though she knew they had only made things worse by riling the old geezer, she was just as pleased as they were to have done it. "I guess all we can do now is sit back and wait until Seth returns with the food."

"And the doctor for my brother," Cody put in eagerly. "Seth told me he'd bring that doctor back with him, too."

"And once we have all had a couple of good meals in our bellies and get some of our strength back, then maybe we can find a way to fight back more effectively," Bill put in and started to laugh, but his laugh quickly turned into hard, rasping coughs that nearly brought the tall man to his knees.

"If nothing else, we'll finally have the strength to walk out of this valley and find work somewhere else," Cody said with a determined thrust of his jaw while he patted his cough-weakened friend on the back. "Things are finally goin' to get better. Just you wait and see."

Audrey's smile dropped when she then remembered the old man's threat. Walking out of this valley, even on a pair of fairly healthy legs, might not prove possible. Gordon Jones had clearly indicated that he, as well as the rest of Marshall's men, would resort to force if they had to. Marshall himself had declared he would gladly send in Pinkerton men if that's what it took to bring his workers back under control. She shuddered, wondering if these people would ever get out of this valley alive. Every muscle in her body tensed. She felt as if she were living a nightmare. None of this could possibly be real.

It was the following afternoon before they heard the distant whistle that indicated a train was finally on its way through the valley. Sitting outside, waiting anxiously for her brother's return, Audrey searched the dingy gray hills in the distance for signs of train smoke, but the heavy afternoon heat had been holding the mill's smoke lower to the ground than usual, making it impossible to detect any smoke that might be coming from another source.

The stagnant smoke from the mill was also making it much harder to breathe and had triggered racking coughs among many of the men, women, and children who waited patiently in their homes for Seth to return. Audrey had already suggested they go ahead and put those mill fires out to help clear the air, but she had been reminded of the company guard posted inside with strict orders to see to it that the fire remained burning. And she knew from personal experience how loyal Marshall's men could be—all except for Jeb, who'd decided all the money in the world was not worth ruining all these men's lives.

Hearing the train whistle a second time, Audrey jumped up from where she'd sat beside Jeb and hurried to the porch steps. "It's a train, all right. I wonder if Seth will be aboard this one."

"Settle down, li'l lady," Jeb cautioned her. He continued to whittle away on a fat stick he'd found near the house. "That train's comin' from the wrong direction for it to be your brother. That's just the afternoon northbound passin' through on its way to Ridgeburg. The southbound won't be through for a couple of hours yet."

Audrey let out a disappointed sigh and sank down on the top step, not caring that she was getting her gray skirts filthy in the process. "What do we do if Seth isn't on that southbound train?"

"Wait until tomorrow, I reckon," Jeb said, trying to sound reassuring.

Audrey watched while the train slowly emerged from around a sharp bend at the southernmost end of the small valley. Though it was not the same train she had ridden on the day before, it was just as dirty and dilapidated, and it clattered just as noisily on the uneven tracks.

Lost in her dismal thoughts, it occurred to Audrey then that even if they were able to get onto one of Marshall's trains, the chances of arriving anywhere unharmed were not good. She noticed that the big iron wheels on both passenger cars and two of the six coal cars on that particular train wobbled in and out, as if they were about to break off. She wondered if her own railroad was as badly in need of repair.

"Jeb, have you ever been up to Ridgeburg?" she asked, thinking perhaps he'd had a reason to ride on the C & A before that last accident had shut it down.

"Yep, I been to Ridgeburg. Twice," he admitted. "At forty dollars a ticket, you can well imagine that I ain't had occasion to go more than that. Besides, there ain't that much there. Just a couple of railroad stations, a half-dozen stores, a post office, a small bank, a boardin' house, and a church that doubles for a school during the winter."

Audrey opened her mouth, planning to ask him if he'd ever seen her railroad, when suddenly she realized the train was slowing down more than was normal for a passing train.

"That train's stopping," she commented aloud, and though she had no reason to think it was bringing trouble, a cold, foreboding chill gripped her stomach. What if it carried a trainload of Pinkerton men?

"Sure looks like it," Jeb said, slowly rising from the bench and coming to stand beside where Audrey sat leaning forward on the top step. "I wonder why. We're not due any shipments of anything that I know about. Now that the iron mill is lying idle, there's no reason to

400

be shippin' in nothin' for it. And with no one able to buy goods at the store right now, there's not a whole lot of reason for Gordon to be stockin' up on any more goods. But with old Gordon, you just never know."

Audrey, too, slowly stood up, watching cautiously. "What if he decides to come out and tell the engineer or the conductor about what has happened here? What if he gets word to them that Seth is out there trying to bring food back?"

Every muscle in Jeb tightened. "I hadn't thought of that." Instantly, he took off, running toward the train.

"Wait," Audrey called out to him, wanting to give him the little derringer she'd taken out of her handbag and slipped into her skirt pocket. But the loud, grinding squeal of the brakes drowned out her voice.

Lifting her skirts as high as she dared, she, too, started to run as fast as she could.

By the time Audrey had crossed the stream and neared the tracks, Jeb had already jumped over them and was headed in a dead run to where the train had slowly come to a halt.

She lost sight of him for a few seconds, until she, too, had crossed the tracks and headed toward the front of the train. When she finally caught sight of Jeb again, he stood near the train, but his gaze was locked on the front door of the store. His huge hands were doubled into determined fists.

By the time Audrey had joined him, she was bent over, coughing from all the soot she'd been forced to breathe, and gasping for breath. Her lungs burned deep in her chest for want of clean air. When she heard a door slide open behind them, she turned to catch a glimpse of whoever was getting off that train. Never had she been more surprised to see Landon Steed.

"Audrey," he said. Spotting her immediately, he dropped his valise on the ground and rushed forward. At that same moment, the front door of the store swung open with a startling bang and out stepped Gordon Jones

401

and his two young henchmen, their rifles and shotgun poised.

Reacting purely on gut fear and survival instinct, Audrey pulled the pistol out of her pocket and pointed it at Landon. Calling out to the three men still standing on the raised platform in front of the store, she shouted, "Toss over all your weapons or I'll shoot Marshall Steed's only son right where he stands."

"Marshall's son?" Gordon responded with a laugh, clearly not believing the handsome young man who'd gotten off the train was Landon Steed. "What would bring Marshall's son out here? Why, Marshall himself has only been here twice that I know anything about."

Landon was too stunned to say anything. His pale eyes were frozen on the gleaming barrel of the small derringer pointed directly at his stomach.

"I don't know what brought him here, but if you don't drop those rifles and that shotgun, I know how he'll be leaving—in a box." She tried to keep her voice loud and strong, hoping to show she meant business, when inside she was such a jumble of twisting nerves that she could barely think straight. All she knew was that she had to do something—for Seth's sake. Blinking hard, in an effort to keep her thoughts clear, she spoke to Landon next. "You want to tell that man up there who you are? Or would you rather wait and have us inform the undertaker of your identity when he comes to collect your body."

"Audrey," Jeb cautioned her, his eyes so wide they looked as if they might burst right out of their sockets. "You sure you know what you're doin'?"

"I'm keeping Gordon from getting any messages out to that train," Audrey said, frowning because her voice had come out strangled. Her throat had closed tight from fear. "I'm just trying to save my brother's life, because if Gordon gets that message out, Seth might very well end up a dead man." She was sweating so hard that she could feel the moisture and the soot collecting on her skin.

"Seth?" Landon said, finally finding his voice.

"What's happened to Seth?"

"Nothing," Audrey answered, aware her hand had started to tremble, clearly revealing the fear she felt. She brought her other hand up to help steady the gun. "Nothing has happened to him yet. But if I can't convince that man exactly who you are and he tries to get a message out by way of that train to those men up at your father's coal mine, which is just a mile or so north of here, my brother could be in very grave danger."

Landon studied her pale expression and the way her entire body trembled, and he realized she spoke the truth—or at least she thought she did. He then noticed the crowd of people gathering in the distance. Some were armed with boards and sticks, but none were quite brave enough to come forward. Finally, he noticed the three men on the platform with rifles and a shotgun held ready and several handguns tucked away within easy grasp.

Confused by what was going on but realizing that he somehow held the key to Seth's safety and probably Audrey's, too, he raised his voice so everyone could hear. "I don't really know what it has to do with anything, but my name *is* Landon Steed. Marshall Steed *is* my father. I have identification in my pocket." He also had a small revolver, which he always carried with him whenever he traveled, but for now he'd leave it where it was. "If Miss Stoane will hold off shooting me long enough to permit me to reach inside my coat and get my wallet, I can prove exactly who I am."

Audrey swallowed hard, wondering what to do. She remembered from previous conversations that Landon usually carried a small handgun beneath his coat when traveling. It was what had made her think to ask Roberta to borrow hers. But she also knew his identification would indeed be in his wallet. It was a hard decision to make. If only she could trust him.

"Okay, but reach in with your left hand and pull it out very, very slowly," she finally said. "Or, so help me, Landon, I'll put a hole right through you."

403

Landon wondered if she really could and knew he had no desire to put her to the test. Slowly, he slipped his left hand into his coat pocket and drew out his wallet. Then, just as slowly, he reached inside the wallet and pulled out his bank signature card, which allowed him to write a bank draft at practically any bank in the nation.

Jeb hurried forward to get the piece of paper, then, after looking at it, carried it to Gordon and held it up for the old man to see. "Looks like she's tellin' the truth. Better toss those guns to the ground. I don't think the boss would take too kindly to havin' his only son gunned down just 'cause you took a notion to be stubborn." He then grinned. "Looks to me like you got ahold of one bad situation here, Gordy. Better go on and do what the li'l lady says."

Gordon's face twisted into an angry glower behind his rounded spectacles. Slowly, he lowered his shotgun, then tossed it forward to the ground. Because of his poor aim, it landed in a large muddy puddle and all but the tip disappeared. The other two men then sent their rifles clattering to the ground nearby. Jeb quickly kicked them all up under the platform so they could not be easily reached.

"Now, for your pistols," Jeb said, stepping closer and putting his hand out. "If you'd be so kind as to fork them over one at a time."

Reluctantly, the three men pulled their handguns out of their holsters and held them, handle out, to Jeb, who quickly took the first two and tucked them into his belt, then reached for Gordon's, only to find out the old man had suddenly had a change of heart. Instead of handing it over willingly, he spun it about in his hand with surprising agility and pointed it at Jeb.

"That little gal ain't gonna shoot that man," he decided with a firm shake of his bald head. "I don't think she has it in her." Slowly, he started backing away, toward the door.

Audrey panicked. She had two choices. She could

either let the old man regain control of the situation by not following through with her threat, or she could shoot Landon. Her fearful brown eyes rose to meet with Landon's questioning blue ones and she knew in that instant that, even as angry as she was with him and even as afraid as she was for her brother, she could never shoot him. Not Landon. She loved him too much.

But she might have the courage to shoot the old man.

With that new thought in mind, she swung her pistol around and aimed it at Gordon. "Maybe you're right. Maybe I can't shoot Landon. But you'd better drop that gun or I'll shoot *you*."

Gordon glanced over to see that the pistol was now aimed at his own stomach and he dropped the gun immediately. His hands flew high into the air as if to show he was now just a harmless old man.

Jeb let out the breath he'd been holding and quickly bent forward to pick up the handgun before it caused any more trouble.

The train engineer, having witnessed the whole strange affair, immediately shouted out for his helper to get the train moving. Barely a second later, the sound of metal creaking and the engine slowly chugging alerted Audrey to the fact that the train was indeed pulling out.

"Oh, no!" she cried out when she saw the huge wheels start to turn. "He'll get to the next telegraph and have them wire Marshall exactly what he saw here. If he does, Marshall will have those Pinkerton men on their way in a matter of hours."

Jeb turned and watched helplessly while the train slowly picked up speed. He was too far away even to hope to catch it.

Landon, still not understanding what was going on but realizing Audrey did not want that train to leave, took off, running beside it, trying to match his speed with its.

"Come back here, you coward," Audrey called out to him, knowing that if he got away, with him went any bargaining power they might still have. As long as they held a gun to his head, Marshall would be reluctant to do anything rash. Still gripping the small pistol in her hand, she took off, running after him, though she had no idea what she would do if and when she caught up with him.

To her horror, when Landon neared one of the passenger cars, he reached out and grabbed hold of a large iron handle attached to the side as the train was accelerating. It was then she realized he was about to get away. Overwhelmed with the need to stop him, she lifted her pistol high into the air and took aim—but discovered she still could not shoot. As she lowered the gun again, feeling like her whole world had crumbled in around her, she saw him loosen his grip and fall off the side of the train. He rolled several times before coming to a stop facedown.

Disbelieving what she saw, Audrey watched for several seconds. Breathlessly, she waited for him to get up, but he did not move. With her heart lodged in her throat, frozen in fear, she ran toward him again.

"Landon?" she cried out. Tears filled her eyes at the thought he might be dead. "Landon, get up!"

Being the closest, she was the first to arrive at his side. She knelt down, sobbing with fear, wanting to touch him but afraid to. "Landon, please, get up. Please, don't be dead."

With trembling hands, she turned him over so she could see his face. When she did, his mouth twisted into a painful grimace as he tried to smile. "I think I missed my train." He blinked hard in a strong effort to remain conscious.

The blood that oozed from a large gash near his temple alerted Audrey to the fact that he was badly hurt and in need of her care. By then, Cody and Bill had come to see what they could do.

"Help me get him to Jeb's house. If we hope to keep Marshall Steed from sending in a whole army of Pinkerton men and armed thugs, we will need this man—and we will need him healthy enough to write a letter."

Her mind was already at work, formulating a plan that might save what until now appeared to be a hopeless situation.

Because Landon could stand on his own feet, all Cody and Bill had to do was give him a little extra support to make the long walk back to Jeb's house without falling again. In his valiant run for the train, Landon had covered quite a distance.

"Put him upstairs in Seth's room," Audrey told them when they entered the front door. She figured they would be able to better hold him for their prisoner by putting him up there. That way, he'd have to either climb out one of the three narrow windows and jump directly to the ground, or he'd have to come down the stairs. Now that they had several guns in their possession, she felt it would not be too hard to keep all four exits covered.

"Take away his boots after you've gotten him in that bed. That way, if he tries to get away, he'll be forced to travel in his stocking feet, and in this rocky terrain, he won't get very far very fast. I'll get some water and a clean cloth to bathe his wounds, then I'll be right up to help."

After quickly gathering the things she needed to cleanse Landon's injuries, she hurried upstairs just in time to see Cody and Bill come out of the bedroom, each carrying a shiny black Hessian boot. Both were eyeing the fancy stitching, as if trying to decide if their own feet might fit into such fine boots but not quite having the courage to try them on.

Catching the door before it had closed behind them, Audrey entered the bedroom with her bowl of water and the assorted cloths she'd gathered for cleansing and for bandaging.

"Audrey, what the hell is going on here?" Landon asked when he glanced up and saw her entering the room.

"You tried to get away but didn't quite succeed," she said as she stepped further into the room.

"I was trying to stop that train," he muttered. "And

you know that is not what I mean. What is going on around here? Why are you at odds with the men in that store and who are they?"

"You'll find that out in due time," she answered evasively, glimpsing him in the bed, half covered with a sheet even though he was still fully clothed. Her heart took a sudden leap just knowing he was really there. "Right now, all you need to be concerned with is the fact that you've been injured and I've come to help."

"There's a lot more for me to be concerned with here than that," he told her, determined not to be put off. If Audrey was in danger, he wanted to help.

"You are right, there is. And when I'm ready for you to know something more, I'll tell you."

"Audrey, please," he tried again, but was interrupted by the sound of boots striking the bare wooden floor outside the room.

Seconds later, Jeb appeared in the doorway. His expression revealed how truly frustrated he felt. "I got bad news."

"What?" Audrey asked, her face tense as she prepared to hear the worst.

"I'm afraid I was so busy watchin' that train take off that old Gordon and his two boys managed to get away from me. They've locked themselves back up in that store again. Now we can't get in there at all."

"Like you told me, that really doesn't change anything. You don't have any less than you had before."

Jeb's expression turned sour. "I know, but I'd sorta hoped we could get to that food before Marshall sent anyone down here to try and force us to do what he wants." His eyes were filled with misery. "By tomorrow afternoon, this place is going to be swarming with all those Pinkerton men you been tellin' us about. You'd think we could at least have one last good meal before that happens."

Audrey set her bowl of water on a table near the bed, then turned to reassure Jeb. "I've got an idea that might keep those Pinkerton men out of here, at least for a while."

"What's that?" he asked eagerly.

"I don't want to talk about it just yet," she said, glancing down at Landon with a meaningful expression. "You go on back downstairs and get several of the men together so we can discuss it at length. I'll be down in just a few minutes."

Jeb also looked at Landon. His eyebrows quirked with uncontainable curiosity. "You really Marshall Steed's boy?"

Though he was not so sure he fit the description of "boy," Landon nodded that he was.

"Well, I'll be. What are you doin' here, anyway? You come to be sure Audrey here was doin' her job right?"

When Landon's only reaction to that question was to look at Audrey with a worried expression, Jeb continued with what he had to say, "Because if you are here to check up on her, you're goin' to find out that she's not exactly doin' what she's been told to do. And I'm damn glad she ain't." Then, turning abruptly away, he nodded to Audrey. "I'll get the men together. We'll be waitin' to hear what this idea of yours is all about."

Landon waited until the heavy footsteps indicated that Jeb was downstairs before slowly lifting his gaze to meet with Audrey's. "What exactly is your idea?"

"You'll find out soon enough," she told him, then immediately set about dipping one of the cloths into the cool water and cleaning the dirt and dried blood away from his wounds. Though he was badly bruised in several places, all together he had only three major injuries that she could see: the large gash on his head; a deep cut on his elbow, where his coat and shirtsleeve had torn away and allowed his skin to come in direct contact with the ground; and the last wound that was easily detectable lay across the back of his left hand, where he'd managed to peel away nearly all the skin. If he had other injuries, he didn't mention them and she certainly did not plan to go looking for them.

"Take your coat off so I can get to that elbow," she commanded sternly, trying to sound more annoyed than anything else. But when he then proceeded to take his shirt off, too, she quickly turned her back and demanded that he keep it on. "All you really need to do is roll up that sleeve," she told him, her voice a little strained at the thought of once again seeing that wonderfully masculine chest of his.

After she carefully washed and bandaged all three of the injured areas and had then turned to leave the bedroom, Landon called out to her. Eager to get away from his intimidating presence, she was reluctant to respond but, at the same time, was too curious to know what he had to say to actually walk out of the room without giving him the chance to speak.

"What do you want?" she asked impatiently.

"Don't you even want to know why I am here?"

"No," she lied, though, in truth, she was bursting to know the reason. "It's really none of my business."

"I came here to apologize to you," he told her bluntly.

"That's very nice, but I don't want to hear any apologies from you," she told him, lifting her chin with a determined air. Finding it hard to trust anything he had to say, she tried to seem unmoved by his words. But deep inside, her heart fluttered with renewed hope. Had he really come all that way just to apologize?

"Then what *do* you want to hear from me? Maybe you want to hear that I love you," Landon said, carefully watching to see what her reaction would be. "Because if that's what you want to hear, I'll gladly say it. Audrey, I love you."

"Oh, you love me all right," she said, angry that he could tell such a bald-faced lie and sound so sincere. Tears of hurt and pure rage filled her eyes as she stepped closer. "You love me so much that you decided to do what you could to ruin me. Landon, do you really think I'm so foolish that I've forgotten everything

410

that you did?"

"No, I don't expect you to forget. My only hope is that you will forgive."

"Forgive? Why should I?" Her voice rose with utter disbelief.

Landon thought carefully about how he should word his answer. "Because I did it out of love."

"You what?" she asked, stunned by such an incredulous statement.

"I did it out of love," he repeated, carefully meeting her tearful gaze, hoping to show how very much he had meant what he'd said. "I thought that by causing you to go broke, I could get you to marry me."

"Of course," she said, angry that he could say something so outlandish and expect her to believe it. "What a clever plan that was."

Landon's expression darkened. "It didn't exactly work out the way I'd hoped it would."

"Well, I'd love to stay here and talk more about this," Audrey said, having heard enough of his nonsense, "but I have people waiting for me downstairs."

She turned to hurry out of the room, but just seconds before she reached the door she heard him call out to her again. For the life of her, she could not simply ignore him and go on. Taking a deep breath, she turned to face him again, just in time to watch him pull a small revolver out from beneath his bedcover and point it at her.

"You *will* hear me out," he said, his voice low with determination. "Now shut that door and get back over here."

chapter twenty-six

Aware it would not really be to her best advantage to argue with Landon at that moment, Audrey slowly closed the door and stepped closer to where he lay propped up on the bed using his good elbow. The revolver was still aimed in the general direction of her midsection, making her feel incredibly stupid for not having warned Cody and Bill about the pistol so they could have taken it away from him at the same time they took his boots.

"Well, if you put it that way," she retorted, tossing her head indignantly. "Just what is it you want to say to me?"

"First, I want a chance to explain why I did what I did. Then, I want to know what is going on around here and what this idea of yours is all about."

"So, go ahead, explain why you so cruelly decided to destroy me financially. Explain how that was really an act of deep devotion and love," she said. Her jaw hardened and her nostrils flared in a hopeless attempt to keep her rage under control. For a brief moment, she thought about her own pistol, which she had returned to her pocket. But she knew she would be senselessly risking personal injury if she tried to get to it. Until he lowered his revolver, she was forced to do exactly what he wanted her to do.

"Sit down," he told her, motioning to a nearby chair. "You make me nervous standing over me like that."

"You're the one who has control of the gun and *I* make you nervous," she repeated for clarification.

He grinned at the illogic in that. "Yes."

Finding his grin contagious, she, too, smiled while she eased her weight into a nearby chair. It took a lot of effort to erase that smile and replace it with what she felt was a far more appropriate frown. "Okay, I'm seated."

Landon then lowered the revolver, setting it on the bed beside him, still within easy reach but making it less of a threat. "I know it doesn't sound very clever, and now that I've had plenty of time to look back on it, even I can see how wrong I was, but when I first decided to spread that rumor about Father needing that little railroad, I did it hoping I could get you to marry me."

"You're right. It doesn't sound like a very clever idea," she agreed wholeheartedly, her eyes trained on the pistol. She wondered how quick he could pick it up and fire, and decided probably a lot quicker than she could pull hers out of her pocket, release the safety, aim, then shoot.

"The whole reason I started that rumor is because I was hoping you would take the bait and sink all your money into that railroad. I knew you had established yourself well enough to be allowed to purchase on margin and your reputation for taking risks was known enough to make your broker think of you as the logical choice to tell. The truth is, I wanted you so broke that you would be forced to go back to living the way you were before, barely having enough money to feed and clothe yourself. Then, after you had a good, long taste of living like that again, I planned to ask you to marry me."

"Thinking I'd jump at the chance to be wealthy again," she concluded, finally starting to understand but still finding the logic a little confusing. "But why go to all that trouble?"

"I could tell you were starting to care for me, but for some reason you were fighting those feelings every step of the way. You were too eager to become rich to allow

413

yourself to concentrate on anything but making it big.
And, because I *was* so certain you had started to care for
me and I knew how very much I was already in love with
you, I decided to try to do something about it. I knew that
if I waited for you to realize your true feelings and be
willing to marry me for all the *right* reasons, it might be
years before I ever convinced you to say "I do." The
thought of waiting that long to make you my wife was
eating me alive. I had to have you. So, I decided to try and
hurry fate along by getting you to marry me for the *wrong*
reason—in this case, money. I knew you had experienced
the sweet life at last and would not want to go back to
living in near poverty, at least not for very long.
Therefore, by ruining you financially, I had hoped to
increase my chances of getting you to marry me. Olivia
knew about it only because I wanted her to understand
how much I had come to care for you."

Audrey stared at him with a blank expression, unable
to believe she had heard him correctly. "Let me get this
straight. You'd have me marry you for your money. It
wouldn't bother you at all that I might not be marrying
you out of love?" Her eyebrows rose slightly. She found
it hard to believe the irony. Not wanting him to think that
the only reason she was in love with him was because of
his money had been the main reason she'd fought her
emotions for so long. Yet, here he had admitted he did
not even care if that was a reason.

"You would come to love me in time," he quickly
explained, and he fully believed it—that is, if she did not
already love him, which he thoroughly suspected she did.
He believed she was too afraid of her own feelings to
admit she loved him yet, even to herself. "I know you
would."

Audrey was now too confused by what he'd told her to
know whether to be angry or happy. He had lied to her,
and he had cheated her out of all that money she was so
proud of; but in his own strange sort of way, he'd done it
because he loved her. Her eyes widened when she looked

414

at him again. "Do you still want me to marry you?"

"Yes, of course I do. That's one of the reasons I came out here. And, believe me, it was not an easy task finding out where you'd gone. If Seth hadn't told Rachel, I'd never have discovered where you two had gone . . . or at least where *you* had ended up. You still haven't told me where Seth is. Rachel was under the impression he intended to stay right here with you."

So that was how he'd found out where she was. Rachel had told him. Thinking only Marshall and James knew of her whereabouts, she'd wondered how Landon had ever gotten that information and had finally decided he must have had other reasons for stopping by there. She knew it would have ruined Marshall's obviously well-conceived plan to trap her there, along with the rest of those people, if he had told anyone, especially Landon. "If you really want me to marry you, then promise to help these people. Promise to do whatever it is we ask of you, and I will indeed marry you."

"When? When will you marry me?"

"Whenever you say. Tomorrow if you want."

"I guess tomorrow will be soon enough," he said with a growing smile, then asked eagerly, "What is it you want me to do?"

Quickly, Audrey filled him in on everything that had happened since her arrival, including the fact that she was determined to help these people, whatever the cost. "You can't imagine how your father has treated them. They live in squalor and can hardly afford food to stay alive, yet he expects a full day of work out of them—six days a week. We've got to make Marshall see how wrong that is."

"But first we have to stop him from sending in a dozen or so Pinkerton agents," Landon said, nodding agreeably. "And I'm not so sure Pinkerton agents are all he'll send in here. You said you have an idea. What is it?"

Audrey smiled sheepishly, hating to admit her willingness to consider such questionable means. "I'd planned to force you to write a letter to your father—at gunpoint if I had to. In the letter, I intended for you to warn your father that if he dared to send anyone in here with either guns or dynamite, your life would be in as much danger as the rest of these people—if not more. I figured if he knew we were holding you here at gunpoint, he'd be less likely to do something rash."

"A letter? That would be too slow. No doubt, by now, the engineer on that train has sent him word of what happened here. We need to send our message by telegraph, and right away."

"I told you. We tore up the lines. Besides, no one but old Gordon himself knows Morse code, and I doubt he feels much like cooperating with us just now. We couldn't send a message even if the wires were repaired."

"I know Morse code," he told her. "And even if I didn't, I'm sure Gordon would have a code book hidden away somewhere."

"You know how to operate a telegraph?" she asked, suddenly hopeful. "And you'd send the message for us?"

"If it will get you to marry me, I'd jump off the ends of the earth," he vowed valiantly, his blue eyes sparkling with devilish intent.

Audrey's hopeful expression fell. "But we destroyed the wires in at least a dozen or so places. And any replacement wire would be inside that store or in the animal shed attached to the back of it. We can't send a message, anyway."

Landon forced himself into a sitting position, grimacing at the dull pain that rolled through his skull. "If we can get the telegraph equipment out of that store, we can carry everything we will need to send our message down to where the wire is still good and reattach it. Then all I have to do is send the message."

Audrey's face lit with excitement. "Then we *can* do it. We can keep your father from sending anyone in here before we've had a chance to get ready for them."

"We can do better than that. I think we can keep him

416

from sending anyone down here at all," Landon told her, smiling, though he knew it really depended on his father's mood and how long he was willing to be put off by their messages. But if his father could eventually be talked into sitting back and letting Landon handle it, they might be able to avoid any violence all together.

"Oh, no!" Audrey cried out, and she looked at him with such a look of total despair that Landon ignored his pain and hurried to her side, needing to comfort her.

"What is it? What's wrong now?" he asked, gently taking her hand in his and rubbing it.

"We've forgotten one other little detail."

"What's that?"

"Three of your father's men are still inside the store with that equipment. Chances are they have rearmed themselves and are just waiting for us to try something."

"Why make them wait?" Landon asked. "Let's go confront them right now."

"Oh, sure. We all just walk right up to that store and demand they give us the telegraph equipment."

"No, not all of us. Just me. They've seen my identification. They know who I am. I doubt very seriously they will want to shoot me. Father wouldn't be too pleased to lose his only son, and it appears that what my Father wants holds a great deal of weight with those men. And if my birthright doesn't get me inside, maybe a little cash money will. I have a few thousand with me that might make them a little more cooperative. They appear to be the type who respect the value of a dollar."

"Then what are we waiting for?" she asked, her hope fully restored. "Let's go."

Within minutes, Landon and Audrey, along with half a dozen others, headed toward the store with long, determined strides. Though Landon was still in pain, the thought that what he was about to do would finally win him his bride kept him from concentrating on anything but the matter at hand. Despite the dull throbbing at his temple and a pulsating ache between his shoulder blades,

417

he bounded across the narrow little walk-bridge at the same hurried gait as everyone else.

"The rest of you stay here," Landon said when they were close to the company store. "I'll go on alone. Although they aren't going to want to shoot me, that old geezer in there would probably take great pleasure in putting a hole through one of you."

Audrey ran her tongue nervously over her lips when she looked up at him. Her heart filled with an overwhelming combination of love and despair. She had to swallow before she could say the words, "Be careful."

"I intend to be," he answered, smiling down at her with an ominous wiggle of his brow. "I plan to be in the very best of health for our wedding night tomorrow."

Audrey felt the color heighten in her cheeks at the mere mention of their wedding night, but she refused to let it distract her. "First you get that telegraph. Then we'll talk about our wedding night."

Jeb and the other men exchanged questioning glances but said nothing when Landon bent forward and placed a kiss at the corner of Audrey's mouth. When he started to straighten back up, she threw her arms around him and held him close. "I mean it. You be very careful, Landon."

"I'll be right back," he assured her. Reluctantly, he pulled free of her warm embrace, then turned and headed toward the store. Though she had still not come right out and told him that she loved him, her actions continued to say it. He was more certain than ever that marriage was the right thing for them.

Several seconds later, when he'd gone about halfway, he thought of his promise to be careful and stopped long enough to clearly identify himself, to make certain the men inside knew exactly who he was. When there was no answer, he walked several dozen yards closer and shouted out to them again. When there was still no answer, he very cautiously stepped up onto the raised walkway in front of the store and called out one more time.

Still, there was no response from inside. He turned to

look at Audrey and Jeb, to see if they had any idea why there were no sounds from inside. Both shrugged to indicate they were as puzzled as he was.

Frowning, he walked cautiously over to one of the windows and peered between the thick iron bars. He immediately noticed the dull patch of daylight coming up out of the floor. After a quick search of the rest of the large, cluttered room, trying to detect any movement, he hurried to the side of the store and dropped to his hands and knees.

There was just enough space beneath the store for a man to crawl through. He called out one last time to anyone who might still be inside, then, when no one answered, he ducked under the building and, using his knees and elbows to propel himself forward, crawled over to the area where he had noticed the large hole in the floor.

Though he felt fairly certain no one was inside, that the three men had already made their escape through this floor hatch, he picked up a bent stick and poked it up through the opening. When that brought no response, he took the stick away and slowly replaced it with his head.

Audrey and Jeb had both wondered aloud what Landon might be up to when he had first started crawling around underneath the store. They exchanged curious glances with the others when his shadowy figure then suddenly disappeared from their sight.

"Where the hell did he go?" Jeb asked, squatting down to try and figure it out, wishing he could see all the way through to the other side, but he couldn't.

"I don't know," Cody said, also squatting low, trying to catch a glimpse of him. "It's like he just disappeared."

Audrey, too, knelt with the others and tried to figure out where Landon could be. She watched carefully for any sign of movement in the dark shadows underneath the building. But, other than the passing pillows of smoke that rolled northward from the mill, she saw no movement at all, nothing to indicate where Landon might have gone.

Several minutes passed.

Jeb stood again, his expression undecided. "Think we should go on up there and see if he's in some sorta trouble?" he finally asked. He turned to look at the other men. "I'm willin' to risk it if you are."

"There he is!" Audrey squealed, jumping immediately to her feet and pointing to the front door as it slowly swung open. "He got inside somehow."

Everyone stared in open-eyed amazement when Landon walked casually out of the store, his clothes dirty and torn, the telegraph equipment balanced in his arms.

"Nobody's home," he shouted out to them. A wide grin spread across his face, causing deep, narrow dimples to form on his dusty cheeks. "I don't know where they've gone, but they sure cleared out of there."

Aware it was now safe to join him, Audrey and the men ran toward him, curious to know more.

While they walked as a group toward the final break in the telegraph wire leading south, he filled them in as best he could. "There's a floor hatch near the back of the store. Obviously, those men decided the odds were more or less against them. I guess that as soon as most of the people had gone over to Jeb's house to find out what could be done next, those three took all the money out of the cash box and some supplies, then took off like a trio of scalded hounds. My next guess is that that's one chunk of ill-gotten money my Father will never see."

Jeb looked concerned. "Should we go after them?"

"I see no reason to bother," Landon said with a shrug. "I imagine their plans are to take the money and run. I really don't think they are headed to a telegraph to warn Marshall of what has happened, because that might hurt their chances of a clean getaway. We'll let Father report them to the authorities after all this is over. Right now, we have more important things to do. We have to get our message to New York before Father has a chance to hire anyone to come in here and cause more trouble."

It took only a few minutes to hook the telegraph to the wire. In another few minutes, Landon was busily sending his message.

"Did you tell them we are holding you at gunpoint?" Audrey asked, wanting to be sure he was sending the right message.

"No," Landon admitted. "I got to thinking about that and realized that Father might decide to send in those Pinkerton agents anyway—to try and rescue me."

"Then, what did your message say?" she asked, eyeing him suspiciously.

"Oh ye of little faith," he said, shaking his head as if offended by her skepticism, though he honestly did not blame her. "I explained that there had been a small misunderstanding when I first arrived, but that the problem has been quickly remedied. I told him you and I now have everything back under control. I also said we'd send Seth back with a full report in a couple of days. That ought to hold him off, at least until he's heard from Seth. And it should give us plenty of time to get married, have one of the grandest celebrations this area has ever seen, and even have enough time left over to plan our strategy against Father."

Audrey was not sure if the electricity that shot through her body was from her lingering fears or from the joy of hearing him mention their marriage; but whatever had caused it, it had set her heart to racing. "What celebration? We haven't won the battle against your father yet."

"A wedding celebration," he answered, frowning at her inability to catch on to the gist of his plans. "We can worry about a victory celebration later."

Then he turned to Jeb and put his arm around the burly man's shoulders. "Who do you know here that can marry us?"

Jeb's brows flattened into a cautious line across his

forehead while he cut his gaze from Landon's hand on his shoulder, to Audrey, then back to Landon's hand. "I can't marry you, mister. We're both men. 'Sides, I'm already married." Though he looked deadly serious in his answer, there was a delighted twinkle in his eye that revealed his real thoughts.

Landon looked skyward for divine strength. "You know very well that's not what I meant. This beautiful woman has finally agreed to become my bride and all I wanted was to know who here could perform the ceremony. I don't want to give her even the slightest chance to change her mind."

"No one that I know of," Jeb answered honestly, aware this man was in no mood for joking around. "Nearest preacher I know anything about is up in Ridgeburg."

"Then we'll have to go to Ridgeburg," he said, as if it were a simple solution.

"Then you'd better be sendin' another message on down to Hartsville to have the next train comin' through stop off and git you, otherwise you'll both have to hoof it all the way to Ridgeburg," Jeb told him, then grinned. "And I doubt you'd feel much like honeymoonin' after a long, hard march like that. Fact, I doubt you'd even feel like standin' up 'fore the preacher after climbin' up and down all those jagged slopes."

Landon turned and immediately sent the message that would get them a train.

"Now, remember, we're leaving you in charge of things while we're gone," Landon said, wincing as he climbed up onto the first step. The muscles in his right leg and both shoulders were still sore from the fall he'd taken the previous afternoon. "I want one humdinger of a celebration ready for us when we get back here tomorrow afternoon. Take whatever you need from the store. Just be sure to leave that dime I gave you on the counter for payment, so no one can accuse us of having stolen anything."

Audrey leaned out over Landon's head, eager to put in her two cents worth. "And when Seth finally gets back here, remember to tell him to send that message Landon taught you and Cody on to the boarding house, so I'll know he's arrived safely. You will have that other wire repaired by then, won't you?"

"Should," Jeb nodded. "Cody and Rade have agreed to get right on it."

"Also, be sure to tell Seth that he'll be getting to go back to New York as soon as we've returned. He'll be carrying a letter to Marshall from Landon. I imagine the thought of seeing Rachel again will make up for whatever hardships he's had to endure while getting those supplies he's gone after."

Jeb's wide smile shrank at the mention of Seth's name; but because he didn't want to upset her when she was about to go off and get married to a man she'd obviously been in love with all along, he decided to keep his big mouth shut. He knew Seth should have been back by now, but there was no way in hell he was going to voice his growing concern. "Anything else?"

"Just remember to send that other message I taught you, if any incoming messages should happen to come across. Chances are, Father will try to get ahold of Gordon to be absolutely sure there are no problems here. It will be reassuring for him to be told that everything is fine, that Seth will indeed be arriving shortly with a letter explaining everything." He grinned and looked back at Audrey. "It'll be reassuring to Rachel, too, should she find out he's returning."

"Will do," Jeb said, going over the sequence of dashes and dots in his head to make sure he remembered it exactly.

"Then, we'll see you tomorrow," Landon told him,

stepping up to join Audrey inside the passenger car. "And when we do, it will be as Mr. and Mrs. Landon Steed."

Audrey had tried to convince herself that the real reason she had so readily agreed to marry Landon was for all the good he could do those people; but by the time they had located the Reverend John Ingram, Ridgeburg's only preacher, she was no longer sure what her reasons were.

By the time they'd returned to the church and stood before the only man in town who could marry them, she was a bundle of confused yet excited emotions. It was not until they stood before the altar, their arms linked, with two strangers standing in attendance, that she finally admitted to herself that she had agreed to marry him because she *wanted* to marry him. Wanted it more than she'd ever wanted anything in her life, even wealth—though it was definitely going to be a pleasant side benefit to their marriage.

While the reverend hurriedly flipped through his bible, looking for a particular passage he sought, she chanced a quick glimpse of her soon-to-be husband and her heart overflowed with the love she felt for him. Landon was right. She did already love him and had for quite some time now. And, if he'd spoken the truth when he'd claimed to be in love with her, they could very well be headed for a long and happy marriage. The thought of that made her shiver with joy, tingling right down to the very tips of her toes.

She felt only a twinge of guilt, knowing she was about to find happiness with the one she loved when her brother would have to wait until December to know such joy. It had just worked out that she had found her niche in life first.

"Are you ready?" the kindly reverend asked once he located the pages he had sought.

"As we'll ever be," Landon assured him.

When he squeezed Audrey's arm, she was not sure if it was a gesture to indicate his love or a silent, unseen warning for her not to back out.

Because the reverend was due at his daughter's house for supper at seven and it was already well after six, the ceremony was short and to the point. Within minutes, Landon and Audrey were pronounced man and wife and were hurried out the door, not even given the opportunity for the traditional kiss afterward.

Feeling cheated, Landon paused on the top step outside the church door and took his kiss anyway. Despite the fact they were in clear sight of anyone who might be passing along the street, Audrey did nothing to stop him. In fact, she, too, had felt disappointed that they'd been cheated of their kiss.

"I love you, Mrs. Steed," he said when he finally pulled away from her to look down into her eyes.

Audrey's head was spinning too rapidly to respond with anything more than a deep, guttural moan.

"And as soon as we've had supper, I plan to take you back to our room and show you how much I do love you," he added, studying her reaction closely. Though he was still convinced that she loved him every bit as much as he loved her, and that they were headed for a very happy, although sometimes stormy, relationship, he would not force Audrey to consummate their marriage that night. Though he well remembered how wonderful it was to make love to her, unless he was absolutely certain it was what she wanted, too, he would be willing to spend his first few married nights simply holding her in his arms. He had rushed her into this marriage, and it might take a while for the idea of their being man and wife to sink in. For tonight, it would be enough to know that she was finally his forever. Making love to her could wait until she was ready.

But Audrey was ready. Having admitted that she was very much in love with Landon and believing now that he truly loved her, she saw no reason for them not to share each other's love to the fullest.

Feeling suddenly shy, she glanced up at him and smiled. "I'm not really that hungry," she admitted. "We could skip supper if you like."

Landon's eyes widened when he realized what she was telling him. He bent forward to study her expression closely. "Are you sure? I realize all this has to be a little overwhelming."

"Of course, I'm sure," she said, meeting his gaze straight on. "I've never been more sure."

Landon's joy was immediate. Taking his new wife's arm in his, he turned toward the boarding house with no intention of stopping in the dining room for supper, though he'd ordered a special feast for their wedding night.

chapter twenty-seven

Aware there was still half an hour of daylight left, Landon crossed the small bedroom to reach through the lace curtains and pull the heavy inner drape across. He wanted to give the illusion of it being nighttime outside, a more normal time to be thinking about going to bed.

"Don't do that," Audrey said. She followed him across the room and placed her hand on his to stop him from drawing the drape. "I want to be able to see."

When he turned to face her, she met his dark, glimmering gaze with an adoring look of her own. She smiled when he bent forward, knowing he wanted to kiss her again. Her heart soared to new and lofty heights when his arms came around her and pulled her near. Tilting her head back, her pulse throbbed with eager expectation while she waited for his lips to close the final inches between them.

Slowly, their mouths came together, and it was as if they were always meant to be that way. Her lips parted willingly, allowing his tongue to enter and lightly tease the sensitive inner edges. Overwhelmed by the thrilling sensations his masterful kiss created, her arms went immediately around his shoulders to bring her husband closer to her. Their bodies met hungrily.

In his eagerness to let her know how he felt, Landon freed his lips from hers to murmur gentle words of love, words that cascaded joyously against Audrey's ears, causing her heart to race harder. She met his tender words of love with an admission of her own love. That admission was all Landon had to hear to set him into a wild frenzy of passion. He'd waited so long to hear those words from her. They meant the world to him.

Greedily, his lips crashed down on hers once more with an even greater fervent desire than before as he sampled again and again the intoxicating sweetness of her mouth . . . the same mouth that had finally admitted her feelings aloud.

No longer afraid, because she no longer had a reason to be afraid, Audrey leaned eagerly against him. She accepted his glorious kiss with all the love and passion she possessed, ready to explore the splendid magic he had created to its fullest. Her blood burned hot trails through her body, urging her forward. She pressed harder against him.

Landon's tongue continued to dip lightly past her lips, gently teasing the tip of her tongue, coaxing her. When she did move her tongue to touch his, the kiss suddenly ignited into something more powerful than she had ever felt. Landon realized that at long last, Audrey's passions were fully aflame and raged eagerly deep inside her. She no longer fought her desires; she did not pull away. Instead, she continued to press her body ever closer, molding herself to him.

As her weight pushed harder against his, crushing her soft curves against the harder planes of his muscular body with astonishing strength, he knew that he could take her right then and that she would let him. But, despite the fiery passion she displayed, he chose to move ahead very slowly. He forced his lips to linger on her sweetly demanding mouth while he eased his hands down the curve of her back, around to the arch of her ribcage, then slowly upward toward her straining breasts.

He was well aware that her breathing had become more labored, more erratic, with each new place he touched, and it delighted him to know he was able to create such powerful responses in her. There was a beautiful sense of accomplishment in knowing he was capable of giving her such complete, basic pleasure. He held back his own swelling response as best he could while he worked to bring her to one new height of arousal after another. This night was for her.

Continuing to do all that was humanly possible to ignore the hard and throbbing ache that had developed low inside him, he moved his hand along the smooth surface of her blouse until at last he was able to feel the firmness of her breasts. Fire shot through him when he slowly cupped his fingers around the precious find.

Gently, he played with the tips of her breasts through the soft fabric until he felt them grow rigid with desire. Taking several deep, quaking breaths in a valiant effort to keep his own shuddering desire under control, he delayed undoing the many buttons that held together the back of her blouse. Instead, he allowed his hand to continue its hungry prowl along the outside of her clothing.

Moaning weakly, Audrey was already so lost to the deep, twisting whirlwind of emotions Landon had so quickly stirred to life inside her that she found it hard to remain standing. A staggering heat rose from her middle and spread quickly through her veins in all directions as her arousal spiraled ever higher, quickly possessing her entire being. Knowing the magic that he held for her, every part of her yearned for more. She wondered what was taking him so long. Why hadn't he attempted to remove her clothing like he had so many times in the past? She tugged at his shirt in an effort to make him hurry.

But Landon was determined to take it slow, to make the moment last, to bring her to her fullest height of arousal. He wanted their first lovemaking as man and wife not only to be wonderful, but also to be everlasting. He continued to tease her sensitive skin through her cloth-ing for several more minutes before finally reaching his breaking point.

With fumbling fingers, he began to slip her tiny buttons from their holes. When the garment parted, his hands dipped inside to touch her warmth before resuming with the last of the contrary buttons.

In his haste to undress her, his knuckles brushed against her heated skin again and again, sending shock wave after shock wave of anticipation through Audrey's body. Her eyes closed and her body trembled with breathless expectation when he finally slipped the blouse off her shoulders, then tugged the sleeves off her arms and the hem out of her waistband. With no concern for the garment, he tossed it haphazardly over his shoulder and reached for the top button of her skirt.

Soon, she stood before him in her camisole and bloomers. Her breasts thrust proudly against the silken fabric. Landon let out a low guttural moan when he then reached for the tiny straps that held the delicate camisole in place. With agonizing slowness, he tugged on the tiny straps until they slipped off her creamy white shoulders. He then allowed himself a leisurely view of her breasts while the fabric slowly drifted to her waist. He then tugged the camisole, along with the waistband of the bloomers, until the material loosened and slipped easily over her slender hips. He allowed the last of her garments to fall to the floor, where they were immediately forgotten.

Enraptured by her beauty, Landon stared at his wife. She was exquisite. Unable to resist, he bent his knees and dipped his head to kiss the straining peaks of her breasts.

Waves of pure ecstasy shot through Audrey. Her legs grew increasingly weaker from the magnificent onslaught. But before her knees could buckle, he'd gathered her into his arms and carried her the short distance to the bed. When he laid her atop the pale blue comforter and gazed down at her, lying there with her arms open to him, his response was overwhelming. Crazed with his desire, he tore out of his clothes like a madman, then hungrily sought her lips again as he gently lowered himself onto the bed beside her and Audrey received her husband willingly. It felt so right to have him there beside her, to hold him in her arms.

While his hands resumed their provocative explorations, this time over bare skin instead of cumbersome fabric, she felt an equal desire to touch him. Eagerly, she allowed her hands to leave his wide, corded neck and slowly ran her palms over his hard, muscular back until she reached the firm curve of his buttocks. She marveled at the feel of his solid muscles as they moved beneath her hands. It was hard to believe that such a man was her husband, that such astonishing pleasure was to be hers forever.

When his lips left hers to trail tiny kisses along her throat, she tossed her head back deep into the pillow and gasped for air. Then, when his mouth moved to take in one of the sensitive tips of her breasts again, she arched her back and allowed him to continue his wondrous torture. While his mouth gently suckled one thrusting breast, his fingertips taunted the other until she thought she would go mad with desire. Believing she could not possibly bear any more of this resplendent torture, she reached down to bring his mouth back up to hers.

Landon obliged her with another long, plundering kiss, but when he brought his lips away again, he returned immediately to the hardened tips of her breasts. Deftly, his tongue teased first one peak, then the other, with short, tantalizing strokes, nipping and suckling until she literally cried aloud with pleasure. Then, just when she was certain she could endure no more, he rose above her, ready at last to bring her the release she sought.

Carefully, he eased inside, then with smooth, lithe movements, Landon brought their wildest longings, their deepest needs, to the ultimate height. When release came for Audrey, it was so wondrous, so deeply stirring, that her head jerked up off the bed as she cried aloud her joy. Only a moment later, the same trembling release came

431

for Landon, leaving him weak and gasping for breath.

With their passions finally spent, the bonds of their marriage made complete, they lay together, perfectly still, in the early darkness that had slowly settled over the room. Bound in each other's arms, they clung together and listened to the steady rhythm of one another's heartbeats. While they continued to languish in the afterglow of their love, their minds overflowed with awe over what had just occurred between them. It was like no other experience in their lives. Nothing else even came close.

"Hungry?" Landon finally asked after several minutes had passed and he had both his breathing and his heartbeat back under control. Though he was not at all interested in food at the moment, he was willing to get dressed again and go downstairs to eat if she was. He knew Ruby, the owner of the boarding house, was supposed to have two steaks with all the trimmings waiting for them.

"Not in the least," she murmured, and snuggled closer to him. It was still so hard for her to believe that they were married . . . that such happiness was to be hers forever. "I just want to lie here in your arms."

Smiling contentedly, Audrey closed her eyes and refused to let any other thoughts enter her mind. She refused to worry about the people at the mill or what Marshall might do to try to return things to the way they were. She also refused to worry about her brother, who had yet to send word verifying his safe return. She could worry about all that later. For now, all she wanted to do was bask in the warm aftermath of their lovemaking and enjoy the feel of her husband at her side. She wanted nothing to interfere with her joy—at least not yet. Tomorrow would be soon enough for that.

Though they had gone to sleep fully sated, Landon and Audrey woke up that following morning voraciously hungry—first for each other, then for food.

It was shortly after nine o'clock when they finally arrived in the dining room, almost too late to expect any breakfast, but they found enough leftover biscuits and eggs to fill their plates and appease their appetites.

Afterward, because their train was not scheduled to depart until one o'clock, they decided to walk to the opposite end of the small town of Ridgeburg, to where the C & A Railroad lay momentarily idle.

Audrey was not too surprised to discover that her railroad equipment was in even worse shape than Marshall's had been. The station itself was nothing more than a twelve-by-fourteen unpainted shed, with a ticket window that had been boarded up and a door that was securely padlocked. They learned that the main train itself was still on the track a little farther up in the mountains. It could be seen from round the first bend, if they'd wanted to walk the half mile to see it. But because of a collapsed section of track, it had been unable to get back to Ridgeburg, and until that broken section was repaired, the major part of her train would remain stalled out in the middle of nowhere, open to vandalism and thieves.

Only two C & A railroad cars sat off to the side of the station where Audrey could inspect them firsthand. Both were large wooden freight cars that looked as if they had not been used in years. But with a little work, she felt certain they could be made useful again.

Later, while waiting for the one o'clock train to take them back to the iron mill encampment, Landon left his wife seated on an outside bench, where she could enjoy a pleasant breeze, while he went to check with the local telegraph operator to see if there had been any messages left for Audrey. Though she had not said anything, he knew she had to be worried that her brother had not sent word of his return, and Landon hoped to learn something that might reassure her that Seth had indeed arrived safely back at the encampment with the food.

433

While they had strolled through the different stores, killing some of the time they still had on their hands after having looked over the railroad, he had thought to ask if a big man had come in and made any major food purchases. They had both been relieved to hear that he had, for it meant Seth had at least arrived in Ridgeburg safely.

Landon had also learned, through the man who sold them their tickets at the train station, that the big man and several large crates of food had left Ridgeburg late the preceding afternoon, about the time he and Audrey were at the church getting married, which meant Seth should have arrived at the encampment before dark, in plenty of time to have sent them a message. But the telegraph operator claimed to have had no incoming messages for anyone named Audrey Steed or Audrey Stoane. Nor did he have any for Landon.

During the time Landon was away, Audrey struck up a conversation with a man who had been busily sweeping off the tiny depot platform and picking up debris that had blown out of a nearby trash box. Having seen her railroad firsthand, she wanted to find out how it had ever gotten to be in such awful disrepair, and Audrey decided this man might be just the one to know.

"That other railroad?" he asked in return to her probing question. He seemed truly puzzled that anyone would care enough to ask. "Well, there just wasn't much use for it after Marshall Steed bought this railroad and made up all his new rules."

The old man's expression had darkened with bitter memories that made Audrey curious to know more. "Why is that? What sort of rules could he come up with for this railroad that would make that other railroad of so little use?"

Leaning heavily on the handle of his broom, the thin man glanced first to his right, then to his left, before daring to answer. "Thing is, that other train was built to go on up into the mountains to those areas where there's not as many rocks and a lot more open space. Used to be

434

several farming communities up there who used the C & A to send their produce on down to Ridgeburg, where it was then loaded up on this railroad and sent on to Hartsville, where it was then loaded up on to the Pennsylvania Railroad and shipped east. But when Marshall Steed bought up this particular railroad so's he could get his goods in and out of his iron mill and his two coal operations, he decided there was to be no more shipping of agricultural products on his train."

"But why?" Audrey asked, wondering what would possess Marshall to give up that added income.

The old man wrinkled his face with disgust. "Don't you see? This here is the only railroad leading out of this entire valley, and by taking away any direct contact with outside food markets, he forced the local farmers to have to go to work in his mill and his mines in order to survive. Oh, a few was lucky enough to find a decent buyer for their farms so they could move somewhere else and start over, but most folks around here found out that no one wanted to buy their land except for Marshall himself, who bought it dirt cheap so he could mine it. But he was only willing to buy the land he figured was rich in iron ore or coal."

"Are you sure of your facts?" Landon asked, startling them both as he let his presence be known.

Seeing the fear in the old man's eyes and the way he then gripped his broom handle with such force his bony knuckles turned pale white, Audrey smiled reassuringly. "Don't worry. That's just my husband."

"Just?" Landon asked, pressing his hand flat against his chest, pretending she'd deeply injured his pride by such a careless remark.

Audrey ignored his dramatics. She tried again to reassure the old man that Landon meant him no trouble. "He looks fierce, but generally he's harmless as a lamb."

"B—but I heared tell he was Marshall Steed's son," the old man said, his face still full of fright. Then when no one denied it, his eyes widened further. "Please don't tell

435

your pa what I said. He'd see me fired, and I need this job. It don't pay much, but it's all I know how to do besides farm."

Audrey's heart went out to the old man. "Don't worry. We won't tell him anything. Besides, we don't even know your name to tell him."

"We're not out to cause anyone to lose his job," Landon added, feeling just as sorry for the old man as Audrey. "I think my wife was just curious to know why her railroad was in such bad shape."

"Her railroad?" He looked again at Audrey with a curious lift of his snowy brow.

"The C & A," Landon verified for him. "She now owns it and was concerned that it was so run-down. So, you see, there's no reason for you to be concerned." Then, as added reassurance, he reached into his pocket and pulled out a coin, pressing it into the old man's hand. "For your trouble."

"Thank you, sir," the man said as he quickly stuffed the coin into his trouser pocket. "Much obliged." Then he quickly took his broom and disappeared into the main building.

On the way back to the encampment, Audrey kept thinking about what the old man had told her. The more she thought about it, the angrier she became. Though she'd always sensed Marshall was a cold and manipulative man, she'd never dreamed he could be so cruel. He had intentionally ruined the lives of hundreds of innocent, hardworking people—and all for his own personal gain.

Dismally, she wondered if there were any way for her to undo even a part of what he had done. While she watched the rocky terrain pass by the small, dingy window beside her, her mind began to formulate the beginnings of a plan. By the time they had arrived in the encampment and discovered that Seth had returned safely but that Cody had been unable to repair the telegraph wire in time to send any messages, she was

436

ready to try her idea out on Jeb.

After getting settled into her room again, she asked Jeb, Cody, Bill, and Seth to join her and Landon out on the front porch for a chat. Aware the chat might last quite a while, she brought several chairs outside so they could all be more comfortable.

After answering the expected questions about their trip and about their wedding, she got right to the point. Audrey told them about having bought the C & A and then about what she had learned from the old man. Jeb verified that the old man had told her the truth. Fact was, he had been one of the farmers who'd been forced to give up farming and go to work at the mill. So had Cody.

"When there was no longer a way for us to get our produce to market and no one to buy our land from us, we had no choice but to leave our homes and look for work elsewhere," Cody told her, agreeing with Jeb. "So, a lot of us ended up here."

"Or working his coal mines," Jeb put in.

"But what if I was able to get my railroad back in good repair, then extended it on over the top of the mountain and continued expanding until the tracks finally reached Lake Erie? You farmers could farm again and ship your produce up to the Great Lakes, where it would then be transferred to barges and shipped on to New York. Shipping by barge would be more economical than shipping it overland, anyway. Therefore, you would end up making more money than you did before."

Jeb, who had sat silently listening to what she had to say, slowly shook his head and glanced from Audrey to Landon, who he noticed looked as surprised by her proposal as the rest of the men had been. "Don't know that it would do us no good no way. We got no money to buy seeds or work animals. And we got no money to have our rusted implements fixed back into workin' order again. You got to remember, those of us who still have some land to go back to haven't had a chance to do nothin' with it in years. It'd take a lot of money and a lot

437

of hard work to git those fields back ready for plantin'.''

"He's right," Cody put in with a grave shake of his head. "Those of us who still got any land don't have the money it would take to get our fields in shape to produce anything worth selling. The land hasn't been worked in years."

Rather than suggest handouts, knowing their prides had taken too much of a beating already, Audrey leaned forward in her chair and spoke in a very businesslike voice. "What if I were to loan you the money?"

"Loan it to us? At what interest?" Jeb wanted to know. For the first time, he seemed truly interested in what she had to say.

"At no interest."

When that seemed to draw a look of distrust and confusion from everyone around her, she quickly added, "That is, if the people I loan any money to will promise in writing to pay me back within a reasonable time and also promise to use my railroad to ship their goods."

Seth and Landon exchanged glances, both knowing from where the money for all this would have to come. Audrey certainly didn't have that kind of money.

"What do you have to say to all this?" Seth wanted to know, before his sister started making a lot of promises Landon might not want to keep.

Landon shrugged, then smiled, clearly not opposed to any of what she was doing. "What can I say? She's my wife."

Aware Audrey and Landon were serious, Jeb pushed his battered hat back and scratched his forehead. His eyebrows lowered into a puzzled expression. He still found it all too good to believe. "But if we were to make you that promise—to use nothin' but your railroad until the loans are paid back—aren't we askin' for more trouble? As soon as we've signed those papers and spent that money, you could hike up your rates until they were impossible to pay. Then where would we be? Right back in the situation we're already in, only we'd owe you

438

money to boot."

Audrey looked at him, disappointed he could think such a thing. "What if I promise to sign an agreement that will establish a set of very reasonable fixed rates— rates that I promise I will not change for at least the first five years?" She was no longer after profit. She simply wanted to help these people in the only way she could. Her insides quivered with eager anticipation at the thought of being able to do something that might get their lives back in order. "And if you agreed to go back to farming and to use my railroad to ship your produce, it wouldn't matter what Marshall Steed did here. You would no longer be at his mercy. You wouldn't be working in his iron mill anymore. And your neighbors wouldn't have to work in his coal mines anymore."

"You'd extend this offer to everyone?" Jeb asked, surprised by the scope of her generosity.

"Everyone who wants to take me up on it."

Landon leaned back in his chair and thought more about it. This could total up into the millions, and he realized Audrey intended to use his money for this business venture yet had not bothered to mention even one word about these plans to him. Still, he thoroughly liked her idea. It was much better than trying to browbeat his father into doing the right thing, which probably wouldn't have worked, anyway. But this could work out to everyone's advantage. After his father no longer had his captive work force, he'd have to offer better wages as well as a fair price at his company stores if he wanted to keep his mill and his mines open. Audrey had come up with the perfect solution.

Caught up in the excitement he saw in both his wife's eyes and in the eyes of the men facing them, Landon quickly added, "And we promise two years of free transportation to the first man to ship a load large enough to fill a railroad car."

Audrey turned to him, clearly amazed that he was willing to be so generous. The look of adoration he saw on her face encouraged him to say more. "And, since it will be six or seven months before planting season and at least a year before the first harvest, in the meantime you men can find good, honest work at an honest wage by helping to lay the track. That way, you can go ahead and quit your jobs here, and also have a hand in seeing the railroad through. We can start by repairing the C & A itself. By the time we've gotten it back into good working order, we should have enough of the land bought and the equipment and supplies brought in to start working on the expansion itself."

"But how are we going to get our farms in workin' order if we're off buildin' that railroad?"

Landon stood, jamming his hands into his pockets while he searched his brain for a logical solution. Finally, he had one. "You could alternate working five days, then taking off for five days. That way, you could continue to work on the railroad and supplement your income right up until planting time. Then, when it did come time for you to quit and go to work full time taking care of your farms, we would replace you with other men as eager as you to find decent work. By the time you harvest that first crop, we should have the railroad completed."

Jeb's eyes sparkled. "You sure that's what you want to do?"

"Yes, I'm quite sure," Landon told him. He smiled when Audrey then rose from her chair and came willingly into his arms. Fact was, he'd do anything to make this woman happy.

Glancing around at the others, Jeb laughed out loud. "Then, I think you two got yourselves a deal."

"Let's start packing and get the hell out of here," Cody added with a boisterous shout, then ducked his head. "Pardon the language, ma'am."

"She's heard worse," Seth assured him, blinking his eyes to clear them of the burning tears of pride that had so quickly filled them. He was deeply pleased that his sister had finally realized there were things in life more important than money.

"But we can't leave just yet," Landon protested, knowing these men needed to eat a few more good, solid meals before tackling any difficult jobs. "What about our wedding celebration? First we feast. Get a good night's sleep. Then we pack up everything and clear out." Turning to Seth, he added, "I've already prepared that letter for you to take to Father, but now that all this has been decided, I really don't think it will be necessary to take it to him. By the time Father realizes exactly what has happened and decides to try to do anything about it, it will be too late. We'll all be gone. And all he'll have left here is an empty mill, a company store, and fifty or so worthless shacks. And one faithful company guard to run it all." Though they'd tried several times, they had never been able to get that one guard out of the mill, and the poor old man worked day and night keeping the fires going.

Seth looked at him, dejected. "You mean I don't have no reason to go back to New York?"

Landon couldn't help but grin at his friend's down-turned face. Clearly, he'd been looking forward to a chance to see Rachel again. "Oh, but you do have a reason to go back to New York. For one thing, we will need to get some tents up here—and lots of them. After we leave here, these men won't have any place to stay while they're working on Audrey's railroad. And we'll need equipment, though I have no idea what we'll be needing. I've never built a railroad before. Any of the railroads I've been connected with in the past were already built. What's more, we'll need for you to get those tents and whatever equipment we're going to need shipped on up here before Father finds out what we are up to and stops any further use of his railroad. It would be almost impossible to carry all that up here by wagon."

"That's true," Seth said, nodding agreeably.

Knowing that it was indeed true, Landon's expression took a serious turn. "In fact, we'd better go ahead and get those supplies here as soon as we can. It won't be too long before Father catches on to what has happened, and I have no desire to go to him and beg on bended knees that he allow our supplies to go through." And he also had no desire to try bullying him into cooperating. He would rather get everything they would need up there and in storage before his father had a real chance to cause any trouble, which he was certain the man would do.

Audrey's eyes widened as her pretty face turned into a thoughtful frown. "I hadn't thought of that. We really do need to get moving on this, don't we?"

"First thing tomorrow. Tonight we celebrate."

And what a celebration it was. With all the food they'd taken from the store added to all the food Seth had brought with him from Ridgeburg, everyone ate and danced and laughed until they were certain they would burst. Even the doctor, who had started all the sickest men on medication to loosen the black phlegm that caked their lungs, joined in the festivities.

After the celebration was over, Landon and Audrey retired to her room and had another little celebration of their own.

chapter twenty-eight

As instructed, Seth and Jeb waited a full twenty-four hours after having shipped the last load of iron rails and cross timbers before approaching Marshall Steed. Having been given a letter, signed by Landon, authorizing the two of them to make the necessary purchases for the newly formed A & L Railroad, they worked long and hard at getting everything needed and on its way to Ridgeburg, including the man Landon had wanted him to hire to help them plan and build their railroad.

The amazing part was that they had managed to get everything bought and the railroad expert hired and on his way in less than five days. During that time, they'd hoped Marshall would continue to hold off doing anything drastic, that he would, in fact, continue to wait for the promised letter from Landon. But knowing how impatient Marshall could be, they realized the chances were slim that he would remain idle for very long.

Exactly twenty-four hours after Jeb and Seth watched the last shipment leave New York, in time to be sure it would indeed reach its destination, Seth cashed the bank draft Landon had okayed for twenty-two thousand dollars, then the two headed straight for Marshall's house. Because of the seriousness of their situation, Seth had been asked to stay away from Rachel until this final step was completed. After they had spoken to Marshall, he could make whatever arrangements were necessary to see her before having to head back to Pennsylvania.

He could hardly wait to hold her in his arms.

"This is some fancy setup," Jeb said of Marshall's house, glancing at their surroundings with openmouthed awe while he followed Seth across the wide walkway and up the steps to the front veranda.

Seth was too nervous about the upcoming confrontation to comment. Instead, he proceeded to the front door with long, steady strides and immediately pulled the leather cord attached to the doorbell. He stepped back to wait for Everett, who should be finishing with breakfast about now and would have to come from the rear of the house.

Meanwhile, Jeb bent over to touch the fancy widemouthed brass urns that sat on either side of the front door. Turning to look at Seth, a wide grin broke across his bearded face. He thumped one of the shiny urns with the back of his finger, as if it were a huge cuspidor. "Makes you want to spit, don't it?"

Seth felt some of the tension leave his body as he looked at the large urn in a whole new light. "Does look a little like a spittoon at that." Remembering that these huge brass pots were all the latest rage among the wealthy, he wondered what Rachel would think of Jeb's assessment of her two prized purchases. Would she agree with him that they did look like oversized spittoons, or would she politely rearrange one of his kneecaps with the pointed toe of her boot? But before he could decide what her reaction would be, he heard the door handle rattle and his thoughts were cut short by the sound of the door opening.

"Seth?" Everett said, eyeing him curiously once he had the door open wide. "What are you doing here? I thought you were off in Pennsylvania somewhere."

"I've come to see Marshall Steed," he answered in a brisk, businesslike tone. "Is he in?"

Everett caught sight of a movement off to one side and

444

turned to see what it might be. He jumped visibly when he saw that the movement had come from an oversized bear in man's clothing. Keeping a cautious eye on Jeb, he stepped back into the house, then led the two men into the library. "I'll tell Mr. Steed that you are here," he said before hurriedly disappearing from the room.

"Whoo-ee," Jeb said as he settled onto one of the plush couches and ran his hand over the satiny material that covered it. "Makes you feel sorta like a king or some'n, don't it?"

At the moment, Seth was too concerned with the footsteps he heard outside the door to listen to Jeb. Rather than join his friend on the couch, Seth stood in the middle of the room with his legs braced and his hands folded behind him.

"Well, it's about time," Marshall muttered when he rushed into the room. James followed only a few steps behind. "I was given the impression you'd be here days ago. And when my last two telegraphs to the mill went unanswered, I'd started to worry that something had gone wrong. I was just about to send someone up there to see what the trouble was."

Seth's shoulders tensed. "No trouble, sir. Everything going just fine," he stated, looking at Jeb, who was draped back across the pillows of the couch grinning from ear to ear.

Unaware of the other man, Marshall stepped closer to Seth, as if expecting him to say more. Finally, he asked, "Well? Don't you have something for me?"

"Oh, yes," Seth said, pulling his gaze from Jeb as he reached into his coat pocket. Carefully, he removed a bulging envelope and handed it to Marshall. "Landon and Audrey told me to give you this."

"A letter explaining what is going on, I hope," Marshall muttered, quickly taking the envelope and popping open the seal.

"No, sir," Seth said, though Marshall had already taken the money out and could see for himself that there

445

was no letter. "That's the twenty-two thousand you gave Audrey the day you asked her to go up to Pennsylvania and break that strike for you. She told me to return it to you. She said to tell you she wouldn't feel right keeping it."

"I gather she wasn't able to break that strike after all," Marshall commented, though he didn't look too surprised as he quickly counted the money to be sure it was all there.

"Oh, she broke it all right," Seth said, being purposely vague, trying not to be distracted by Jeb, who had discovered a small porcelain statuette of a nude woman and had picked it up to examine it more closely.

"I don't understand. If she broke the strike, then why is she refusing this money?" Marshall asked. "And why don't you have a letter for me from Landon?"

"Don't know. All I was told to do was bring you that money. And to tell you that I'm not working for you anymore."

"What? Why not?"

"Got me a new job," is all he would say. "And since we've now done what we came here to do, I guess we'll be on our way."

"We?" Marshall asked, and for the first time he noticed Jeb. Though the man looked vaguely familiar, he could not place him.

Aware the time had come to leave, Jeb quickly set the figurine back down and stood, adjusting his new store-bought clothes over his broad, muscular body. "Good to see you again, Mr. Steed," he said with a brisk nod. Then to Seth, he asked, "Ready?"

Immediately, the two large men started toward the door.

"Wait a minute," Marshall said in an effort to stop them. "I've got some questions."

"Another time perhaps," Seth said, and turned to leave. "Right now we've got to get going. We've got some very important things to get done today." The most

446

important of which was to see Rachel. His heart fluttered at the thought.

"But who are you working for? You can at least tell me that." Marshall followed them out into the hall. "And where is Landon? How can I get in touch with him? Is he still at the mill?"

"No, he's not at the mill anymore," Seth told him, never breaking his stride, taking great pleasure in not giving the man any of the information he so obviously wanted. "Maybe you'll hear from him soon."

"Seth! Come back here," Marshall demanded when the two men continued to the door, opened it themselves, and stepped outside. "I'm not through with you yet."

Jeb cut his gaze from Seth's determined expression to look back over his shoulder at Marshall's, and he chuckled. "That's too bad, 'cause I think he's more'n through with you."

Seth felt a chuckle bubble up in his throat, but because he was trying to seem very strong and dignified at the moment, he fought the urge to laugh. Instead, he continued to walk toward the front gate with long, resolute strides.

"Seth!" Marshall tried one more time, so furious with his former employee that he shook with rage. "Damn you, get back here!"

When that had failed to stop the oversized buffoon from climbing into an awaiting cab with the other man, Marshall spun about and stalked back inside the house. It was bad enough that Landon had refused to listen to him, but now even his former help was renouncing him. Well, someone had damn well better listen to him—or there would be pure hell to pay!

"Everett!" he shouted at the top of his voice. "Everett, get out here!"

"Sir?" the elderly butler responded as he promptly but cautiously appeared in the hallway.

"Find Gene Haught and send him into the library! I've got to get to the bottom of all this!"

"Yes, sir," Everett said, bobbing his head agreeably, not wanting to do anything that might upset his boss more. "Right away, sir."

Less than five minutes later, Gene Haught entered the library, his heavy brows pulled together with curious concern. "Ol' stiff-lip out there said you were very eager to see me, mate. Wot 'ave ya got in mind for me this time?"

"You are going on a little trip."

Gene reached up and scratched his unshaven jaw. "Where to?"

"My iron mill near Ridgeburg. I want you to find out just exactly what's going on out there."

"Why don't ya just send a wire to one of yer men? 'Ave ya thought of that?"

"Of course I've thought of that. And I have sent wires, but until late yesterday afternoon, I kept getting the same response. That everything was fine. Only now I feel certain everything is not so fine. Something's wrong. Very wrong. And I want you to find out what it is."

"Ya can count on me, mate," Gene vowed. "I'll be on me way within the hour."

"Take a couple of men with you. There could be trouble."

"Aye, I'll do that," he said with a pleased grin. Nothing delighted Gene Haught more than the possibility of trouble.

Because the only person working for Marshall that Seth could trust to take a message to Rachel was Kelly, he had given her the letter that would explain to his ladylove that he was back in town and staying at Audrey's house. Though he had given Kelly the letter early that morning, knowing that the only chance he'd have of catching her alone would be while she was at the market doing the morning shopping, he had asked her not to give the letter to Rachel until after he'd seen Marshall. He hadn't dared

448

take the chance of Marshall finding out he was back from the mill until after he'd completed all the things Landon and Audrey had asked him to do.

But now, not only had he and Jeb finished each and every task, but there were still five hours remaining before they had to catch the train that would take them back toward Ridgeburg. How he wished Rachel could be on that train with them, but he would not ask that of her. He would simply enjoy whatever time they had together and promise to return as soon as he could.

Knowing Kelly had promised to give Rachel the note as soon as she'd learned Seth and Jeb had been there and gone, the two men went directly back to Audrey's house to wait. Seth knew that if there were any way at all for her to get out of the house, she would come to him, and he didn't want to chance missing even a minute of their time together.

Restlessly, he paced the front parlor, glancing out the windows from time to time, though he had no idea if she'd use the front door or slip around to the back. He could hardly wait to hold her in his arms again and kiss her sweet lips. His heart hammered wildly at the mere thought of it, causing him to pace even harder.

"Why don't you sit down for a while?" Jeb suggested, having grown tired of watching his friend walk back and forth from window to window. "Keep that up an' you're goin' to be too tired to do nothin' once she gits here."

"I can't sit. I haven't seen her in more than two weeks," Seth tried to explain as he twisted his hands restlessly in front of him.

"I 'magine she looks 'bout the same," he offered back. "Can't have changed too much in two weeks."

Seth flattened his mouth into an exasperated expression when he then turned to face Jeb. "Don't you have something better to do than sit here and make dumb remarks?"

"Nope."

"Don't you have somewhere you'd like to go,

someplace you'd like to see before leaving the city? You realize it may be months before we get the chance to come back."

"Nope."

Seth's eyebrows arched, then slowly lowered. "You do plan to make yourself scarce once Rachel gets here, don't you?"

"You mean *if* she gets here. You got to keep in mind that that li'l gal has had two whole weeks to get over you. By now, I 'magine she's forgot all about you," Jeb teased, then glanced at the clock. "'Sides, if she don't get here soon, you ain't goin' to have time for much more than a quick peck on the cheek. Our train leaves in just over an hour."

Seth shifted his weight restlessly while he studied the clock. Jeb was right. They barely had over an hour. What could be keeping her? His heart sank to the pit of his stomach at the thought that Kelly might not have gotten his message to Rachel in time. But she had to have! They needed to discuss their wedding plans. He might not have a chance to see her again before December.

Just then, he heard a carriage pull into the drive. With a burst of renewed hope, he bounded for the front door. Ready to sweep Rachel up into a big bear hug, he jerked open the door and rushed outside just in time to see Everett climb down out of the carriage. With a cold lump of dread firmly lodged in his throat, he walked out into the yard to meet Everett halfway.

"What are you doing here?" he wanted to know, glancing curiously at the piece of paper the little man carried in his hand.

"I've a message for you," Everett responded, and quickly thrust the paper into Seth's hands.

"What does it say?" he asked, staring at the folded paper, afraid to open it. If it was from Rachel and had been sent through Everett instead of Kelly, then it had to be a letter refusing to see him. Maybe Jeb had been right. And even if it was from Marshall, it was probably a threat

450

of some sort meant to convince Audrey and Landon not to build their railroad—that is, if Marshall even knew about their railroad yet.

"I'm quite sure I wouldn't know what it says," Everett answered with an insulted lift of his narrow chin. "It is not my place to read someone else's messages." Then, with a haughty shake of his head, he made two brisk quarter turns and marched back to the carriage, as if going off to war.

Seth waited until the carriage had circled on through the driveway before returning to the house to open the letter. Sitting down in a chair near the front door, he studied the outside of the folded paper for a moment, then slowly opened it and peered inside. His heart sank to the depths of his soul when he glanced over the words inside.

"What's that?" Jeb asked, upon entering the hallway where Seth sat staring at the page.

"It's the letter I sent Rachel asking her to meet me here," he answered without glancing up.

"She sent it back to you?"

"No, *she* didn't," he said, then handed the page over to Jeb. Sadly, he shook his head and tried to keep his anger in check. "Somehow, Marshall must have gotten his hands on it."

Jeb studied the page for a minute, then handed it back. "How do you know?"

Aware then that Jeb did not know how to read, Seth held it up to him and pointed to the dark lettering at the bottom. "Because right there, in Marshall's own handwriting, it says: *Over my dead body!*"

Jeb looked at the letter for a long moment before reaching up to scratch his jaw. "Dead, huh? What you goin' to do about it?"

"There's nothing much I can do about it," Seth admitted dismally. "If I went over there and demanded to see her, he'd probably have me arrested and thrown in jail. A lot of good that would do."

"Yeah," Jeb agreed with an understanding nod. "And he'd probably do the same thing if you murdered him."

Seth covered his face with his hand and peered at his friend between a small gap in his fingers. What was it about Jeb that made him want to laugh even in the worst of situations? "Well, I guess we might as well get on to the train station. We need to try and get to Ridgeburg before Marshall finds out what has happened and shuts his railroad down to through travel."

Even with fifty-three men hard at work, Seth was amazed at what they had accomplished in just eight days. When he'd left, they had started to get organized into work teams, but as he and Jeb rode up to where the main camp had been established a half mile north of Ridgeburg, he was astonished to see that the collapsed trestle had been completely replaced and that new rails were already being laid across it.

"Look at that," Jeb said. He pointed to the elaborate new structure that stretched across the deep, wooded ravine. "They built her out of metal instead of timber."

"That ought to hold for a good long while," Seth commented as he climbed down from the wagon, then eagerly searched the many people for sight of either his sister or Landon.

"At this rate, they'll have that entire railroad repaired within the week," Jeb added, shaking his head in wonder at all the activity around them. While several of the men worked to lay the rails across the new trestle, others worked at replacing some of the damaged or worn-out rails farther up the mountain. Off in the distance, hidden in among the dense trees, they could see the front of the train that had lain idle for almost two months now. Beyond that, even more work was going on. Soon, Audrey's train would be able to make its first run up to Twin Peaks. A surge of excitement filled him as he thought about it.

"I wonder if your sister will let us ride with her on that first run," he said, voicing his thoughts out loud just before he, too, stepped down off the wagon. He knew his chances of being included were good, since he was one of the only three working for her who knew how to operate the thing and she probably wouldn't be hiring a full-time crew until they were a little farther along.

"Seth! Jeb!" they heard Audrey call from the distance. Her voice had almost been drowned completely by all the hammering and clanking going on around them.

Turning toward the sound, they saw her standing beside a large work table near the tracks, studying what appeared to be some charts. "Over here!"

"Where's Landon?" Seth asked when they were closer. He glanced back toward the different areas where the men were working to see if he could locate him.

"He's gone to Philadelphia to hire someone to take care of the land purchases we are going to have to make. He says there are men who do that sort of thing for a living."

"When do you expect him back?"

Audrey's welcoming smile faded at the thought of having to be without him for two more days. He had only been gone for thirty-two hours and already she missed him dreadfully. "He hopes to be back sometime Saturday." Then, forcing her smile back into place, she pointed to the drawings in front of her. "Come look at the plans as they are now. We have two possible routes mapped out."

Finding her excitement contagious, Seth and Jeb eagerly crowded around the table and listened while she explained step by step what they had accomplished thus far and what they still had to do.

"I hate to interrupt your meal, sir, but there's a young man here with a telegraph message for you," Everett said, approaching the dining table cautiously. Ever since

Seth's brief visit Tuesday morning, Marshall had been in one hell of a mood, and Everett had learned long ago that it was best to stay clear of him as much as possible whenever he was like this. Obviously, Miss Rachel felt the same way he did about her father's mood, because she had taken to her room and refused to leave for any reason, even to come down to dinner. "Shall I accept the message for you?"

"No, I'll get it," Marshall said, quickly rising from the table and hurrying toward the door. "See to it Kelly keeps my plate warm until I get back."

Rather than bother Kelly, who was also in one hell of a mood these days—ever since Marshall had taken that mysterious letter away from her—Everett picked up his master's plate and carried it into the kitchen himself. He then hurried back to the entrance, eager to know what the message might be about. He hated being so completely in the dark about what was going on—especially when he felt certain Kelly knew plenty. If only he could get her to tell him, but he couldn't, so he was reduced to snooping in order to get his facts.

By the time he had returned to the entrance hall, the young man was gone. Marshall stood in the center of the hallway, intently reading the message in his hand. Everett felt the skin along his neck prickle at the fury he saw slowly developing across his master's face.

"How can they do this to me?" he shouted angrily.

Everett's curiosity had gotten the best of him. Though he knew Marshall's question had not really been directed to him, he asked, "How can who do what to you, sir?"

"Landon and Audrey! They are trying to ruin me!" he shouted, so angry that the veins in his neck bulged. Spinning about, he glared at Everett. "My own son has taken sides with that—that woman. They are working together to ruin me. Pack my things. I'm going up there to see about this myself! Surely this can't be true!"

chapter twenty-nine

Marshall was furious after he had the train make a brief stop at the mill and discovered that only one man had remained. Seeing for himself how deserted the place was meant only one thing: Gene Haught's message had been true. The workers had indeed quit working for him and had gone to work for Audrey, repairing her railroad with Landon helping her.

Though he now believed it, he could not understand why they had bothered repairing that eleven miles of track, because without full cooperation of his railroad, her railroad was only good for getting from Ridgeburg up to Twin Peaks and back. It was worthless as far as being able to ship anything out of the area. Couldn't those men see that? Didn't they know that as soon as the track was repaired and the train was running again, their new jobs would have run their course and they would be right back where they were, eager for him to hire them back? Only when he did hire them back, he planned to see to it they weren't paid as well. He'd have Gordon Jones reduce their wages by at least ten percent. They damn well were going to pay for having deserted his mill.

And that was to be one of his first orders of business: locate Gordon Jones and find out exactly what had happened. But before that, he wanted to talk with Gene Haught.

Knowing Gene was staying on a cot in the storage room at his depot in Ridgeburg, so no one would know he'd come up there and was snooping around, Marshall planned to make that his very next stop. And because he also did not want anyone to realize he was there, either, at least not right away, if Gene was not at the depot, he planned to wait right there for him until he returned.

Fortunately, Gene was there taking a nap when he arrived. Startling him awake, Marshall demanded to know what he had found out. "Your telegraph was not very clear. You said Landon was helping Audrey in her attempt to steal my workers away. How is he helping?"

"Best I can figure, 'e is the money be'ind it all," Gene told him, rubbing his blooodshot eyes and blinking them hard as he sat slumped at the edge of his cot. He tried to focus on the dirty footprints on the wooden floor. "Right now, 'e's in Philadelphia hiring some man to start buying up the land she's going to need."

"Land? What is she going to need land for?"

"That's right." He sat up a little straighter and looked directly at Marshall. "You don't know. I wasn't too sure when I sent that message, but it seems that Miss Stoane is planning to extend her little railroad on over the mountains and across to Lake Erie. That way, these farmers around 'ere can go back to farming and won't 'ave to be working for you anymore."

"She's what?"

"Looks to me like she's out to ruin your entire operation 'ere. She's not only got all your mill workers on her payroll, but she's got a good lot of your coal miners working for her, too."

"And she has Landon helping her?"

"Like a little trained puppy, 'e is," Gene commented with a disgusted twist of his fat lips. "But I gather 'e's being well rewarded for 'is 'elp."

"Why do you say that?"

"Because I've followed them back to the boardin' 'ouse where they are staying and watched them disappear into the same room together. Later, I checked with the proprietor, a Mrs. Ruby Brooks, and learned that those two 'ave signed in as man and wife so it wouldn't be raising any eyebrows."

"Man and wife?" Marshall shouted, and felt a sharp twist in his stomach. Narrowing his eyes into thin slits of steely blue, he slammed his fist against the wall. "Damn that woman! What she won't do to get even with me. She's caused me nothing but trouble since that first day we met. She has to be stopped!"

"I'll see wot I can do," Gene said with a sinister smile pulling his mouth full width. His eyes sparkled while his thoughts raced ahead.

Audrey squealed with delight when Jeb told her that the train was working again.

"You are a miracle worker," she cried, hugging him close, unable to contain her delight.

"Not no miracle worker, I just figured out what was wrong with her is all," Jeb insisted, wiping at his grease-streaked face with the back of his hand, then brushing at the dirt on his sleeve, afraid she might get some of it on her pretty yellow dress. "We should be ready to try her out as soon as you get the go-ahead on that new trestle."

"I can hardly wait!" she squealed again, then turned to Seth, who had stopped what he was doing to find out what all the excitement was about. "We are going to take the train across the trestle later today."

"We?" Seth asked, peering quizzically down at her, then back toward where the main portion of supplies was stored.

"Yes, of course, *we*. I certainly can't run that train by myself!"

"But you just told me to go get another wagonload of cross timbers and distribute them to the different areas still being repaired. That'll take a good four hours. Some of those crews are miles from here."

"I've changed my mind. Let someone else do it. This afternoon, you, Jeb, and I are going to drive that train across that trestle, then down the tracks to the station. That's where that train belongs, anyway. At the station. And *we* are going to be the ones to take it there! Won't Landon be surprised when he gets back tomorrow and finds the train already sitting at the station." The color rose prettily to her cheeks.

"And by next Tuesday, we should be ready to take her all the way up to Twin Peaks," Jeb put in, also excited. "Then we can get started layin' that new track."

Audrey squealed again with delight. "I can't believe this is all happening so quickly. Sometimes I have to pinch myself to make sure I'm not dreaming."

"Uh-oh," Seth said, having glanced up from his sister's beaming face toward a rapidly approaching buggy. "Looks like we've got trouble."

"What sort of trouble?" she asked, and turned in the direction her brother's gaze had gone. Her heart froze in mid-beat. "Marshall! What's he doing here?"

"Don't rightly know," Jeb muttered with a dark scowl. "But I reckon you're 'bout to find out."

"Come on, let's go see what he has to say," Seth said, stepping bravely forward. "Might as well get it over with."

"No," Audrey insisted with a proud toss of her chin. "I'll face him alone." She took a deep breath and headed off toward where the buggy had come to a dusty stop a few hundred feet from where they stood.

"Oh, no, you won't," Seth argued, quickly following.

Audrey stopped and grabbed her brother by his arms as she peered up into his face. "Please, Seth. I want to show him that I'm not afraid of him. Now that I am married to Landon, I'm going to find myself at odds with him over and over. He has to know now that I'll always be willing to stand my own ground. I will not cower to him or to anyone."

Reluctantly, Seth stepped back and allowed her to go

458

on alone.

"Your sister's some'n' else," Jeb said, watching proudly as she marched staunchly toward Marshall Steed.

"Yeah, she's something else all right, but what?" Seth muttered, afraid she was trying to take on more than she could handle. He stood with his legs ready to spring into action while he watched from a distance.

"Marshall, what brings you here?" Audrey asked sweetly, reaching out her hand in greeting as she approached him. "Landon will be so disappointed when he finds out he missed you."

Marshall looked down at the proffered hand, then crossed his arms to indicate he had no intention of accepting any show of friendship from her. "I think you know what brought me here."

Aware of his anger, Audrey dropped her hand to her side. "I gather you've found out about our plans."

"*Our* plans?" Marshall responded, his expression turning rock hard. "Don't you mean *your* plans? Why don't you just admit that this railroad idea was yours and yours alone? Don't go trying to make it seem like my son had anything to do with it."

"Originally, it was all my—" she started to answer, but was quickly cut short.

"You've been out to get me ever since we met," he accused Audrey, taking a menacing step toward her. "I should have done something to stop you months ago. You and that overgrown brother of yours."

"I'm sorry you feel that way," she said, not wanting to antagonize him further. At the same time, she did not step back to give him more room for his tirade. Thrusting her chin forward, she stood right where she was, her heart pounding so hard she could hear it.

"Not as sorry as you are going to be," Marshall told Audrey, taking another step toward her. Now, only inches separated the two. "I've come here to tell you that I am not going to allow you to get away with this. I don't care if Landon is helping you or not. I plan to do everything within my power to stop you."

"And Landon and I will do everything within our power to see this thing through," she responded, surprised at how calm her voice sounded.

Marshall stared at her for a long moment. His body vibrated with anger. "I can't believe my son is a part of this. I can't believe he'd be willing to go against me like this."

"And he couldn't believe you were capable of treating these men the way you treated them," she returned. "When he saw the horrible conditions at the mill and discovered how you were cheating the workers out of every cent they earned, he was more than willing to help me do something to make things right again."

"Cheating the workers out of their money?" he asked, furious she would say something like that to his face.

"Yes, by forcing them to spend every cent of their money in your store," she retorted.

"I've never forced anyone to buy anything in my store. Those men were free to purchase their goods wherever they wanted."

Audrey met his angry gaze straight on. "Look, I don't plan to stand here and argue with you about this. I've got work to do. With Landon gone, I'm having to make all the decisions myself. If you have something to say to me, then say it. Otherwise, get out of here and leave me alone."

"I've already said most of what I came here to say. I just have one other thing I wanted to make clear: Leave my son alone. I have already heard from a pretty reliable source how you are allowing Landon to sleep with you in return for his help."

Audrey's eyebrows shot up. Apparently, his source had not mentioned the fact that they were married. "You are right. I am letting your son sleep with me, because he's my husband."

460

Marshall looked as if she'd struck him. "You are a liar!"

Smiling prettily, Audrey lifted her left hand high enough so he could see the beautiful wedding ring Landon had brought with him. "If I'm a liar, then why do I have this?"

Marshall hesitated, then answered in a defiant tone. "To convince these other people you are married so they won't know what a true harlot you are."

"I happen to be family now. You really shouldn't be calling me a harlot," she taunted. "And if you have any doubts about the validity of our marriage, then why don't you have a nice little talk with the local preacher. His name is Reverend John Ingram. I'm sure he'll be willing to tell you all about it."

Marshall's face was beet-red when he turned around and stalked back to the buggy . . . so red that for a brief moment, Audrey had wondered if he might explode. Sadly, she watched him drive away, her shoulders slumped. She had expected to feel some sort of deep satisfaction over having made him so angry, yet she didn't. All she felt was a deep feeling of loss—for Landon. And a strong, muscle-tightening sense of foreboding.

Marshall did indeed pay the local reverend a visit and was infuriated even more to learn that Audrey had told him the truth. She and Landon were married. Legally married. And there was nothing he could do about it.

By the time he'd located Gene Haught at his railroad station, hoping the man would help him decide what he should do next, Marshall was livid with rage.

"That woman is really married to my son," he announced to a not-too-surprised Gene Haught. "They were married almost two weeks ago right here in Ridgeburg. I talked to the preacher himself and he showed me his record of the ceremony."

"Really married, are they?" Gene commented, lifting his shaggy eyebrow at a private thought that obviously pleased him. "Until *death* they do part?"

"I can't imagine Landon marrying her. Not when he had someone like Olivia Arlington waiting for him back home. She must have tricked him into it. She had to have."

"Doesn't really matter if she did or not," Gene told him with a shrug as he sank heavily onto his cot.

"What do you mean it doesn't really matter? Of course it matters. My son is now married to her. That woman is now a part of my own family." He paused with bulging eyes while he thought more about that. "She's now my very own daughter-in-law. She'll be the mother of my grandchildren."

"No, she won't," Gene assured him. "That's wot I come back 'ere to tell you about. I've got your problem solved."

"You do? How is it solved?" he asked, clearly doubtful.

"Because little Miss Audrey Stoane," he started to explain, but then corrected himself, "—I mean, Mrs. Audrey Steed—is not going to be around much longer."

Marshall's eyes widened. "What are you planning to do, kidnap her?" His stomach knotted. He wasn't so sure he wanted to take his vengeance quite that far. Driving her away was one thing, but taking her away completely against her will was quite another.

"Kidnap her? 'ell, no. I've got a better plan than that. Wot I've got in mind for 'er is a lot more permanent than a bloody little kidnapping."

Marshall felt a sickening prickle of apprehension in the pit of his stomach. "What is it you have in mind?"

"I 'eard that she 'as plans this afternoon to take that train of 'ers over that new trestle they've just completed. Fact is, she could be climbing aboard that train right now." He paused to consider the possibility.

"So? What has the train to do with anything?"

"That train is never going to reach the other side of that ravine." An eerie smile crossed his face. "I've ordered me men to plant dynamite along the base of that new trestle and then gave them orders to blow 'er up about the time that train is 'alfway across."

"You what?" Marshall asked, hoping he had misunderstood. True, he hated the woman, but he didn't want her murdered.

"It's all set. The men are sittin' down there just waitin' for that train to start across. When she does," he paused for effect, "then *boom*, the trestle comes tumbling down, train and all. As deep as that gorge is, there's no way she'll survive. By the time your son gets back 'ere from Philly, 'e'll be a widower."

"You didn't!"

Gene looked confused. "Of course I did. It was the perfect answer. This way, you get rid of 'er for good, and with no one to pay those men their wages anymore, they will 'ave no choice but to go back to work for you."

Marshall felt a painful tightening in his chest, cutting his breath short. He had to stop her. She was his son's wife, for God's sake. Clutching his hands into fists, he ran as hard as he could back to the buggy and slapped the reins sharply against the horse's back. Fervently, he prayed he would get there in time.

Driving the buggy as hard as he dared, he heard the train's whistle even before he had the locomotive in sight. His throat closed in over the scream that welled up inside him. He was too late.

As the buggy bumped over the narrow wooden carriage bridge that spanned the same huge ravine as the newly replaced railroad trestle, he spotted the train and noticed smoke billowing up out of the smokestack. The train had not started to move yet but was only seconds away from taking off. He heard the whistle again and knew they were issuing a warning to clear the track. Biting into his lower lip until he tasted blood, he slapped the reins against the back of the horse again and again. There was still a chance, however slight, of catching that train.

"Get on!" he shouted to the horse, though the animal was already running as hard as it could. He watched in horror as the train, which was only a few hundred yards away by now, started to move. The huge metal wheels spun once, then gripped the newly laid track and slowly began to propel the small train forward.

"No!" he shouted, and slapped the reins down again.

His insides wrenched with fear when he saw Audrey lean out of the locomotive and wave to the small gathering of men who stood on the other side of the deep gorge happily cheering her on.

Aware time was all but gone, Marshall pulled the buggy to a halt beside the track only seconds behind the train and started to run, still hoping to catch it before it was too late. Running as hard as he could, he slowly shortened the distance between himself and the train, which was traveling at a reduced speed as it approached a sharp bend in the track.

He knew that once it cleared that bend, the trestle lay directly ahead, only a few hundred yards away.

Still running with all his might, Marshall stumbled but didn't lose his balance. He continued to run as hard as he could, until finally his hand touched the back of the train. Making a wild grab for the railing, he managed to pull himself up onto the back platform of the caboose.

Tears filled his eyes when he realized there was still time to stop the train, though barely. There were only five railroad cars he'd have to pass through, then he would be in the locomotive with the rest of them. On trembling legs, he reached to jerk open the back door. He screamed aloud his anguish when he found out it would not budge. It was locked. There was no getting through.

"Landon, what are you doin' back here already?" Cody asked when he'd felt a hand on his shoulder. There was too much noise from all the cheering and hollering to have heard his approach or noticed his voice.

"I managed to find someone to handle the land purchases almost immediately," Landon leaned toward him and shouted, glancing around curiously at all the cheering men. "What's going on? Where's Audrey?"

Cody pointed across the wide ravine to where the train was now slowly coming around the bend, headed for the trestle. "She and Seth and Jeb are testing out the new trestle."

Landon's eyes widened. "When did they get the train running?"

"A couple of hours ago. Jeb figured out what was wrong with it and fixed it. I think your wife wanted to surprise you by havin' it sittin' at the station when you returned."

Landon chuckled and glanced back at the station, which was only a half mile behind them. "Now I can surprise her by being out front waiting for her when she gets there." He turned to get back on his horse. "I'll talk to you later."

Cody nodded, then quickly turned his attention back to the approaching train. "There she goes. She's crossing the trestle."

Landon had just settled into the saddle and turned back to catch a glimpse of the train when he heard the screech of wheels, which was followed immediately by a loud explosion. His horse reared back on hind legs, but Landon was able to bring him under control while he watched in horrified disbelief.

The entire south end of the trestle slowly collapsed into a billowing cloud of dust and smoke.

"My God! No!" he cried out, watching helplessly, his heart frozen in fear, while the train slowly slid off into what was now empty space.

Driving his heels into the sides of his horse, he spurred the animal into a dead run.

"Audrey, no! Please, Audrey, no!" he cried out, still too stunned to believe what had happened. In his mind, he hoped to get to the edge of the ravine, look down, and find the train sitting perfectly upright, with Audrey standing beside it with her hands on her hips, angry over the delay. But in his heart, he knew that would not be the case. He knew he'd find a mangled heap of twisted metal. He'd seen train wrecks before.

When Landon did reach the edge of the huge ravine and looked down and saw the train through the broken trees at the bottom, it was worse than he had feared. Not only was the train twisted and broken, but a fire had broken out inside the locomotive. Huge yellow flames licked high into the sky. Another fire burned off in the distance, near where the trestle had once stood but now lay in pieces.

Landon's attention focused on the burning locomotive. He watched for some sort of movement. Something to indicate that there were survivors. He saw nothing.

With his heart now racing in panic, he dismounted from the horse and slid, half standing, half sitting, down the steep sides of the embankment. Other men were doing the same. Crashing through the underbrush, everyone struggled to get to the wreckage as quickly as possible, hoping to find Audrey, Seth, and Jeb still alive.

chapter thirty

Debris was strewn everywhere. Smoke and steam hissed from the twisted wreckage of the train while the flames spread from the inside, quickly catching the trees, bushes, and grass on fire. Slowly, Audrey tried to stand but her legs were too numb. The sound of the splintering explosion still rang in her ears.

Hanging onto the side of the steep slope, she looked again at the burning wreckage below and willed herself to stand. When she finally found her footing, white lights danced before her eyes, and for a moment, she thought she would faint. But she couldn't faint. She refused to faint. She had to find Seth. She had to find Jeb. She had to know if they were still alive.

Ignoring the pain that knifed through her shoulder, she quickly slid several feet down the steep mountainside, calling out her brother's name as she went. On the opposite side of the wide ravine, she saw others catapulting down the rugged slopes. Clouds of dust filled the sky as they caused tiny avalanches to cascade beneath their feet in their haste to reach the bottom.

She paused in her descent to watch and smiled weakly, despite the dull white haze that slowly closed in over her, forcing her to her knees. Her last thought before she lost consciousness and fell, crashing endlessly to the bottom of the ravine, was that she hoped one of them would reach the wreckage in time.

Seth woke up to the choking smell of smoke, his thoughts dazed by the pain in his leg and chest. Blinking to clear his mind, he remembered the train wreck and realized that he was trapped inside the train. He looked around, trying to orient himself to his surroundings, aware the train must be resting on its side for him to be lying against a window filled with crumpled brush.

While studying the direction of the smoke, he heard someone cough. Seth looked toward the sound but saw only more smoke, then suddenly huge yellow flames blared out of the broken furnace.

"Jeb?" he called out, wondering what had become of his friend. Was he near those flames? Had he been able to get away on his own? "Jeb? Where are you?"

"Seth," he heard a panic-filled voice call out to him. "Seth, help me." It was Marshall.

Seth peered through the smoke and flames and saw Marshall pinned up against what had at one time been the side of the train but now served as the ceiling. The flames from the furnace licked up at him as if to taunt him with cruel threats of a gruesome death.

"Seth, help me. Get me down."

"Where's Jeb?" he asked. He knew he would need help. "Can you see Jeb?" Then he shouted, "Jeb! Where are you? I need your help here!"

There was no response, just the hiss of smoke and the angry crackling of the fire. Fear tightened his throat. "Jeb? Jeb! Where the hell are you?"

"I don't see him," Marshall said, coughing again. "He must have been thrown from the train. Help me get down, Seth. We have to get out of here."

Seth forced himself into a crouching position, then after pausing to fight the resulting pain, he pushed himself to his feet. Smoke had filled a large portion of the cab, causing his eyes to burn and his lungs to rebel.

The resulting cough sent spasms of pain so severe through his chest that he cried out in pure anguish. Instinctively, he reached down to put a protective arm over the area and discovered the bottom half of his shirt had been torn away and his lower ribs were caved in. Bent forward to keep his head beneath the smoke, he stared down at the deformity with stunned fascination.

"Hurry, Seth!"

With no time to worry about his own injuries, Seth quickly sized up the fact that Marshall was being held up against the wall by a piece of the trestle that had penetrated both the side and the floor of the locomotive like a huge spear. Had the ten-inch wide strip of metal slashed through the wall any further to the left, it would have sliced Marshall in two. He then noticed that the fire was only a few feet to the right of him.

"Get me down! Please!" Marshall tried to wiggle his way out of the trap but couldn't. The metal piece held him too tightly.

"How?" Seth knew he was not strong enough to bend the stout metal.

"Tug on my legs while I stretch my arms up over my head. I think I can wriggle my way out."

Seth's attempt to do as he had been told met with a pain so severe he almost passed out; but he managed to get hold of Marshall's legs and pulled down on them, using his weight more than he did his muscles. He had to save the man for Rachel's sake.

He felt his first ray of hope when Marshall's body slipped down several inches. He pulled on the legs again and again, and each time Marshall slipped several more inches. The heat from the fire, which was spreading out in all directions, scorched his skin while he gave Marshall one last pull. This time Marshall came crashing down on top of him. Another white-hot shaft of pain tore through Seth, but he managed to push Marshall off him and to stand again. Sweat ran down his face while he tried to remain lucid enough to figure out what to do next.

"The only way out is through the window," he said, pointing directly overhead to a large rectangular hole where smoke was pouring out in a steady stream. "Hold your breath and I'll help you out."

Locking his hands into a stirrup, Seth bent over and gave Marshall a boost up. Through his dizziness, he heard Marshall scream with pain as he pulled himself up through the window and rolled over the scalding metal to drop quickly onto the ground.

Seth landed only a few inches from Marshall, and only a few feet from where the grass and underbrush had already caught fire. Able to see nothing but smoke and flames around them, he helped Marshall to his feet and together they stumbled away from the train. When they had finally cleared the worst of the smoke, Seth heard voices and he called out.

"We're over here."

Instantly, they were surrounded by panic-stricken faces. He turned to glimpse the burning train and wondered how they had ever survived.

"Seth." He heard his name. Still dazed by pain and blinded by tears from the smoke, he turned toward the voice.

"Landon, thank God you're here. Where's Audrey?"

"Wasn't she on the train with you?" he asked, studying his brother-in-law's smoke-streaked face with sudden hope. Maybe Cody had been wrong. Maybe she had never gotten on that train at all.

"She was until your father came down from out of nowhere and pushed her off. Barely half a minute before the explosion. Just when we were starting across the trestle."

Then, as if just noticing the injured man who clung weakly to Seth's arm, Landon narrowed his eyes. His stomach burned with acid. "What were you doing on that train?"

"I had to try to save her," Marshall tried to explain, bursting into sobs. "I crawled over the top of that train to

470

do it. I never wanted her to die. You've got to believe me, Landon. I never wanted her dead."

"Dead?" A cold chill pierced Landon's heart. "Audrey!" he shouted in a voice that did not sound like his. Panic filled him while he quickly scanned the opposite side of the ravine, desperately searching for a glimpse of her. His blood ran ice-cold trails through his body when he saw nothing but trees, twisted metal, and smoke. "Audrey! Can you hear me?"

His voice echoed back to him, unanswered.

"Audrey!"

A few minutes passed before someone shouted, "There she is!" Landon looked toward the voice and saw a man pointing off into the distance to where a small patch of lemon-yellow could be seen through the underbrush.

Landon took off in a dead run, tearing through the trees and bushes as if they did not exist.

When he reached her and saw the blood flowing thick and red from the side of her head, he fell to his knees. His heart no longer functioned, but his mind continued to race with panic.

"Get the doctor!" he shouted to Cody, who was the next to arrive at the scene. "Hurry!"

His heart sprang back to life, hammering with intense fear while he ripped his shirt off and tore it into strips. Quickly, he bound the ugly head wound, then lifted her into his arms. By the time he'd stood up to carry her back toward the encampment, the makeshift bandage was already soaked with blood.

"Oh, my God, no!" Marshall cried out, weeping bitterly at the sight. He stepped forward to help in some way, only to be pushed aside by his half-crazed son.

"Get out of my way, damn it! I have to get her to the doctor." He glanced down at her face and saw that she was already turning an ashen gray. Cradling her against his bare chest, he moved carefully through the underbrush toward the area along the embankment that looked to be the easiest to climb. His heart pounded, frantic with

471

the knowledge she was dying. She had to have help.

By the time he'd reached the slope and begun his climb upward, his chest was heaving from a combination of stark fear and exertion. Still, he managed to make it to the top with her in his arms and hurried toward his horse. He felt the sticky dampness of her blood against his skin. Tears of anguish had started to fill his eyes, blurring his vision, but he continued toward the horse, carrying his limp, beloved burden tenderly in his arms. He prayed they would find the doctor waiting for them when they finally reached the encampment.

The men helped them onto the horse, then balancing Audrey carefully in his arms, Landon urged the animal into a quick walk. He did not want to jar her injuries by making the horse run, though he did want to get her there as quickly as possible. Several of the men ran along behind him, not quite able to keep up but not too far behind. The other men returned to the train wreckage to try to put out the fire and look for Jeb.

The doctor arrived at the supervisor's tent at almost the same time Landon did. Hurrying forward, he helped Landon lower Audrey's limp body from the horse and together the two men carried her inside to a cot near the back of the tent. The other men, who had come along hoping to assist, watched helplessly from outside the opening. Landon looked out among them for Seth, so he could order the young man inside to be examined by the doctor next, but he discovered that his brother-in-law was not among the men who had returned. Despite his injuries, Seth was still out there looking for Jeb.

"How bad is it?" he asked the doctor after he'd had enough time to take the blood-soaked bandage off her head and examine the wound.

"Pretty bad," he commented, then quickly jerked open his medical bag and reached inside. "She's got a lot of swelling and has lost a lot of blood. Still losing it. You wouldn't happen to have any ice around here, would you?"

472

Dismally, Landon shook his head no. "But I can send for some." Immediately, he was on his feet, ordering Cody to go back into town and bring back all the ice he could get his hands on. He shoved his wallet into the young man's hands. "I don't care what it costs."

The doctor was already at work, cleansing the wound, when Landon returned to his side. "Is there anything I can do, Doc?" He felt so helpless.

"Pray," he said, his voice low and earnest, never looking up from the wound where he was busily rinsing away all the dirt and excess blood with a mild solution of carbolic acid.

Seth's hands trembled with a combination of fear, anger, and pain while he helped the other men rummage through the wreckage. His tortured thoughts were pulled in so many different directions that it was becoming harder for him to concentrate on any one thing. Having seen how much blood his sister had lost, he was worried that her injuries might be so serious that she would die. They had been through too much for her to die now.

He was also worried about Jeb, who had not surfaced from the burning wreckage of the train; nor had they located him anywhere nearby. And in between the tormenting thoughts of his sister and his friend, he allowed his anger to flare up and grab hold of him, making him want to take off and try to find the men who had caused the explosion. He wanted to beat their names out of Marshall Steed, then find them and rip them apart one at a time. But, at the moment, the thing he wanted most was to find Jeb—and he wanted to find him still alive.

Ignoring his own pain, he continued to sift through the twisted metal and broken tree limbs, hoping to uncover his friend. Finally, when he was about to give up hope, he pulled away a huge tree limb and there he was.

Seth dropped to his knees and pulled off several other tree limbs that were in his way. Blood had soaked Jeb's shirtfront from his shoulder to his waist and his face was deathly pale. Horrified, Seth reached out to touch his friend's face and found his skin cold. At the same moment, he noticed a broken tree branch protruding through Jeb's burly chest. A scream welled up inside of him, forcing its way up and out in a bloodcurdling yell. Seth had reached the limit of his endurance and sagged slowly forward over his friend's body. He wept until all of his strength was gone. When the other men hurried to his side and tried to pull him off Jeb, he screamed out one last time, then succumbed to the dull gray fog that was hovering over him.

Landon's heart felt as if it were pumping pure ice water the whole time he watched the doctor work. He pressed his hands against the sides of his head to keep from crying aloud his anguish when the doctor finally sat back with a defeated expression and said, "There, that's all I can do. It's up to God now."

All the color drained from Landon's face. He wanted to talk but couldn't. All he could do was listen.

"The only reassuring thing I can say to you now is that if she dies, she'll feel no pain. If she did not feel anything while I was cleansing her wound and then stitched it closed, or when I applied the ice to the swelling, then she should not feel anything when the time comes to meet her Maker."

Tears spilled from Landon's pale eyes in steady streams while he looked down at his beloved wife. Somewhere, deep inside of him, he found his voice again, though it was choked with emotion. "Then you think she will die."

"I have no way of knowing," the doctor said, neither falsely reassuring Landon nor verifying his worst fears. "I told you. It's totally up to God now. If it's her time to go, she'll die. If not, she'll eventually come to. But if and when she does come to, she's going to have one monster

474

of a headache. Now, where are the other patients?"

Landon shrugged. He had not left the tent to find out what had happened to Seth or whether or not they had ever found Jeb. But his father was outside with burns on his face and hands. He pointed toward the men standing outside the tent but did not watch the doctor get up to leave.

"Doctor?" he asked, his voice barely above a tormented whisper. "Would you close the flap behind you?"

Once he was alone with her, Landon sank to his knees beside her cot. Gently, he lifted her hand to his face and rubbed it against his cheek, cherishing the feel of her skin against his.

"Don't die." he said. His body shook uncontrollably while hot tears coursed down his cheeks, wetting her hand. "Audrey, please don't die. I can't bear the thought of ever living without you."

"Git the hell off me, you heavy ox. I can't breathe," Jeb wheezed, grimacing with pain. When that brought no response from the sagging weight on top of him, Jeb looked to the startled faces hovering over his head. "Git him the hell off me."

Quickly, the men did what they were told. Together, they lifted Seth and stared in horror at the wooden spear protruding grotesquely from Jeb's chest. Jeb arched his neck to see what had drawn their attention and frowned when he, too, saw the jagged piece of wood sticking through his chest, just inches below his shoulder.

"Damn, how'd I do that?" he muttered, his face a dark scowl. He blinked with frustration when his attempt to sit up brought him a severe stab of pain, forcing him to stay put. "You men are goin' to have to help me sit up."

Again, they hurried to do as they were told, staring at him in disbelief.

"Quit lookin' at me like that. I ain't no ghost," Jeb protested, feeling a little dizzy-headed now that he was sitting straight up. "Bill, do me a favor, would you? Break off any of the branch that's still stickin' out of my back. I can feel it pullin' down on me."

Bill swallowed hard, but he stepped around behind Jeb and quickly but gently broke off the twigs so that only a few inches of the branch stuck out through his back. When Bill stepped back again, his hands were splotched with blood and he looked as if he might faint.

Jeb glanced down at Seth's prone form and chewed on his lower lip for a moment. "I'd never have thought that of him," he said, shaking his head with disappointment. "Faints like a woman at the sight of blood. Better see if you can wake him up, 'cause we're goin' to have a hell of a time tryin' to carry him out of here. I'm goin' to be doin' good gittin' myself out."

As it turned out, it took twelve men to get the both of them out of the deep ravine. Even after they'd revived Seth, he was too weak from his injuries and from the strain of having saved Marshall and then having found Jeb supposedly already dead to stand on his own. And Jeb was too weak from having lost so much blood, so weak that when they crested to the top of the ravine, his legs gave out on him and he nearly fell backward again.

Rather than try to carry the two men any farther, Bill ran back to the encampment and got a wagon. Jeb and Seth had just enough strength left when he returned to climb into the back.

Jeb found it too painful to lie down and sat with his shoulder slumped against the side of the wagon. Seth lay on his side, staring with morbid fascination at the bloody nub of wood coming out of Jeb's chest, then slowly shook his head with disbelief.

"You say one word about roastin' me over a fire like some skewered pig and you'll be walkin' back to camp on two broke legs," Jeb warned in a weak voice, his eyebrows low with warning, only seconds before he passed out.

*   *   *

Driven by anger and frustration, Landon pressed Audrey's hand tighter against his cheek. His tone had gone from quiet desperation to loud, vocal anger as his frustration grew to unbearable proportions. "I swear to you, I'll make my father tell me exactly who set off that dynamite and I'll kill them with my bare hands."

Landon's emotion-filled voice broke through the gray-white haze that enshrouded Audrey's brain. She felt a damp pressure on her hand and realized it was being held. Still groggy with pain and weak from her blood loss, she tried to answer him but couldn't. Her throat was too dry. She swallowed, then tried again, this time managing a soft, guttural moan.

"Audrey?" Landon cried out, staring down at her with sudden hope. He patted her hand to help revive her. "Audrey, what is it? Speak to me. What are you trying to say?"

She swallowed again. "Isn't that a little drastic?" she finally said in a throaty whisper.

Landon's heart soared. "Isn't what a little drastic?" he wanted to know, already having forgotten his mindless ramblings of just moments before.

"Killing them with your bare hands. Won't a severe beating do?" she asked, then slowly opened her eyes to look into Landon's surprised face. She tried to smile, but it hurt too much.

Overwhelmed by relief, Landon clutched her hand to his chest, tossed his head back, and laughed. He laughed so hard that tears filled his eyes and his shoulders shook helplessly. He laughed so loud that several of the men outside the tent lifted back the flap and peeked in, curious to know if Audrey had shown any signs of recovery or if Landon had simply become so overcome by his grief that he'd finally lost his mind. When they saw that Audrey was awake, staring questioningly up at her laughing husband, a cheer went up that could be heard all the way into town.

*   *   *

Audrey was startled awake by the sound of the door opening, and she smiled when she saw Landon enter their bedroom with a large serving tray.

"Another offering of chicken soup?" she asked, feeling deeply touched that Landon had stayed by her side nearly the entire time of her recovery.

"It's what the doctor said he wanted you to have," he reminded her with a firm nod as he pushed the door closed behind him with the heel of his boot. "He said you could probably start eating real food sometime tomorrow—that is, if everything continues to go as well as it has so far."

"What about Seth and Jeb? Has he started them on solid food yet?"

"Just Seth. Jeb is still pretty weak," he told her, setting the tray down on the table beside their bed. "But, if Jeb doesn't see real food soon, he's already warned the doctor that he plans to go looking for the kitchen in this place and help himself."

Audrey nodded. That certainly sounded like Jeb. "How's your father? Has he talked to the sheriff yet?"

"Yes, and they are looking everywhere for Gene Haught and the two men who were helping him," Landon told her. "Though I really do believe Father, that he didn't know what Gene was planning, he has decided to take full responsibility for everything anyway. He's paying the doctor for all his services that have resulted from the train wreck, and he's having the trestle repaired himself."

Audrey's eyes widened. Even though she remembered how he had dropped down from the top of the train and thrown her off in a last minute effort to save her, she found that a lot of what Landon had just told her was a little too hard to believe.

"Talk about a complete turnaround," she muttered, her tone skeptical.

"Not really," Landon said, then sat down on the bed

beside her and took her hand into his, glad to see color back in her fingertips. "Father has told me that he had no idea Gordon Jones was overcharging those men in his store. Fact is, he's visited that mill only twice since it began operating, and neither time did anyone mention the outrageous prices to him. Nor was he aware of the dreadful conditions of the mill itself. He'd trusted Gordon to keep him informed of everything that was happening, and as long as he was receiving his weekly profits from the mill and no reports of problems, he never questioned the job old Gordon was doing."

"Well, that's just as bad," she protested, not ready to be as forgiving as Landon seemed to be. "Why didn't he make it his business to find out what was going on at his mills? Didn't he know that was his responsibility?"

Landon shrugged, his expression sullen. "He was too busy with all his other investments, I guess. He's admitted he was wrong and is very sorry for his part in all this. And he wants permission to see you so he can apologize to your personally."

"He needs to apologize to the men first," she said, starting to become angry that Landon seemed so willing to forget all the tragedy his father was responsible for— whether he'd been aware of what was going on or not.

"He has. He's apologized to them all. He's also doing what he can to compensate for all the injuries and the deaths that have occurred in his mill. Whether the men decide to go back to work for him or return to their farms, he's giving them all a month's wages to help them get back on their feet. For the ones who do decide to return to the mills, he's promising fair prices and better safety practices. He's also promising to prosecute Gordon Jones to the fullest if he's ever caught."

Audrey's mouth fell open. "He did all that?" Suddenly, she felt guilty for her burst of anger. "And he's going to have the trestle replaced?"

"Just like it was before. They've already started on it."

Audrey smiled with renewed excitement. "Then we should still be able to complete our railroad by next summer."

"Maybe sooner," Landon said, bending forward to place a husbandly kiss at her temple, on the opposite side of her head from her injury. Though she no longer complained of any pain and the swelling had gone down considerably, he did not want to take any chances. "There's one more thing he did that is going to shock you."

"What's that?" she asked, turning her head so she could receive his next kiss on her lips.

"He's sent for Rachel. Now that Seth has saved his life and nearly killed himself in the process, Father has got a whole new outlook about those two. He told me that if they really wanted to get married, it would be with his blessing."

Audrey's heart soared with joy. That would solve all of Seth and Rachel's problems. They could be married and not worry about losing her trust, her mother's jewelry, or her father's love. Their destinies were set. "And has your father come to accept me, too?"

Landon smiled wickedly. "How can he not? You happen to have a mysterious way of getting up under a man's skin when he's not looking."

Audrey's eyes widened when she felt a light touch against the side of her breast. "And you, sir, happen to have a mysterious way of getting up under your wife's bedcovers when she's not looking."

Landon laughed, his pale eyes full of pure devilment. "Ooh, what I plan to do to you once you finally get better."

"I was better the minute you walked into this room," she purred as she reached up and drew him down on top of her.